SURVIVOR'S GUILT

MICHAEL WOOD

One More Chapter
a division of HarperCollins*Publishers*
1 London Bridge Street
London SE1 9GF
www.harpercollins.co.uk

HarperCollins*Publishers*
1st Floor, Watermarque Building, Ringsend Road
Dublin 4, Ireland

This paperback edition 2021
1
First published in Great Britain in ebook format
by HarperCollins*Publishers* 2021

A catalogue record of this book
is available from the British Library

ISBN: 978-0-00-846065-5

Printed and bound in the UK using 100% Renewable Electricity
by CPI Group (UK) Ltd

To Philip Lumb.
Eminent pathologist and the man behind the science of my gory murder scenes.

Also, Carolyn and Elizabeth Lumb. Avid readers. Apologies for making you cry.

Prologue

Wednesday 25th March 2015 - Dore, Sheffield

The white Mercedes Sprinter van had seen better days. Its body work was dented, the windscreen wipers didn't work, a couple of the wheel trims were missing, the back door was a different colour to the rest of the van, and it was caked in mud. This was all intentional. The van was relatively new and would be returned to its showroom condition within twenty-four hours.

It was parked at the bottom of the driveway to a rather grand-looking house with perfectly manicured lawns. The engine was turned off and the two occupants sunk in their seats.

'What time have you got?' the man in the front passenger seat asked. He tried to angle his wrist to catch the light from a nearby lamppost, but it was no use. He couldn't see a thing.

'Just gone half eleven,' the driver whispered.

Both didn't take their eyes off the house.

The curtains were drawn in every room. It appeared to be

in total darkness apart from a chink of light at the corner of a downstairs room which they took to be the lounge. Someone was obviously still up, probably watching a film.

'Right, here's what we're going to do,' the driver began. 'The moment we're inside and the door is closed behind us, I'll grab the old woman, you tie her up. While I'm getting the kid, you bring the van to the door. We'll be out in three minutes tops. Understand?'

The passenger looked to the driver, taking his eyes off the house for the first time. Even in the dull light of the spring night, it was evident by his wide-eyed stare he was nervous.

'Yeah.'

'You okay?'

'Fine.'

'Not having second thoughts?'

'Of course I'm having second fucking thoughts. I'm having third and fourth thoughts, too.'

The driver sighed. 'We've been over this again and again.'

'I don't want to go back to prison,' the passenger said, a catch in his voice.

'You won't. As soon as we get the money, we'll leave the country, start over somewhere else. Now, are you ready before some nosy bastard walking their dogs spots us?'

The passenger took a deep breath. 'I'm ready.'

'Good man.'

They both left the van quietly, closed the doors carefully and made their way as professionally as they could up the paved driveway.

The house was elegant and simple in its red brick design. It sat in its own grounds but was open to its surroundings in an affluent part of Sheffield. It was easily five bedrooms, several en suite bathrooms, huge dining room, utility room and a couple of reception rooms. This was a property that would sell for way over a million. It was obscene that a couple with one small child would be rattling around in this space when some families were cramped into shitty council houses not a five-minute drive away.

The men reached the doorstep. They took one last look at each other and nodded. Game on.

The driver rang the doorbell.

Annabel Meagan was curled up on the Chesterfield sofa with a blanket around her shoulders. She had a glass of wine on the coffee table in front of her and an open box of chocolates on her lap. She was watching her favourite film, *Brief Encounter*. She stifled a yawn. She wasn't tired but playing with an energetic seven-year-old all evening took its toll on a woman who was thirteen months shy of the dreaded seventieth birthday. After watching *Toy Story*, *Toy Story 2* and more episodes of *The Simpsons* than she could count, not to mention the endless games of Mouse Trap, KerPlunk and the aptly titled Frustration, she was enjoying the quietness of the night. Her grandson, Carl, was in bed and fast asleep and she was enraptured in one of the greatest love stories of all time.

The doorbell rang.

Annabel reached for the remote and paused the film. She looked at the clock on the mantlepiece. 11:37. She hated calls to the house after dark. Nobody ever popped round for a visit and a chat at this time. Only bad news was delivered at this hour. The last time someone knocked on her door late at night it was a policewoman to tell her Charlie had been involved in a car accident. Fifteen years ago this August, and the memory was still as fresh as it was back then.

Annabel walked silently to the door, fishing the keys out of the pocket of her oversized cardigan. She fumbled for the right one and secured the chain as she unlocked it. As she pulled open the door, a cool breath of air came in, causing her to shiver. The security light above the door came on automatically. She squinted in the brilliant white light. When her eyes adjusted, she saw two uniformed police officers standing on the doorstep. Her heart sank. History was repeating itself.

Both men removed their hats in sync. Their faces were grim.

'Annabel Meagan?' The taller one of the two said.

'Yes,' she said quietly, swallowing hard.

'PC Bevan. This is PC Yorke. I'm sorry to call so late. Would it be possible to have a word?'

Annabel's bottom lip began to wobble. 'Oh my God, something's happened, hasn't it?'

'I'm afraid we do have some unpleasant news. I think it would be better if we came in and told you.'

She stared at them, her face expressionless. Her eyes darted from one to the other as if committing their faces to memory.

'Mrs Meagan?' the taller one prompted when she didn't move.

'Of course. Sorry.'

Annabel stepped back. She closed the door, removed the chain, and opened it.

'Come on in.'

The two men in police uniform slowly entered the house. They wiped their feet on the mat and stood in the vast hallway, taking in their surroundings.

Annabel closed the door, locked it and pocketed the key.

'I'm in the living room watching a film,' she said, leading the way.

She didn't notice the men in uniform place their hats on the hall table. She didn't register one of them walking so closely behind her as she entered the living room. She picked up the remote from the coffee table, pointed it at the television and turned it off. In the reflection of the blank screen, she saw, over her shoulders, one of the men raising something high above his head. That's when she realised she hadn't seen any identification.

Annabel Meagan, who had been widowed for fifteen years, an independent woman with a sharp mind and a blue belt in karate, turned on her heels, and with as much energy as she could muster kicked the man hard between the legs.

His cries could have woken the whole neighbourhood. He dropped the truncheon, bent double, hands between his legs.

'Who the hell …?' She didn't get time to finish her question. The second man, truncheon raised in his left hand, stepped forward, and hit her on the side of the face. She stumbled backwards, lost her balance and fell, banging her head hard on the edge of the glass-topped coffee table. She was dead before she hit the floor.

'Fucking bitch,' the first man said through gritted teeth as the pain from the kick rose up his body. He felt sick.

'Shit. Rob, she's not moving.'

'Who cares!'

'Rob, look, there's blood,' the other man said, pointing to Annabel. 'Fuck! Look at all that blood coming from her head. Jesus Christ, Rob, I think I've killed her.'

'Who gives a shit?' he wheezed. 'Look, go and bring the van up to the door, I'll go and get the kid.'

The man stood still staring down at the lifeless woman. The pool of blood around her head was growing as it leaked out of the gaping wound.

'Now, for fuck's sake,' the first man said in a loud whisper.

'Right, yes. Sorry, Rob.'

'And stop using my name,' he shouted quietly.

Rob was left alone in the house. He took several deep breaths, but the feeling of sickness wouldn't go away. He looked down at the woman. He laughed to himself. He had known the boy would be looked after by his grandmother tonight. He expected a grey-haired frail old woman. When he saw the taxi pull up earlier and spotted the slim woman, no taller than five-foot, step out, he assumed she wouldn't take much to overpower. He never expected her to be so feisty.

The other man came back into the house.

'Haven't you got him yet?'

'Have you ever been kicked in the bollocks? It's fucking painful. Want me to show you?'

The man jumped back. 'You said we'd only be three minutes maximum. It's been more than five already.'

'Yes, well, I didn't expect the door to be answered by Batman's grandmother, did I?'

'Are you all right?'

'No. I'm in fucking agony,' he seethed.

'Shit. What are we going to do?'

———

Carl Meagan was fast asleep. His bedroom, at the back of the house, was large and even had its own en suite shower room, though he didn't use it, except for the toilet, as he preferred to have baths. He had a built-in wardrobe and bookcases brimming with books. At the bottom of the single bed, a two-year-old golden Labrador, Woody, was wide awake and staring at the closed door, his ears alert, his head tilting at every sound.

The door began to open slowly and a sliver of light crept around it, lighting up the room in a dim glow from a distant bulb. Woody barked. The boy didn't even stir.

A gloved hand fumbled on the wall for a light switch. It found it, flicked it on, and the whole room was ablaze in a harsh yellow.

Woody barked again, louder this time.

The boy woke up.

Carl rubbed at his eyes as he sat up in bed. When he saw two uniformed police officers enter his room, his eyes widened and he cowered slightly.

'Carl? It is Carl, isn't it?'

'Who are you?' He asked, quietly.

'I'm PC Bevan. This is PC Yorke. I'm afraid there's been an accident and you need to come with us.'

'Where's my gran?'

'She's downstairs in the police car. She's coming too.'

'What's happened?'

'There's been a crash involving your mum and dad,' he said in a mock-calming tone. 'They're all right, but they want to see you.'

A tear escaped Carl's eye. He didn't brush it away.

'Where?'

The man swallowed hard. 'They're … at the hospital. Come on, we don't have much time.'

He stepped forward and pulled back the duvet. Carl swung his legs out of bed. He looked from the kindly-faced policeman stood over him to the nervous-looking one by the door.

He slipped his bare feet into slippers then went over to the chest of drawers by the window on the opposite side of the room.

'What are you doing?'

'Getting dressed.'

'We don't have time for that, Carl. Just put your dressing gown on. Your mum won't mind.'

'But I'm not wearing any pants.'

'For fuck's sake, Rob, just grab him and let's go,' the man by the door said.

Woody barked.

Carl's face filled with fear.

The kindly-looking police officer rolled his eyes. The comforting smile dropped as he stormed towards Carl, picked him up and threw him over his shoulder.

'What are you doing? Get off. Put me down. I want to get dressed first.'

'Shut up, you little bastard.'

Woody barked and followed as Rob took huge strides across the landing towards the stairs and ran down.

Carl struggled to break free. He beat the man's back with his fists, but it was no use. There was no way a seven-year-old could overpower a tall man with granite-hard muscles and a vice-like grip.

Woody bit at the man's trousers and tried to pull. He stumbled. He turned and gave the dog a hard kick, sending him flying to the other side of the hallway. He landed with a painful yelp.

'Woody!' Carl screamed. Tears ran down his face and he continued to beat the man harder. 'Woody!'

The man turned to look at the stricken dog. As he did so, Carl saw into the living room. His gran was lying on the floor, her eyes closed, a large pool of blood surrounding her head.

'Gran?' he asked.

Rob left the house. The van was as close as possible to the front door. The side door was open. He threw Carl onto a mound of blankets and jumped in after him. The tools he needed were already waiting. He tore off a strip of duct tape and sealed it across his mouth. Using plastic ties, he secured his ankles and wrists together.

'One sound from you and I'll do to you what I did to your gran. Understand?'

Carl nodded. Tears poured down his pale, terrified face.

Rob backed out of the van and slammed it closed. He turned back to see his partner closing the door to the house.

'Well, that could have gone better.'

Friday 27th March 2015

The phone rang.

Sally Meagan jumped up from the sofa and grabbed for the phone. As she did so, a hand was placed on top of hers.

'You need to keep him talking for as long as possible,' DCI Matilda Darke said. 'Ask to speak to Carl. Ask how he is. Tell him he needs medication. Remember everything we talked about.'

She nodded firmly. She looked to her husband, Philip, by her side. He held her hand. Matilda removed hers and Sally picked up the phone.

'Hello,' she answered. Her mouth was dry. She was physically and mentally drained. She wanted her son home so badly. This was a nightmare. How could this be happening to them?

'Sally Meagan?'

'Yes.'

'We've got your son, Sally.'

'Oh God,' she said under her breath. She didn't think she had any more tears left to cry, but they came and ran down her face.

'We want two hundred and fifty thousand pounds, or we sell him to the highest bidder.'

She swallowed hard. It was painful. 'We don't have that kind of money.'

'Let's not play these games, Sally. I know you've contacted the police. Stop listening to them and pay attention. Get the money sorted or your pretty little boy ends up in some paedo's basement.'

Sally closed her eyes tightly shut and squeezed her husband's hand tighter.

'Please. Can I speak to him?'

'No.'

'Then ... how ... how do I know he's still alive?'

'You just have to take my word on that.'

'Wait, erm, Carl's ill. He takes regular medication. He needs...'

'What?' the kidnapper interrupted. 'Is he diabetic? Does he need regular injections of insulin? Does he have allergies and requires special food? Is he claustrophobic and has panic attacks? Or maybe he has epilepsy and is likely to have a fit. Don't try and play games with me, Sally. Carl is perfectly healthy. You've got a day to get the money. I'll call back in twenty-four hours.'

The line went dead.

Sally crumpled. Her husband caught her and sat her down on the sofa. She wailed and beat his chest with lifeless fists. She was living in hell.

'You did very well, Sally,' Matilda said. 'I know it can't have been easy.' She waited for a long moment, watching the married couple fall to pieces in front of her.

She stepped back and out of the room, giving the nod to a family liaison officer to watch over them.

In the large kitchen, a team set up with computers on the central island hammered away on keyboards.

'Please tell me we were able to trace the call?'

'Sorry. It wasn't long enough.'

Matilda bowed her head. She looked as shattered as the Meagans did.

Saturday 28th March 2015

DCI Matilda Darke was sat behind the wheel of an unmarked Peugeot in a dark car park. A fine rain was falling. On the passenger seat next to her sat a large bag containing two hundred and fifty thousand pounds in used bank notes. Her mobile was on the dashboard.

The ransom drop had been arranged for nine o'clock. The deadline came and went. Matilda didn't notice. She sat impassively looking somewhere far into the distance. Her mind was anywhere but where it should be.

The phone rang, making her jump. She looked around and suddenly remembered where she was, why she was here. She picked up her mobile and swiped to answer.

'Where are you?' a deep voice asked.

'I'm in the car park, as arranged.'

'Liar,' he shouted.

'No. I'm not.' She turned the key in the ignition and flashed her headlights. 'See. I'm over here by the tennis courts.'

'I said the car park by the animal farm.'

'What?' Matilda's eyes widened. Her whole body began to shake.

'Are you fucking playing games with me?'

'No. No, I'm not. Honest. I thought you said by the tennis courts. Look, I'm sorry. I'm sorry. I can be with you in less than five minutes.' The line went dead. 'Hello. Are you still there? Fuck!'

There was no way Matilda could drive to the car park on the opposite side of the park in less than five minutes. There was no direct route. She'd have to go there on foot.

She threw off her seatbelt, pushed open the door and almost fell into the cold night air. She grabbed the bag from the front passenger seat. It was heavier than she expected it to be. Matilda started running.

The park was empty. In the distance she could hear the sound of traffic on Meadowhead and somewhere a car alarm was blaring, but she ignored it. She pounded the concrete pavement in painful, sensible shoes, turned left and ran past the river and up through the trees by the café shrouded in darkness. Her legs were heavy with lactic acid. She wanted to stop. No, she wanted to keep going. She wanted to run and run and never stop. The weight of the emotion of the past few days, weeks and months was too much for one person to cope with, and she wanted to run away from everything.

Matilda heard the sound of a car starting. Tyres crunched over gravel. Surely there wouldn't be another car in the park at this time of night. She tried to run faster but felt as if she was slowing down. A seven-year-old boy was relying on her.

She came out from under the trees and saw the car park up ahead. It was empty. She could smell petrol in the air.

'Carl,' she called out.

She rotated three hundred and sixty degrees to look for the small blond-haired, blue-eyed boy.

'Carl!' she called. 'CARL!!!'

Her mobile started ringing. She grabbed it out of her inside pocket and looked at the display. Her boss was calling her.

'Shit.'

The kidnappers had gone.

Carl was gone.

Chapter One

Carly Roberts was freezing. Dressed in a short, faded black skirt, knock-off Skechers trainers and an off-white sleeveless top with a short pink puffer jacket over the top, she walked slowly up and down the cracked pavement, glancing all around her. There was a chilly wind coming from somewhere and the clouds were heavy with rain. She hoped it held off for a few more hours yet. She'd only made twenty quid so far tonight and the rent was due next week.

'Carly, is that you?'

She looked up at the sound of her name being called. Across the street, Bev and Sarah, two of Sheffield's longest serving street prostitutes, came trotting towards her. She could smell Bev's perfume from the other side of the road.

'I didn't think you were back on the streets,' Bev said. 'I thought you were at that brothel down Shalesmoor.'

'I was. He was taking too big of a cut. I couldn't live on what I was earning. Bastard. At least here I get all the money.'

'You mean your Paul does. Did he do that to you?' Bev held Carly by the chin and tilted her head towards the lamppost to get a better view of her black eye.

'No, he didn't, actually. Some foreigner last week tried to do me out of a tenner. I scratched him and he gave me this.'

'Did you get his number?'

'He was on foot. Are you all right, Sarah? You don't look well.'

Bev and Sarah went everywhere together. The only time they were apart was when one of them was with a punter. There was nothing they hadn't seen on the grimy streets of Sheffield and they were hardened to a life of prostitution. Tonight, Sarah looked pale.

'She's not feeling too well. I'm just taking her home actually. There's no point being out here on a cold night like this. Besides, Mondays are nearly always dead.'

'Tell me about it. Two hours I've been out here, and I've only had one hand job and a blowie.'

'Listen, I'm going to take Sarah to the flat, get her settled, then I'll be right back. There aren't many out tonight, so don't go with anyone you don't know until I've returned, you hear me?' Bev said, pointing a warning finger at Carly.

'Loud and clear,' she smiled. 'Hope you feel better soon, Sarah,' she said as they walked in the direction of their flat.

There was something reassuring about having someone looking out for you, Carly thought. There was never any jealousy or resentment from Bev and Sarah if another woman had more business than they did. They liked to make sure all the girls were safe and not taken advantage of.

Carly shuddered as a gust of wind whipped around her. She could understand people not coming out tonight. She liked the winter as it went dark early and there were more hours to work, but it was bloody cold. It didn't help that she hadn't had a decent hot meal in weeks.

A car drove slowly by. Carly waited for it to stop. It didn't.

From her pleather handbag she took out her battered iPhone with the cracked screen. There was a text from Paul she hadn't heard come through: *On your way home pick up a few cans.* There was no asking how she was, if she was taking care of herself or if she'd been busy; just thinking of himself as usual. Selfish prick. Paul had been good to her, though. He looked after her when no one else would. She'd come to Sheffield at the age of seventeen, fleeing her abusive father. Paul was the first person she'd spoken to at the train station. He said he saw her and thought she looked lost. He also thought she was pretty, and he wanted to take care of her. That made her smile. Even now, three years later, she smiled when she remembered him telling her how much he wanted to protect her.

Protect her? That was a joke. He was now in a grotty bed sit watching shit films and smoking grass while she was out on the damp streets selling her arse to feed the habit he'd got her addicted to.

'Eh up, Carly, love,'

She jumped at the sound of her name being called. It was only Dermot. Bev didn't trust him. Sarah thought he was sweet. Carly couldn't make her mind up. He came down to see the women most nights, offering a hot cup of tea to warm them up or something to eat. He never asked for anything in return, he was simply being charitable. Occasionally he looked menacing, but that could have been the dullness of the street lighting.

'Hello,' she smiled. 'You all right?'

'*I* am. You look perished.'

'It is a bit parky,' she said, pulling her jacket tighter around her.

'Not many out tonight.'

'No. Mondays are always quiet,' she said, her eyes gazing up and down the road.

'I've got a flask of coffee in my car if you want a drink – some sandwiches too.' He stepped forward, standing right next to her. She could feel his coffee breath on her face.

She turned to look at him, his glassy eyes sparkling beneath the lamppost, every wrinkle seeming cavernous in the shadows. He was a tall, thin man and always had a smile on his face which never quite reached his eyes. They were permanently sad, as if he was about to burst into tears at any moment.

A silver Vauxhall Astra pulled up across the road and flashed its headlights. 'Duty calls. I'll see you later, Dermot,' she said over her shoulder as she trotted across the road. She was thankful she didn't have to endure being in his car drinking that cheap nasty coffee. Bev was right, he was sinister.

'Hello, Carly. On your own tonight?'

'Looks that way, doesn't it?' she said, leaning into the window and giving him her famous pout.

'You look cold.'

'That's because I am. You want to warm me up, Tom?'

'I'd love to. Hop in.'

———————————

Tom was a regular and all the women knew him. Carly had been with him a number of times, and, strangely, she liked him. He was a kind man, attentive, loving, gentle, and he was handsome too. He was in his forties, she surmised, had a shaved head and permanent stubble. He was solidly built, had big hands which she enjoyed having placed on her hips as she rode him. He wasn't like the others, only out for a quick shag, Tom seemed to make sure she had as much pleasure as he had, and although she didn't orgasm every time, he was the only man to make her do so in the past three years. Even Paul hadn't achieved that, and he was supposed to be her boyfriend. But then, Paul had issues. It wasn't his fault.

They drove ten miles in just under twenty minutes and parked in woodland close to Tankersley. He turned off the engine and removed his seatbelt.

'So, what can I do for you tonight, Tom, the full monty?' She smiled without revealing her teeth. She was self-conscious about how they'd browned over the past couple of years.

'Would you ...' he stuttered. He was quieter tonight. Usually in the car he asked her how she was, how her day had been, how Paul was doing, but this evening he'd remained quiet. His hands were fixed on the steering wheel and he hadn't looked at her once.

Carly knew he was married. There was a mark where his wedding ring usually was. Maybe he was feeling remorse for cheating on his wife. There was a first time for everything.

'Are you all right?'

'I'm fine.' He gave a weak smile.

'If you just want to chat, that's okay with me, Tom,' she said. She placed a hand on his lap and he winced. 'Is everything okay?'

'Yeah. I'm just a bit ... I don't know.'

'Do you know what you need?' she asked, playfully.

'What's that?'

'A cuddle. How about I sit on your knee and we have a bit of a cuddle. It might make us both feel better.'

'I'd like that,' he smiled.

Carly took off her seat belt and Tom pushed back his seat. She climbed on top of him, sat on his muscular thighs and rested her head on his chest. It felt warm, cosy, comfortable. She felt safe. This was how she should have felt with Paul except she couldn't remember the last time he'd touched her, let alone given her a cuddle.

'This is nice,' Tom said.

'It really is,' she replied. She could hear his heart beating as she snuggled into him. As much as she enjoyed it, she wanted him to relax, turn him on. Tom was a good payer and always gave her extra if they had full sex, and she needed the money.

Tom wrapped his arms around her. He brushed her greasy hair with his large hands and slowly ran them down her back.

'I like being with you, Tom,' she said, and surprised herself that she was telling the truth.

'I'm glad.'

'You make me feel like a woman.'

'That's what you are.'

She sat up and looked him in the eye. 'To most men I'm just a piece of meat.'

'I don't think that at all.'

Carly leaned forward and kissed him on the lips. She tried to avoid kissing wherever possible, but she genuinely liked Tom.

'You look after me. You're a good man.'

His smiled dropped. 'And you're a dirty cunt.'

His huge hands wrapped themselves around her throat and started to squeeze. Her brain didn't have time to realise what was happening. She started to choke. Her small hands tried to pull Tom off her but his were so big and muscular that she couldn't get hers around his wrists. Her vision began to blur as the oxygen supply to her brain was cut off. She expected her young life to flash before her eyes, but it didn't. Nothing happened. A warmth began to spread over her and for a moment she was relieved as she'd been cold ever since she left the flat, but then she realised it was the slow release of death, enveloping her. Her tragic life was ebbing away. Despite her hating what she had turned into, she wasn't ready to die just yet.

'Tom, please . . .' she squealed.

The look on Tom's face was alien to Carly. She had never seen him look so cold, so heartless, so evil. His eyes were wide and staring. There was a devilish grin on his wet lips. He was enjoying himself. All those times they'd been together, when they'd laid back in the glow of sexual excitement on the back seat of his car, panting, basking in their ecstasy, and it had all been a lie. He'd been building up to this, to killing her.

Tom suddenly let go of Carly's throat. She coughed and gasped for breath. She felt light-headed and wanted to climb off him, get out of the car and run away, but she didn't have the energy.

Her breathing began to return to normal, as did her vision.

'Tom, please, I don't do tricks like that, you know I don't.'

'This isn't a trick, Carly.'

Once again, he wrapped his huge hands around her throat and squeezed harder this time. His thumbs pressed into her windpipe. She choked. Her mouth opened and her tongue stuck out. Her eyes rolled into the back of her head and her body began to give in to impending death. She eventually closed her eyes and went limp. Life had been extinguished.

Life. The most precious thing on the planet and it had been snuffed out in less than five minutes.

He shoved Carly off his lap and into the front passenger seat. He looked at his large hands and his sausage-like fingers. They were shaking with adrenaline. The power surging through his body right now was immense. He closed his eyes and leaned back in the seat.

There was a noise. It sounded like the car door being opened.

He opened his eyes just in time to see Carly fall out onto the ground. She wasn't dead. She was fucking playing him.

'Come back here, you bitch,' he growled as he flung open his door and stepped out into the cold night air. He ran around the car as he saw Carly disappear into the trees, fleeing for her life.

Carly couldn't believe what was happening to her. She knew the dangers of the job. She knew several of her fellow prostitutes had gone missing, one of whom, Denise, had been found dead just over a year ago. Despite being desperate, she thought she was sensible enough to be able to judge who was a threat to her and who was a regular punter. She thought Tom was one of the nice ones. How could she have got him so wrong?

She ran as fast as her thin legs could take her. She stumbled over uneven ground and tried not to let the branches hitting her in the face slow her down. She had no idea where she was, or where she was running to. If she could just find a road, flag down a passing car, she would be safe.

'Carly, get back here right now,' she heard Tom wheeze as he ran after her. 'Fucking slag!'

It was Tom's voice, but they weren't his words. He had always been so kind, respectful and gentle with her. Where had this evil suddenly come from?

Ahead, she saw the safety of a road. It wasn't much further. She found the energy from somewhere to thrust herself through the thicket of trees. Out in the open, she took one last glance over her shoulder to make sure there was enough distance between her and Tom before taking a risk by stopping to wave down a car. He was still in the trees.

She almost made it to the road when she felt a hand grab a handful of hair and pull her down to the ground. She rolled over, looked up and saw the angry face of Tom looming over her. Surely this wasn't real. Tom was kind, caring, loving, considerate. He'd given her extra money when she faced having her electricity cut off. He bought her a new pair of shoes when her last pair had a hole in them. He paid to have her mobile repaired. He didn't call her horrible names and try to kill her. What had happened to him? What had caused him to turn so evil?

'Please, Tom, don't do this. I promise, I won't tell anyone,' she cried.

Tom leaned down. He wrapped both hands around her throat and squeezed harder than he'd ever done in his life. In the silence of the woods, he heard her neck crack. Her felt her body go limp. She was dead, he was sure of it, but she'd pretended before. He wasn't going to risk her trying to escape again. He continued to squeeze her neck, harder, harder.

Chapter Two

Tuesday 22nd October 2019. 03:05

Detective Chief Inspector Matilda Darke stood in the car park of South Yorkshire Police Headquarters. It was a chilly, rainy day. The sky was grey, and a heavy mist hung low over the steel city. Around her, her colleagues were dropping to the wet ground as a gunman on the roof of a building overlooking the car park opened fire and mercilessly picked them off one by one.

Matilda was deaf to the cries, the screams, and the shouts. She didn't acknowledge the sound of glass breaking as bullets hit the windows of the station behind her. She didn't feel the blood spatter hit her face, or which of her colleagues – her friends – had lost their lives. She stood perfectly still and looked up at the gunman.

Not five minutes earlier, she had received a phone call in her office. *'You're a survivor, aren't you, Matilda? But what's the point of surviving, when everyone around you is dead?'* The caller hung up before she had a chance to respond. Was it a threat or a prank? She assumed the latter, put the phone down and went into the main suite of the Homicide and Major Enquiry Team to begin the morning briefing. Moments later, the fire alarm sounded, and everyone filed out of the building in an orderly fashion. Then, the shooting began.

Matilda should have sprung into action. She should have taken control and directed everyone to safety, but she couldn't. Fear took hold. She looked up to where the gunman was firing from and knew straight away it was the man who'd made the call.

I am a survivor. But what's the point, when everyone I care about is dead?

She looked around her. The dead face of her boss, Assistance Chief Constable Valerie Masterson, glared at her. DC Ranjeet Deshwal had recently become a father for the first time. He was excited about his wife returning to work so they could solve crimes together like an ethnic Tommy and Tuppence. He was face down on the tarmac, bullet holes in his back.

Come on, you bastard.

Out of the corner of her eye, she saw DC Rory Fleming cradling the dead body of his fiancée, PC Natasha Tranter. Two young people with their whole lives ahead of them. They were so in love, so happy, and it had been ripped from them so cruelly. She doubted Rory would ever get over such a loss. He would be a changed man.

Do it.

Later that day, the gunman would cause more atrocities throughout Sheffield, claiming dozens more innocent lives. DC Rory Fleming would lose his life as would Chris Kean, the son of her best friend, Adele. Most importantly, the one constant reliability in her life, her own father, Frank Doyle, would die trying to protect her as she lay comatose in her hospital bed.

Kill me.

Everyone Matilda cared about was affected by the events of Tuesday the eighth of January 2019. Those who survived would be scarred psychologically. A part of everyone Matilda knew would die that day.

What's the point of surviving, if everyone around me is dead?

The gunman looked at Matilda through the viewfinder on his rifle. She looked at him. She knew he was here to kill her. And she didn't care.

The first bullet hit her in the shoulder. She staggered backwards. Strangely, she didn't feel any pain. She regained her composure and looked back up at the gunman.

Is that the best you can do? Fucking kill me!

The second bullet took off the back of her head.

Matilda screamed and woke herself up.

She sat up in bed. Her T-shirt was wet with sweat. She was breathless and cold. She picked up her mobile on the bedside table and looked at the time. It was a little after three o'clock. She sighed and flopped back down on the bed.

The nightmares were a constant visitor to her sleep. She dreaded going to bed at night as she knew that within minutes of nodding off, she would be back to that chilly day in January in the car park. Sometimes she dreamed about being shot again, other times she was stood on the sidelines watching her colleagues die. One particularly vivid nightmare was of her on the operating table and surgeons were panicking as she was losing blood at an alarming rate. She had no idea if this was a flashback or whether her mind was playing a cruel game with her. She didn't want to know the truth.

Matilda was in hospital for six weeks following the shooting. She'd undergone several operations to remove bone fragments from her brain, relieve the pressure and swelling, and then to repair the broken skull. Followed by another operation on her shoulder and further reconstructive surgery.

Unfortunately, her recovery was far from over. Matilda need rehabilitative care. The part of her brain that controlled her cognitive and motor skills was damaged. The good news was it was repairable through therapy. She had to learn how to walk again and see a speech therapist to improve her now slurred way of talking.

When she was discharged at the end of February, she was moved into the Dame Charlotte Montgomery Rehabilitation Centre on the outskirts of Sheffield. She spent eight weeks there, and despite seeing Dame Charlotte Montgomery's severe face looking at her from a framed photo in almost every treatment room, she still had no idea who the woman was. Every day she was in the gym or the pool trying to strengthen her body. When she wasn't having physical therapy, she was working on her speech and seeing a psychotherapist to talk through her trauma, to try and make sense of how she was feeling and how she would cope with normal life, whatever that was. By the time she left, her body was stronger, and she'd never felt fitter before in her whole life. She had even returned to the target weight she had been longing for and would once more be able to fit into her designer size-ten clothing she had been clinging on to. Her priorities, however, had changed. She no longer cared that she could wear her Armani suit. All her woes before the shooting seemed somewhat insignificant and baseless now. People whom she loved and cared for were dead and, what, she should smile because she could now wear a designer jacket with ease?

Matilda left the rehabilitation centre on the eighteenth of April. Surprisingly, it was an emotional event. She wanted life to return to normal but there was a sense of safety and comfort in living in such a place. She returned home for the first time since she left it on that fateful morning in early January. It was a sombre affair and as soon as the car turned the corner and her house was revealed, she burst into a flood of tears. She was relieved to be home. She was sad she was able to go home when so many people she knew and loved had died.

Survivor's guilt was Matilda's main issue and one she downplayed most of all. The gunman, the brother of a former police officer turned serial killer, had come for her. She was his target, yet he wanted the glory and horror of a spree killer. He'd mercilessly shot at random, not caring whom he murdered, and while Matilda was seriously injured, she had survived. So many hadn't. She shouldn't have either. She would happily give up her life so that Rory could be back, or Chris, or Ranjeet, or Valerie. Or her father.

———————————

Matilda's bedroom door was flung open and her sister, Harriet, entered. She was wearing a dusky pink dressing gown that was hanging off her shoulders and a pair of Winnie the Pooh pyjamas. Her hair was a mess, and her eyes were half open.

'I heard a scream. Are you all right?'

'Bad dream. Sorry. I didn't mean to wake you.'

Matilda's speech had more or less returned to normal. When upset, she often stumbled over her words but apart from the nightmares, the flashbacks, the psychological torment, she was, physically, dramatically improved.

'That's okay.' She went and sat on the bed next to her.

Harriet was two years younger than Matilda at forty-three years old. She'd been married to Brian for seventeen years, though the divorce was almost finalised following her discovery he'd been seeing a hairdresser called Beatrice for seven years and they'd had a three-year-old daughter together.

Upon Matilda being shot, Harriet had moved to Sheffield to help with her older sister's recuperation. Her two sons, Joseph, seventeen, and Nathan, fifteen, had stayed in Grimsby while they finished their education. They both had important exams coming up. Once they were over, they planned to leave their father to his new life and move to Sheffield to be with their mother. Hopefully, by then, Matilda would be able to live on her own again and Harriet would have found somewhere for the three of them to live. That was the plan, at least.

'Do you want to talk about it?' Harriet asked.

She sighed. 'I'm tired of talking. That's all I do.'

'Didn't your therapist say it was important to talk about things?'

'She did, but I'm starting to piss myself off so I'm sure it's not helping.' She ran her fingers through her close-cropped hair. They came away damp with sweat.

'Cup of tea and a Bourbon?' Harriet asked with a smile.

'Sounds good to me.'

———

While Harriet set about making a pot of tea, Matilda slipped on her dressing gown and went into the living room to make a fire in the wood burner. She turned on the light and saw the mound of cards and letters from well-wishers on the coffee table she hadn't got around to replying to.

Fire lit, she went over to the window, peeled back the curtain and looked out into the blackness of the dark autumnal night. There was a strange car parked outside the garage, above which was an apartment DC Scott Andrews had shared with his boyfriend, Chris Kean. Scott had yet to open up about his loss and was dealing with grief in his own way. It was the wrong way, but he'd need to see that for himself. Only then could he begin to recover.

Matilda shuddered in the cold and went over to the fire that was slowly heating up the room. It was October. *Nine months since the shooting*. She had lost the whole of this year to her recovery. Everything seemed to be going so slowly with her therapist. Diana Coopersmith had told her, on many occasions, there were no quick fixes to what Matilda was going through and baby steps were needed. *Baby steps*. While living at the rehabilitation centre, Matilda had pushed her body to its limits and beyond in order to physically recover. Her mind, however, was completely independent and would decide for itself how long her mental recovery would take.

Nine months. Baby steps.

When Matilda woke up in hospital, her sister had taken her hand in hers and asked her if she knew she was pregnant. Matilda had no idea. She'd felt different in recent weeks and put it down to the onset of menopause. She had lost the baby in the shooting. It had died before it had lived.

Matilda shuddered. Whenever she thought of the baby she

thought of Daniel and was sad their relationship had come to such an abrupt end. She took a deep breath and mentally chastised herself for allowing emotions to grip her once more when she'd promised herself she wouldn't allow any more hurt into her life.

Harriet brought the tea and biscuits in on a tray, pushed the cards and letters on the coffee table aside with it and set it down.

'What was the dream about?' Harriet asked, getting comfortable on the sofa.

'I was being shot again,' Matilda replied quietly. 'It happened in slow motion this time and I could see what was happening to everyone around me. I saw Ranjeet get hit as he tried to save Sian. But I didn't really see that happen.'

'But you know it happened. *That* is not helping,' she said, nodding to a pile of cardboard files on an end table.

'I thought it would.'

'You've read every report, every statement, looked at every crime scene photograph. Your own attempted murder could be your specialist subject on *Mastermind*. It's not doing you any good.'

'I know,' she said, looking down as if she'd been told off for stealing a cookie before tea.

'Remember when I found out Brian was sleeping with that thick tart, Beatrice?'

'I thought it was Bernice?'

'Who cares! Anyway, I wanted to know all about her, what was so special about her that a married man would risk losing everything, his family, to be with her. Remember what you said to me?'

'Actually, I don't,' Matilda said with half a smile.

'You said that knowing about her wouldn't make me feel any better about being betrayed, that I could end up feeling worse.'

'Did you?'

'Of course I did. The bimbo applied to go on *Love Island*, for crying out loud. When Brian told her I was naming her as a co-respondent on the divorce papers she asked if she'd have to take an exam.'

Matilda laughed.

'She calls her hairdressing salon Blow and Go and wonders why she gets so many dodgy phone calls.'

Matilda continued to laugh.

'I'm pleased you're finding my pain so funny.'

'I'm sorry. I'm not laughing at you.'

'It's okay. It's good to see you laugh.'

Matilda took a breath. 'It's been a while.'

Harriet studied her fragile sister. 'Do you think you've maybe gone back to work too soon?'

'I've only been back a week.'

'Exactly. And look at what's happened in that week. You've done more work in seven days than most people do in a month.'

'Someone is out there targeting prostitutes. We have four of them dead over the past three years. There has to be an official investigation.'

'But why do you need to lead it? And why now?'

'Because it's my job.'

'And what's happening tomorrow, is that your job too?'

'Yes. It is,' Matilda replied firmly.

'You're taking too much on. You're running before you can walk.'

'If I stop I …' Her voice broke.

'If you stop, you'll think about everything you've lost,' Harriet finished the sentence for her.

'Precisely.'

'Oh, Mat.' Harriet went over to the other sofa, sat by her sister and put an arm around her shoulders. 'You can't try and ignore what happened to you.'

'I'm not ignoring it,' she said. Her head was bowed and there was a catch in her throat.

'Nobody will think anything less of you if you decide to take more time off.'

'I will. Besides, Diana Coopersmith said that the psychological effects, the PTSD, the nightmares, could be lifelong. I'm never going to be fully back to normal. I've accepted that. I just,' she swallowed her emotion, 'I just think that if I could get into some form of a routine, bring some normalcy back into my life, it may help.'

'And if it doesn't?'

'I'd rather not answer that.'

'I hope you don't have to.'

A tear rolled down Matilda's cheek. 'This is too hard.'

'That's why I'm here. You don't have to go through all of this on your own.'

'I'm so glad you're here,' Matilda said with a hint of a smile. She ate a biscuit and reached for another one. 'I think this is the closest we've been since we were teenagers.'

'And all it took was a near-death experience to bring us back together.'

'If I'd known that I'd have got shot in the head years ago.'

They both laughed, but it didn't last long. Matilda was never able to laugh for long before she realised there were people she loved who wouldn't be laughing again. She felt guilty for being able to enjoy the freedom of living when others hadn't survived. Diana bloody Coopersmith was helping her with survivor's guilt, among other things. Matilda hadn't told Harriet, or anyone outside of her therapy sessions, exactly what she was going through. And she had no intention of doing so, either.

Chapter Three

DS Sian Mills and DI Christian Brady pulled into the car park at South Yorkshire Police HQ at the same time.

'You're early,' Sian said, stepping out into the cool, bright air. She tucked her red hair behind her ear and buttoned up her coat.

'So are you,' he replied, beanie hat pulled down low, resting on his eyebrows.

'I've hardly slept.'

'Me neither.'

'We don't get many success stories but this one really is the best news ever, isn't it?' A light was dancing in Sian's eyes. There was a genuine smile on her face. She was excited, like a child on Christmas morning.

'I never thought this day would come,' Christian said.

Sian linked arms with Christian and they headed for the entrance.

'I bet you know the whole itinerary for today, don't you?' Christian said.

'It's emblazoned on my mind.' She looked at her watch.

'They'll be at Charles de Gaulle airport right now. The EasyJet flight leaves at 10:07 and they'll land in Manchester at 11:32.'

'You wish you were there, don't you?'

'If I had my way, we'd have a huge welcoming committee at the terminal, but we need to be practical about these things.'

'And we have a press conference at 10:30.'

'True.' She shuddered. 'I hate press conferences.'

'It's all right for you. You're on the sidelines watching. It's me that'll have the lights flashing in my eyes and the journalists shouting questions at me. And we all know what the first question will be.'

He held the door open for Sian. She entered the building and began unbuttoning her coat as the warmth of the station enveloped her. They headed for their new offices.

––––––––––––––

The Homicide and Major Enquiry Team had lost two officers in the shooting, DC Ranjeet Deshwal and DC Rory Fleming. Ranjeet's wife, Kesinka, also a DC, was on maternity leave at the time, and decided not to return to work. She resigned from the force and, when little Hemant was old enough for full-time school, she would look for a new job, something a world away from policing. In the aftermath of the shooting, DS Aaron Connolly had realised his life was more important than his career. He threw himself at the feet of his wife, who had begun divorce proceedings following an affair he had, and said he would quit policing if she would take him back. She agreed. They had even left Sheffield to start a new life together. HMET was now missing four good officers.

DI Christian Brady – acting DCI during Matilda's absence – had been to many meetings with the new ACC to discuss the future of the team. Firstly, Christian said they should move to a new suite. There were too many ghosts in the existing one, and although it was a superficial change, a new name should be given to the team. Start afresh. The Homicide and Major Enquiry Team was now The Homicide and Major Crime Unit.

Sian pushed open the glass doors and stepped in. 'I think Matilda's right, you know, there is a smell.'

'It's just your imagination. You didn't notice a smell until Matilda brought it up.'

'I think it's damp,' she said as she flicked on the overhead lights with her elbow.

'It's not damp.'

The suite was half the size of the previous one. The walls were painted a sickly yellow colour, the lighting was too bright and intrusive, and the carpet tiles were so old, their colour had faded beyond all recognition. The team had adapted and got used to their new surroundings. When Matilda returned to work, nine months later, she hated it on sight. And she picked up on the smell straight away.

'I'd open a window but it's cold this morning,' Sian said. She pulled open the bottom drawer of her desk, grabbed a can of air freshener and began spraying liberally around the room.

Christian coughed. 'That's just making it worse. What is it?'

'Verbena and waterlily, apparently,' she said, looking at the can.

'What the hell's verbena?'

'I haven't a clue. It smells better than fragrance of damp.'

'It's not damp!' Christian exclaimed.

'I'm going to get a damp meter from Stuart and then we'll know for sure. Coffee?'

'Please,' he nodded before going into Matilda's office, which had been his office until last week.

DC Finn Cotton was the next to arrive. He stood in the doorway and pulled a face.

'What's that smell? It's like someone is trying to mask a nasty fart with cheap perfume.'

'It's verbena and waterlily,' Sian said.

'Am I supposed to know what that means?'

'Sod it, I'm opening a window.' Christian came out of the small office and pushed a window wide open, letting in a cold draught of air.

'I bought a big box of Mars bars for the snack drawer, Sian, but I left them at home. I'll bring them in tomorrow,' Finn said, taking off his coat and squeezing between Scott's desk and Sian's to get to his own.

'No worries.'

'Big day today, isn't it?' He smiled. 'I can't believe this is happening.'

'Yes, well, it's a big day for us too,' Christian said. He glanced out of the window. 'Journalists are arriving already. Bloody vultures.'

'They can smell a big story brewing,' Sian said.

'I wonder if it smells like verbena and waterlily,' Christian smiled.

Chapter Four

Harriet was driving Matilda's Range Rover. Matilda was usually protective over who drove her car. However, since the shooting, her reactions were somewhat reduced. It would be a while before she was cleared to drive. The worst-case scenario was that she'd never be allowed to drive again. When going to work, she had Scott to drive her there and back. It was handy with him living above her garage, but at the weekends, if she wanted to go anywhere, she had to rely on her sister or be at the mercy of taxis.

In the back of the car sat retired detective Pat Campbell. She was a good friend of Matilda's and had helped her with this cold case when Matilda was consumed with active cases. It was only fitting she should join her on the journey.

'So, how is it being back at work?' Pat asked.

The trip to Manchester was due to take just over one and a half hours. They left Sheffield behind them and were driving through the stunning scenery of the Peak District National Park, a large area of natural beauty that separated two of Britain's larger cities.

'It's wonderful,' Matilda said, only half-lying. 'I was going crazy at home.'

'Thank you very much,' Harriet butted in.

'I didn't mean that. I hate not having anything to do. I had to get back for my own sanity.'

'Again, thank you,' Harriet said.

Pat laughed. 'I'd stop talking if I were you, Mat. You're only digging a bigger hole for yourself.'

'You know what I mean, though.'

'I do.' She watched the scenery pass by in a blur for a few moments. 'I still can't get over what happened back in January. I remember watching it unfold on the television; it was like a nightmare and it kept getting worse as the day went on. I haven't cried like that since 9/11.'

Matilda sat quietly in the front, her head angled so neither Harriet nor Pat could see the look of torment on her face. She should have been with her officers on that day as they faced evil head on. They'd run into a school with an active gunman, a hospital with a mad man holding hostages, been caught up in an explosion and the aftermath of watching dozens of innocent people brutally murdered. She should have been with them. She hated herself for that.

'How is everyone?' Pat asked.

'They're fine,' Matilda replied. 'They've all had counselling. Christian still goes. Only once a month now, but he says it helps to talk about things, even if he's talking about nothing in particular. Sian didn't go to many sessions, but she's got her Stuart. They've always shared everything.'

'Is Stuart the tall bloke, built like a rugby player?' Harriet asked.

'Yes.'

'Ooh, I like him. If Sian ever gets fed up with him, she can send him my way.'

'Harriet! Your divorce isn't even final yet.'

'So, I'm not dead. I still have urges.'

'I can't remember the last time I had an urge,' Pat said. 'Actually, I tell a lie, I can. But it certainly wasn't for my Anton.'

Matilda laughed. 'Still getting on your nerves?'

'The man's impossible. Next April is our thirty-eighth wedding anniversary. Thirty-eight years. Once I got over the shock that I'd have served less time if I'd blown up Parliament, I said we should do something special. I mean, neither of us are getting younger, and in this day and age, who knows what's around the corner. We may not make our fortieth. Anyway, I suggested a long holiday, somewhere we've never been before: New Zealand or Japan. Hawaii or Jamaica. Guess where he wants to go?'

Matilda smiled. 'I shudder to think.'

'Whitby. Sodding Whitby.'

'Whitby's ... nice,' Harriet said.

'I've nothing against Whitby. It's a lovely place. I've been there many times, but it's not somewhere you go to commiserate being married to someone for thirty-eight bloody years, is it? Whitby's a day out. I've told him, it doesn't have to be as far away as New Zealand, but it's got to be a plane journey or I'm filing for divorce.'

'I know a very good divorce lawyer,' Harriet said.

'I know plenty myself. I've been googling them since I retired.'

The lightness of the conversation made Matilda relax. She was looking out of the window, watching the countryside in its gorgeous autumnal colours glide by, and she was content. It

was only when the talking stopped that her brain reminded
her of what she had been through in the past nine months: shot
twice, almost dying on the operating table, a miscarriage,
months of rehab, the nightmares, the dark thoughts, the
flashbacks, the ongoing battle with survivor's guilt, Daniel…

'How about Morocco?' Matilda said, silencing the
screaming voice in her head.

Chapter Five

Plantation Woods, Tankersley, Barnsley

Rosie Shepherd was tired and annoyed. She was tired because she had just worked a double shift at the Northern General Hospital and was due on again in six hours, giving her very little time to catch up on much-needed sleep and play with her two-year-old son. She was annoyed because, as she predicted, the dog she didn't want, which her useless husband said he would walk, needed walking and Graham had typically fallen into his usual routine of leaving everything to someone else. Bloody men!

She pulled up beside the woods in her aging Ford Focus and opened the back door for the hyperactive spaniel to jump out. Within seconds, Buttons was lost to the trees. All she could hear was his yapping as he chased floating leaves and frightened sparrows.

As much as she protested about getting a dog, she had grown to like the bouncy pup and Buttons had soon realised who the real master of the house was. Buttons followed Rosie around everywhere and when Rosie woke up in the afternoons when she was on nights, she often found the small dog curled up at the bottom of the bed. It was comforting, and the spaniel gave her more affection than Graham had done in a long time. Useless lump. Graham, not Buttons.

'Buttons, come here, boy,' Rosie called once the barking had stopped and he'd run out of sight.

It was a chilly morning. The clocks were put back at the weekend. Winter was on its way. She hated the dark mornings and the early dark evenings, and she didn't relish coming to the woods alone to exercise Buttons. He wasn't even a year old yet, so he wouldn't be able to tackle someone if she was attacked.

'Buttons?' she called again. 'You want your ball?'

She heard a yap and followed the noise. There was no denying having a dog was good exercise for her, too, but right now, all she wanted was to go to bed and wrap that big duvet around her.

Up ahead, she found the spaniel lying down in a clearing. He never did that. It was almost as if he'd had enough running around and playing and wanted to rest. She hoped he wasn't injured or had eaten something he shouldn't have. It was only a few years ago she read about some sick bastard putting meat laced with broken glass in Meersbrook Park to injure cats and dogs.

'Buttons, are you all right?' She ran towards him and stopped before she reached him.

He wasn't injured at all. He was lying at the side of a woman who, judging by her appearance, was dead, and had clearly been dead for some time.

Chapter Six

Last year, Sian Mills had been given the task of liaising with the prostitutes of Sheffield. With Finn's help, they had worked together in creating a database of the women so, should any of them go missing, or come to harm, they would immediately have their details to hand and be able to inform next of kin. It wasn't a one hundred per cent success as some of the women were reluctant to talk to the police. They didn't trust them and thought this was a ploy so they could easily be arrested. No amount of reassurance from Sian, Finn, or the charities the police worked with would help change their mind.

Since 2016, seven prostitutes had gone missing. Four had been confirmed dead, murdered, and the cases had gone cold very quickly. When Matilda returned to work, she decided a full investigation needed to be launched. The women who worked the streets needed to feel safe. They needed to know that somebody cared about what they had to face on a daily basis, and that someone would be her.

The press conference was to inform the media of what they

would be doing and how the newspapers and the public could help. Unfortunately, other events had forced Matilda to pull out. Privately, she was pleased. It was to be her first public appearance back at work, and she knew many of the questions coming from the eager press would be about her and how she was feeling. The murders of four women needed to be headline news, not her.

Christian stood in front of the mirror in the men's changing rooms. Before the shooting, he'd been paranoid about getting old. His hair was thinning and receding, and he had a bald spot forming on the crown of his head. He was getting softer around the middle, too, and he hated it. However, the death of two of his colleagues, both of them in their twenties, had brought about a change in his outlook. Rory and Ranjeet would never get old. They'd never worry over losing their hair or putting on a bit of weight in their middle years. Suddenly, age didn't scare Christian. On his next visit to the barber's, he asked for a full head shave. Surprisingly, he liked what he saw looking back at him, and so did everyone else. Sian even commented that it made him look younger. He should have done this years ago.

He washed his face, straightened his tie and smoothed down his jacket. He didn't mind speaking in front of a room full of people; it was the questions the journalists would ask that he didn't like, especially if he couldn't answer what they wanted to know.

The door opened and Scott poked his head around.

'Are you ready?'

'As I'll ever be.'

'I have some news for you. Do you want the good or the bad first?'

'Oh God,' he said, his face paling. 'Give me the bad first.'

'The press conference is going to be shown live on the BBC News channel.'

'Please tell me you're joking.'

'I'm afraid not.'

'Jesus Christ!' he exclaimed. 'What's the good news?'

'Sian told me to tell you that she's managed to book us a table at the Mercure for our team Christmas meal.'

'And that's supposed to cheer me up, is it?'

'Well, it's better than a piss-up and a kebab.'

Christian glanced at his reflection one more time. In the space of less than a minute he'd gone from looking like a confident DI to a rabbit caught in the headlights. He rolled his eyes at Scott, pushed past him, and out into the corridor where Sian was waiting for him.

'Here you go,' she said, handing him the prepared statement. 'I've increased the font and line spaces, so you don't have to squint. You know what those bright lights are like and the flashes from the cameras can make your eyes go funny.'

'Thanks.'

'Remember, speak slowly, calmly and clearly.'

He took a deep breath. 'I wish Matilda was doing this. Bloody journalists.'

They turned a corner and entered the small anteroom where the ACC was waiting for him.

Assistant Chief Constable Benjamin Ridley had enormously tiny shoes to fill. His predecessor, Valerie Masterson, was only a small person – just over five feet tall in heels – but her personality was titanic. She was liked and respected by everyone at South Yorkshire Police HQ and her loss was greatly felt.

Ridley had taken the job as promotion, moving across the Pennines from Manchester, bringing with him his wife and three children. He was in his late forties, tall, slim, black hair trimmed into a military buzzcut, deep, dark brown eyes and an expressionless face which made reading his mood almost impossible. Maybe he was nervous about taking over the role from such a formidable woman. Maybe he was worried about joining a grieving team and not feeling their emotions. Maybe he was a stern man with strong principles and moral rectitude that made him unapproachable on a personal level. It didn't help that he kept himself hidden in his office, rarely appearing amidst the action.

'Good of you to step into the breach at the last minute, DI Brady,' he said, his voice deep and smooth.

'Not a problem,' he said, smiling nervously.

'It's a packed room. I'm afraid the news of an urgent investigation mixed with the return of DCI Darke has brought the reporters in their dozens.'

'I suppose it's for the best that Matilda isn't here then. We don't want the focus to be on her, do we?' Christian said.

'No. Well, when you're ready.'

Ridley opened the door and stepped out into the press room. Sian and Scott wished him luck. He looked down and checked his trousers were zipped up before following the ACC onto the stage. The cameras began to flash immediately and stopped just as quickly when they realised DCI Matilda Darke wouldn't be putting in an appearance.

'Ladies and gentlemen, thank you for coming,' Ridley began. 'Today, South Yorkshire Police is launching a major investigation, reopening several cold cases the Homicide and

Major Crimes Unit believe are connected. We require the help of the nation's press, and the public, in order to solve these crimes. I shall now hand over to Detective Inspector Christian Brady, who shall provide the details.'

Christian's mouth had dried. He swallowed hard, but it hurt. He reached for the plastic cup of water, took a large sip, and with a shaking hand, put it back on the table, far enough away so he wouldn't knock it over.

He looked up and smiled into the camera glaring at him. There was a sea of expectant faces, eagerly awaiting his words. He didn't recognise any of them, but this wasn't a group of school children listening to a lecture on the importance of online safety, or uniformed officers being given tasks in a manhunt, this was a room full of hardened journalists who were trained to spot every twitch, shake, stumble and hesitation and read more into it than just a nervous DI who didn't want to be there.

He cleared his throat, which, through the microphone, resounded around the room.

'Today, the Homicide and Major Crime Unit is launching an investigation into the deaths of four women in Sheffield over a period of three years.' DI Christian Brady spoke calmly and professionally into the microphone. 'These women all had one thing in common; they worked as street prostitutes. In a recent cold case review, we have concluded that all women were killed by the same individual and we are working hard to establish a timeline of events leading up to each woman's death so a suspect can be identified and apprehended.'

On the large screen behind Christian, the faces of four women were brought up.

'The dead women are identified as Ella Morse, Rachel Pickering, Deborah Monroe and Denise Jones. Anyone who has any information about these women or think they know anything about their deaths, or the person responsible should call South Yorkshire Police, *CrimeStoppers* or 111. Calls will be taken in strictest confidence. Details of each of the women, including dates and times of when they disappeared and were found, will be available at the end of this briefing.'

'We are also seeking the whereabouts of three women who also work as prostitutes in Sheffield.' Behind Christian, on the screen, the faces of the four dead women were replaced with photographs of the three missing women. 'Lucy Fletcher was last seen in December 2016. Fiona Bridger was last seen in January 2018 and Jackie Barclay was reported missing in April 2018. We have no information on whether these women are dead or alive. However, we know they worked in Sheffield and they may simply have moved on. Again, if anyone knows where these women are, please contact us. I will now take a few questions.'

Christian glanced over the ACC. They both braced themselves. They knew what kind of questions they were about to face.

'Stephanie Bishop, *The Sun*. Is there a serial killer targeting prostitutes operating in Sheffield? If so, why are we only hearing about this now, especially as, in your own words, the victims span a few years?'

Christian licked his lips and swallowed before he replied. 'As I said, in the light of a cold case review we have only just discovered all the victims share a common trait in the manner of their deaths.'

'What is that common trait?' the same reporter asked.

'That would be remiss of me to comment on at this stage.'

'Can you confirm or deny if this is the work of a serial killer?' Stephanie Bishop continued.

'I'm aware how much the media like to sensationalise these events, however, I implore you to remember these are dead young women we are dealing with here who have loved ones who are grieving for them,' Christian said. 'I can confirm the killings all bear a startling similarity, causing us to believe one person is responsible, but until we have more information, I am not going to tag the killer with a headline-grabbing label. Next question, please.'

'Jason Fairfax, ITN. What year was the first victim killed and why has it taken until now for you to realise one person has been killing throughout this whole time?'

'The first victim was Ella Morse. She was found dead in October 2016. I am aware that three years is a long time. Also, Ella's death was extensively investigated and although the trail soon went cold, it was never forgotten. The remit of the Homicide and Major Crime Unit is to investigate active murders and cold cases. We are launching this investigation today in the hope new evidence and witnesses may finally reveal the person responsible.'

'Clara Edwards, Sky News. What steps are being taken to protect the women working as prostitutes within South Yorkshire?'

'We have dedicated officers who have been working alongside the women over recent years. We're also working with Sheffield City Council and various local charities to make sure the women are as safe as possible.'

'Anna Pritchard, *Daily Mail*. It was reported in the summer that following the shooting at South Yorkshire Police earlier this year, you are several officers down. Have those officers been replaced and are you equipped to deal with an investigation into serial murder at this time?'

ACC Ridley cleared his throat and signalled to Christian

that he'd answer this question. Christian took this opportunity to have a long drink of water. His mouth was parched.

'It is true that we are still a number of officers short of where we were this time last year,' Ridley said. 'The recruitment process is ongoing. However, members of the Homicide and Major Crime Unit, along with CID, are long-standing professional detectives who are more than capable of investigating this crime. Should we need more officers, we will draft others in from neighbouring forces. We are not too proud to ask for help,' he said with a smile.

A man towards the back of the room stood up. He was tall and broad with a stylishly messy mound of jet-black hair. He wore a navy blue sweater with a white shirt beneath. 'I have the names of seven women who worked as prostitutes in Sheffield who have gone missing, all since 2016. Four of whom you didn't read out the names of. Do you know the whereabouts of these women? Do you presume them to be dead? If so, that would make eleven dead women over a space of three years. If that's not the work of a serial killer, I don't know what is.'

The room fell silent and all eyes were turned to the handsome young man at the back of the room.

Christian squinted in the bright lights. He couldn't make out the man asking the question. 'I didn't catch your name and the organisation you work for.'

'Danny Hanson. BBC News.'

Christian's heart sank. Danny had been a thorn in the side of the unit for a number of years when he was a journalist on the local newspaper, *The Star*. When he'd broken out into broadcast journalism and started working for the BBC, they all thought they'd heard the last of him. Obviously not.

'I wrote a piece last year about the long-lasting effects of austerity Britain and the lengths people have gone to in order to make ends meet. While interviewing a number of prostitutes on the streets of Sheffield I discovered seven women who have gone missing, only three of whom you've named.'

Christian hoped his expression wasn't giving away what was running around his mind. Could this possibly be correct? That would make for a very prolific serial killer. He wished Matilda were by his side right now.

He couldn't speak. He could feel everyone was looking at him, watching, waiting for him to say something, to put the power of control and order back into the hands of the police, but Christian's mind was blank. He had no idea what to say.

'Mr Hanson,' Ridley spoke up. 'We would be more than happy to discuss your research with you if you'd like to stay behind at the end of this press conference. I'm sure we can answer some of your concerns without mentioning the names of people you believe to be victims in front of the media and unnecessarily causing upset.'

Danny gave a rueful smile.

'Any more questions?' Ridley asked.

'I have one more,' Danny said, remaining on his feet. 'Does the launch of this investigation have anything to do with the return to work of DCI Matilda Darke and, if so, why isn't she here leading this press conference?'

Christian looked up and saw the annoying grinning face of Danny Hanson glaring back at him.

Chapter Seven

Matilda had known the time of the press conference and switched the radio on to catch it. She wanted to see how Christian handled it, and how the journalists reacted to what was, in all intents and purposes, a serial killer operating in Sheffield. She turned it off before Christian could answer the final question.

'I was listening to that,' Harriet said.

'That bloody man,' Matilda fumed.

'Who?'

'Danny fucking Hanson.'

'Who's he?

'A shit journalist who's been using my career to get himself out of a dying local paper and onto TV. He's the BBC's North of England Correspondent. Wanker,' she sat back, arms folded firmly across her chest. 'Everywhere I turn, there he is, glaring at me, watching me, waiting for me to say something to fuck up.'

'Is he the one who posed as a doctor to try to get into your hospital room?' Harriet asked.

'Yes, he bloody is.'

'Can't you get an injunction out against him or something?'

'He's doing his job. He's a journalist, after all. It's just I wish he'd piss off and do it elsewhere.'

'Why should he when he knows he can get great copy from you?' Pat said.

'Exactly. He's leeched onto me and I can't seem to shake him off.'

'He's very popular. He's often trending on Twitter when he's reporting,' Pat said. 'The women love him.'

'Why?'

'It's the dark floppy hair and the smiling eyes, apparently. You should read some of the things they say about him. I used to think I was unshockable.'

'That's just what that narcissist needs: an ego boost.'

'Is that right, what that reporter said?' Harriet asked. 'About there being seven other women missing?'

Matilda bit her bottom lip. 'As far as I'm aware there's only three.' She dug her phone out of her inside pocket and unlocked it. 'I'll ask Sian to look into it.'

'I know he enjoys the limelight,' Pat began from the back. 'Why not bring it to you sooner? Why wait until a press conference?'

'I've no idea.'

'And how did he know there was going to be a press conference about it? You only decided yourself last week when you returned to work. These women must have been missing for months, years maybe. Has he been sitting on this information all this time?'

Matilda frowned as she thought. 'That's a good point, Pat. You're wasted in retirement.'

'Tell me about it. I'll invoice you my consultant's fee,' she grinned.

A sign ahead indicated they should turn right at the roundabout for Manchester Airport. They were almost here. Matilda looked at her watch. The plane would be landing in half an hour. She could feel the butterflies fluttering around her stomach.

Chapter Eight

DS Scott Andrews and new recruit DC Zofia Nowak were sent out to Plantation Woods to investigate the discovery of a body.

The HMCU had lost two officers in the shooting, and another two had left shortly afterwards. However, they were only given one replacement, in the form of twenty-four-year-old Zofia, who had joined South Yorkshire Police just over a year ago. She was keen and eager to impress and was the first name on her sergeant's lips when it came to promoting someone to the prestigious team. Her boundless energy and constant questions were unrivalled, and she fitted into HMCU with ease.

Despite seeming confident and strong, Zofia was a mixed bag of worry. She joined the team when it was as its most vulnerable. The survivors were hurt, grieving and banded together to help lick each other's wounds. Only those who had been involved in the horrors of that day in January knew how the others felt. The biggest task Zofia faced on the day of the shooting was redirecting traffic from the Parkway.

She felt she was intruding on their grief. When they spoke of their fallen colleagues and remembered the good times, she didn't get the in-jokes and the stories they told. It was like they had their own secret language, and she couldn't understand a single word. She was an outsider.

She liked Scott. The blond hair, the blue eyes, the athletic build and the firm jawline. He was the definition of everything she wanted in a man. She knew he was gay from the talk around the station, but it didn't stop her having a soft spot for him. Grieving the loss of his boyfriend made him even more attractive. He had a sullen, brooding vibe going on that she found irresistible.

At only five foot four, Zofia was almost a foot shorter than Scott and had to trot alongside him to keep up as they made their way over the uneven ground of Plantation Woods to where the body had been found.

Zofia was wearing the wrong shoes. She stumbled and managed to right herself before she fell over and made a fool of herself. She tried to engage Scott in conversation, but he only gave monosyllabic replies.

They reached the scene of crime tent which covered the body. A swarm of white suited CSIs examined the area for evidence. Scott and Zofia were handed paper suits of their own to put on. Scott slipped into his with ease. Zofia took a little while longer. He didn't wait for her and disappeared through the flap in the tent while she was struggling with the overshoes.

Inside, Home Office Pathologist Adele Kean and her technical assistant Lucy Dauman were crouched over the body. A photographer was snapping away where Adele directed him to take pictures.

Adele and Scott had a personal connection. Scott's

boyfriend was Chris Kean, Adele's son. He was killed in the shooting at Stannington Secondary School when he put himself in the firing line to protect a group of students. Scott was there. He watched the man he loved die. He and Adele had never spoken about that day and they were each dealing with their grief alone and in their own way. For them both, it was the wrong way.

'What can you tell me?' Scott asked. His voice was low and quiet, a world away from the cheery dedicated detective of old.

'A young woman, early twenties, evidence of regular drug use,' Adele said, pointing out the track marks on a bare left arm. 'She was manually strangled. There are finger shape indentations and bruising around her neck. No skin samples under her nails, but she bit them so I can't tell if she tried to fight back. She was strangled from the front as the thumb print was pressed hard against the trachea.'

'Was she killed here, do you think?'

'Sorry, I couldn't get the overshoes on,' Zofia said, bursting into the tent.

'Adele, Lucy, have you met DC Zofia Nowak?'

Lucy smiled, but Adele didn't acknowledge her.

'We've already met,' Zofia said. 'I attended a post mortem a few weeks back.'

'You were saying, Adele.'

'I think she was murdered here. The ground beneath her is dry and there's evidence of a struggle around her. Then again, a dog bounded all over her, so he could have caused most of this.'

'Any identification on her?'

'Nothing at all. No bag, no purse, no mobile.'

Scott turned to Zofia. 'Call the station, ask if anyone matching her description has been reported missing.'

'Will do. Nice to see you both again,' she said with a smile, before leaving the tent.

'She's very willing, isn't she?' Lucy asked.

'It's like being followed around by a puppy,' Scott said.

'It could be worse; she could—'

'Are you two finished?' Adele asked standing up. 'I only ask because I have a great deal of work to do and don't particularly enjoying kneeling on the ground in a cold wood for hours on end.' There was an iciness to Adele's tone.

'Sorry, Adele,' Scott said. 'What else can you tell me about her? Was she sexually assaulted?'

'It doesn't look like it, though she doesn't have any knickers on. She's also very poorly dressed for the time of year, if you ask me.'

Scott looked down, taking in the short skirt and bare legs for the first time.

'Maybe she was wearing tights and pants and the killer stole them, for whatever reason?'

'And put her shoes back on her?'

Scott looked at the dead woman's feet. She was wearing well-worn Skechers trainers; the laces were done up.

'Maybe not then.'

'We'll take her prints and run them through the system. If anything comes up, we'll let you know. I can do the PM this afternoon if anyone wants to attend.'

'We're a bit short staffed at the moment.'

'Still? I thought Matilda would have found extra officers by now,' Adele said, snapping off her latex gloves.

'If only it were that easy. Besides, Matilda's away for the day too now.'

'Why? She only came back last week.'

'Hasn't she told you?'

Adele made eye contact with Scott for the first time. She quickly lowered her gaze, tore off her mask and left the tent.

'Is there something I should know about?'

Lucy stood up. 'Matilda and Adele haven't spoken to each other since before the shooting.'

'What? But that was months ago.'

'I know.'

'But why? They're best mates.'

'Not anymore by the looks of it.'

Lucy left the tent, leaving Scott alone with the dead body. He hadn't heard of Matilda and Adele falling out. Why weren't they talking to each other?

Scott shuddered as he opened the car door and climbed inside.

'It's getting colder out there.'

'I've just got off the phone with Sian. Nobody's been reported missing matching the woman's description.'

'I can't say I'm surprised. Okay, Zofia, answer me this one: a young woman with a history of drug use, out and about in the woods wearing skimpy, inappropriate clothing for the time of year, no tights and no knickers on. Who is she?'

Zofia thought for a moment. Her eyes darted around the car. She blew out her cheeks. 'I don't know. Maybe she's a prostitute.'

'That's what I thought too.'

'So, you think she was out here with a punter who killed her and robbed her of her mobile and what little cash she had on her?'

'Possibly.'

'But didn't Adele say she wasn't sexually assaulted?

Wouldn't a punter have had sex with her first, or raped her, before killing her?'

'Maybe he didn't want to kill her for sex. Maybe he just wanted to kill her,' Scott said, starting the car.

'Surely the sole purpose of killing a prostitute is sexually related. Someone just out to kill someone can kill anyone. You only target a prostitute if sex is involved. Don't you?'

'I've no idea. But I've got a strange feeling this young woman might be one of the missing women that Danny Hanson was talking about.'

Chapter Nine

'Have you dressed up?'

'Of course. It's a special occasion.'

Pat Campbell had been to the hairdressers yesterday to ask them to do something with the white mound that was growing in wild abandon on the top of her head. She'd pressed her best black trousers and bought a new cream sweater. She had a light black jacket over the top, and, unusually for Pat, she was wearing a touch of make-up. She looked elegant and fashionable.

'Are you expecting photographers?' Matilda asked as she noticed Pat looking around her as they stood at the entrance to the gate where the flight from Paris was arriving.

'No,' she said, almost disappointed.

Matilda had decided to soften her image. There was nothing she could do about her hair. It was growing back slowly and the scars from the gunshot and subsequent operations were strikingly visible. When she went out to the shops she put on a hat, but for work, and occasions like this, a hat wouldn't do. She often received lingering stares from strangers, but she was getting used to them, and, hopefully, it wouldn't be long before her hair grew back completely and covered up the scars. Out of sight, out of mind.

Matilda usually wore black, charcoal grey or navy. There was a dark, heavy colour to her wardrobe. Today, the severe look was inappropriate. She wore black trousers and a white shirt, open at the neck.

They both stood there, impatient, surrounded by the melee of airport noise. Around them, people were welcoming home relatives from holiday or business trips, or they were dashing to catch their flights. Little did they know they were mere inches away from an event that would be splashed all over the front pages of the newspapers tomorrow morning, and the following days to come.

'I feel nervous,' Matilda said.

'So do I. It makes you wonder how he feels, poor sod. How did he sound to you on the phone?'

Matilda's tensed face relaxed into a warm smile. 'He said he felt like he knew me. He's read all the stories about the case and he's read all about me. He even knew about me being shot and asked how I was feeling.'

'Bless him.'

'He has a very old head on his shoulders.'

'He's had a lot of growing up to do.'

'He's nervous, obviously, but that's only to be expected. He said...'

Matilda stopped when she saw the first people begin to come through the gate. She took a deep breath and waited.

People in business suits with laptop bags, the young and old returning with overnight bags after a mini break in Europe, and the absolutely shattered for whom the flight from Paris was the final leg in their long journey home, all dragged themselves past Matilda and Pat and on their way to collect their luggage.

'He's not here,' Pat said, disappointed, when the trickle of people stopped. 'Please tell me we've got the right airport.'

'Of course we have.' She looked at her watch.

A dog barked somewhere.

Matilda turned as something caught the corner of her eye. Her heart skipped a beat.

'Oh my God,' Pat said.

Matilda's throat dried. She began to shake and couldn't take her eyes from what she was seeing. She thought this day would never come. She tried to smile, but her face was frozen in shock.

'DCI Darke?' a woman with a thick Swedish accent asked.

'That's right.'

'And you know who this is?'

'I certainly do.' Matilda held out a hand. 'It's lovely to finally meet you, Carl.'

Chapter Ten

Christian and DC Finn Cotton made their way along the corridor on the top floor of South Yorkshire Police HQ to ACC Ridley's office.

'I've done some digging,' Finn said, reading from his iPad. 'Danny Hanson may work for the BBC but he's classed as freelance. Anything that comes up in this neck of the woods he's used. However, since his reporting on the shooting earlier this year, his stock value has risen. He's written articles for *The Guardian*, the *Sunday Times* and he's had a couple of features published in *The Observer*. He's doing very well for himself.'

'Annoying little runt,' Christian said with venom.

'He was shortlisted for an award this summer for a feature he wrote about the MP Vanessa Maitland. Remember her?'

'Vaguely.'

'She was caught on camera accepting money from a private company so they could get a contract on a children's hospital extension in Dorset. Also, he exposed Jonathan McDonald, MP for Blaydon in the North West, who was caught using a prostitute while his wife, also an MP, was undergoing treatment for cancer.'

Christian stopped in his tracks. 'He likes uncovering scandals then?'

'Yes. Do you want to know what he did in Essex that caused the Chief Constable to resign?'

'No, thank you, Finn. You know, there is such a thing as too much research.'

'I found it interesting.'

'And I bet you had Sian reading over your shoulder, too,' he said with a smirk.

'She did take an interest.'

'I bet she did. Hang on a minute,' Christian stopped dead in his tracks. 'He uncovered an MP seeing a prostitute?'

'Yes.'

'And suddenly he's come to us about missing prostitutes. Do we think Danny Hanson has an unhealthy interest in prostitutes?'

'I hadn't thought of that.'

They turned the corner and Christian knocked on the highly polished door. It was strange to hear a deep voice telling them to enter. He still expected to hear Valerie calling for him to come in.

Benjamin Ridley was sat behind his desk and Danny Hanson in front of it, a large folder on his lap. Both had relaxed, smiling faces, as if they'd shared a joke. Christian found this highly unsettling.

Ridley stood up. 'I believe you two already know each other.'

'We do,' Christian said through almost gritted teeth.

Danny stepped forward and held his hand out. 'It's a pleasure to meet you again.'

Reluctantly, Christian took his hand and briefly shook it.

'I was expecting DCI Matilda Darke. I believe she's back at work now.'

'She is,' Christian said.

'Isn't this something she would be heading?'

'DCI Darke is the head of the Homicide and Major Crime Unit. However, today, she is taking charge of another investigation. DI Brady stepped, very comfortably, into DCI Darke's shoes while she was recovering,' Ridley said.

'But Matilda is definitely working on this case?' Danny asked.

'It's DCI Darke to you,' Christian said. 'And yes, she is.'

'Maybe I could speak to her when she gets back.'

'Why?'

'She's in charge.'

'Danny, why the theatrics? I'm guessing it's taken a while for you to compile your list of missing women, why not come to us before now? Why wait until there is a press conference?'

Danny cleared his throat. 'I'm aware that I'm not well respected among the team, DI Brady. I'm also aware that as a journalist I'm seen as something akin to pond life by the police.'

'You think very highly of yourself,' Christian smirked.

Danny gave him an icy glare. 'If I'd tried to contact you, I'd have been ignored.'

'You really do have a chip on your shoulder, don't you, Danny?' Christian asked. 'If you'd approached us with legitimate information, we would have given it the respect it deserved. The reason you stood up in front of the nation's press was because you wanted the limelight on you. You wanted to show off in front of your contemporaries.'

'That is not true,' Danny smiled.

'You thought DCI Darke would be leading the press conference. All eyes would be on her, and you thought she'd be scared, nervous, her first big case since her return, and you wanted to show her up with your research.'

Danny slumped back in his chair, his face reddening. 'That is so not true.'

'It so is.'

'Look, I think we're getting away from why we're here,' ACC Ridley said, stepping in. 'I'm guessing there is some history between you both, however, we all have one common interest and that is seeking the truth in an investigation. Now, Mr Hanson, if you do have some information for us, I believe it's in everyone's interest for you to share it.'

It was a while before Danny spoke. He refused to take his eyes from Christian.

'You're right,' he smiled, turning to the ACC. He opened his folder and took out a single sheet of paper. 'I have the names of seven women, all of whom worked as prostitutes on the streets of Sheffield, all of whom are missing.'

'May I see the list?' Christian asked, trying to remain calm and professional.

He leaned across and handed it to him. 'Keep it. It's a copy.'

He glanced at it and handed it to Finn. He cast his eye down it, looked to his boss and shook his head slightly.

'Where did you get these names from?' Christian asked.

'By talking to the women.'

'We've been talking to them,' Finn spoke up.

'I think it's safe to say that some prostitutes are reluctant to talk to the police,' Ridley said. 'Many of them are working the streets to feed a drug habit. Despite DC Cotton and others saying they're looking out for them, wanting them to be safe, they may suspect an ulterior motive for police questioning. I don't think we can attribute blame anywhere in this.'

'I'm not blaming anyone,' Danny said.

'Your tone suggests otherwise,' Christian stated.

'I apologise for my speaking voice.' Danny's reply oozed with sarcasm. 'However, I'm sure South Yorkshire Police isn't unfamiliar with the concept of undercover work. I'm sure your officers could have talked to these women posing as a charity worker, a fellow prostitute, or even a journalist to uncover more information.'

'We believed we were being told the truth,' Finn said. 'You can't probe someone, force them into giving you information when they're vulnerable and fragile. You'd scare them away.'

Christian looked at Finn and smiled.

'No, you can't,' Danny agreed. 'Which is where undercover work comes in.'

'If you go undercover and your cover is exposed that will make them mistrust the police even more,' Finn said, his voice growing in volume, clearly angry with Danny questioning the work he had done with Sian over the years.

'Look, I think things are getting a little heated here,' Ridley said. 'Mr Hanson, I thank you for bringing this matter to our attention and we will of course investigate the names you have given us.'

'I'd like to sit in on the investigation,' Danny said, staring directly at Christian.

'Out of the question,' he said firmly.

'Why?'

'I have never had a journalist shadowing me and I refuse to start now.'

'I won't be shadowing you, merely observing the investigative process.'

'No.'

Danny looked to Ridley.

'It's DCI Darke and DI Brady's investigation,' Ridley said, removing himself from the debate.

'Maybe I should speak to DCI Darke when she returns.'

'Danny, you do not have the ability to sit in a room full of detectives for an eight-hour shift and remain quiet while they work around you. It's not in your nature. I also won't have you commenting on, instructing and belittling my officers. We're a highly skilled and dedicated team. We work together and we get results. We're searching for a serial—' He stopped himself dead.

Danny grinned. 'So now you admit you have a serial killer on your hands?'

Christian cleared his throat a couple of times. He needed a drink, and not necessarily water. 'I... I...' he stuttered.

'We are looking for a man who has committed multiple murders.' Finn spoke up for Christian. 'His victims of choice seem to be prostitutes. If you want to lower yourself to the standards of the red-tops and call him a serial killer, you're free to do so. We don't believe in panicking the public with tabloid jargon. And, you're correct, we do think you're akin to pond life.'

For the first time in the whole discussion, Danny's smile dropped.

———

'Where did that come from?' Christian asked Finn once they were out of Ridley's office and in the corridor.

'I've no idea. I'm so sorry. It's just when he started saying how we weren't doing our job properly, I saw red. I'm sorry,' Finn said quickly.

'Don't apologise. You did magnificently. I couldn't have said it better myself,' he smiled.

'Really?' He looked concerned.

'Absolutely. You stood up for yourself, and your team. I'm proud of you.'

He beamed. 'Thanks. Ridley won't give me a bollocking, will he?'

'I won't let him. Come on, let's go and raid Sian's snack drawer while she's out. We've earned it.'

He put his arm around Finn's shoulders and headed down the corridor towards the stairs.

Chapter Eleven

Adele Kean was sat in her small office, her head in her hands. She needed a few minutes to herself after attending the crime scene at Plantation Woods this morning.

Adele had always had a heavy workload, but in recent months she had thrown herself head-first into it. Apart from her full-time work at the Medico-Legal Centre, she decided to return to lecturing the next generation of pathologists at the University of Sheffield. She was also writing a book detailing the life and procedures of a Home Office Pathologist. She had received a healthy advance from her publisher and the deadline was looming. Adele had never been so busy, and it was this work that kept her mind active and stopped her drifting into the darkness.

Over the past year, her work had noticeably changed, and she'd taken on tougher cases that had ingrained themselves in her memory. Never before had death lingered following a post mortem, but the world had changed, not for the better, and Adele was only human, after all.

Adele had been chief pathologist on the Westminster

Bridge terrorist attack in March 2017. Two months later she coordinated the autopsies on the twenty-two victims of the Manchester Arena bombing. Less than two weeks later she was back in London dealing with the aftermath of the London Bridge attack in which eight people were murdered.

She had a strong support network around her. Her parents were no longer around, but her son, Chris, was a young man with a sensible head on his shoulders. He was able to provide his mother with help whenever she needed it. And in 2017, she needed a great deal of comfort. Her best friend, Matilda, was more like a sister. They had a strong bond. They were always there for each other whenever needed. No questions asked.

Chris's senseless murder and almost losing Matilda had a terrible effect on Adele. Matilda was in an induced coma for a number of weeks and she hadn't been able to attend Chris's funeral. Adele went home every night to a large empty house. She had nobody to talk to, nobody to cry with, to reminisce about the good times and help her come to terms with the biggest catastrophe she had ever faced. She was coping by not coping.

There was a light tapping on the door. She looked up and saw her technical assistant Lucy Dauman through the glass. She tucked her blonde hair behind her ear and pushed the door open.

'We're ready when you are,' Lucy said in a soft voice.

'Right,' she smiled. In the few minutes she allowed herself to relax, her thoughts drifted. She pictured her son as he was the last time she saw him, laid out in his coffin. He looked peaceful, clean, smart in his favourite designer suit. Death had robbed him of his personality. It wasn't her son lying there, just a figure who happened to look like him. She cried when the funeral director stepped forward to put the lid into place and began screwing it down. She'd been crying ever since.

She took a deep breath to steady herself. It didn't work. She was tense, emotional and could feel her professionalism slowly ebbing away from her.

'Adele,' Lucy said, stepping into the office, 'I know … well, I know you're not in a good place at the moment, but, well, it's my hen weekend in a few weeks. I'd really like you to come.'

Adele tried to smile, but she could feel her lips wobbling, her cheeks shaking. 'I don't think you'll want someone my age cramping your style.'

'Don't be silly. There are all ages going. My gran's coming and she's in her eighties. She's such a party animal. She'll probably be the last one of us to go to bed,' she laughed. 'I'd love you to come.'

'Thanks, but I'm really busy at the moment. I've got two lectures to prepare for and I'm almost finished with the first draft of the book I'm writing.'

'Adele, don't you think you're taking on too much work?'

She frowned. 'No. Did you say the next one is prepped?'

'Yes.'

'I'll go and scrub up then,' she said, turning off her laptop.

'I'd really love you to come to the hen weekend, Adele,' Lucy said with genuine warmth.

Adele stopped as if thinking for a moment. 'I appreciate you asking me, Lucy, but I'm not up to it right now. Thanks anyway.'

'Adele.' Lucy sat on the edge of her desk. 'I wish you'd talk to me. I know you're hurting, but you need to open up. You'll go mad if you don't.'

It didn't take much to bring Adele to tears these days. It only took the briefest mention of the shooting for the emotions she was struggling to suppress to come hurtling back to the surface. She didn't dare risk speaking. She knew her words would be lost to tears if she tried. She proffered a weak smile and nodded.

'Why don't you go and see Matilda? You haven't visited her since she went back home from the rehab centre. I'm sure she'd love to see you.'

'I can't,' she croaked.

'Why not?'

She shrugged, fearing to say anything else in case it unleashed a torrent of tears.

'Are you worried about seeing Scott?'

'No, it's not that.'

'What is it then?'

'I can't say,' she said with a painful lump in her throat.

'Adele.' Lucy leaned forward and placed a hand on her boss's shoulder. 'I know I'm not Matilda, but I'd like to think we're friends. You can tell me anything. It won't go any further.'

Adele took another deep breath. She braced herself but didn't dare look at Lucy.

'The gunman was after Matilda. He didn't get her. But he got my Chris.' She cried. Tears rushed down her cheeks. 'I hate myself for thinking it but…'

'Hello!' A call came out from the entrance to the autopsy suite. It was DS Sian Mills.

'Shit,' Adele uttered under her breath and turned away, quickly wiping her eyes.

Lucy ran out into the suite to stop Sian from stepping into the office and seeing Adele crying. 'Hi, Sian, you're a bit late if you've come for the post mortem. We had all the fun without you,' she said with a smile, tucking her hair behind her ear.

'You've been working here too long, Lucy, you're getting as ghoulish as Adele.'

'Oh my God, I am, aren't I?' She frowned. 'Maybe I should have gone into catering after all.'

Adele came out of her office. She said hello to Sian and avoided eye contact at all costs, keeping her head down and going about her business at a hundred miles per hour. She went over to the bank of fridges, opened the door and pulled out the runner with Carly Roberts on it, her body covered with a white sheet. She folded it back to reveal the head and shoulders.

Carly looked younger than her twenty years. She was pale, clean and her dark brown hair was neatly combed.

'Cause of death isn't easy to determine, I'm afraid. She was strangled as you can see by the bruising around her neck, but have a look here,' Adele pushed the sheet down lower to reveal her naked torso. It was a map of bruises. 'She was severely beaten. By the shape and size of the bruises I'd say she was kicked. There are a few broken ribs which resulted in a pneumothorax in both lungs. However, you'll be more interested in the neck. As you can see there are thumb marks on the front of her neck and her windpipe was bruised. There are also fingernail indentations in the back of her neck. Her attacker had a very tight grip.' Not once did Adele look at Sian, preferring to keep her eyes on Carly. Her voice was a tired monotone.

'Any guess as to male or female?'

'Male. His hands wrapped around her neck and his fingers overlapped around the back. I've never seen a woman with such big hands. She has the beginning of petechial haemorrhage in the skin on her face and the lining of her eyelids.'

'Was she raped?'

'I don't think so. Though she had performed oral sex not long before she died. I swabbed around her mouth and found traces of semen between her teeth, at the back of her mouth, in the trachea and upper oesophagus.'

'Enough for a DNA sample?'

'I'm not sure yet. I've sent it off for analysis. I'll have to get back to you on that one.'

'Any drugs in her system?'

Adele pushed the white sheet further down the body to reveal Carly's arm. 'Several needle marks, old and new, on the inside of both arms.'

'Is there anything else you can tell me about how she died?' Sian asked, not taking her eyes off the young woman.

'No. However, I can tell you something about the killer.'

'Go on.'

'I was doing some research for the book I'm writing, and my publisher asked for a chapter about unsolved murder cases and how often we relook at forensics and post mortem results as technology advances. I had a look back through my reports, and I was using Rachel Pickering as an example. I'm not sure if you recall but she was found murdered in Graves Park in June 2017. She was a prostitute working the red-light district.'

'Of course I remember. I have her details on my desk,' Sian said.

'Looking at the injuries to Carly's neck and those to Rachel's neck I would say the same person inflicted both sets of injuries.'

'Really?'

'They also match the injuries which killed Ella Morse and Deborah Monroe.'

'Oh my God,' Sian said. 'How sure are you?'

'Let me show you.'

Back in Adele's small and chaotic office, she put her hands straightaway on what she was seeking among the mess of folders, files and textbooks.

'This is a photograph of Ella Morse,' Adele said, placing a coloured picture of Ella on the table. It had been taken before the post mortem began and showed a close-up of the young woman's neck. 'She'd been missing for two months before she was found so obviously the marks around her neck aren't as clear as Carly's, but we were able to see bruising where the killer had pressed down on her throat. Thumbprints on the windpipe, fingerprints around the back of the neck and fingernail indentations overlapping each other. Exactly the same with Carly Roberts this morning.'

'Can you get fingerprints from the skin?'

'Not in these cases, I'm afraid.'

'Shame.'

'However, you can link Carly Roberts to your four women with the positioning of the fingers. I doubt you'd find two killers with an identical way of murdering their victims.'

The door to the suite opened and Lucy came back in carrying a supply of latex gloves.

'Lucy, have you got a minute?' Adele called.

'Sure.'

'I forgot to ask,' Sian said. 'How long until the big day?'

'Two months, two weeks and four days. Not that I'm counting or anything,' Lucy said with a huge grin on her face.

'Lucy, come here, I want to strangle you,' Adele said, remaining on topic.

'I'd rather you didn't. I've spent a fortune on this wedding already,' she laughed.

Adele rolled her eyes. 'Let me show you how the killer

gripped his victims,' she said to Sian. 'Lucy, just drop to your knees. I think it's safe to say that the killer will be much taller than his victims.'

Adele placed her cold hands around Lucy's warm neck. She pressed her thumbs against the windpipe and removed them, showing a slight reddening where they'd been.

'See, that would have caused the bruising. Also, notice my fingers on the side of her neck as they wrap around. Now, my fingertips won't go all the way around Lucy's neck, but if I show you how the killer's would have looked...' She interlocked her fingers at the tips and pressed them to the back of Lucy's neck, where Lucy had pulled her hair up out of the way. Adele pressed her fingers firmly into the skin.

'Ouch!' Lucy exclaimed.

'Sorry. I didn't mean to press so hard. But, if you see the fingernail indentations, it gives you some idea of how much longer and bigger the killer's hands are. He was able to wrap both hands quite comfortably around each victim's neck.'

'So he's a powerful man?'

'I'd say so. I take a size medium glove, so just imagine how big his hands are.'

'Jesus!' Sian muttered.

'Can I get up now?' Lucy asked.

'Yes. Thank you, Lucy.'

'I'd say you're welcome, but I think you might have enjoyed that a little too much.' She turned and left, rubbing at her neck.

'If she goes on any more about this sodding wedding, I may have to throttle her for real.'

Sian laughed. 'Why do people seem to think their good news is something everyone else wants to hear about over and over?'

'I know. Anyone would think she's the first person ever to marry.'

'Well, thanks for this, Adele. You've confirmed what I was dreading, but at least we know where we stand.'

'Erm, how's ... how's Matilda getting on?' Adele asked, hesitantly.

'Fine. Hasn't she kept you up to date on things?'

'No. We haven't spoken much since ... well, we haven't spoken at all really.'

'What? Since when?'

'I went to see her in the hospital just after she'd come out of the coma.'

'You haven't seen her for nine months?'

'No.'

'Why not?'

'It's ... complicated. I just... No, it doesn't matter. I'd better be getting on.' With her head down, Adele turned and went into her office, closing the door behind her.

Sian followed. 'Adele, is everything all right?'

'Yes, fine,' she said, her back to Sian.

'We both know that's a lie. You haven't seen Matilda since she was in hospital in January. You're best friends. You're closer to her than her sister is. Why haven't you been to see her?'

'I've been busy,' she said, picking up a stack of files and wondering what to do with them.

'You're always busy, but you've always found time to go round with a couple of bottles of wine and watch a bad film in the past.'

'I'm writing a book, Sian. Do you have any idea how time-consuming that is? Now, I'm sorry, but I must get on.'

Sian studied the pathologist. There was so much pain in her

expression, but it was hidden behind a stony facade. 'Right. Okay. Well, thanks for all this.' Sian stepped back, turned and headed for the doors. She stopped and looked back. Through the slats of the Venetian blinds in Adele's office, Sian could see the stoic pathologist was crying.

Chapter Twelve

Carl Meagan was incredibly important to Matilda Darke. At the time he was kidnapped, Matilda was struggling to cope with her husband, James, dying from a brain tumour. She told no one and threw herself into her work to avoid confronting the fact she was losing him. On the day of the ransom drop, James had died in the early hours of the morning. Matilda should have handed the case over but continued as if everything was fine. Her mind wasn't on the case. She messed up. Carl disappeared and whenever she thought of Carl, she thought of James. She'd done everything in her power to keep the Meagan case alive. If she could atone and bring him home, maybe she'd be able to salvage some happiness from her wreck of a life.

A room at Manchester Airport had been booked for Matilda and Pat to have a chat with Carl Meagan before they headed back to Sheffield. It was a simple room, mostly used to interview people who were suspected of smuggling something illegal into the country.

Crammed around a small table, Matilda and Pat were on

one side, and Carl was on the other with the detective from Sweden, Alva Olsson, who had been the one to rescue Carl and remained by his side ever since. She was a tall, homely-looking woman with a lived-in face and dyed blonde hair. Her eyes were a pale blue and her permanent smile was warm. She spoke in heavily accented English and in the few days they had been together, she seemed to have struck a bond with Carl.

At his feet laid his golden Labrador, Woody. He had been bought for Carl by his captors and, although they didn't know it, he was a reminder of what he had waiting for him at home in Sheffield. Matilda had been informed the dog had a passport and didn't need to be quarantined. Carl had no intention of letting Woody go; he'd been the only ray of light in the darkness. He was his security blanket and judging by how close the young dog stayed to Carl, the same could be applied in reverse.

Matilda had never met Carl in person. She only knew about him once he'd been kidnapped. However, she'd seen countless photographs of him from when he was born until he disappeared at the age of seven. He was constantly smiling in them. His blond hair was soft and floppy. His blue eyes were wide. He was happy and healthy and enjoying his young life. His face had filled her nightmares when the kidnapping went awry, and she failed to return him home to his parents. She dreamed this day would come, but never expected it to. Now that it was here, she almost had to pinch herself. Matilda wanted nothing more than to wrap her arms around the now eleven-year-old boy.

His appearance had changed over the years. He was taller and thinner, but still looked healthy. He had obviously been looked after by whoever had bought him from the kidnappers.

There was a sadness to his eyes. Every time he looked up and smiled at Matilda, it didn't reach his eyes. He looked lost.

'How are you feeling?' Matilda asked.

'I'm fine. Tired,' he said. His voice was quiet and there was a Nordic hint to his Sheffield accent.

'Carl, this is Pat. She's a retired detective, but she's helped me, and your mum and dad, a great deal in trying to find you.'

Pat grinned. 'I've been so excited to meet you, Carl.'

Carl gave his eye-less smile again.

'Carl,' Matilda began. 'Alva informed me that you've read all about your disappearance and the investigation. You know what happened to your gran, but when you were taken, what happened to you?'

Carl looked to Alva. She smiled and tilted her head to one side. She placed a comforting hand on top of his.

He took a deep breath. 'I was taken to a house. I don't know where it was. It was dark. I think I was in a cellar, though.'

'The men who took you, do you remember what they looked like?'

He shook his head. 'When I close my eyes, I try to remember, but I don't see them. I can hear them, but their faces aren't there.'

'Okay. Did they talk to you, tell you what was happening?'

'Not much. They brought me meals and something to drink. They brought me a blanket and books to read. After a while they said they were waiting for Mum and Dad to pay them and I could go back home.' His eyes filled with tears. He looked up. 'I heard you.'

'Sorry?'

'When I was in the back of the car. I heard you shouting my name.'

Matilda's bottom lip wobbled, and tears fell from her eyes. Pat held her hand under the table.

'I shouted back, but ...' His voice broke as emotion took over.

'Carl, I am so sorry,' Matilda said. She leaned forward across the table and took his hands in hers. 'I really am sorry I couldn't save you.'

'They said ... they said that Mum and Dad didn't want me as they didn't pay.'

He cried. Woody jumped up from the floor and placed his head on Carl's lap.

'That's not true, Carl. They did want you back. I did everything I could to get you home.'

'I know. I've read the book.'

'You read the book your mum wrote?' Pat asked.

He nodded.

'It doesn't paint me in a very good light, I'm afraid,' Matilda said through the tears.

'Were you in Sweden when you read the book?' Pat asked.

'Yes. I only read it last year.'

'Why didn't you go to the police and tell them who you were?'

'I couldn't.'

'Why not?'

'The man who I was supposed to call my dad, he ... he used to have someone come to the house, to visit. He wore a police uniform.'

'The couple we arrested,' Alva said. 'Theo and Hanna Sandberg. Theo's brother, Arvid, worked for the local police.'

'Did he know they'd bought Carl?'

'No. I don't know Arvid personally, but he's been extensively questioned, and he knew nothing about this.'

'Whenever he came to the house, I had to hide in the attic,' Carl said. 'I saw him coming and going. They were always laughing and smiling. I thought that if I'd gone to the police, he would have taken me back to them.'

Matilda shook her head. 'You must have been so scared,' she said, gripping his hands firmer.

'I was at first. Woody helped me.'

'Do you think Woody back in Sheffield will get on with your new dog?'

'I hope so,' he said with a genuine smile, the first one to reach his eyes.

'I'm sure they will,' Pat said. 'Every time I visit, I take him a Bonio. He's really missed you.'

'I've missed him, too. Will I be going back home now?' he asked. He looked nervous.

'Yes,' Matilda said. 'We will need to speak to you more about what happened as we need to get the men who took you, and we're going to arrange for you to speak to a professional, a therapist, who will help you settle back in.'

'Do Mum and Dad know I'm coming home today?'

'Yes, they do. And they're very excited.'

'Will you be coming too?' Carl asked Alva.

'I'm afraid not. I have to go back to Sweden. But I'm going to keep in contact with Matilda, and she is going to tell me how you're getting on.'

'Could you…?'

'Carl,' Pat interrupted. 'How about we take Woody for a walk outside. He's not done anything since he got off the plane. I bet he's bursting.'

'Okay.' He stood up. He wiped his eyes with the back of his right hand before holding it out for Alva to shake. 'Thank you for everything you've done for me.'

'It's been my pleasure, Carl,' she said, struggling to hold back the tears. 'Will you promise me one thing?'

'What's that?'

'To go back home, enjoy your life and make all those who love you proud.'

He smiled. 'I will.'

Pat led the way, taking Carl and Woody out of the room. She closed the door firmly behind her.

Matilda wiped her eyes. 'He was going to ask you to keep in touch.'

'He already has done. Several times on plane over here.'

'What did you say?'

'I told him that it would remind him of what happened, and it would be better if he tried to move forward.'

'Did he mind?'

'At first, but he's been through a great deal. He just wants some stability. He'll get that at home.'

'Did you know it was Carl when you went into the house?'

'No. A neighbour said she'd seen a young boy in the garden a few times but knew they didn't have any children of their own. She said she'd vaguely asked about a child, but they denied that one was there. That's when she contacted us. We watched the house for a few days and decided to swoop in. When we realised who he was, we couldn't believe it,' she grinned.

'And he's fine, no physical injuries or anything?'

'Nothing at all. Two doctors have looked him over. He's fine. He hasn't been mistreated. Hanna Sandberg had six miscarriages. All she wanted was a child.'

'What about adopting? Surely you have children in Sweden who need adopting.'

'Many. Their ages went against them. They felt this was their only way.'

Matilda suddenly felt sympathy for Hanna Sandberg. She had suffered a miscarriage earlier this year. She had never wanted children and often wondered how she would have reacted had she found out she was pregnant and not been shot. And there was Hanna, desperate for a baby at any cost.

'Have they given a description of the men they bought Carl from?'

'Not great descriptions. We have a mobile number that no longer works.'

'Any help you require, just let me know. I think these men are likely to be local. They knew the Meagans were going to be out that night. I want them caught for the murder of his grandmother.'

Alva stood up and went over to the window. Outside, Pat had found a patch of grass. Woody was sniffing at a tree before he cocked his leg. She was chatting to Carl and he was chatting back. It looked a picture of normality.

'He was preparing to run away, you know?' Alva said.

'Really?'

'He'd been stealing the odd can of food and money from Hanna's wallet. When he had enough, he was going to try to get back to England on his own.'

'Oh God,' Matilda said, slapping a hand to her chest. 'Who knows what would have happened to him.'

'He had more than enough money under his bed for a plane ticket. I think he was scared.'

'I suppose he thought he was doing something positive.'

'Probably. How do you think he'll cope with returning home?' Alva asked.

Matilda thought for a while. 'I have absolutely no idea.'

Chapter Thirteen

Sian entered the HMCU suite. Her hair was windswept and her cheeks red from the cold breeze that had picked up outside.

'Any news from Matilda?'

'Not yet,' Finn answered.

'It's a shame we couldn't all have taken the day off and had some kind of party.'

'I know I wasn't on the original investigation or anything,' Finn said, leaning back in his seat. 'But I've got a special bottle of wine at home that I may have to crack open tonight. A mini celebration, just me and Stephanie.'

'That's a good idea. I may have to do something special with Stuart. He'll be just as pleased, after all the crying I've done over that little lad these past years. Anyway, getting back to topic,' she said, shaking off her coat and flicking the kettle on. 'We have an ID on the dead body found this morning.'

'Really? Who?'

'Carly Roberts.'

'She's one of our prostitutes,' Finn said.

'I know. And she's not listed as missing either which means...'

'Which means our killer has struck again.'

'My thoughts exactly. Christian!' she called out.

Christian was in Matilda's office. He stuck his head out of the door. 'Yes.'

'Any chance of rallying the troops for a briefing?'

'I've been researching the seven names Danny Hanson gave us,' Zofia said. 'We know about three of them going missing, Lucy, Fiona and Jackie, so that only leaves four. Two of them have turned up. Julia Forsythe is working as a prostitute in Bradford and Angela Whitaker is working at a brothel in Leeds.'

'Who are we left with?' Finn asked.

'Caroline Richardson and Monica Yates.'

'So, that's five missing and if we add the woman found dead this morning, Carly Roberts, that makes five confirmed murdered prostitutes,' Sian said.

'Bloody hell! Ten potential victims,' Scott said.

'Before we get ahead of ourselves,' Christian said, standing up. 'We have five murdered women. Let's try and keep those who are missing separate until we know otherwise. It's bad enough they're missing without us writing them off as being murdered. Two have turned up in other cities, maybe the others will, too.'

'I should probably go and talk to Bev,' Sian said.

'Who's Bev?' Zofia asked.

'She's been working the streets longer than anyone. She knows all the women.'

'How reliable is she going to be, though?' Christian asked. 'She didn't tell us about the four we didn't know about.'

'Maybe she didn't know.'

'You just said she knows all the women.'

'Then I'll ask her about them. Now, back to Carly. Scott, anything from the scene?'

'No,' he said. 'Forensics are still out there, but we all know what an outdoor crime scene is like when left overnight to the elements. They're not very hopeful.'

'No houses nearby?'

'None.'

'Has she been reported missing?'

'No,' Zofia said.

'Well, she has a record for two assaults last year. I'll check out the address we have for her, see if she still lives there,' Sian said.

'Can we go over these murders again?' Finn asked. 'I want to try something.'

When Finn teamed up with Sian in liaising with the prostitutes, he took an interest in the four they knew had been murdered over the past three years. He wanted to understand what kind of a person they should be looking for. There was no forensic evidence and no eyewitnesses to the killings. The only way to try and catch this killer, Finn surmised, was from a psychological point of view. He took it upon himself to enrol in a criminal psychology course with the Open University. He'd been working hard at it for over a year but kept it quiet in case he failed. However, once the dust had settled following the shootings, he decided to be more open with his colleagues and shared his news.

Sian picked up her iPad and went over to the murder board where photographs of the four dead women were placed.

'Our first victim is Ella Morse,' Sian began. 'She went missing in August 2016 and was found in October in Endcliffe Woods by a council worker. She'd been strangled. She lived in a council flat in Pitsmoor with Lucy Fletcher who also worked as a prostitute. She went missing in December 2016 and is still missing.' She moved along the board and pointed at a photograph of a young woman with dark hair and a dark complexion. 'Victim number two is Rachel Pickering. She was reported missing in February 2017. She was found in June partially buried in woodland in Graves Park. Again, she'd been strangled. Victim number three is Deborah Monroe. She was reported missing in July 2017 and found in November. Here, the cause of death differs. There is evidence she was strangled as she has the same marks on her neck as the others, but the official cause of death is she was beaten to death.'

'Bastard,' Zofia said quietly, bowing her head.

'Are you all right?' Scott asked.

She nodded. 'You can picture it, can't you? Some hulking bloke who thinks he can treat these women however he wants. He's strangled and kicked them to death like they're nothing; something to be used for his own sick pleasure.'

'I know it's easier said than done, Zofia,' Christian said, 'but try not to let it get to you like that. Our job is to make sure he's caught so other women don't suffer the same fate. We can't bring them back, but we can make sure he's convicted for what he's done.'

Zofia gave a pained smile of thanks.

Sian waited a long moment before continuing. 'There are three missing women in between victims three and four, that we know of: Lucy, Fiona and Jackie. Victim number four is Denise Jones. She was killed in September 2018. She was found the day after she was reported missing. Like the third victim she had been strangled and beaten to death. She was found in Chelsea Park by a dog walker. There was no evidence the killer had tried to conceal her body. She was left exposed to the elements. Now, after September 2018, the killer seems to stop. We have no reports of women going missing until Carly Roberts yesterday. That's thirteen months of silence.'

'Killers don't just stop, though, do they?' Zofia asked.

'Yes,' Finn said. All eyes turned to him. 'Serial killers commit their crimes as an outlet for something. It's possible that their circumstances changed, for whatever reason, and they were able to get the same gratification elsewhere. Dennis Radar, the BTK Killer, murdered ten people from 1974 until 1991. He wasn't captured until 2005. That's fourteen years without committing a murder. He simply stopped.'

'Why?' Zofia asked, genuinely interested.

'Well, if memory serves me correctly, the reason Radar gave for stopping was that he turned to, erm, autoerotic activities to quench his thirsts.'

'And he got the same buzz from that as from killing?' she asked.

'Yes.'

'But in this case, it was only thirteen months. Surely that isn't long enough to find another outlet only for it to not give him the same kick as killing.'

'Not necessarily. Say this killer turned to autoerotica. Maybe the high didn't last as long. He gave it a good try and after thirteen months decided to go back to killing. Or, maybe, he was sent to prison for a lesser crime, was released, and decided to pick up where he left off. There are many reasons why a killer stops and starts again.'

'It's like having Robbie Coltrane in the room with us,' Sian said with a smile.

'Who?' Zofia asked.

'You're showing your age, Sian,' Christian grinned.

'How many women are listed simply as missing again?' Scott asked, looking back at the murder wall.

'We know of three. Danny Hanson has given us potentially two more,' Christian said.

'I'll update the board in a bit,' Sian said.

'How can a man murder so many people and we're only just putting all this together?' Scott said.

'Ask Fitz,' Sian said, nodding towards Finn.

'Who?' Zofia asked.

'Oh my God.'

'The majority of people who are killed by serial killers come from five groups,' Finn began, counting them off on his fingers. 'Prostitutes, babies and small children, the elderly, young people leaving home and moving to another part of the country, say to go to university or something, and,' he looked over to Scott, 'gay men.'

'Why those people?' Zofia asked.

'They all have one thing in common. They're vulnerable,' Finn said. 'They're easy targets. A killer will go for a victim who is easy for them to get access to.'

'And this killer has chosen prostitutes?'

'It would appear so.'

'Do we know how many prostitutes are working the streets of Sheffield?' Zofia asked.

'As far as we know, there are between forty and fifty women currently working in Sheffield,' Sian said. 'However, it will be much higher. There are women working in brothels and saunas, those who meet men via an app, those who have a pimp who arranges meets via mobile phone. The women we have in our database are all those we've spoken to who work the streets.'

'So, where do we go from here?'

'If you look at the victims,' Finn stood up and went over to the murder board, 'the first three were either buried or partially buried. Number four, Denise Jones, and our new one, Carly Roberts, were left out in the open. It seems that he's decided he wants recognition for his crimes.'

'How do you know that?' Zofia asked.

'Because he made no attempt to hide them. The previous three were found by accident. Denise and Carly couldn't have been missed. Just killing no longer gives him the kick it used to, he now needs the chase. The press conference this morning has alerted him that we're now on his scent. He knows we're going to be hunting for him, and this will give him his next high.'

'But surely the press conference was the wrong thing to do then,' Zofia said. 'Surely the best thing would be to analyse what we've got and, hopefully, take him by surprise.'

'No. By alerting the killer, we're also alerting everyone who knows him. People are going to start wondering who the killer is. They'll look around them, see who has started behaving differently and changed in their personality over the years. We've opened him up to everyone. He'll start getting paranoid. That's when he'll make a mistake.'

'You mean he'll kill again?' Zofia asked.

'He'll try.'

'How do we stop him?'

'By protecting his targets.'

'Surely we can't protect them all.'

'We need to give it a bloody good try,' Sian said.

Chapter Fourteen

Sian arranged to meet Bev in a café in the city centre just after four o'clock. She knew she'd arrive with Sarah in tow. The two were inseparable. When she arrived at the Blue Moon Café on St James' Street next to the cathedral, they were already waiting outside for her.

Bev was forty-eight years old but looked a great deal older. She'd been working the streets since she was twenty-five and a lifetime of being out in all weathers, surviving on very little money and alcohol addiction, had taken its toll on her appearance. From the outside, she looked a hard-faced, no-nonsense woman, but she had a heart of gold and cared for each and every one of the girls who were prostituting themselves on the streets of Sheffield. She was wearing her customary shiny faded black leggings and had a pink and black zebra print sweater on beneath a fake-fur coat. Her skin was the colour of leather. Her thin hair was dyed blonde and she over-plucked her eyebrows, giving her a permanently perplexed expression. She stood five feet nine inches tall and was painfully thin.

'Afternoon. Are you both well?'

'Well, I woke up this morning, so I assume so,' Bev said with a chuckle. Sarah rarely spoke so simply smiled.

'Shall we go in?' Sian said, shivering slightly in the cold breeze.

Bev and Sarah entered the café first and went to sit down while Sian went to order.

Sarah was a good deal shorter than Bev and slightly older at fifty-one. She didn't speak much and lacked confidence, always allowing Bev to take the lead and make decisions for her. Originally from Barnsley, Sarah had been in Sheffield for more than thirty years. She had an ex-husband and children somewhere, but they didn't want anything to do with their ex-junkie, alcoholic mother. She spent every night clutching an old and fragile photograph of her two kids and cried herself to sleep. She was a slave to her addictions and had fallen off the wagon on a number of occasions; so much so, she had decided long ago not to try and get back on it.

Sian carried the tray of teas and sandwiches over, and Bev and Sarah quickly helped themselves.

'I'm bloody starving,' Bev said. 'Don't wolf that lot down, Sarah. Your stomach's still recovering.'

'Haven't you been well?' Sian asked.

'She had some noodles from a van the other night,' Bev answered for her. 'I told her the bloke had dirty fingernails, but she wouldn't listen. She spent two nights vomiting. Street food, it's called. That's where it belongs in my opinion. I wouldn't give it to a starving dog.'

'Bev,' Sian began after clearing her throat. 'Do you know someone by the name of Carly Roberts?'

'Carly? Aye.' She looked up and saw Sian's pained expression. 'She hasn't got herself arrested, has she?'

'Nothing like that. I'm afraid she was killed late last night.'

'What?' Both Bev and Sarah stopped eating and looked at Sian with their mouths open. 'Where?'

'In woods out towards Tankersley. Just off Westwood New Road. Do you know what she would have been doing there?'

They looked at each other.

'No.' Bev shook her head. 'We only saw her last night, too. Sarah said she was okay to go out, so we did, but it wasn't long before she was heaving again so I took her back home. We passed Carly. Chatted for a bit. I said I was going to go back out, but, well, you know what it's like when you get home and you've put your feet up for five minutes, you can't be arsed, can you? What happened to her?'

Sian took a sip of her tea. It was hot so she blew on it, purposely using up time before having to break the news that the killer of five prostitutes was possibly back at work.

'She was strangled.'

'Oh my God,' Bev said, bowing her head. 'It's not like last time, is it?'

'That's the theory we're working on.'

'Bloody hell. I thought he'd given up or moved on or something.'

'So did we.'

'Carly murdered. Poor cow.'

'Bev, what can you tell me about Carly?' Sian asked, taking a note pad and pen out of her pocket.

Bev thought while she chewed. 'Well, she said she was twenty-four, but I thought she was younger. I could be wrong. Make-up hides all kinds of secrets. We know that only too well. She had a bit of a Liverpudlian accent.'

'Boyfriend?'

'Aye. Paul Chattle. I wouldn't trust him as far as I could throw him.'

Sian made a note of his name in her notebook. 'Why?'

'He's a shit. Takes all Carly's money off her to buy drugs and leaves her with nothing. Many a time she's come out and she's practically fainted, she's been so hungry. We've often had to buy her something to eat, haven't we, Sarah?'

Sarah nodded.

'I kept telling her to leave him,' Bev continued. 'I offered her a bed at ours for a few weeks until she got herself sorted, but she wouldn't have it. Said she loved him. Silly mare.'

'How long has she been on the streets?'

'We've only seen her in the last year or so. She did say she was working in that brothel down Shalesmoor, but they were taking a large percentage of what she earned. That so-called boyfriend of hers told her to get back out on the streets then what she'd earn she'd keep. More money to inject in his arm.'

'Do you know where I'd find this Paul Chattle?'

'Pass me my book, Sarah.'

Sarah lifted up a large shoulder bag from the floor. It had seen better days and had a plaster over a large hole at the bottom. She rummaged around inside it, dumping items onto the table, hairbrush, make-up, a little bottle of mouthwash, a packet of condoms. Sian looked around her, embarrassed. Sarah handed over the battered notebook and swept the rest back inside.

'I keep this to jot down registration numbers of blokes we've not seen before and anything else that might come in useful.' Bev turned to Sarah, tapping a page in the book. 'We never got the money for those straighteners from Abby. Remind me. Here we go.' She handed the book to Sian for her to copy down the address.

'Do you know why she came to Sheffield in the first place?' Sian asked.

'She said her father threw her out. They all say that, though, don't they? She didn't go into it and I didn't ask. They tell you when they're ready. She did mention that her mother died when she was twelve.'

'Bev, does the name Danny Hanson mean anything to you?'

'No,' she said instantly. 'Who is he?'

'He's a journalist. He said he was working on a story about prostitutes in Sheffield last year.'

'Oh, him? I remember him. He wasn't calling himself Danny Hanson. Hang on.' Bev licked her fingers clean then flicked through her book again. 'Here we are: Alistair Tripp.' She snapped the book closed and handed it back to Sarah.

Sian frowned. 'Can you describe him?'

Bev thought for a moment. 'Tall, thin, mousey hair, blue eyes.'

Sian looked on her phone and googled for a photo of Danny Hanson. She showed it to Bev.

'No. That wasn't him.'

Sian's frowned deepened. 'And this guy definitely said he was a journalist?'

'Yes. He said he was researching about why women turned to prostitution.'

'Did you talk to him?'

'Yes. I'm not shy.' She gave a throaty laugh. 'He was offering ten pound and a cup of tea for anyone who'd talk.'

'Do you know who else spoke to him?'

'A few of them. He took a shine to Denise.'

'Really?'

'Yes. She gave him a blowie a few times.'

Sian's eye widened in shock. She scribbled it down in her notebook. 'Did he pressure her?'

'No. She liked him. She said it made a change to go with someone who smelled nice.'

Sian looked as confused as Bev did with her overplucked eyebrows. 'Bev, we've been given a list of names: seven women who have gone missing. Now, we already know about three of them and two others we've discovered have moved away. The other two, Caroline Richardson and Monica Yates, do you know them?'

'Caroline, I do, yes. But she said she was going back home.'

'Where's home?'

She thought for a moment, picking up another sandwich and tearing out a large bite. 'Somewhere up north. I want to say Sunderland.'

'But she lived in Sheffield?'

'Yes. Give me my book back, Sarah.'

Sarah rummaged around in her bag again, took out the book and handed it over.

Bev flicked through it. 'Here you go.' She pushed it across the table to Sian. 'She lived at Wincobank. She said she was going back as she couldn't stand Sheffield.'

Sian made a note of the address. 'And Monica?'

'Name doesn't ring any bells.'

'Will you have a think, maybe have a chat with the other women, as well?'

'Course I will,' she said with a smile.

'Now, have you noticed anyone hanging around lately or someone behaving suspiciously?'

Bev thought for a moment, slurped her tea and wiped her mouth with the back of her hand. 'No.'

'What about any of the regulars? Have they... I'm not sure how to put it,' Sian said, almost blushing.

'Turned kinky?' Bev suggested. 'If any of them had started putting their hands around our throats while shagging us, I'd know about it and I'd have told you.'

Sian could feel herself blushing. Bev didn't lower her voice when talking and people from the next table were glancing over at them.

'Right,' she said, making a note and bowing her head.

'Anyway, how are things with you, Sian, family all right?' Bev asked, her tone brightening.

'They're fine, thanks.'

'Kids growing up fast?'

'Too fast for my liking,' she smiled. 'Anyway, I'd better be getting back. Thanks for all your help, Bev. I'll go and order a couple more teas, get them to send it over.'

'Thanks, Sian, you're a love.'

'Let me know if you hear anything, and take care of yourselves, won't you?'

'Of course we will. Don't worry about us. We've got bigger balls than most of the blokes round here, haven't we, Sarah?'

Sarah blushed and smiled.

Sian left the café and hunted for her mobile in her bag. She pulled it out and dialled a number.

'Homicide and Major Crime Unit, Detective Constable Nowak speaking. Can I help you?'

'Bloody hell, Zofia, take a breath,' Sian said.

'Sorry. I'm still trying to get my tongue round what to say.'

'Just say Homicide and Major Crime. It doesn't matter who you are.'

'Sorry. What can I do for you?'

'Is Scott or Finn there?'

'No. Finn's popped out and Scott's left early.'

'Right. Well, I suppose it can wait until the morning. Although…' She thought for a moment. 'Actually, pop along to CID and have a word with DS Cleeves. Tall bloke, grey hair, bad teeth.'

'I know him.'

'Ask him to send a couple of DCs around to Carly Roberts' flat. She lives with her boyfriend. I'm guessing he won't know she's dead yet, so they need to deliver the death message. I'd also like to know why he hasn't reported her missing. Then, tomorrow morning, you and I can pop around to question him about Carly.'

'Will do.'

'I've got another call coming through. I'll text you his address. Bye for now.' She ended the call with Zofia and answered one from her husband. 'Hello,' she said, softening her voice.

'I got your text earlier. A celebratory evening without the kids is fine with me,' Stuart said. 'Do you want me to cook?'

'I was thinking of a couple of pizzas, a few bottles of wine and a snuggle on the sofa in front of a film that we won't see the ending of.'

'My kind of evening. And seeing as the celebration is in connection with your work, I'll let you choose the Bruce Willis film we watch.'

Sian rolled her eyes. 'How about…' She paused playfully. 'Hudson Hawk?'

'I think we should start seeing other people,' Stuart said.

Sian gave a throaty laugh.

Zofia was clearing up her desk when her phone buzzed an incoming text. It was from Sian, the address of Carly's boyfriend. She scribbled it down on a post-it note and was about to leave the suite when an idea came to mind. She looked at the address again. It wasn't close by, but it was on her way home. She could pop along and see this Paul Chattle herself, break the news and get his alibi and some background information on Carly in the process. She hadn't had the chance to show her initiative yet and she'd been with HMCU for four months now. It was about time she proved what she was capable of.

Chapter Fifteen

Philip and Sally Meagan were different people from who they were before their only child was kidnapped in 2015. They worked long hours building up their restaurant empire, and when it came to opening a new site, they worked even harder.

Both came from humble backgrounds and both wanted to create a future and a comfortable lifestyle for Carl. It was important to them that he had all the advantages growing up that they didn't. When he was kidnapped, they realised they'd been wrong. What Carl needed was family.

Sally gave up working in the restaurant to focus on finding Carl. She held interviews with every news programme, newspaper and magazine in Britain, Europe and around the world. She emailed as many missing person charities as she could find from New York City to Sydney and everywhere in between. She organised for Carl's picture to be shown at major sporting events, had it printed on T-shirts, and took out full-page adverts in the national press. She needed to keep Carl's memory alive in people's consciousness. She needed them to be able to recognise him at a glance in case they walked past him in Seattle, Helsinki, St Petersburg or Reykjavik. When the trail started to go cold, she wrote a book and tore into South Yorkshire Police, DCI Matilda Darke in particular, for their handling of the investigation and allowing an unstable woman who was grieving the loss of her husband to be in charge of the ransom drop. The book was an instant bestseller and sold in its millions around the world. The sightings came flooding in. None of them successful.

Sally knew that the only person who could help find her son was the person she blamed for losing him – Matilda Darke. At first, the relationship between the two women was fractious, to say the least, but as the months and years dragged on, a grudging respect for each other was forged. They were both fighting for the same cause and, with the help of retired detective Pat Campbell, they worked together to formulate a plan to keep Carl at the forefront of people's minds. It had obviously worked.

The neighbour of Theo and Hanna Sandberg had spotted a blond-haired child in their back garden late at night on two occasions. She knew they didn't have children of their own so he couldn't belong to them, or even be a grandchild. She immediately thought of Carl and sent an email to Sally Meagan with a blurred photograph. Sally contacted Matilda and Pat. Their hopes weren't high as they'd been in this position before. However, there was something about this photograph that Sally fixated on and she couldn't put her finger on what it was. She called the neighbour and asked her immediately to contact the police. Less than twenty-four hours later, Matilda came round to bring her the good news. Carl was safe. He was coming home.

Sally sat at the island in the kitchen. There was an

untouched mug of coffee going cold in front of her. She was dressed in jeans and a deep red sweater. She'd hardly slept. As much as she wanted Carl to come bursting through that front door, she wouldn't believe it was actually happening until she saw him. Her right leg was jiggling involuntarily. She kept biting her bottom lip, and her stomach was performing somersaults.

Around her, Woody was pacing the kitchen. He could sense something was wrong but didn't know what. He'd only eaten half of his breakfast. He'd been bought for Carl as a gift for his fifth birthday. The two were inseparable. When Carl was kidnapped, Woody became despondent. He hadn't barked once in the four years he'd been away.

'What time is it now?' Philip asked as he came into the kitchen. He was informally dressed in jeans and a white shirt. He'd lost a great deal of weight since Carl disappeared from worrying and trying to single-handedly keep the business afloat.

'I don't know, Philip,' she almost snapped. 'Probably about two minutes later than when you last asked me.'

'I'm worried,' he said, pulling out a stool next to her and sitting down.

'What about?'

'In my head, he's still seven years old. I still see him how he was the last time we saw him and he's not, is he? He's eleven. He'll have grown. Changed. What if...?'

'What?'

'What if he doesn't ... fit back in?' he asked, his eyes darting around the room.

'Fit back in? This is his home. We're his parents. He doesn't need to fit back in. He's as much a part of this house as we are. We'll just continue as before.'

'That's just it, we can't, can we? It's four years later. He's changed. We've changed. Everything's going to be different.'

A heavy frown formed on Sally's face as she thought. Philip was right. Did she honestly expect things to be how they were before? She wouldn't walk him to school with Woody as he was no longer seven. Would he still enjoy *Toy Story* and *The Incredibles*? She used to read to him at night when he was tucked up in bed, that was no longer necessary. Would he still want to be a fireman when he grew up?

'What if he doesn't like us?' Sally said.

'Sally?'

'Like you said, we've all changed. We might not get on anymore. He might not like who we are now. Oh my God, what if we don't like him?' She slapped a hand to her chest. The tears came and ran down her made-up face.

Philip jumped off his stool and put his arms around his wife. He rested her head against his chest and held her close. They had both dreamed of their son coming home but had no idea how wrong everything could go. The nightmare had always been the unthinkable, what had happened to him in the aftermath of him being kidnapped, but what if the real nightmare was his return?

'We should have gone to the airport to meet him. This is agony,' Sally said, pushing herself out of her husband's embrace.

'Matilda explained we wouldn't have seen him straightaway as he'd need to be interviewed. We'd have just been hanging around. Someone would have seen us, called the press and it would have been a frenzy. This is the best way. We don't want out first meeting with him to be captured on camera, do we?'

'No. Bloody journalists.' She looked at her watch.

The buzzer to the video entry system sounded throughout the house. They both froze. Carl was home.

Slowly, they walked over to the monitor in the corner of the kitchen. Sally pressed the 'accept' button. The small screen lit up. They could see Matilda's car at the gates.

'I feel sick,' she said. She watched as the gates yawned open and the car began to slowly climb the drive.

'Remember,' Philip began, taking his wife by the shoulders and looking deep into her eyes, 'he's our son. Whatever's happened to him, however he's changed, he's still our child, our Carl, and we love him.'

'We do,' she replied firmly.

As Philip moved to open the front door, Sally could feel the tsunami of emotions rise up inside her. She wanted to cry. She felt sick and dizzy and didn't think her legs would hold her up. She was in the vast hallway, facing the double front door, Woody by her side, pining and looking up at her, wondering what was going on. She needed to be strong for Carl. She had no idea how he was feeling right now but she needed to reassure him, show him that everything was going to be all right.

The front door opened. Sally felt the cool autumn air hit. She heard the heavy tyres crunch over the gravel driveway and eventually the Range Rover came into view. Pat was in the front passenger seat. She guessed the woman driving was Matilda's sister, Harriet. That meant behind the tinted windows in the back was Matilda and … her son.

She swallowed hard, but it was painful. She tried to smile but her lips were quivering and wouldn't stay still.

Pat climbed out of the car. She said something to Philip, but Sally didn't hear. Her attention was fixed on the door at the back.

Matilda came around the front of the car. They locked eyes. Matilda was smiling. It had been a long time since Sally had seen that. The recovery from her gunshot wounds had been long and arduous, but now she was smiling. That could only be a good thing.

Sally braced herself.

The back door opened.

She saw Carl as he manoeuvred himself to jump down from the high back seat. She stopped breathing.

Everything seemed to happen in slow motion.

She felt Woody brush past her as he spotted his best friend. He ran out of the door and for the first time in four years began to bark. Another dog jumped out of the back.

As Philip embraced his son, Sally very slowly walked towards the door. She had to hold onto the walls to keep herself upright. She looked at her husband gripping his son tight. It didn't seem real.

Her breath was shaking. She tried to speak, to call out her son's name, but nothing would come.

Eventually, Carl broke free from his father's hold and looked up. His face was wet with tears. He looked completely different to how he was when he disappeared, but there was no denying he was her son.

'Carl,' she croaked, holding her arms out.

'Mum,' he said, his voice barely above a whisper.

He came towards her, stepped into her embrace, and she wrapped her arms around him, holding him to her chest, squeezing hard, breathing in his strange scent. This didn't feel real, yet it felt right.

'I never thought this day would come,' Matilda said.

Matilda, Pat and Harriet were stood by the Range Rover. All had tears in their eyes.

'Look at their faces,' Pat said.

Sally and Philip were huddled together, Carl lost in the middle. They looked blissfully content. All three of their lives had been on hold for the past four years; now, they could begin again.

'What happens now?' Harriet asked.

Matilda released a heavy sigh and wiped her eyes. 'Everything. Everything happens now.'

Chapter Sixteen

Zofia Nowak was Sheffield born and bred. Her parents moved to Yorkshire from Poland in 1992 to start a new life and their only child came along four years later. Her father, Tomasz, was a business studies lecturer at the University of Sheffield while her mother, Magdalena was a theatre nurse at the Northern General Hospital. Knowing they only came to Sheffield with what they could cram into two suitcases and very little money, Zofia was incredibly proud of what her parents had achieved and hoped to emulate their success in her own chosen field.

Zofia had wanted to be a police officer from a young age. When she was seven, she was woken one night by blue flashing lights dancing around her bedroom. She pulled back the curtains and saw an active crime scene across the road. At the time, she was unaware of the severity of the case (a man was holding his wife and daughters hostage with a meat cleaver upon learning of his wife's affair) and was in awe of the police's actions. She watched with rapt attention into the small hours of the morning until the man was eventually arrested and led away in handcuffs. She knew then that she wanted to be a detective. And she'd be a bloody good one, too.

Tomasz and Magdalena beamed with pride when their daughter qualified and she still had the photo in a frame in her bedroom of her first day at work in her uniform, a parent either side of her, grinning to the camera. It made her smile every time she looked at it. She wanted to prove to them how successful she was. Zofia was dedicated, ambitious and eager to impress.

She left the station and shivered in the cool October air. She buttoned up her coat and checked for Pye Bank Road on her mobile. It was further away than she thought so she booked an Uber which arrived within three minutes. It was a short journey and when she told the driver where to pull up, he asked if she was sure. That question sent her confidence plummeting. No, she wasn't sure. Zofia knew what she was doing was breaking all the rules she had been taught. She could almost hear Sian giving her a bollocking. However, she had come this far.

Surrounded by bare trees, she shivered. It was cold and dark, and a fine drizzle was falling. Wearing a waist-length black woollen coat and short black skirt, she felt the chill and hoped Paul Chattle, despite grieving for his girlfriend, would be receptive enough to offer her a cuppa, or would at least have the fire on.

She checked the address again on her phone, found the house number and walked up the few steep steps to the front door. It was a large house that had been split into five small flats. She pressed the buzzer marked 'Chattle'. The front door was grubby. The paint was chipped and one of the glass panels boarded up. There was a dark atmosphere leaching out of the brick work, but Zofia chastised herself for being overly cautious. Being a detective was not an easy job. Of course there were dangerous areas of Sheffield, there were dangerous areas in every city. If she was going to get scared every time she came to a house she didn't feel right about then she was in the wrong job.

Zofia identified herself through the crackling intercom and there were a few long seconds before she was buzzed in. She walked up the narrow, dimly lit staircase, taking in the threadbare brown carpet and trying not to breathe in the rank odour.

Paul Chattle stood on the landing at the top. He was a tall, skinny young man in his mid-twenties. His head was shaved, his cheeks were sunken, and his clothes hung off his shoulders. His dull blue eyes were wide and staring and when he spoke, Zofia caught a whiff of stale alcohol on his breath.

'Mr Chattle, I'm sorry to bother you at this time, but I'd like to ask you a few questions, if I may?' she asked, looking up at him.

He gave a painful smile then headed to his flat. She followed.

Calling it a flat was a slight overstatement. The main room acted as a living room, dining room and kitchen. A door led to a single bedroom and the bathroom was down the corridor and shared with everyone else in the house.

The room was poorly lit. A dark-coloured sheet was pinned up to the window to act as a curtain. Anaglypta wallpaper was peeling away at the corners where the rising damp was eating into it. The carpet obviously hadn't been vacuumed for a long time and the single sofa and armchair were long overdue for the skip. She turned to see the kitchen; every surface was a mess with takeaway boxes and food stains, the sink piled high with dirty dishes. She wanted to leave. This place made her feel sad.

Paul Chattle slumped himself down onto the sofa and offered Zofia the armchair. She carefully perched on the edge.

'Mr Chattle, do you know a woman by the name of Carly Roberts?'

He looked up at her with heavy eyes. 'Carly? Yes, she's my girlfriend.'

'When was the last time you saw her?'

'Last night. She went out to … she went out.'

'Were you expecting her back?'

'Yes.'

'But she didn't?'

'No.'

'Is that unusual?'

His eyes darted around the room. 'Not… No. She sometimes slept out overnight, with a friend or someone.'

Zofia swallowed the painful lump in her throat. She could taste the rank smell from the flat. 'Mr Chattle, I'm afraid I have some bad news. A body of a woman was found in woodland out towards Tankersley. We took her fingerprints and they're a match for your girlfriend. I'm so sorry.'

Paul remained impassive, as if he hadn't heard what Zofia had said.

'Mr Chattle,' Zofia prompted.

'Sorry, I'm just… Carly's dead?'

'I'm afraid so.'

'How?'

'We think she may have been murdered. If I could ask you some questions about Carly…'

'Murdered?' He looked up at her. His eyes were wide; the tiny pupils darting around the room. 'How? Who by?'

'We don't know yet. We're still in the early stages of the enquiry. Mr Chattle, do you know of anyone who may have wished to do her harm?'

'This is unbelievable,' he said, standing up and moving over to the window. 'I only saw her last night. She... You know what she did for work?'

'We do, yes.'

'Was it a punter who did this?'

'Did Carly mention any punters who she felt were threatening?'

'No.' He went back over to the sofa and slumped into it. He placed his head in his hands. 'I loved her,' he said, his voice muffled.

'Was she working as a prostitute when you met?'

He shook his head.

'You didn't mind what she did?'

He sat up, sniffled and wiped his nose on his sleeve. 'It helped pay the bills,' he said with a shrug.

'What do you do for work?'

'I don't. I'm on disability with my back.'

'Oh. I'm sorry.' He didn't limp when he walked or seem to be in any pain with his back. She guessed it was probably a condition that came and went whenever the benefits office needed proof of his injury. 'Mr Chattle, do you know if Carly had any enemies or people who didn't like her?'

'No. Everyone liked Carly. She was a good lass,' he said. He picked up a scratched and battered tin from the stained coffee table and began to roll a slim cigarette.

'Had she mentioned any unwanted attention she'd received lately?'

'No,' he replied quickly.

'Any punters who had been aggressive or threatening?'

'You've already asked me that,' he said, his voice hardening.

'Sorry.' She quickly searched her brain for another question. 'How did she get on with the other women who worked the streets?'

This time, he looked up. His stare looked straight through her. 'You mean prostitutes?'

'Well, yes.'

'You can say it, you know. She was a prostitute. A hooker. A whore. A slag.'

'Mr Chattle...'

'She let men use her body for a few quid. They fucked her, had their fun, then dumped her. She was the lowest of the low, but do you know what, she was my girlfriend, and I loved her,' he said with a catch in his throat. 'And what are you going to do about it?'

'We're making extensive inquiries...'

'For now, yes,' he interrupted. 'But you'll soon come up against a brick wall and you'll stop looking because why should you waste resources on a whore?'

'Mr Chattle, it's not like that at all.'

'Isn't it? Do you know how many prostitutes have gone missing in Sheffield in the last few years? There are women dying out there and you lot are doing fuck all about it.'

'Mr Chattle, please, I know you're upset...'

'Do you?' he snapped. 'I saw your face when you came in here. You looked around, saw the state of the place and turned your nose up. We can't all live like you in your fancy apartments with your open-plan living and en-suite bathrooms, your big fuck-off TVs and those fancy boiling hot water taps. Don't think you can come in here and try to pretend you understand what I'm going through.'

Zofia swallowed hard. She knew it had been a mistake to come here alone. She should have listened to her inner voice, and the Uber driver.

'I should probably go,' she said, standing up.

'No. Don't go. I'm sorry.' Paul jumped up from the sofa and stood in front of the doorway, blocking her exit. 'I shouldn't have said those things. I really am sorry. It's just... I don't know how I'm feeling right now. Yesterday, we were sat on the sofa watching a film and everything was fine. We knew we didn't have much, that life wasn't easy, but we had each other, and that made things a little bit more bearable, you know? Now, she's gone. I don't know what I'm going to do without her.'

He started to cry. He collapsed back onto the sofa and held his head in his hands as he sobbed.

'Mr Chattle,' Zofia said quietly. She went over to him and sat on the arm of the sofa. She rubbed his back lightly. 'I really am sorry for your loss. There are people you can talk to about how you're feeling. I can get you the number of a grief counsellor.'

He nodded and sniffled. He looked up at her with wet eyes.

'I loved her.'

'I know. I can tell.'

'I'm really going to miss her.'

'Is there anyone I can call for you?'

'No. There was only me and Carly.'

Zofia bit her bottom lip. She hadn't delivered the death message before and had no idea what to say next. 'Is there anything I can do?'

'No.' He said, placing a hand on her lap.

Zofia immediately felt uncomfortable but allowed him to keep his hand there. He'd just been told his girlfriend had been murdered. His mind was all over the place, trying to take in the unthinkable.

'Mr Chattle,' Zofia said, her voice barely above a whisper. 'We will need to ask you some questions, about Carly, so we can understand who may have been responsible for her death.'

He nodded.

'I can leave you my card,' she said, rummaging around in her inside pockets for one. 'If you have any questions, or think of anything that may help us, you're welcome to give me a call.' She jumped up from the sofa and placed the card on top of his tobacco tin on the coffee table. 'I should go.'

'Please,' he began, standing up and blocking her exit. 'Can you stay with me? Just a little while longer.'

She looked up at him, at the hopelessness and desperation in his eyes. She felt sorry for him, but also felt slightly afraid at being in a small space, alone.

'I have other inquiries to make, but myself and a colleague will come again tomorrow morning.'

She made her way to the door, hoping Paul Chattle would step to one side. He didn't.

'Mr Chattle, please, I'd like to leave now.'

It was a long few seconds before he moved. Carefully, Zofia stepped around him. She opened the door and went out onto the landing.

'Wait,' he called after her.

She walked faster, heading for the stairs.

'Will you come back inside? Will you stay with me?'

He grabbed her shoulder and turned her around. He was so close she could see the spots around his mouth, his chapped lips, the dry flakes of skin, the dilated pupils.

Zofia shook her arm free from his grasp with such force she lost her balance and hurtled headfirst down the steep staircase, landing with a heavy thud at the bottom.

Chapter Seventeen

Sian had missed most of the first *Die Hard* film by having a long soak in the bath. When she came out, the second film was just starting, and the kids were heading for their rooms.

'What is it with Dad and Bruce Willis?' Belinda asked from the entrance to her bedroom.

Sian laughed. 'Years ago, me and your dad were at a party. There was a woman there who'd had a few to drink and she was really flirting with your dad. Anyway, she's got her hand on his arm, she leans into him and says, "Has anyone ever told you that you look like Bruce Willis?" Well, that was it for your dad. Ever since he's thought he's some kind of hunky hard man.'

'Hunky?'

'I know. It's a shame what goes on inside some men's heads, bless them.'

'I'm going to FaceTime Tina. If Dad comes up, tell him not to sing when he passes my room.'

'Will do.'

Wrapped up in her dressing gown, Sian went downstairs.

She headed for the kitchen, picked up a bottle of wine, a glass and a tube of Pringles before bracing herself to go into the living room and endure one man taking on a whole terrorist organisation. She had no idea what enjoyment people got from these kinds of films.

Stuart was on the sofa, a can of Fosters in hand. He looked relaxed and comfortable. Sian didn't see Bruce Willis when she saw her husband, she saw a cuddly bear of a man with a pillowy chest to rest her head on.

As she sat down, he raised his left arm for her to snuggle into him.

'Has the fake British woman been on yet?' she asked once she was settled.

'Not yet,' he laughed. 'How was your bath?'

'Just what I needed. I'm shattered.'

'Busy day?'

She thought for a moment. 'It feels like it, but at the same time I don't feel like I've achieved that much.'

'Have you heard from Matilda?'

She smiled. 'Yes. She spent about an hour with Sally and Philip, told them all about what'll happen next and left them together to get reacquainted again.'

'I can't imagine what they must be going through,' Stuart said, gripping his wife tighter.

'It's not often we get a happy ending. We're certainly due one after the shite year this has been. Fingers crossed 2020 will be quieter.'

'How's Matilda now she's back at work?'

It was a while before Sian answered. 'You know, I'm not sure.'

'What do you mean?'

'Well, physically, she seems fine, but there's something underlying that I can't put my finger on.'

'She's bound to be a bit different; she was shot in the head. Remember when you were stabbed last year, you were quiet for weeks.'

'I know. I didn't expect the same old Matilda to come breezing back in, but she seems to have lost all her confidence. She's got this intense stare like she's seeing us all for the first time and she's unsure who we all are.'

'What does everyone else think?'

'I haven't asked. Christian's trying to act like everything's normal.'

'That's the best way to be, surely. It'll help her to ease back into things.'

Sian sighed. 'I'm ... I'm worried.'

'What about?'

It was a while before Sian answered. 'I'm worried she's no longer up to the job.'

Chapter Eighteen

Scott had spent the evening running. He'd always been a keen runner. He and Chris entered half marathons and ten-kilometre races as a way of winding down after a stressful week at work. While most people sent out for a pizza and watched a terrible film on Netflix, drinking a couple of bottles of wine and sleeping until noon the following day, Scott and Chris would set their alarms for seven o'clock, even on a Sunday, and be out in the countryside surrounding Sheffield, pounding the rough terrain to improve on their previous race times, trim what little body fat they had, and add more definition to their already impressive bodies.

Following Chris's death in January, Scott had thrown himself more into running, but he wasn't preparing for a race. Those days of competing for medals were over. He no longer cared for a piece of cheap metal on a colourful ribbon, he just wanted the pain of losing the man he loved to go away.

Every day after work, he came home and changed out of his suit and into his running top and trousers. Then he'd drive out towards the Derbyshire Dales, park at Upper Burbage, and set off on foot along the makeshift trails. He didn't listen to music. He didn't take his mobile with him and he'd stopped wearing his Apple Watch that kept a record of the calories he'd burnt or his heart rate. He simply ran and allowed his tears to mingle with the beads of sweat dripping down his face. He ran until he literally couldn't run anymore, and collapsed to the ground a tormented wreck. Then, he'd look around him, wonder where he was and slowly make his way, somehow, back to the car.

Back at the flat, he'd shower, once again allowing his tears to mix with the scalding hot water, before slumping onto the sofa, listening to the sound of the clock ticking, trying to ignore the miasma of thoughts racing around his head, and waiting to pass out from exhaustion until he woke in the morning and started all over again.

There were times, however, like tonight, when running wasn't enough to silence the screams in his head. He felt angry, frustrated, and he needed something to stop him descending into depression.

He logged on to Grindr, the gay dating app, dating being one of the last things most members were looking for. He had a message waiting for him from a twenty-one-year-old whose profile picture showed him in a pub with a pint in his hand, smiling at the camera. He was good-looking with black spikey hair, blue eyes and a smooth complexion, and seemed relatively fit in his fitted grey sweater.

Scott opened the message which simply said 'Hi'. Hardly imaginative, but Scott wasn't interested in brain power. Scott said 'Hi' back and the conversation started.

'Nice abs,' came the reply. Scott's profile photo was of him naked from the waist up in front of the bathroom mirror. He'd always been toned thanks to the running, but lately, with the excessive workouts on the road and in the gym, he'd gone from toned to ripped.

Within four exchanges of chat, Scott had given the young man his address and told him to come straight round. He didn't want to know this man's name, what he did for a living, his hopes and dreams for the future, he was just looking for some stress relief, and right now, he couldn't think of anything better than giving someone a good hard fucking.

Fifteen minutes later, he heard a car crunching the gravel driveway. Scott went downstairs to open the door in case Matilda was looking out of the window and saw he had another visitor, or if the young lad had ignored his instructions and gone to the main house rather than the flat above the garage.

'Up here,' Scott said, heading back indoors. The young man followed.

'This is nice,' he said. 'I didn't know this place existed. It's quiet, out of the way, isn't it? Wow, nice flat,' he said, upon entering at the top of the stairs.

Scott looked him up and down. He was wearing tracksuit bottoms and a hooded sweater. His hair, swept by the breeze, gave him a boyish charm. He smiled; his whole face lit up. He really was very handsome.

'Your pictures don't do you justice, mate,' the young lad said. 'You're hot.'

'Bedroom's this way,' Scott said, turning his back and heading for the master bedroom.

Half an hour ago, there were two framed photographs on the bedside table. One held a picture of Chris on his own, the other was of the two of them on a beach in Devon. They were now face down in the drawer.

Scott began removing his T-shirt while kicking off his

trainers and undoing his jeans. The young man stood in the doorway.

'Look, I haven't got all night.'

'You're not one for chatting then?' He laughed nervously.

'No,' Scott replied honestly. 'Are you up for this or not?'

'Sure,' he said and began to undress.

Scott was on the bed naked. He'd taken a Viagra twenty minutes ago, and despite not feeling sexually aroused, he knew it wouldn't take much for something to start to happen down there.

The young man, now naked, joined Scott on the bed. He leaned in close to kiss before Scott slapped a hand on his chest and pushed him away.

'No kissing.'

'What?'

'I don't do kissing.'

'Why not?'

'I just don't.'

Kissing was important to Scott. He and Chris would spend hours in bed or curled up on the sofa in each other's arms. It was passionate, sensual and sexual. Kissing was as special as love-making.

Scott grabbed a handful of his hair and pushed him down, thrusting his crotch into his face. As he felt himself being taken into the young lad's mouth, Scott closed his eyes tightly shut and a single tear escaped his left eye. He felt sick as a wave of powerful, raw emotion swept over him. This was wrong. He shouldn't be doing this. He pushed the lad away.

'Go.'

'What?'

'I said go. Let's forget it.'

Scott jumped off the bed and quickly turned away.

'What's going on?'

'Nothing's going on. I've changed my mind. Go.'

'But ...'

'Just go now before I fucking throw you out,' Scott screamed at him.

'Jesus Christ! All right,' he said, stumbling around in the dark for his clothes. 'I hate you repressed straight blokes. Make your fucking mind up about what you want instead of wasting people's time.'

He left the room, having pulled his tracksuit bottoms and trainers on. He began putting the hoody on as he slammed the door and charged down the stairs.

He left the front door to the flat wide open, got into his car and drove off at speed, kicking up gravel with his back tyres.

Matilda was in bed reading. Well, she had the book open, but she wasn't taking any of the story in. *Sorry, Miss Marple*. The brief nap she had when she came in had completely thrown out her sleeping pattern. Not that she had much of a pattern; it was irregular at the best of times. She heard the sound of a car pulling away at speed and got out of bed to investigate.

'What's going on?' Harriet asked, coming out of her bedroom with hair standing wildly on end.

'Nothing. Go back to sleep,' Matilda said, looking out of the window on the landing and seeing the flat door open.

'Where are you going?' Harriet asked as Matilda made her way downstairs.

'Nowhere.'

'Thanks for filling me in. I love being informed of what's

going on in the middle of the night,' she said, her voice laced with sarcasm.

Matilda ran down the stairs, picked up the keys from the ceramic bowl on the hallway table and unlocked the door. She stepped out into the clear night air. It was cold and she shivered as she pulled her dressing gown tighter around her.

She made her way over the gravel, which was painful to walk on wearing only carpet slippers. She entered the flat, closed the door behind her to keep out the cold and walked slowly up the stairs. She listened intently for any sound, but there was none. As she reached the top, she heard something. She frowned as she listened. Whimpering. It was a sound she knew well. She had done a great deal of it herself in the past few months.

Matilda called out Scott's name. He exited his bedroom wearing Chris's dressing gown. His eyes were red, and tears streamed down his face.

She held out her arms and he walked towards her as if his legs were made of lead. He rested his head on her shoulder and sobbed loudly. She held him tight.

'It's all right, Scott. Everything is going to be all right.'

'It's not, though, is it?' he asked through the tears.

She thought for a moment. 'No. I'm afraid it's not.'

———————————

In Matilda's living room, the fire roared, the room was warm and the DCI on hiatus and the newly promoted DS sat on the sofa with a glass of wine each.

'You should delete that app,' she said.

'I already have done.'

'Good. That's the first step.'

'How many steps do I have to take?'

'You never stop taking them.'

'I miss him, Mat.'

'I know you do.'

Scott looked up at the framed photo of James Darke on the railway sleeper above the wood burner. 'How long was it before you could think of James without crying?'

She blew out her cheeks. 'I honestly have no idea. A long time. I still get upset now when I think about him. Not all the time, obviously, but occasionally. Like you with Chris, I loved James so much that it physically hurt. When he was gone, well, it was like I'd lost a limb. I had no idea how I was going to function without him. But Adele told me that I have people around me to help. There was her, my parents, you guys at work. And she was right. It's not the same, no way is it the same, but being surrounded by people I knew were genuine and cared for me made me realise that I wasn't alone. I was hurting and in pain but knowing there were others out there who are willing to help me through the grief was the first hurdle.'

Scott took a deep breath and gave a weak smile. 'Usually, when things have gone bad, I've had Rory to turn to. And when I remember that he's not there either, I hate myself for grieving more for Chris than for him. I knew Rory much longer than I knew Chris.'

'Don't beat yourself up, Scott. You can't quantify grief. You can't say I'll cry for an hour for Chris on Monday and an hour for Rory on Tuesday. It doesn't work like that. You've been dealt such a blow and I can't even begin to understand what's going on in your head, but you need to realise that you're not on your own. You've got me. You've got your parents. You've got Sian and Christian and everyone at work. I will always be here for you, Scott. Always.'

He tried to say thank you, but his emotion wouldn't allow it.

She pulled him towards her, his head on her shoulder once again.

'I wish I were dead,' he said, his words muffled in her dressing gown.

Matilda pretended she hadn't heard. She knew exactly how he felt.

Chapter Nineteen

Wednesday 23rd October 2019

After chatting with Scott into the small hours of the morning, when he returned to bed in the flat above the garage, Matilda had gone upstairs, yet sleep had eluded her. She tried reading but couldn't concentrate. She must have nodded off at some point because she woke with a start and a feeling of fear deep within. She couldn't recall what she had been dreaming about, and she was glad of it.

At five o'clock, Matilda decided to get up. She wrapped her dressing gown around her and padded down the stairs. She went into the kitchen and flicked on the kettle. While waiting for it to boil she unlocked the back door and stepped out into the dark, cool morning.

Despite her house being on the edge of the countryside, no neighbours around for miles, cut off during a harsh winter snowfall with a feeling of isolation and loneliness, Matilda loved it. Standing in the doorway, looking up at the black sky with countless twinkling stars and a sharp crescent moon, she felt content and all the problems she had rattling around her mind were silenced. Briefly.

A smile spread on her face when she thought of the Meagans. She wondered what kind of a night they'd had. They were in for a busy time as a press release was being issued this morning, then the vultures from the media would descend. Matilda had promised to help and so would the press team at the station.

'You're a survivor, aren't you, Matilda?'

She caught her breath as Jake's voice came into her head from somewhere deep in her psyche. She wished she knew of a way to silence these thoughts for good.

'But what's the point of surviving, when everyone around you is dead?'

She heard the gunshot and closed her eyes, screwing them tightly shut.

'You're a survivor, aren't you, Matilda?'

'Leave me alone,' she said to herself as she clamped her hands around her head, squeezing it hard.

There was a bang.

She opened her eyes, looked up and out into the dark morning. That bang wasn't in her head. It was real.

She stood in silence and waited for it to happen again. Her heart was pounding in her chest, the blood rushing around her brain.

Another bang resounded through the darkness. It was a familiar sound. A gunshot. *Is this real?* She could smell cordite. It must be real. There was a rustling in the distant trees. Someone was coming for her.

Matilda practically fell into the house. She slammed the back door closed, locked it with the key and turned out the light.

'Harriet!' she called out.

Matilda ran through the house and charged up the stairs two at a time. She didn't knock on her sister's door but turned the handle and burst into the room.

'Harriet. Harriet, wake up,' she said, shaking her sister's sleeping figure.

'What is it? What's wrong?' she asked, dazed at being woken up.

'Jake's outside.'

'What?'

'He's out there. He's shooting at me.'

'Who is?'

'Jake. Who else?'

Harriet sat up and turned on the bedside light. 'Matilda, calm down. Jake's dead. He can't be shooting out you.'

'Then someone else is. It's Steve. He's paid someone to shoot me.'

'Matilda, it's just a dream.'

'It's not. I was outside…'

'Outside? What time is it?'

'I don't know. I couldn't sleep. I went to make a drink. I opened the back door for some air. Someone took a shot at me.'

Harriet, more alert now, looked worried. 'Are you sure?'

'Of course I'm sure,' she shouted.

'All right, all right. Calm down.'

She threw the duvet back and swung her legs out of bed, shoving her feet into her slippers and picking up the dressing gown from the bottom of the bed to wrap around her shoulders.

'What are you doing?' Matilda asked.

'I'm going to have a look.'

'Are you crazy? There's someone out there shooting at me.

We should call Christian. He can get an armed response round.'

Harriet held Matilda by her shoulders and looked into her wide, staring eyes. All she saw was worry and fear.

'Matilda, listen to yourself. You live on the edge of the countryside, it's only natural for you to hear a gunshot from time to time. If someone was going to shoot at you, do you think they'd hang around in the middle of the night on the off-chance you'll get up to make a cup of tea?'

'Well, I suppose…' she said, calming down slightly.

'It was probably a farmer warning a predator off his sheep or something. And it was probably miles away. You know how sound travels at night.'

'Do you think?' Matilda asked, not looking convinced.

'Yes, I do. However, if you want to make yourself a laughing stock at the station, by all means give Christian a call and get him to send a squad of armed officers to tear through the countryside.'

'Oh my God,' Matilda said, her face reddening in embarrassment. 'I overreacted.'

'It's only natural after everything you've been through.'

'I feel so stupid.'

'Don't. There's only me who knows. I don't think you're stupid at all. Look, write it down, like that Coopersmith woman told you to, and discuss it with her at your next session.'

Matilda took a deep breath. 'I will. You're right. I just… I panicked. I heard the shot and thought…'

'It's perfectly normal. I'm the same whenever I see a bottle-blonde bimbo hairdresser. I just want to smash her face in with a hairdryer.'

Matilda smiled.

'Do you want to get in with me until it's time to get up?'

'No. Thanks. I think I'll go and read a book or something.'

Matilda slowly walked out of Harriet's room, closed the door and stood on the dark, silent landing. She couldn't believe she thought someone was outside shooting at her. It was preposterous.

My God, what if that had happened at work?

She shook the thought from her head. There were bound to be cases involving guns at some point. Hopefully she would be in a better frame of mind by then. Or maybe she should rethink her future before it reached the stage where she lost the respect of her colleagues. Was there a place within the police for someone so physically and mentally damaged? She had reached the rank she always wanted to, the Carl Meagan case was finally solved – what was there left for her here?

Chapter Twenty

Simon and Adam Warburton had got away with sneaking to the woods for three days in a row. They were pushing their luck to make it four, but having to spend half term with their grandmother, who spent most of her days nodding off in front of interminably dull repeats on ITV3 with the volume on high, was not their idea of fun. When their parents, Beth and Andrew, split up in the summer they had thought it would mean two holidays, two lots of birthday presents and two Christmases. Unfortunately, Andrew hadn't been heard of since he slammed the door on that hot Friday night in July and Beth was left with a full-time job at Sainsbury's, two children under ten and a mortgage to pay by herself. It was a logistical nightmare. Her aging mother helped where she could and her home was a haven for the kids during the school holidays, but she didn't have a clue how to keep an eight- and ten-year-old entertained. After breakfast, she gave them a ten-pound note each in case they wanted to buy something to eat or drink, then said they could go out, providing they didn't stray too far from the house.

Once they heard the theme tune to *Heartbeat* blasting from the living room, they knew their gran would be settled in her recliner and wouldn't be getting up any time soon. They headed for Plantation Woods.

The trees were dense, and the woods were often cool in summer under the canopy of leaves that were blocking out the sky and the heat from the sun's rays. In autumn, the ground was a carpet of leaves, all in different stages of decomposition. They crackled underfoot as the boys, inappropriately dressed, headed on an adventure. They walked for miles picking up fallen branches, stripping them of their bark, fighting as if they were swords, breaking them against trees, kicking leaves and daring each other to see who had the guts to climb a tree the furthest. Simon, being the oldest, always won.

Sitting ten feet in the air on the creaking branch of an oak tree, they surveyed the woods. It was quiet. The only sound came when a breeze rustled the leaves and branches clacked together.

'Do you think Gran's rich?' Adam asked.

'Probably. I heard her saying to Mum that when she dies the house would be hers. She said it was all paid for so she could do what she wanted with it.'

Adam pulled a face. 'Does that mean we'll have to move into it? I hope not. It smells upstairs.'

'No. Mum'll probably sell it.'

'Who'd buy it? It's horrible.'

'Someone's bound to buy it. It's big.'

'I think it's haunted,' Adam said, shuddering.

'You're scared of everything.'

'I am not.'

'You are.'

'I'm not.'

'Prove it.'

'How?'

Simon thought for a moment. 'Jump to the ground from here.'

'What?' Adam exclaimed. 'It's miles to the ground.'

'It is not.'

'I could break my legs.'

'Not if you land properly.'

'How do you land properly?'

'Well, aim for those leaves over there and as you land you roll onto your side so your legs don't take the impact. It's called tuck and roll.'

'How do you know that?'

Simon shrugged. 'I dunno. I just do.'

'Show me?'

He rolled his eyes. 'You've going to get eaten alive when you move schools.'

'That's years away. I'll have grown up more by then.'

'Right. Watch me, okay?'

Simon spat on both hands and rubbed them together. He took a deep breath and braced himself, all the while keeping his eyes on the patch of leaves on the ground.

'One, two, three.' He lunged off the branch, landed, grabbed his knees and rolled over several times as he came to rest in the mound of dry leaves. He looked back up to the tree. 'Piece of piss. Your turn.'

Adam looked scared. His eyes were wide, and his heart was thumping loudly in his chest. He'd jumped from a tree before, but never this high up.

'We go back to school on Monday, Adam, hurry up,' Simon called.

'Don't rush me.'

He copied his older brother by spitting on both hands and rubbing them together. He counted to three, much slower, and before he threw himself off the branch, he closed his eyes.

As he landed, Simon grabbed him and helped him to roll.

'I did it,' Adam said, a huge grin on his face. 'I did it.'

Simon began to kick the leaves over his brother, burying him under the mound.

Adam spat. 'Give over. They're going in my mouth.' He scrambled to free himself, arms and legs flaying widely. He reached for a stick, but it was stuck on something so had to yank it harder. It eventually broke free and he used it as a weapon to threaten his older brother.

He looked up and saw Simon glaring at him, his eyes wide, his face pale.

'What's up?' Adam asked.

'Where did you get that?'

'What?'

Adam looked at what he was holding in his hands. It wasn't a stick. It was a bone, and there was a hand dangling off the end of it.

Chapter Twenty-One

Matilda was the first one to arrive at the HMCU. Scott dropped her off early then went to the gym for a quick workout before the day truly began. There was definitely a fusty smell in the room, and she was sure it was coming from the grubby carpet tiles. She opened a window and shuddered as a cold breeze enveloped her. She flicked on the kettle and returned to stand by the window. She'd had less than two hours' sleep and needed the cold air and a strong coffee to get her through the day.

Less than an hour, and two cups of coffee, later, Sian breezed into the suite, a huge smile on her face.

'I'm so pleased you're in early. Tell me everything that happened with the Meagans yesterday. I've hardly slept, I was so excited.'

The kettle was turned on again and Matilda filled her in on all the gossip. Sian grabbed a tissue from the box on her desk and wiped away the tears as she heard the story of the reunion.

'I'd have loved to have been there. They've been through so

much, bless them. I hope they can try to put it all behind them and move on.'

'I hope so, too,' Matilda said, a slight smile on her face.

'When is the press release going out?'

'About ten o'clock-ish. We're going to arrange for there to be an exclusive interview so they can just tell the story once and that's it. I don't think any of them want to be paraded in front of the cameras for weeks on end.'

'If there was ever a sign to never give up hope, this is certainly it,' Sian said. 'It's given me a lovely warm feeling. I think we can all say this year has been one of the worst for a long time, but when something like this comes along, it puts things into perspective, doesn't it?'

'I suppose it does,' Matilda said, turning to look out of the window at the grey, dank view of Sheffield.

'What are you thinking about?' Sian asked,

'I just thought for a moment that if the shooting had never have happened, I wouldn't have lost the baby, who knows what would have happened between me and Daniel, and I'd have been a mother by now.'

'Would you have had the baby?'

Matilda took a deep breath and held it while she thought. 'I don't know. Probably.'

'Do you hear from Daniel?'

She shook her head. 'He wanted us to carry on seeing each other, but I knew my recovery was going to be long and difficult. I didn't want to put him through all that.'

'But he loved you.'

'I know. But I didn't love him, not enough, anyway.' Her eyes filled with tears.

'Oh, Mat,' Sian said, leaning down and giving her a hug. 'Why is life so difficult for you?'

'I certainly don't help myself. I dwell on everything too much. I keep everything stored up here,' she said, tapping her temple. 'I can't let things go. I've got James, Carl, Ben and the guilt from...'

'You are not to blame for the shooting, Matilda, you need to believe that.'

'I'm trying.'

Sian pulled a chair closer to Matilda and sat down. She reached out and held her hands. 'When you were in the coma, and we didn't know if you were going to survive or not, me and Stuart were at home and I was in pieces. Stuart said to me that despite being emotionally fragile, you were tougher than you gave yourself credit for. You've been through so much in the past few years, more so since James died, and you've always survived. There was no doubt in his mind you'd survive this, and he convinced me of the same. He's right. You're the strongest person I know, yet you don't believe it.'

Matilda smiled. 'I never realised your Stuart was so wise.'

'No. He surprised me, too,' she laughed. 'It's true though. You're incredibly strong. And if anyone can survive being shot twice, it's you.'

'Thanks Sian. You're a good friend,' Matilda said.

'I know. And I know your favourite chocolate too,' she said, reaching into her snack drawer and bringing out a large bag of Maltesers. 'Shall I stick the kettle back on and we can snaffle these before everyone else gets here.'

'Go on then. Thank Stuart for me, won't you?'

'What for?'

'For believing in me.'

'We all believe in you, Mat. You just need to believe in yourself.'

'I'm getting there.'

'So, who is this mystery journalist?' Matilda asked.

She, Christian and Sian were squeezed into the DCI's office as Sian filled them all in on her meeting with Bev and Sarah yesterday evening.

'I've no idea,' Sian said.

'And Bev is definitely sure it's not Danny Hanson?'

'One hundred per cent.'

'That's a shame. I'd like to have seen him disgraced in public,' she said with a cruel glint in her eye.

'I think we need to bring Danny in,' Christian said. 'Ask if he knows this man.'

'I'd rather not,' Matilda said, folding her arms. 'Danny isn't the type of person to spend night after night walking the streets of Sheffield chatting to prostitutes. He thinks he's this big reporter since he's been on TV. I bet he paid this other guy to do the research for him.'

'I wouldn't put it past him,' Sian agreed.

'I don't want Danny knowing more about this case than he should do,' Matilda stated.

'He won't. However, we've got someone who was obviously abusing his position with the women. It's the first lead we've had. We need to capitalise on it.'

The room fell silent while Matilda thought. Christian and Sian exchanged glances. Christian was clearly frustrated, and was struggling to hide it.

'Has anyone looked online for this Alistair ... what is it?'

'Tripp. I have. I can't find anything,' Sian said. 'There are several on Twitter and LinkedIn. I agree with Christian, we should bring Danny Hanson in.'

It was a while before Matilda replied. 'Fine,' she said with as much hatred and bile as she could attach to one word.

'By the way, I requested the files of the four women be sent up yesterday. They should be around here somewhere,' Christian said, looking around at the mess of the office. There didn't seem to be an area free for anything in such a cramped space.

'I found them, thanks.'

There was a knock on the glass door. Scott opened it and popped his head in.

'Sorry to interrupt, though I'm not going to mention being hurt that I'm the same rank as Sian and haven't been included in this private meeting, but Zofia has just arrived, and she has a black eye.'

They all filed out of the room.

'You were at the gym when we started,' Sian said, tapping Scott's firm stomach as she passed him.

Zofia was sat at her desk. Her head was bent over her keyboard as if she was seeing it for the first time.

'Zofia, is everything all right?' Sian asked.

'Yes. Fine. Sorry I'm late. The bus didn't turn up.'

'Zofia, look at me.'

It was a while before she did. Slowly, she lifted her head. Her left eye was bruised and swollen, and she had a cut along the bridge of her nose.

'Oh my God, what happened?'

'I slipped on a magazine and fell,' she said.

'And the truth?' Christian asked.

Zofia started to cry. Sian went around to her side of the desk and hugged her.

'Zofia, it doesn't matter what happened, you're among friends here. We can help you. We won't judge you.'

'You'll hate me.'

'No we won't. Why would we hate you?'

'On my way home last night, I went to see ... Paul Chattle.'

'Paul Chattle? Who's he?' Christian asked.

'You did what?' Sian asked, her voice stern.

'Who is he?' Matilda asked.

'Paul Chattle was Carly Roberts' boyfriend. Bev told me all about him. She said he was using Carly. He made her work the streets to pay for his drug habit.'

'And you went to see him alone?' Christian said.

Zofia nodded.

'It was on my way home. I thought that I'd break the news to him and find out more about Carly. I thought it would give us a head start on finding her killer.'

'What the hell?' Matilda asked. Her face was red with rage. 'Do you have any idea how stupid that was? The man was pimping his girlfriend out, for fuck's sake. What did you think he was going to do, welcome you with a pot of tea and a Mr Kipling? He could have killed you,' she shouted.

'I'm sorry,' Zofia whimpered.

'Sorry? We're a team, DC Nowak. We work together. If you're not able to do that I suggest you rethink your career.'

'Okay, calm down, everyone,' Christian said. 'Finn,' he called out across the room, 'get on to uniform and ask them to pick up this Paul Chattle and bring him in.'

'I really am sorry,' Zofia said again, struggling to hold in her tears.

'I should bloody think so,' Matilda barked.

'Have you seen anyone about your eye?' Christian asked.

'No.'

'Well, pop up to A&E. They'll probably want to give you an x-ray.'

'Now?'

'Yes. Now.'

'But, there's work to do.'

'Don't worry, it'll still be here when you get back,' Matilda said before turning on her heel and marching back into her office, slamming the door behind her.

As Zofia left the suite, her head down, tail between her legs, a phone rang. Scott answered.

'I can't believe how reckless she was being,' Sian said.

'We've all been there, Sian,' said Christian. 'She's young. She—'

'That was the control room,' Scott said. 'We've just had a phone call from a member of the public. Two bodies have been found in Plantation Woods.'

Chapter Twenty-Two

It was decided that Christian, Sian and Scott would head out to Plantation Woods while Matilda and Finn, who worked closely with Sian on building the database of Sheffield's prostitutes, would see what Danny Hanson could tell them and why he felt he needed to so publicly reveal his information.

Plantation Woods wasn't easy for a team of forensic officers to work in. Trees were very close together, the ground was uneven, and lighting was dull. It took a few hours for them to carry the equipment they needed from the road to where the bodies had been found.

By the time Scott pulled up behind a car he recognised as belonging to Adele, work on the bodies was already underway.

'I'm wearing the wrong shoes,' Sian said as she trod carefully over a carpet of fallen leaves.

'I thought you always kept a pair of walking shoes at work?' Scott asked.

'I had to throw them away. I've had them that long they

were falling to pieces. I meant to get a new pair but never got around to it.'

'Would you like me to give you a piggyback?'

'Yes, please.'

Scott laughed. 'You'd let me as well, wouldn't you?'

As they turned a corner, they saw the white forensic tent up ahead. There was no clearing and CSIs had to traverse trees to perform their tasks. It wasn't an easy crime scene.

'Who found them again?' Christian asked.

'Two brothers,' Sian said.

'Shouldn't they have been at school?' Scott asked.

'It's half term.'

'Oh. I thought the traffic was quieter this week. Where are the brothers now?'

'Apparently their gran is looking after them. She doesn't live far away. A family liaison officer is with them.'

They changed into white paper forensic suits, pulled up the hood, covered their shoes with matching overshoes and gloved up, before opening the flaps of the tent and stepping inside. All three squinted at the brilliant, unnatural light.

On the ground, Home Office Pathologist Adele Kean and her technician Lucy Dauman were working alongside CSIs to preserve as much of the scene as possible while trying to remove the bodies, which were badly decomposed and fragile.

'Two bodies buried together. How did we not know about two people going missing at the same time?' Sian asked no one in particular.

'They weren't buried together,' Adele said, leaning back on her haunches. 'When we arrived, we found the body where the young lad said it was and did some digging. Less than a metre away, we found another body.'

'Could they have been buried together?'

She shook her head. 'Different levels of decomposition.'

'Were they murdered?' Christian asked.

'This first one was. Have a look at this.' She leaned further into the shallow grave. 'You've got the skull and the basic skeleton. I don't need an x-ray to tell me the hyoid bone is broken.'

'Strangled?' Sian asked.

Adele nodded.

'With the other body not far away, could they have been lovers and maybe someone objected to them being together?' Scott asked.

'The other body is also a young female,' Adele said. 'Her body isn't as decomposed. She seems to have been buried deeper and the grave was dug and filled more carefully; different compaction of the soil.'

'Maybe he'd improved on his first kill,' Sian said, looking from one body to another.

'I'm guessing it's too much to hope for any form of identification, a tattoo or something?' Christian asked.

'First body, absolutely,' Adele said. 'However, there are some fillings in her mouth and she's missing a few back teeth on her upper jaw. There's bound to be a record of that somewhere. As for the second body, she's in a much better condition. I need to get her back to the lab, get her clothes off her and see what we can get under a UV light or x-ray. There is one significant piece of information you might be interested in now. The second body has dirt in her mouth.'

'Meaning?'

'Meaning, she wasn't dead when she was buried.'

Chapter Twenty-Three

'Danny Hanson is in interview room number one and Paul Chattle is behind door number two. Who would you like to chat with first?' Finn Cotton asked.

'I love it when I have a choice,' Matilda smiled. 'Let's leave the scumbag to stew for a little longer.'

'You're going to have to narrow it down.'

Matilda gave a genuine laugh. She slapped Finn on the arm. 'You've really come out of your shell over the last few months. I'm loving the new Finn.'

'Knowledge is power. Isn't that what they say?'

'So I've heard. Let's chat to the journalist.'

Danny Hanson hadn't been told why his presence was requested at South Yorkshire Police HQ. When Matilda opened the door and entered, Danny stood up and held out his hand. He had a huge grin on his face like he was the one with all the answers, as if he held the key to the mystery of the missing women.

'DCI Darke, it really is a pleasure to see you once again. You're looking … well,' he said.

Matilda had no intention of shaking the man's hand. She pulled out a chair and sat down.

'Those scars are still quite prominent,' Danny said as he returned to his seat and leaned in to get a better look at Matilda. 'How many operations was it? Three? Four?'

'Mr Hanson, we'd like to know where you got your information from regarding the missing women,' Matilda began.

'Good old-fashioned journalism,' Danny said with a smile, looking from Matilda to Finn and back again. 'You'll be surprised how much people are prepared to talk to you once you've been on TV. I couldn't shut some of them up.'

'It's strange, but I can't picture you hanging around the red-light district in all weathers chatting to prostitutes.'

'Journalism isn't a glamorous job.'

'Does the name Alistair Tripp mean anything to you?'

The smile finally dropped. 'I can't say it does, no.'

'Tall, young, messy mousey hair, blue eyes.'

'Nope.'

'You see, this Alistair character was seen hanging around the women last year asking all kinds of questions, posing as a journalist. When we showed some of the women your photo, they didn't recognise you at all.'

'Well, it was dark, and during the winter I was wearing a beanie hat and layers to keep warm.'

'Even when I told them you were the insufferable prick on the TV news, they didn't remember you. So you couldn't have gathered all this information yourself. My theory is that you paid someone to do the leg work and you'll take all the glory if anything comes of it. Am I right?'

'Absolutely not,' Danny said, sitting back in his chair and folding his arms.

'So, you're stating that you did all the research yourself?'

'Yes.'

'Fine. Finn?' Matilda turned to DC Cotton.

'We've looked into the list of names you gave us,' Finn said, opening the slim file in front of him. 'Two of the women have been found safe and well. They're still working as street prostitutes but have left Sheffield. Three others we already knew about and are looking into as part of this new investigation. The remaining two are new names to us and we will be opening new inquiries.'

Danny looked crestfallen. 'Oh. That still leaves you with five missing women, all working as street prostitutes. Do you believe they're dead?'

'Do you mind if I ask you a question?' Matilda asked.

'Go ahead.'

'Does the name Denise Jones mean anything to you?'

'Yes. She's one of the dead women.'

'And you spoke to her during your research?'

'Yes.'

'What did she speak about?'

He blew out his cheeks and looked up as if searching his memory. He loosened his posture and tried to act nonchalant. 'She told me all about herself: why she became a prostitute, what the job was like, about some of her regular punters. The usual.'

'Did you like her?'

'I can't say I formed much of an opinion.'

Finn opened the file once more, took out a photograph and placed it on the table in front of Danny. 'She's pretty, isn't she?' he asked.

He didn't reply.

'Obviously, this photo was taken some time before she

died,' Matilda chipped in. 'This is before the prostitution and drug addiction had ravaged her body. Finn's right, though, she *was* pretty. Bright eyes, cute smile, dimples. She's very sweet looking.'

'I'm not sure where you're going with this,' Danny said, frowning.

'We've been informed that Denise was attracted to the journalist hanging around.'

He raised an eyebrow.

'She spoke many times with you, told you a great deal. I'm guessing she flirted with you.'

'If she did, she wasn't very good at it as I never picked up on any flirting.'

'Really? Not even while she was deep throating you?' Matilda asked.

'What?' Danny asked, his eyes widening as if in shock.

'Did you have to pay for the blow jobs, or were they free?'

'What are you talking about?'

'She said she enjoyed being with you as you were clean and smelled nice. He does smell nice, doesn't he?' She asked Finn.

'Yes, very nice. What is that, Jean Paul Gaultier?'

Danny gave a hollow laugh. 'So, because she said she liked me and talked about going with a man who was clean and smelled nice you assume that's me?'

'Well,' Matilda said, leaning forward. 'I was told that Denise was sweet on the young journalist, who was asking a lot of questions, and was seen blowing him off a couple of times. I used my detective brain to guess that she was talking about you, seeing as you're a journalist and claim to have spent time with these women.'

Danny pursed his full lips. He seemed to be running his tongue around his mouth. His eyes wouldn't settle as they darted around the room. 'Okay,' he eventually said. 'I admit, I didn't spend all my time with the women. I'm sorry but, well, it's horrible down there. I was chatting to this one woman when she got a text. She looked at her phone and said she was needed, and off she went. I thought I'd follow, see what she was up to, you know, the life of a street prostitute, nothing sordid. Anyway, she went around the back of this office in a badly lit car park and there's this big bloke waiting. They didn't talk, he just unzipped and she dropped to her knees. He … well, he wasn't exactly gentle with her and it didn't take long for him to finish. She turned, spat it out, he flung a note at her and went off zipping himself back up. I felt physically sick just watching it.'

'Would you recognise the man if you saw him again?' Matilda asked.

'No. It was pitch dark. It's really badly lit down there.'

'Did you talk to the woman anymore?'

'No. I couldn't, not after I'd seen what she'd done. Look, I know I come across as this wanker journalist to you, but I'm really not. Yes, I want to get on in this job, I want the big stories, I want to uncover corruption and write about the reality of life in twenty-first century Britain, but the truth is, I don't have the bloody stomach for it. I couldn't get out of there quick enough.'

Danny's entire body language had altered since Matilda entered the room. He'd started out as a cocksure journalist, full of himself, chest puffed out with bravado, but within the space of ten minutes he'd revealed his true personality. The Danny he showed on television was a character he was playing. The real Danny was a mouse.

'So, you paid someone to do the digging for you?'

He nodded.

'Alistair Tripp?'

'Yes.'

'Who is he?'

'He's a journalism student at uni. He's a friend of a friend and I said I'd help him, once he'd qualified, to get a job if he did some work for me,' Danny admitted, looking ashamed.

'It would appear this Alistair took his research a little too far.'

'I had no idea…'

'No, I don't believe you did,' Matilda said. 'We'll need to talk to Alistair.'

'I can't give up my sources.'

'He's not a source, he's a student you're paying. For fuck's sake, Danny, he could be the killer for all you know.'

'He's not a killer,' he scoffed.

'Really? You know that for a fact, do you?'

'Well, no.'

'No. We have it on record that Alistair was seen with more than one woman, trousers round his ankles, his dick down their throats,' she said, hoping Danny never found out they only knew of one woman Alistair had been with. 'You paid him to ask questions and he was abusing his position to manipulate and violate those women,' Matilda said, raising her voice. 'You sent him down there, and if he harmed or killed any of them, it's on your conscience.'

'DCI Darke,' Finn said as a way of alerting his boss she was going too far.

She looked at Finn, saw the worry in his eyes. 'I think we should stop there, for now. However, if you don't produce Alistair within twenty-four hours, I'll charge you with obstructing an investigation. Do you understand me?'

Danny nodded.

Matilda stood up and headed for the door. She stopped and turned on her heels. 'By the way, from now on, any press conference I or any member of my team holds will be by invitation only, and your name will be nowhere near the list.'

She yanked open the door and stormed out, slamming it behind her.

Chapter Twenty-Four

At Plantation Woods, the forensic team, the detectives and Adele and Lucy were taking a break. Adele was sat behind the wheel of her car drinking coffee from a flask she'd brought with her. Sian tapped on the glass and asked if she could sit in the passenger seat. Adele nodded.

'It's chilly in those woods,' Sian said, climbing into the car. 'How's it going?'

'Fine,' she said, looking dead ahead.

'How long does a body take to skeletonise?'

'It depends on many factors. How deep is the body buried? What's the climate like? Weather conditions. Are they wearing clothes? Are they in a coffin? If so, what kind of wood?'

'Okay, okay, I get all that, but these two women here, how long are we talking?'

Adele blew out her cheeks. 'I don't know. I need to do some tests.'

'Months? Years?'

'Sian, you know I don't make guesses,' she said, a slight edge to her voice.

'No. I know. I'm sorry. I just... I don't know how someone can be buried for so long, however long that is, and for us not to know about it. Surely someone was missing those women.'

'Maybe you do. You have missing persons going back years.'

Sian fell silent.

Adele looked across at her. She sighed. 'The first body was in a shallow grave. The earth around her was disturbed, many times I'd say, over the years. The smell from decomposition would have attracted wildlife. The fact she's buried in a densely packed area shows that few people went there, probably only inquisitive kids and animals. Any rain will have soaked through the soil and aided the decomposition process. I'd estimate a couple of years, but that's a wide estimate.'

'Thanks, Adele.'

They both fell silent and Adele went back to looking at her phone.

'I see the news has been leaked about Carl Meagan being found,' she said, holding up her phone.

'Yes. We issued a press release this morning. Excellent news, isn't it?'

'It is. I'm sure Matilda is on top of the world,' she replied in a flat monotone. 'Well, I'd better be getting back.'

Christian was stood by his car, a worried frown on his face.

'What's wrong?' Sian asked.

'Did you notice how Matilda kicked off at Zofia this morning? I've never known her go into such a rage like that before.'

'No. It was... I don't know.'

'Frightening.'

'Really?'

'She flipped in a matter of seconds. I was watching her. I saw the change happen like a switch had been flicked. Her entire face just changed.'

'Christian,' Sian began, sidling up next to him, leaning on his car. 'Do you think Matilda should be back at work?'

He took a deep breath and exhaled slowly as he thought. 'I love having her back. I've missed her, but ... I don't think she's ready.'

'I've been thinking the same. What are we going to do?'

'I'm buggered if I know.' He looked around him and into the woods at the hive of activity taking place as the two bodies were lifted out of the ground. 'I'm worried about these two as well.'

'What about them?'

'They're found in a wood where Carly Roberts was found a day ago. What if they are two of our missing prostitutes? How many more bodies could be buried in there?'

'You think this is the killer's dumping ground?' she asked, looking back at the innocuous-seeming woodland.

'It's possible.'

'We can't dig up the whole wood.'

'We won't need to. I'm having someone come out with a couple of cadaver dogs to have a sniff around. Also, I'm thinking of sending a drone up so we can film the woods from above and then zoom in on certain areas. I'm sure there's a way you can tell if there's a buried body. I know grass discolours if one is buried in a field or something. We should probably get an expert in.'

'Should we seal the woods off?'

'Not yet. We may need to try and get hold of one of those ground penetrator radar machines.'

'Don't you think you should run this all past Matilda before you begin? All that is going to be very costly.'

'The last thing she needs right now is a case as big as this.'

A gust of wind caused Sian to shudder. She was looking deep into the darkness of the woods.

'I don't like serial killers,' Sian said, holding herself rigid.

'I don't think they're supposed to be liked.'

'It's the whole planning and stalking their victims; the fact that they've set out to kill someone, and the enjoyment they get out of it. What's wrong with these people?'

'Well, fortunately we don't get many in this country,' Christian said.

Sian moved over to the entrance to the woods. She watched as the fragile body of the first victim was placed inside a body bag.

'One is too many. Life is precious. We know that more than anyone in the job we do, and after the shooting, we certainly know how short life can be. I don't think I'll ever understand how someone can kill another person and get some kind of pleasure out of it.'

'There are some jobs that should be left to specific people. Look at Adele and the things she does all day. I'd never want to cut open a body to find out how they died, and I don't want to try to get inside the head of a serial killer. I'll stick to reading reports, looking at evidence and tracking the killer that way.'

'Good old-fashioned detective work, eh?' She half-smiled.

'Sian!'

She heard her name being called and looked back into the woods. Scott beckoned her over. She and Christian headed for him, walking over wet leaves and into the darkness of the woods.

'We've found something,' Scott said. 'They've moved the second body out of the grave. Underneath her was a bag.'

'What kind of bag?'

'A handbag type of bag.'

Christian was snapping on a pair of latex gloves. The bag had been placed on a large plastic sheet. He squatted and picked it up. The bag was covered in dirt. He carefully unzipped it and looked inside. Next to him, Scott appeared with an evidence bag open.

Christian pulled out several condoms. He looked inside, found a purse and handed the bag to Sian while he looked inside it. There were two ten-pound notes and a fiver, a few coins of loose change and a driver's licence.

'Oh God,' he said.

'Who is she?' Scott asked.

'Lucy Fletcher.'

'One of the missing prostitutes,' Sian said.

'I wonder who the other one is, then,' Scott said.

'That's two found. Three more to go.'

Christian stood up. 'And I wouldn't be surprised if the remaining three are all buried in Plantation Woods.'

Chapter Twenty-Five

Matilda: Hello. Just a quick text to see how you all are and how your first night back together went.

Sally: We all stayed up until very late. There were a lot of tears. Carl's still in bed. He was shattered. He was telling us about the couple he was living with. They really were looking after him well. That's a bonus I suppose. The two dogs are getting on fine.

'He didn't give a toss about Carly, did he?' Matilda said as she left the interview room and slammed the door behind her. She quickly read Sally's reply to her text and squirrelled the mobile away.

Paul Chattle's responses to most of Matilda's questions were either shrugs or monosyllabic. The fact his girlfriend had recently been murdered didn't seem to faze him in the slightest. There was no emotion on his face, no tears in his eyes. He sat at the table, playing with his fingers, picking at the loose skin around his nails. It was difficult to read if he'd taken something, was on a come-down or simply didn't care.

'It doesn't look like it,' Finn agreed. 'He was practically pimping her out.' He looked disgusted. 'He said he loved her and she meant the world to him, but how can she have? I don't understand.'

'If we hadn't told him she was dead he wouldn't have noticed until he realised there was no money for his next fix.'

'What do you want me to do with him?'

'Put a couple of rocks in his pocket and throw him into the Don.'

'I think the new ACC may frown upon that.'

'I'd claim diminished responsibility and blame the effects of the shooting,' she smiled. 'Send him home. He's no use to us. He's no use to anyone.'

'What about what he did to Zofia?'

'He didn't do anything to Zofia,' she said, her voice terse. 'She tripped over the carpet. Silly cow; shouldn't have been there in the first place.'

She took off down the corridor before realising she was heading for the former suite. She turned on her heels and headed back the way she came.

'You weren't gone long,' Matilda said when she entered and saw Zofia sat at her desk.

'No. I flashed my warrant card and said I'd been injured in the line of duty. They rushed me through.'

'I don't think you should be telling me that. How did it go? Any lasting damage?'

'No. Just a bruise. Nothing broken or fractured, apart from my pride.'

'Well, remember what I said earlier about going off on your own.'

'I know. I really am sorry.'

'We'll put it down to experience and move on.' Her voice softened. 'We've just been chatting to Paul Chattle downstairs. Charming man, isn't he?'

'Absolutely. I'm sure my mum would be over the moon if I took him home to meet her.' She smiled then winced as her split lip hurt. 'Did he say anything useful?'

'Not a single thing.'

'I'm not surprised.'

'Me neither. Zofia, the thinking is that Carly went out to Plantation Woods with a punter. If that's the case, they'll have gone there by car. Look at a map and find the roads circling the woods, then see if we can trace a car on CCTV or ANPR.'

'What time frame am I looking at?'

'I don't know. From when it was dark, I suppose. Get someone from uniform to help if it's a big job.'

Matilda's mobile rang. She looked at it. The number was withheld. Her heart skipped a beat.

'You're a survivor, aren't you, Matilda?'

'Aren't you going to answer that?' Zofia asked after the fourth ring.

Matilda was stood still, glaring at the phone. She swallowed hard and swiped to answer.

'Hello,' she said tentatively as she made her way to her small office.

'Matilda? It's me, Pat,' Pat Campbell said.

Matilda looked back at her phone. 'Where are you calling from? Your name didn't come up on my phone.'

'I'm using Anton's. I forgot to charge mine. I've just been speaking to Sally Meagan. She's had a call from the BBC about that interview they're going to be doing. You'll never guess who they're sending round.'

'Oh God, do I really want to know?'

'Danny Hanson,' Pat said.

'What? Why?'

'Well, he's written a few stories about them, he's from Sheffield.'

'He bloody isn't from Sheffield. He studied here and does a poor imitation of the accent.'

'Well, the BBC think he's perfect for the job.'

'The BBC also axed *Spooks*, *The Hour* and *The Fades*. I don't think their judgement should be taken as gospel,' she said, making her way to her office. 'Pat, will you do me a favour? Ask Sally if you can sit in on the interview; keep an eye on that Danny prick and call him out if he crosses a line.'

'Sally's already asked me if I'll be there.'

'Good. I'll talk to you later.'

Matilda ended the call, walked into her office and closed the door behind her. As she did so, her hand slipped off the handle and the door slammed shut with a loud bang, resounding around the thin walls. Matilda squeezed her eyes closed as she pictured the bullet hurtling through the air in slow motion towards her, hitting the side of her head. How much longer was she going to be plagued by these sodding flashbacks?

Chapter Twenty-Six

When Matilda returned to work in 2015 following the death of her husband and the botched Carl Meagan case, she was a shadow of her former self and was clinging onto the then named Murder Investigation Team by the tips of her fingers. Whenever she needed a moment to herself to cry or inwardly scream, or felt the symptoms of an encroaching panic attack, she took herself off to the toilets, locked the door to the furthest cubicle and waited for the panic to pass.

Over the following four years, she had improved and grown stronger with every day and every investigation. Those four short years sometimes felt like a lifetime. Now, as she sat on the familiar toilet lid, it felt like it was 2015 all over again. This time, it wasn't panic or self-doubt; she had evidence to the contrary that she was more than capable of the job, but the flashbacks, the dark thoughts, the worry every time an unfamiliar number came up on her phone, a banging door sounding like a gunshot, they all added to the feeling of intense despair that her mind wasn't going to win this time. Physically, she was recovered, but mentally, she felt lost.

Several deep breaths and a few splashes of cold water on the face later, and Matilda felt well enough to return to her office and fake it once more in front of her team. Fortunately, Christian, Sian and Scott were still at Plantation Woods, Finn was out and Zofia was on the phone. She was able to creep back to her office and close the door behind her without being seen.

She pulled the first file of the four murdered women from the pile and opened it to reveal a photograph of Ella Morse smiling up at her. The Barnsley woman had gone missing in August 2016 and found two months later hidden in woodland. She'd been strangled. At just twenty, she had been working as a prostitute for little over a year. A statement from her parents described her as a shy and quiet child growing up. She was quite open with them and told them all about her first real boyfriend when she was seventeen. He was twenty and they didn't approve of him (no qualifications, never had a job, tattoos on his neck) yet didn't tell Ella that. They felt it was important for her to discover what he was really like for herself. By the time they intervened, it was too late. Ella had been using heroin for six months and stopped going to college. It was only when her mother caught her stealing from her father's wallet that things came to a head. Ella stormed out and, despite returning now and then, begging for money, they didn't see her alive again.

According to the police report, Ella's mother was inconsolable when given the news of Ella's death. Her father, calm and staid, had been expecting it.

Matilda looked back at the photograph supplied by Ella's parents. She was a beautiful young woman, with blonde straight hair, blue eyes, a fair complexion. Nobody had forced her to take heroin, but she had been won over by the charms of one man who had used her naivety to introduce her to a dangerous world she knew nothing about. Whoever strangled her needed finding and punishing for what he did, but the man who introduced her to this lifestyle should take some responsibility for her untimely death.

Matilda read the witness statements and post-mortem and forensic reports. The case had been investigated as fully as possible, but it quickly went cold. The man with the tattooed neck had a perfect alibi for the night of her disappearance. He was in a cell at a police station in Doncaster. Nobody knew her whereabouts on the night she was taken. Nobody knew who her clients were. She disappeared. She died. She was found. A sad, tragic and pointless end.

Matilda closed the file and let out a sigh. She wondered what had been lacking in Ella's young life that she had fallen under the spell of the man who destroyed everything she had. She obviously came from a loving home, and, according to her parents, she was well liked among her peers, performed well in her exams and was hoping to go into nursing. She was always smiling, enjoyed socialising and dancing. But what was missing that, when offered heroin, she simply took it willingly?

'I'm popping out for a sandwich. Do you want anything?' Zofia asked from the open doorway.

'No, thanks. Zofia, before you go, let me ask you something. What were you like as a teenager, around sixteen?'

Zofia almost blushed and turned her head. 'You don't want to know.'

'Oh dear. That bad?'

'No. The opposite. I was probably the dullest teenager ever.'

'Go on.'

'I did my schoolwork on time, I revised for exams, I didn't

go out drinking or smoking. I didn't have a boyfriend until I was seventeen.'

'You see, Ella Morse was like that,' Matilda said, holding up the tragic girl's photo. 'Then she met a bloke who introduced her to heroin, and she was lost. Do you think something like that could have possibly happened to you?'

'With my dad? You're joking!' she scoffed. 'If anyone had shown an interest in me around exam time, my dad would have thrown him into the next county.'

'So, he was strict?'

'Not strict, just… I don't know… My parents wanted me to do well. I wasn't thick, but I wasn't a straight A student. I needed to concentrate, and they didn't want any distractions.'

'It seems like Ella Morse came from a similar kind of family, yet she quickly had her head turned. I'm trying to understand why.'

'Maybe her parents were *too* strict. Maybe they didn't show her as much love and affection as she wanted. I hate to say this about someone who was only twenty when she died, especially as she was murdered, but Ella knew what she was doing. I'm sure her parents would have welcomed her home with open arms if she'd gone back and asked for help to kick the drugs and prostitution habit. Maybe she just didn't want to.'

'Or maybe she'd gone too far down the rabbit hole to turn back.'

'It's never too late to turn back, especially if you have people willing to help you, like Ella obviously had. Anyway, are you sure I can't get you anything?'

'Screw it. I'll have a bacon butty.'

The second victim, Rachel Pickering, was completely different from Ella Morse. Rachel went missing in February

2017 and was found strangled four months later. She'd been dumped in thick woodland. Her next of kin was her grandmother, Angie Pickering, who, when told of her granddaughter's death simply said, 'I can't say I'm surprised.'

Rachel's mother, Noreen, was also a prostitute and Rachel was an unwanted surprise from one of her clients. She made three appointments to have an abortion but couldn't go through with any of them. At the back of her mind, she hoped having a child would change her focus, and she'd put the child's needs before her own and become a decent mother with a dull job and an overdraft. Unfortunately, it didn't work out that way. Within weeks of giving birth, Noreen was back on the streets, dumping the baby on Angie. Noreen overdosed just days after Rachel's first birthday, leaving Angie to raise her alone. Angie did not waste an opportunity to bring Noreen up and tell Rachel all about her trollop of a mother and the things she'd do for a packet of fags.

Rumours of what Rachel's mother did for a living swept through the school like a case of head lice and the young, impressionable Rachel was ridiculed. If she was to survive the bullies, she needed to develop a thick skin, and quickly. A kindly PE teacher took her under his wing, spotted her talent for netball and made her captain of the school team. She excelled and enjoyed herself, but it wasn't long before the teacher wanted something in return for everything he'd been doing for her. Rachel rapidly understood what her grandmother had been telling her all these years – all men are bastards and only want one thing. Rachel had it. And if men wanted it, they'd have to pay for it.

There were no photographs of Rachel smiling. She always seemed to have a permanent scowl, a hardened look of icy disdain. She had shoulder-length dark hair, dull, dark eyes and thin lips. She wasn't attractive. She wasn't ugly. She was a tragic figure with a disturbing start in life and a violent end.

Matilda leaned back in her chair. Was there any hope for Rachel Pickering or had her cards been marked from the day she was born? The subject of serial killers being born or made often came up, but what about everyone else? Will the daughter of a prostitute follow in her mother's footsteps or will she carve out a career in something more worthwhile? The world was full of examples of people shining in the face of adversity, it was possible, but in Rachel's case she was slighted at every turn. Her grandmother continually told her how useless her mother was, she was bullied at school because of it, and the one person she thought could help her, the PE teacher, took advantage of her. In the end, Rachel succumbed to her fate. Angie discovered she was selling her body when she was sixteen but guessed it had started long before. Five years later, she crossed paths with a killer and her life was obliterated.

Chapter Twenty-Seven

Christian and Sian watched as a car pulled up and a uniformed officer climbed out. He was well over six feet tall and judging by the way he held himself and walked, he was no stranger to the gym. How he managed to squeeze himself into the car with all the paraphernalia the uniform afforded was anyone's guess.

'DI Brady?' he asked, his voice deep and pure Yorkshire.

'That's me,' Christian said, looking up.

'Sergeant Inneson. Toby,' he said. 'You've requested a cadaver dog?'

'That's right. I didn't expect you so soon.'

'We were due at a training site this afternoon but thought this would be better experience for him.'

'He is qualified then?' Sian asked.

'He is, but he needs regular training.'

Sergeant Inneson went to the back of the car and opened the boot. His cadaver dog, Dexter, was a three-year-old Labrador Retriever. Once he was fully harnessed up, he was let out of the van.

'I don't suppose I'm allowed to have a cuddle,' Sian asked.

'The dog or me?' Inneson asked.

Sian blushed. 'I wouldn't say no to either.'

Inneson gave her a crooked smile that caused his blue eyes to twinkle then headed into the woods.

'Oh my God, I think my ovaries have just popped,' she said, fanning herself.

'Bloody hell, Sian, control yourself,' Christian said with a smile.

'He's gorgeous. And that voice. It was more of a growl. He sent a shiver down my spine.'

'Do I need to throw cold water over you?' he said as he headed into the woods, following Inneson.

'It's not cold water I need throwing at me.'

'Down, girl,' he said over his shoulder. 'We don't know if there are any more bodies buried in the woods,' he continued, trotting to keep up with the striding dog handler. 'It's just a theory. If there are, we've no idea how long they'll have been there. We could be talking years.'

'That won't bother Dexter,' Inneson called out. 'If there's something here, he'll find it. Human bodies decompose in five stages and each stage has its own unique smell. Dexter knows each and every one of them. His nose is about a thousand times more sensitive than ours.'

'Maybe we should let him into our office and he can tell us what that smell is,' Sian commented.

Dexter was pulling on the lead and dragging Inneson to the site where the two bodies had already been found.

There are many factors in the decomposition of a body and the various smells that emanate from it. The most obvious one is the absence of oxygen. Left to the elements, a body will rot quicker than one buried underground. Decomposition, therefore, will be completely different above and below ground.

Christian and Sian watched as Inneson unhooked the lead and Dexter was allowed to roam freely. Nose to the ground, tail high and wagging, he set off at pace. He had a lot of ground to cover.

'Amazing animals, aren't they?' Christian said.

'Yes. Their handlers aren't bad either.'

With bacon butty consumed and washed down with a mug of tea and two fun-size packets of Maltesers, Matilda returned to the files of the dead women.

Victim number three was twenty-five-year-old Deborah Monroe. She lived alone with her three-year-old son Lucas. He was the product of a one-night stand with a man she met in a nightclub one New Year's Eve while she was out with the girls from the supermarket where she worked. When she found out she was pregnant and counted back the date to when the baby was conceived, she couldn't remember what the man looked like let alone if she knew his name or not. All she could recall was that he was generous with his cash and was a decent kisser. Not exactly something you put on a birth certificate.

She quit her job a month before she was due to give birth, deciding to be a full-time mother and realising she'd get more money in benefits than she would working part time. Unfortunately, money soon ran out, and when Lucas was only five months old, she asked her boss if she could have her old job back. There were no vacancies, but he wrote her a good reference, not that it did much good. Companies just weren't hiring staff with the uncertainty of Brexit looming over the economy.

Life as a new mother wasn't fun. She rarely went out, except to the shop to buy nappies and baby milk. She could no longer afford to have her hair dyed or her nails done. Her mates stopped calling as she didn't have the money for a night out and every time her mother called all she did was ask how her grandson was. What about her? Why did nobody care how she was doing?

On one visit by her mother, the bottled-up emotions over spilled and once the tears came, they refused to stop. Her mother had the answer: "You need a night out, love. Here's fifty quid, give your mates a ring."

Deborah squeezed herself into her best "going out" clothes, slapped on the make-up and arranged to meet her former colleagues at a pub in town. By eleven o'clock, she was drunk and shattered and falling asleep at the bar. She looked around and couldn't find her friends, but she did find someone to talk to; an overweight leering man in his fifties bought her a drink, took her by the arm and led her to the sofas at the back of the nightclub. He asked her back to his place, but she said she needed to get back for Lucas. He told her to get a taxi. She said she couldn't afford a taxi. She needed every spare penny for Lucas.

'I tell you what,' he said, leaning in, breathing his rancid, smoky breath on her. 'Come to mine, we'll have some fun, and I'll pay for your taxi home. Depending on how much fun we have, I might give you a bit extra.' He winked.

By the time Deborah fell into her council flat at three o'clock in the morning she had more money than she originally went out with. A new career was born.

Deborah's move into prostitution was out of desperation.

She needed money to pay for her child's welfare. She couldn't get a job during the daytime as Lucas was only a baby and needed looking after. At night, the only jobs available were waitressing and bar work, and she couldn't do either. She told her mother she'd got a job behind the counter in her local takeaway three nights a week if she'd look after Lucas for her. When Deborah saw how much money she could earn in three nights, she wondered how much she'd earn in five.

Deborah was slim, pretty, short, and looked younger than her years. She could pass for someone in their mid-teens, if not younger, and some of the men liked that. She told one bloke she was fourteen and this turned him on more. He even paid her extra. She started playing the schoolgirl trick and it wasn't long before she had punters queuing up for her services. And they paid her very generously.

When Deborah went missing and the police were notified, her mother found out the truth. There was no job in a takeaway, Deborah was a street prostitute. Her mother felt sick, betrayed and horrified. How could she sink so low? Four months after she disappeared in July 2017, what was left of Deborah Monroe was found. She'd been strangled and dumped in woodland. There had been no effort to hide her body and the local wildlife had nibbled away at what they could.

The crime scene photographs Matilda looked at made her stomach turn and her bacon butty came back to haunt her. A beautiful, petite, twenty-five-year-old mother had been ravaged, torn apart and partially eaten. Animals were just doing what animals do in order to survive. To call a killer an animal was wrong. In Matilda's eyes, this killer was inhuman. He was sick. He was evil.

The fourth victim was slightly different to the previous

three. Denise Jones was found a day after she disappeared. Her body was found in Chelsea Park by joggers. She'd been left where she was killed, her body purposely left to be found. Why had the three victims before her been buried, or well hidden, yet this one hadn't? Had the killer been interrupted and fled the scene? Or had he upped his game? Deborah Monroe hadn't been buried, but she had been placed out of sight. Was this a transition in the game of this particular sadistic killer?

Denise was only nineteen years old. She was also an enigma. Nobody knew anything about her. The file included a statement from Bev in which she said Denise just turned up one day on the streets. She didn't seem afraid of selling herself; she wasn't nervous or repulsed by what she was doing. It was as if she'd been prostituting herself her whole life. Bev doubted Denise Jones was even her real name.

Denise was a quiet young girl. She rarely spoke about her life away from the streets. She didn't say where she'd come from or where she laid her head at night. She joined in the gossip about the other women and some of the punters, but that was it. When the journalist Alistair Tripp showed up, she seemed to change. She was smitten with the good-looking young man. She helped him with his research, there was a bounce in her step, and she was smiling more. He left as mysteriously as he arrived, and the old Denise returned.

She was murdered in September 2018, the last assumed victim of the killer before his thirteen-month break. In Bev's statement, she said she was incredibly sad as she liked Denise, but it was obvious she was sad, lonely and hurting. Bev hoped she was now at peace with whatever demons had brought her to the streets.

What Matilda found difficult to digest was the fact that a

nationwide appeal had been put out for Denise Jones following her murder and not one single phone call had come into the station. In life, nobody missed her. In death, nobody claimed her.

Matilda looked down at the only photograph they had of her, taken in the mortuary. She'd been washed and cleaned up. Her eyes were closed, there was a hint of a smile on her pale face and there was almost a serenity about her. It did seem that she was at peace.

Matilda wiped away a tear. 'I'll find the man who did this to you, Denise, to all of you. It took a while for Carl to be found, but I never gave up. I'll never give up on you either.'

Chapter Twenty-Eight

Bev was in the kitchen of her small flat making a sandwich. The kettle was boiling but it didn't click itself off as that part of the mechanism was broken. She unplugged it and poured the hot water into two mismatched mugs: one for her, one for Sarah. She placed the mugs on a tin tray stolen from a nearby pub, along with her sandwich, and went into the living room.

Sarah was sat on the sofa reading a well-thumbed romance novel.

'Are you sure you don't want anything to eat?' Bev asked.

'No. I'm not hungry.'

'Are you all right? Ever since you had that food poisoning you've hardly touched anything.'

Bev sat on a brown armchair, crossed her legs and tucked into the potted meat sandwich.

'I had a big breakfast. Besides, I'm trying to lose weight.'

'I thought you'd have lost plenty with all that vomiting and shitting you were doing.'

'I did, and I'd like to keep it off.'

'Are you coming out tonight?'

Sarah sighed and closed the book. 'Better had. I'm skint.'

'Well, I've had a couple of texts so I should make about sixty quid tonight,' Bev said. 'Then there's anyone else who's out and about on top of that. I can always let you have some if you're short.'

'I'm worried about the heating,' Sarah said. 'It cost a bomb last winter. If we have another cold one, we won't be able to afford it. I was thinking maybe if we went halves and got some heavier curtains, especially in here, there's a right draft coming through the gap in the window.'

'Do you have any idea how much decent curtains cost? Even going halves it won't be cheap.'

'Well, maybe we could ask Brandon to—'

'No!' Bev almost snapped.

'He is our landlord.'

'Yes, and we're paying way less than we should be doing for this place. If I ask him to do all the things that need fixing, he'll put the rent right up.'

'He gets plenty out of us,' Sarah said, a look of disgust on her face. 'I hate it when he comes round here, pawing over us like he does. He could at least have a wash first.'

'I was thinking—' Bev was interrupted by the doorbell ringing.

She placed her plate on the coffee table, dusted her hands and got up to answer the door. She looked through the spyhole.

'Shit, it's Paul Chattle,' she whispered.

'What does he want?'

'How do I know?'

'Pretend we're not here.'

'He'll know we're here. Where else are we going to be at this time of day?'

The doorbell rang again following by a loud hammering on the door.

'Maybe he wants to ask about Carly,' Bev said. 'You know, who she was with on the night she died.'

'Come on, Bev, open up. I can hear you through the door. I know you're in there.'

'Fuck,' Bev mouthed. 'Hang on,' she called. 'I'm just getting dressed.'

She motioned to Sarah to keep calm and relaxed. She took the security chain off, turned the Yale lock and pulled open the door. Paul barged his way past and into the flat.

'Come in, why don't you?' Bev said, closing the door after him.

'Which one of you two has been jawing to the police?'

'What are you talking about?' Bev asked, standing her ground. She stood by the door, her hands on her hips, while Sarah cowered on the sofa.

'I'm not thick. I know you two talk to the police. You think you're doing good by being all pally and friendly with them, thinking they'll look after you in return, well, they won't. You're scum to them. They're just using you for information. So, which one of you slags has told them about me?'

'Excuse me! When you've done calling us names, perhaps you'd like to tell us what you're talking about.'

'I've been at the station all morning, answering questions. Did I know Carly was a prostitute? Who were her regular clients? Did I know she was on drugs? Did I supply her with them? Where was I when she died?'

'Paul, you know me and Sarah have nothing to do with drugs. We haven't told the police anything about you.'

'You've never liked me, have you, Bev?' Paul said. His tone was threatening, and he spat as he talked. 'I've seen how you've looked down at me, all high and mighty just because you used to be an accountant. Well, you're fuck-all good now, are you? You're a cheap old dirty slag. Just like Sarah and just like Carly was.'

The closer he came to Bev the more alcohol she could smell on his stale breath.

'Look, Paul, I know you're upset about Carly dying, but there's no need to be like that. Why don't you go home, sleep it off and come back round when you're sober? We can talk then.'

'The day I take advice from an old slag is the day I help the police with their enquiries. Oh, wait, that's what you two do, isn't it?' he said, his nose almost touching Bev's face.

'Paul, please, I'd like you to leave,' she said, fear shaking in her voice.

'I'm not going anywhere until I get some answers.'

'Then you'll have a long wait because I'm not talking to you when you're like this.'

'You'll talk. Or I'll fucking make you talk.'

'You can't bully me like you did Carly.'

'Can't I?'

Paul grabbed Bev by the throat with his left hand and wrapped his dirty fat fingers around her neck. He pinned her up against the wall and started to squeeze tight.

Bev used both hands to grab his wrist and tried to pull him off her. It was no use; his grip was like a vice. She choked and gasped for breath.

'Paul, leave her alone,' Sarah called out, tears in her eyes. 'She hasn't told the police anything about you. We wouldn't do that. You know us.'

'You're a pair of fucking slags who'll do anything for a few quid. If the police flashed a tenner at you, you'd sell your own mother.'

'That's not true. Paul, please, you're hurting her,' Sarah pleaded, tears filling her eyes.

'Good. Dirty bitch tried to turn Carly against me. Tried to get her to leave me.'

'She didn't say anything like that. We liked Carly. We were looking after her.'

'She didn't need you. She had me to look after her.'

'Fat lot of good it did. You made her go back on the streets. She got kicked, punched, battered, bruised, bitten, spat at and raped just so you could buy your fucking drugs,' Sarah shouted. 'You didn't look after her. You used her for your own ends. Now let go of Bev right now,' she screamed.

Paul turned to look at her. His whole face had changed. There was pure evil staring at her.

Sarah backed off. She had found the courage from somewhere to scream at him when her best friend was in danger, but it was all she had. He could kill Bev and come for her. He could kill them both right here, right now.

Paul released his hold on Bev. She dropped to the floor with a heavy thud, not moving.

'Bev?' Sarah whimpered. 'You've killed her,' she cried.

'One less whore in the world. They'll be another one in a few minutes.'

Sarah backed up, her legs hitting the flatpack sideboard they'd bought from a charity shop and carried between them all the way from Attercliffe. Bev and Sarah sometimes brought men back to the flat, if they didn't have a car or if the weather was bad. However, they always thought one step ahead and were prepared for any eventuality in case one of the punters turned violent or refused to pay.

Sarah lowered herself down the wall and reached behind the sideboard where a wooden rounders bat was waiting to be used to defend herself with.

She swallowed hard. She'd never used it before. She'd never had anyone be violent with her in the past and always worried if she had to guts to stand up for herself if anyone did. She was about to find out.

She wrapped her small hand around the thin end of the bat and pulled it out of its hiding place. As soon as it was free, she raised it and with one swing she smacked Paul around the head with it.

Chapter Twenty-Nine

Christian entered Matilda's office without knocking. He pulled off his beanie hat. 'I'm absolutely bollocking... Oh, hello, sir,' he said when he noticed ACC Ridley standing by the door.

Matilda stifled a smile.

'Good afternoon DI Brady,' Ridley said. 'You have cadaver dogs out at Plantation Woods, I hear.'

'That's right, sir. One of the bodies found had the ID belonging to one of the missing prostitutes on her. Obviously, we don't know if it is really her until we can get a positive ID, but we need to know if Plantation Woods is a dumping ground or not.'

'Matilda, how do you want to play this?' Ridley asked, turning to her.

Christian turned his back to take his coat off. He rolled his eyes and inwardly sighed.

'I suppose we wait and see if the cadaver dog tells us anything. If so, we dig.'

'It might be worth contacting a specialist to take a look at the woods as a whole. When I was in Manchester, we frequently looked for Keith Bennett, the missing victim of the Moors Murderers. I was invited to visit the so-called Body Farm in Tennessee to look at how plant growth and ground depressions differ when a body is buried. It was fascinating as well as being macabre. Plant growth is suppressed for around one year after the body is buried. After three years, when the soft tissue has broken down and enriched the soil, plant growth thrives, and you get a rich abundance of plant life. The human body is made up of seventy per cent water, after all. That alone will feed the soil as the cadaver decomposes. I'm sure there are some gardening experts who can help.'

'I was thinking of sending a drone up, sir,' Christian said. 'If we film the woods from above, we can zoom in on specific areas.'

'We'd still need to send an expert into the woods to have a close-up look at the vegetation,' Matilda said. 'We may as well miss out the drone stage completely. It's a needless expense. As I was saying, sir,' Matilda turned to the ACC, 'the first victim that we know about was Ella Morse in 2016. She was found, but we have five women who went missing after that time. If they're buried in Plantation Woods, the vegetation should stand out, don't you think?'

'It's possible. Obviously, there are many contributing factors: weather conditions during the time the body has been buried, the type of soil, wildlife, the depth the body was buried, the state the body was in when it was buried. If the body was in a shallow grave, there are chances local wildlife could have been attracted by the smell of decomposition.'

'Adele did say the first body had been disturbed,' Christian said.

'In that case, any areas with a disturbed ground, animal faeces, feathers, animal fur, should all be seriously looked at.'

'What about those ground penetrating radar machines?' Christian asked.

'They work best when the body has been wrapped in something as the wrapping won't have broken down and will provide a good reflective surface.'

'Neither of these two bodies were wrapped,' Christian said.

'In that case,' Ridley continued, 'a machine that measures electrical resistivity will be better. If the body is still decomposing, the bodily fluids will seep into the soil and these machines will measure how the fluids disrupt the flow of the electrical current.'

'Fascinating,' Matilda said.

'I was going to say gruesome,' Christian smiled.

'I'll get on to the universities and see if we can find an expert in topography who can help with our search.'

'Thank you,' Matilda said.

As Ridley headed for the door he stopped and turned back. 'You may want to try and find someone who knows Plantation Woods quite well. A woodsman or something. They may be able to point you in the area of recent changes. Let me know if you need anything,' he said with a smile before leaving the room.

'Quite a knowledgeable bloke,' Christian said.

'Yes. Not as scary as when he first appeared.'

'That was probably nerves. I didn't want to ask him for a full description of topography as I didn't want to look stupid. I'm assuming you know.'

Matilda smiled. 'It's a field of geoscience and the study of the shape and features of the ground at a local level. They help with the drawing up of maps, too.'

Sian knocked on the door and popped her head through the small gap. 'I've been having a think…'

'I thought I could smell burning,' Christian smiled.

She gave him a look and continued. 'The child, here, mentioned about possibly sending up a drone over Plantation Woods to take a look at the ground from above. Using high-definition cameras, you can feed the footage into the computer and select different areas to focus on and how they differ to others.'

'We've more or less discounted that stage. Besides, I doubt we have access to cameras like that,' Matilda said.

'I'm not sure. However, do you remember the manhunt for Raoul Moat? Police had the RAF do a flyover of the area they thought he was hiding in and used one of those heat-seeking cameras to find him. I know someone who works at RAF Syerston. We could ask them to go up in a Tornado and film Plantation Woods for us.'

'How do you know so many people?' Christian asked.

'I'm a very friendly person,' she smiled.

'This case is going to cost a bloody fortune,' Matilda said. 'Before we start scaring the locals by having the RAF flying low over their houses let's wait to see what the cadaver dogs find. Then we'll take it from there.'

'Sergeant Inneson said he's going back out there tomorrow as it's starting to get dark now. He's going to bring another one out, too.'

'What about the two bodies we've found? When are the PMs?'

'Tomorrow.'

'Do we know cause of death yet? Are we looking at two more strangulations?'

'No,' Christian said. 'Adele said it appears one of them was buried alive.'

Matilda leaned forward on her desk and rested her head on her steepled hands. 'Why would the same killer change from strangling to burying someone alive?'

'Maybe it's not the same killer,' Sian suggested.

'Two unrelated killers with the same target? That's a bit of a stretch, isn't it?' Christian asked.

'Not necessarily.' Matilda stood up and left her small office, entering the main suite. 'Finn, you're our resident criminologist, answer me this question: why would a serial killer switch his method of killing?'

'Is that what he's done?' Zofia asked.

Matilda put a hand up to silence her.

Finn leaned back in his chair. There was a heavy frown on his face as he thought. 'Well, I'm not fully up on all this at the moment, so this will just be a guess based on what I've learned so far.'

'That's enough for me.'

'Okay. This type of killer is killing for some kind of thrill. He's enjoying himself and getting a kick out of the murders. We've seen with the earlier victims that he buried them or put them in a place where they'd be difficult to find. With Denise and Carly, he left them out in the open, showing us that merely killing them wasn't enough. He wants the police to know that we're dealing with a serial killer rather than missing people. He wants the public to be scared.'

'I get that, but why change from strangulation to burying someone alive?'

'Or vice versa,' Christian said.

'What?'

'Well, we don't know how long this victim has been in the ground. Maybe she predates our first known victim,' he said.

'That's true. Either way, he changed the method he used to kill them – why?' she asked, turning back to Finn.

'If she was an earlier victim, maybe he found that method of killing too difficult, or maybe he didn't get the kick he wanted from it. If she's a later victim, maybe he wasn't getting the same kick out of strangling so needed to up his game.'

'So,' Sian began, 'the more victims a killer murders using the same method, the more he'll become immune to what he's doing, and it'll become banal?'

'Precisely. I remember when I was a child, I told my mum I wanted to work in an M&Ms factory so I could eat as many as I wanted to. She said I'd soon get sick of the sight of M&Ms and it would no longer be fun.'

'I wonder if the same could be said for any job?' Scott mused.

'What do you mean?' Sian asked.

'Well, I joined the police because I wanted to catch killers. How long before that becomes banal and I turn to the dark side myself in order to make things more interesting?'

'Bloody hell, Scott, that's turned things dark,' Christian said.

'Our job is a tad different from packing M&Ms, Scott,' Matilda said. 'We don't get the same kind of killer, victims and motive. Every case is different, that's what keeps us on our toes. It's the banality of the norm that needs shaking up.'

'So, what does all this tell us about our killer?' Zofia asked. 'Is he easily bored and that's why he changed methods?'

Matilda turned to the murder board. 'We need to discover what order the killings came in. We have five strangulations, but whereabouts on the list does the burying alive come?'

'It does help us get a snapshot of our killer, however,' Finn said. 'If he did change so quickly from strangling to another method of killing, maybe his life outside of murdering is very dull and routine. He could have a job packing M&Ms or something and is frightened of getting stuck in a rut.'

'That could be anyone,' Sian said. 'Every mature adult male I know hates routine.'

'That's an oxymoron, Sian. There's no such thing as a mature adult male,' Matilda said with a smile.

'That's true. There are times I feel like a single mother raising five kids.'

Matilda clapped her hands together. 'Right, here's where I think we should go next with this: obviously the first task is to discover how these two women died and roughly when. We need to talk to Bev and Sarah about these other missing women and get as much information as we can about them, then talk to their families and friends and see if they've been in touch. We need to keep an eye on Plantation Woods. Is this the killer's dumping ground? If so, why? What's in the local vicinity? We'll get the dates of the women disappearing then knock on doors to see if the surrounding neighbours remember anything unusual about those days. This is going to be a huge investigation, but I know we're all capable of succeeding here.'

Matilda surprised herself by how positive she suddenly felt. This was what she needed, though. A demanding investigation would occupy her mind, stop her from dwelling in the pity of her own recovery. It would help to dispel the nightmares, the flashbacks and the overreactions whenever she heard a loud noise.

Matilda sent everyone home early. The coming days would be long and arduous so when the opportunity to finish at a decent time came, it should be grabbed with both hands. Matilda and Scott were the last to leave the suite.

'What do you think to the new office?' Matilda asked as they walked down the stairs to the car park.

'I don't like it. It's too small. And what the hell is that smell?'

'I know. It's rank, isn't it?'

'Do you think we've got a dead body under the floorboards?'

Matilda laughed. 'Can you imagine the headlines if there was a dead body discovered in a police station?'

They walked in silence for a few moments. 'Can I ask you a personal question?' Scott asked.

'Sure.'

'While you were recovering, did you ever think about not coming back to work, changing career altogether?'

'I did. I'm still questioning myself even now. But what else would I do? All I ever wanted to do since I was a child was join the police force. What about you?'

'In the aftermath of the shooting, I was planning to quit every day. I even wrote my resignation out once.'

'What changed your mind?'

'Similar reason to you, really. It's all I've ever wanted to do. I wouldn't be happy in another job.'

'But you're not happy now, are you?'

He looked at her. 'No. I'm not. But I know that Rory and Chris would be sticking pins into a doll of me if I quit the force.'

Matilda linked arms with Scott. They reached the exit to the car park and Scott pushed open the door. They stepped out into the cold, dark night.

'I'm not the best person to give you advice on how to be happy, Scott. I haven't been happy since James died.'

'You were happy with Daniel.'

'Yes, but looking back, it was a different kind of happiness.' She squeezed Scott's arm harder. 'I know for a fact that you'll find love again, and you'll laugh again, and be happy again, but it will be different to what you had with Chris.'

'It's a long road, this grief malarkey, isn't it?'

'Long, bumpy and painful.'

'How long until the exit?'

'Only you can answer that. I turned off at the Daniel junction, but I've got back on it again.'

'I haven't even stopped for petrol yet.'

Matilda smiled. 'How long do you think we can hammer at this metaphor for?'

'At least until we get home. Then I'll text you just as you're falling asleep when I think of another one,' he grinned.

They reached Matilda's car and were just about to climb in when Matilda's name was called. She turned quickly but couldn't make out the dark figure standing at the entrance to the car park.

You're a survivor, aren't you, Matilda?

'Who's that?' she asked, her voice quivering.

He stepped forward and into the light. It was Danny Hanson.

'Jesus Christ, Danny,' Matilda said.

The smug smile was back on his annoying face. 'Can I ask you a few questions about Carl Meagan?'

'No. You cannot,' she replied firmly.

'I'd just like your take on his return.' She ignored him. 'His disappearance has haunted you for four years. Now he's been found and back where he belongs, how do you feel?'

Matilda opened the front passenger door, got in and slammed the door behind her. Scott remained standing by the driver's side.

Danny continued, raising his voice slightly so she could still hear him. 'I'm guessing you're relieved. You blamed yourself. Sally and Philip blamed you. Did your colleagues blame you, too?' He asked looking at Scott. 'I'm guessing the people of Sheffield did. Every time the case was highlighted in the press the reason for the botched ransom drop was mentioned. It must have brought all the buried emotions back to the surface.'

'Go away, Danny,' Scott said.

Danny approached the car and bent down to look at Matilda. She refused to make eye contact with him.

'You can sleep at night now, can't you? A huge weight off your mind. You must have more lives than a cat, Matilda. Everything seems to work out all right for you in the end, doesn't it? I've put in a request with my bosses at the BBC and with South Yorkshire Police to have a full interview with you; get your side of the story. I'm sure they will grant me permission. I am, after all, the official interviewer on this case,' he grinned. 'I shall look forward to sitting down and chatting with you.'

Scott grabbed Danny by the collar. The detective loomed over the journalist, and practically picked him off the ground. He dragged him away from the car and threw him towards the exit. He stumbled and fell onto the damp, hard tarmac.

'Staff personnel only. The sign is perfectly clear, Danny. For a journalist, you don't notice much. Now piss off before I arrest you.'

Danny picked himself up and dusted himself down. He grinned, blew Scott a kiss and headed for the exit.

Scott got into the car. 'Are you all right?'

Matilda looked at him. 'There is no way I am being interviewed by that reptile.'

'I'm sure the ACC won't make you do it if you don't want to.'

'I hate that man so much,' she said through gritted teeth.

'Look, it's dark, there aren't many people around, how about we run him over on the way home?'

Matilda laughed. 'I honestly don't think anything will kill him. He's like the sodding Terminator.'

'I love those films. Well, only the first two.'

'Is there some kind of power plant in Sheffield where we can crush him?'

Scott reversed out of the car park and began the drive home.

'Plenty of steels works. Maybe we can drop him into molten steel.'

Matilda sat back in the passenger seat and looked out at the dark streets of Sheffield as they passed by in a blur. She wondered if this was what the killer of the street prostitutes did: plot and think of new and ingenious ways to kill his victims. Strangulation had become the norm after a while, so he switched to burying one alive. Had he sat in his car, watching the women work, and imagine how he was going to end their lives? She shivered. Was it so easy for a normal, upstanding member of society to descend into being a killer? If Matilda could get away with it, would she kill Danny Hanson? She honestly couldn't answer that question, and that scared her. Had this killer thought the same about killing prostitutes?

Chapter Thirty

Pat: I went to visit Sally this afternoon and see how Carl is. I had both dogs jumping all over me. Loved it. Carl's hardly left his room. He's very quiet.

Matilda: Understandable. Hopefully when his therapy starts he'll open up more.

Matilda opened the front door and kicked it closed behind her. She'd asked Scott if he wanted to join her and Harriet for tea but when she identified the strange car as belonging to her mother he politely declined.

It felt strange coming home after a long day at work to a warm house and the sound of conversation rippling through the rooms. Usually, it was cold and all she could hear was the humming of the fridge and a ticking clock from the living room. She had never thought of herself as being lonely, but, looking back, she supposed she was. When Harriet found a house and moved out, would the loneliness return, and would she feel worse than before? Maybe she should contact Adele, try and repair some bridges.

She went into the living room. Harriet and their mother, Penny, were on the sofa. The coffee table was a mess of get-well letters and cards Matilda hadn't got around to answering yet as well as a plethora of newspapers.

Penny stood up, went over to her eldest daughter and gave her an awkward hug and a kiss on the cheek.

Since the shooting in January which resulted in the death of her husband, Penny had changed from being a harsh, stubborn woman to a more relaxed one. In the immediate aftermath, she sank into a depression, she lost weight and there were days she refused to get out of bed. It was only the breakdown of Harriet's marriage and relocating to Sheffield that made her realise the family was falling apart and needed a matriarch to pull it back together. She sold the cottage in Bakewell that was littered with memories of her marriage to Frank and returned to Sheffield in a beautiful stone-built two-bedroom cottage in Greenhill.

When Matilda lost James, Penny had a lot to say about coming to terms with her grief and moving on. Now that Penny was on the receiving end of losing the man she loved, she understood what Matilda had gone through and how the grieving process was far from simple. She felt she had a great deal of ground to cover in repairing the fractious relationship with Matilda. Like grief, it was a long and slow process, but it was one she was prepared to commit to.

'Hello, sweetheart, have you had a good day?' Penny asked.

'Fine. Thanks. Busy,' Matilda said, shrugging off her jacket and slumping down on the opposite sofa.

'The papers are full of Carl Meagan being found. You must be ever so pleased.'

'I didn't find him myself.' Matilda glanced at the front pages and the famous image of the smiling seven-year-old glaring up at her. The press had obviously not managed to get an updated picture yet. 'If it wasn't for a vigilant neighbour, he'd still be missing.'

'True, but you've kept the case in the spotlight. This is a good result for you.'

Matilda glanced to her mother's overly made-up, grinning face, then back down to the papers. 'Am I mentioned?'

'Yes. Briefly.'

'What happens next?' Harriet asked.

'Well, his parents are doing an exclusive interview with the BBC. There'll be counselling and therapy offered to them all. It's a big shock for them.'

'Will you keep in touch?' Penny asked.

Matilda shrugged.

Harriet and Penny exchanged glances.

'You've had some lovely cards and letters,' Penny said after a lengthy, awkward silence. 'You'll be replying to all of them, I hope.'

'Of course I will. I'm a bit preoccupied at the moment with two dead bodies and four missing women,' she almost snapped.

'Matilda, I'm showing an interest. Isn't that what you wanted?' Penny asked.

Matilda rolled her eyes. 'A natural interest.'

'What does that mean?'

'You should ask about things because you actually want to know, not just because it's something you think I want to hear. If you genuinely want to know how my day has been then I'll tell you in glorious technicolour, but if you're just being polite, then I'm not going to waste my breath.' She stood up and headed for the door.

'Where are you going?' Harriet asked.

'I'm tired. I'm going to bed.'

'But you've only just arrived home. Have you eaten?'

'I'm not hungry.'

Matilda had to use the bannister to get her upstairs. She was tired. Her body was tired, and she didn't have the energy to get up them on her own. As much as she was grateful for Harriet moving in and helping her with her recovery, she knew that it was partly for selfish reasons that Harriet had agreed in the first place. She had left her husband and was living in a grotty flat with two teenage boys. It wasn't ideal, whereas a five-bedroom house in Sheffield was.

Matilda went over to the window and sat on the armchair where she sometimes read in the evenings. The view, in daylight, was sprawling and took in the splendour of the Sheffield countryside and the Peak District National Park. There wasn't a house in sight and Matilda could pretend she really was in the middle of nowhere; just her and the wilderness. In darkness, all she saw was her own spent reflection looking back at her. She looked old, grey and listless. Everything had fallen apart with the shooting. She had lost many people she truly cared about.

You're a survivor, aren't you, Matilda?

She kept hearing Jake's voice when he called her, threatened her, on that cold January morning. Yes, she was a survivor. She had been through a great deal over the years and had always managed to bounce back. Even being shot in the head hadn't killed her. She *was* a survivor.

What's the point in surviving, when everyone around you is dead?

Matilda couldn't answer that question. People had told her that you honour the victims by surviving and continuing to live your best life. That is the only way to defeat the Jake Harrisons of this world. The problem was Matilda had no idea how to live. The raw pain was agony.

'You bastard, Jake. Why didn't you just kill me?' she cried.

Chapter Thirty-One

'Mum, will you tell that lizard if he ever goes in my room again, I'm going to break his fingers.'

Sian was in the kitchen dicing chicken breasts for their tea. In the background, competing with Radio Four, were her four children. Anthony was home from university having broken an ankle playing rugby and wanting the round-the-clock attention he wouldn't receive in the halls. Danny was struggling with his revision and shouting at Gregory to keep the noise down, while Gregory was riling Belinda, who was trying to get ready for a date.

'Belinda, please don't threaten to break your brother's fingers,' Sian said.

'Mum, I'm trying to put my make-up on and I can't concentrate with him gawping at me all the time.'

'Gregory, I've warned you about going into your sister's room. It's out of bounds to you,' she said, pointing at him with the carving knife.

'Are you threatening me with a knife, Mum?'

'No,' she said, quickly putting it down. 'Just … keep out of your sister's hair.'

'It's not fair. I want my own room.'

'Not this again.' Sian rolled her eyes. 'We don't have the space for everyone to have their own room.'

'I hate sharing with Danny.'

'Do you think I enjoy sharing with your dad?'

'I heard that,' Stuart said, entering the kitchen. He had just had a shower and smelled clean and fresh rather than of grease and oil.

'Dad, can you give me a lift to Tina's? I'm going to be late thanks to this reptile,' Belinda said, looking daggers at Gregory.

'Remember all those baby books we read when you were pregnant with Anthony?' Stuart asked Sian, leaning on the counter.

'Ye-es,' she said, wondering where this was going.

'Did any one of them ever mention that being a parent is basically being a taxi or a cash machine?'

Sian smiled. 'Not to my recollection.'

'That reminds me,' Belinda said. 'Dad, I don't think I've got enough money, can I borrow twenty quid?'

'And when did the word "borrow" change its meaning into "you'll never see this money ever again"?'

'Please.' Belinda went over to her dad and gave him a hug, resting her head on his chest. 'I'll love you for ever and I'll help you wash the car this weekend.'

He reached into his back pocket, took out his wallet and handed Belinda a twenty-pound note. She took it, reached up to kiss him on his stubbled cheek and ran out of the room.

'Hang on,' Sian called out. 'You told me you were going on

a date. Now you've said you're going round to Tina's. Which is it?'

She came back into the doorway. 'Both.'

'A double date?'

'No. Me and Tina are going on a date together.'

'Oh,' Sian said.

'You don't mind, do you?' Belinda asked, looking from one parent to the other.

'No. We don't mind. As long as you're happy.'

'Cool. I'll be ready in about ten minutes, Dad.'

Belinda ran up the stairs.

'Did I hear that correctly?' Stuart asked. 'Did Belinda just tell us she's gay?'

'I think she did, yes,' Sian said, looking stunned.

'And we're really not bothered about it, are we?'

'No.'

'Wow, look at us two – modern parents,' he said, smiling and putting his arms around Sian.

Adele Kean had converted the dining room into a study. It was only used as a dining room on special occasions such as birthdays, Christmas and for a celebratory meal. Since Chris's death, there was nothing to celebrate and Adele couldn't imagine cooking a full Christmas meal just for herself. It would look sad sitting at a table for six with a turkey and all the trimmings. The room would be much better used as a place for Adele to write her lectures and her book.

The table was covered with textbooks and notepads. She was nearing the end of the first draft of the book. She had one more chapter then a conclusion to write. The final chapter was about the intricacies of the post-mortem examination and how even the smallest detail can aid the police in difficult murder investigations when killers believe they have covered their tracks. Matilda would have been a great source of information for this chapter, but that wasn't possible now.

The case she was using was that of two-year-old Daisy Chapman, who had been rushed to hospital by her parents after falling down the stairs. She was unconscious when she arrived at Sheffield's Children's Hospital and never woke up. During the post mortem, Adele noticed a small faded bruise on her lower back. A scan of the body also revealed a broken bone in her arm which hadn't healed correctly yet her medical records didn't refer to any hospital visits following an incident resulting in a broken bone. Adele had decided on a full invasive post mortem, and upon dissecting the sexual organs, she found severe bruising and tearing, both vaginally and anally. Daisy Chapman had suffered sustained sexual abuse over a long period of time. Adele contacted the police, who launched an investigation. The result was that Daisy's mother, father and uncle were all arrested and charged with sexual abuse. Two further children in the extended Chapman family had since come forward with allegations of sexual abuse.

At the time, Adele performed her duties with professional care, and although it was difficult performing a post mortem on a two-year-old child and the discovery she made was incredibly dark, she had remained stoic throughout. Now, as she re-read the case and her notes, and looked into the sweet, smiling face of the victim, the floodgates opened, and Adele had to stop work. She felt sick.

She pushed back her chair and stood up too quickly. Her surroundings blurred and she felt light-headed. She couldn't remember the last time she'd had something to eat. There hadn't been time for a full lunch break with everything going on at Plantation Woods. She'd eaten an apple while ordering supplies, but it wasn't a substantial meal.

She went into the kitchen and opened the cupboards. Apart from a few cans of soup and a packet of dried pasta, there was little there to tempt her. The fridge was just as empty, and all the freezer contained was a full ice cube tray.

Adele headed for the living room and stood in the doorway. The silence wrapped itself around her like a shroud; she could feel it gripping her, squeezing her. The living room, once large and spacious, a hive of activity, the centre of the home, was barren of life. The curtains were drawn, and the lights were out. Adele went over to the sofa and sat gently in the middle of it.

There was a time she and Matilda would spend hours watching films, debating which superhero in the Marvel films was the best looking, why Hollywood was obsessed with remakes and reboots, and whether there would ever be a decent Superman film again, but not anymore. Those days were long gone.

Since Chris had been murdered, Adele had covered the walls with more framed photographs of the son she had brought up alone, the son she was proud of and loved with all her heart. It was nine months since he'd been killed. No time at all, yet sometimes it felt like years. She ached to see him once more, to hold him, to kiss him.

Adele reached out for her mobile on the table by the sofa. She picked it up and, with cold hands, dialled the voicemail.

'You have no new messages and one saved voice message.'

Adele swallowed hard and braced herself.

'Mum, it's me. There's a shooting at the school. I'm inside with some of the students, but we're hiding. I've called Scott and the police *are outside. They're trying to find a way to get us all out. I'm sure everything's going to be fine. It's just... If it isn't, I want you to know that I couldn't have asked for a better mum than you. You've been amazing. You brought me up on your own as well as working hard at a career. You're a bloody superhero. I love you. I know I don't say it often, but I do. I love you, Mum.'*

Tears ran down her face. She couldn't help it. Her entire body was in agony with grief. She loved her son more than anything else in the world. She'd do anything to be with him once again.

Chapter Thirty-Two

Matilda woke to the sound of her mobile ringing. She'd fallen asleep in the chair by the window. She ached from the uncomfortable position she'd been slumped in. The room was in total darkness, lit only by the screen of her mobile. She reached across for it and looked at the display. It was a number she didn't have saved in her contacts and one she didn't recognise.

'You're a survivor, aren't you, Matilda?'

'Hello?' she asked tentatively as she swiped to answer.

'Is this Matilda Darke?'

'But what's the point of surviving, when everyone around you is dead?'

She swallowed hard. 'Yes. Who's this?'

'It's Sarah.'

'Who?'

'Sarah. I'm Bev's friend. We work together.'

Matilda visibly relaxed. 'Sarah, of course. I didn't recognise your voice, sorry.' It was probably the first time she had ever heard Sarah speak. Bev usually did the talking for them both.

'I need your help. Bev's been attacked.'

Matilda sat up. 'What? Who by? Where is she?'

'Shit. I don't have much money left on my phone. We're at the Hallamshire. Can you come?'

'Of course. I'll be right there.'

The line went dead. Matilda didn't know if Sarah's phone had cut out or if she'd simply ended the call now she knew Matilda was on her way.

It was a little after half past eleven. Matilda had been asleep for five hours. That was more sleep than she sometimes had in a whole night.

She left her bedroom and was halfway down the stairs when she realised she was unable to drive.

'Shit.'

She turned, ran back upstairs, knocked on her sister's door and walked in without waiting for a reply. Fortunately, Harriet was sat up in bed, reading.

'Harriet, I need you to drive me to the hospital.'

'Why? Are you in pain?'

'What? No. It's not me. Look, I'll explain on the way. Please. It's important.'

Matilda explained everything while Harriet was pulling on a pair of jeans and a wrinkled sweater she picked up from the floor. By the time they were in the car and headed down the drive, the conversation had ended, and an awkward silence descended.

'Are you going to apologise to Mum?' Harriet asked.

'Why?'

'You were rude to her.'

Matilda looked out of the window. Sheffield in the dark looked peaceful and serene. 'Mum is only suddenly interested in how I'm doing since Dad died. He badgered her for years to understand the job I do, the dangers I face, and she wouldn't. Now he's dead she thinks by acting the caring mother she's honouring his wishes in some way. It's so transparent.'

'She cares.'

'No. She doesn't,' Matilda replied firmly.

'So … what, then? Are you going to cut her out of your life completely?'

'Of course not. I want her to be how she was before. She hates me being a detective, always has done. How can Dad being murdered change her feelings on the matter? She still hates my job. I don't want her fake concern and plastic smiles.' She sat back in her seat, arms folded tight across her chest.

'Do you want me to have a word with her?'

'It's entirely up to you.'

'You're as stubborn as each other,' Harriet said under her breath.

They pulled up at the Royal Hallamshire Hospital and seemed to find a parking space easily, which made a refreshing change. Matilda looked up at the building. She had been in a coma in this hospital when Jake went on his final rampage, killing her father in the process. She felt sad, momentarily, but Matilda had a degree in suppressing her emotions and right now, she had more important things on her mind.

Matilda flashed her warrant card to a passing nurse who told her where to go to find Bev. She was still in a cubicle in A&E waiting for a bed on a ward. Matilda pulled back the curtain and saw Bev sat up in bed with a smile on her face chatting animatedly to a worried-looking Sarah by her side.

'Bev, what happened?' Matilda asked. She squatted down

to look at the bruising on her neck. 'Oh, sorry, this is my sister, Harriet.'

Greetings were exchanged and Harriet stepped back but remained within earshot.

'I was…' It obviously caused Bev pain to talk. She reached for a plastic glass of water and took a lengthy drink. When she did speak, her voice was hoarse. 'He tried to strangle me.'

'Who?'

'Paul Chattle,' Sarah said.

'Why?'

'He came barging into the flat, wanted to know what we'd said to the police about him. He's never liked us. He always said we were interfering in him and Carly, trying to get her to leave him. We told him to get out, but he wouldn't. He had this evil look in his eye. If I hadn't have hit him, I honestly think he would have killed Bev,' Sarah said, reaching out and taking Bev's hand.

Matilda thought that was the most she'd ever heard Sarah speak in one go. 'You hit him?'

'Yes. We've got this rounders bat hidden in case … well, just in case. I grabbed for it and hit him around the head.'

'Where is he now?'

'I've no idea.'

'Have you known Paul to be violent before?' Matilda asked.

'Carly never mentioned it,' Bev croaked.

'He was always more of a verbal bully, apparently,' Sarah continued. 'He said some nasty things to Carly, really put her down, made her feel useless. He did it to keep her on the streets. He did it so she'd think there was only him who could take care of her when in fact it was him who needed her. It was her money he used.'

'Has he ever been with any of the women?'

Bev shook her head.

'No,' Sarah said. 'He can't get it up, according to Carly. It's all them drugs he takes; they've made him impotent. Best thing for the human race if you ask me.'

Matilda looked back at Bev. 'What have the doctors said?'

'Bruised larynx. I'll be fine in a few days. They're only keeping me in for observation because I was unconscious when the paramedics came.'

'I'll get onto uniform and get someone to go to Paul's flat, see if he's there. I'll make sure he's charged with assault and we'll get a restraining order out on him so he can't come anywhere near you.'

Bev smiled.

'Erm, will I get into trouble?' Sarah asked, looking worried. 'I hit him pretty hard.'

'It was self-defence, Sarah. I'm sure when police go around to his flat, they'll find all sorts of drugs there, too. We'll have plenty to charge him with. Do you want a lift back?'

Sarah looked to Bev then back to Matilda. 'No. I'm going to hang around here for a while. I'll head back later.'

'Okay. Well, you two take care. I'll be in touch.'

'Before you go…' Bev began. 'I meant to phone Sian earlier, but obviously I didn't get a chance. She asked me if there was anyone suspicious I could think of hanging around the women. I don't know why I haven't thought of him before.'

'Who?' Matilda asked.

'Dermot Salter.'

'Who's he?'

'Dermot Salter isn't suspicious,' Sarah chimed up. 'He's a harmless old man.'

Bev waved her quiet. 'He's been hanging around for years, off and on. He never uses any of the women, but he lets them use his house for a safe place to sleep or if they want a hot bath. When it's cold, he'll bring flasks of soup and old clothes. At first I thought he was some kind of religious nut wanting to save our souls, but he's never mentioned God once.' She stopped to have another sip of water and rest her bruised throat. 'Nobody's that sympathetic for nothing.'

'Did he know any of the victims?' Matilda asked.

'All of them. Even Sarah's been to his house a couple of times, haven't you?'

'I went once when our heating packed in and I wanted a decent shower.'

'Did you get any feeling about him?'

'No. He's a lovely bloke,' she said loudly. 'There are some people in this world who are kind and charitable.'

'There bloody aren't,' Bev said. 'Everyone is selfish. I can't believe you're still so naïve after all these years. Look,' she turned to Matilda, 'I'm not saying he's a killer or anything, but even if he is on the level and wanting us to repent so we can enter the kingdom of heaven, he may have seen something we haven't. You know what I mean?'

Matilda nodded. 'I'll look into it. I don't suppose you know where he lives?'

Bev looked to Sarah and nodded for her to answer.

'He's got a big house out near Bradfield,' she said, almost reluctantly. 'It's quite private, big garden.'

'In the middle of nowhere is what she's trying not to say,' Bev said. 'Perfect place for luring women back to and strangling them.'

'Okay. Well, you get some rest and I'll be in touch. Take care of both of you.'

She left the cubicle, pulled the curtain to and rejoined her sister.

'Sarah's going to stay here all night, isn't she?' Harriet asked, her voice barely above a whisper.

'I think so.'

'Are they, you know, lovers?'

Matilda smiled. 'No. They're practically family. They only have each other.'

They began walking towards the exit.

'Why do they do it?'

'What?'

'Prostitution. What made them think that was all there was for them?'

'I've no idea.'

'You've never asked?'

'If they want to tell me, they will. The thing is, Harriet, it's not something you choose to do. It really is a last resort. The majority of women do it to feed a habit, drugs or drink. I know Sarah has a drink problem, but I don't know about Bev. I don't know what happened to her that caused her to lose everything.'

'You think she lost everything?'

'She used to be an accountant. She had a house, nice clothes, car. She was a respectable woman. She showed me a photo of herself once when she was in her mid-twenties. I didn't recognise her.'

'Didn't you ask what happened?'

'I tried to, but it was difficult for her to talk about, so I didn't push it.'

'Poor woman,' Harriet said as they left the hospital and stepped out into the cold night air. 'So, what now?'

'I need to make a phone call. Put out an arrest warrant for Paul Chattle, and then I need to get something to eat.'

'Sausage sandwich?'

'Ooh, lovely.' Matilda linked arms with her sister, and they headed for the car park.

Chapter Thirty-Three

'Hello, Robert, long time no see,' Lisa said as she leaned down to look through the open car window.

'I've been working away,' he replied.

'Anywhere nice?'

'It depends how you feel about Durham.'

'Better than this dump, I'm guessing.'

'You look cold. Are you getting in?'

Lisa smiled. She pulled open the door and climbed into the car, making a show of her long legs. She sat down on the heated leather seat and put on her seatbelt.

'Another new car? You must be doing well for yourself,' she said with a smile.

He smiled back, put the car into first and headed down the road, turning left at the junction.

He'd liked using Plantation Woods. It was out of the way and it didn't matter if he was there to kill or fuck, he was never interrupted. It was a shame it had been cordoned off by police. Still, it had to happen at some point. He'd used plenty of other woods in Sheffield over the years. That was the beauty of the

Steel City. It was right on the edge of the countryside and had some amazing parkland, perfect for hiding his crimes from the public but right under the noses of the police.

Earlier, during his lunch break, he'd popped into town to go into the bank and passed Plantation Woods. He saw the police presence and, for the life of him, he couldn't remember who he'd buried in there. Was it two women or three? What were their names? When had he killed them? He gave himself a headache racking his brain, then he realised it didn't matter. They were dead. Who gives a flying fuck what they were called?

So the police were obviously on to him. It was about time. Three years he'd been killing and not once had he been questioned. He did think police would have come to his work to interview staff, especially after his third victim had been found, seeing as it was close by where he'd dumped her, but no. He was very disappointed. He'd love to have been questioned by police about his whereabouts on the night of the murder. He'd have enjoyed lying. They'd have bought it, too. Of that, he was in no doubt.

As he couldn't use Plantation Woods, he headed for Grenoside Crematorium and pulled off at Côte de Oughtibridge. It was called The Birley Stone until the Tour De France got their hands on it and decided to ride through Yorkshire.

He parked clear off the road. He hadn't passed another vehicle for a while. Should one come around the corner, he doubted they'd be able to see where he'd parked.

Lisa took off her seatbelt and unzipped her jacket. She turned towards Robert and smiled. 'What are you up for tonight?'

'I know it's October,' he said, 'but how about we do it outside?'

'Really? It's cold out there.'

'I'll soon warm you up.'

Her smiled dropped but soon spread across her thin lips again. 'Okay.'

The sky was black and clear. An infinite number of stars pierced the darkness. It was cold, and they could both see their breath in front of them. Lisa shivered beneath her thin layers of clothing. Robert was warm and comfortable in his North Face padded jacket.

Once in the woods, away from the sight of the road, Robert stopped. He grabbed Lisa and pushed her against a solid oak tree. She smiled at him, trying to hide her stained teeth.

'You're a very handsome man, Robert,' she said.

He'd heard that many times in the past. When his wife said it, he knew it was true. When a prostitute said it, he knew they were hoping for a bit of extra cash.

He held her by the chin and angled her head to the moonlight.

'How old are you?' he asked.

'You should never ask a lady her age,' she said with a smile in her voice.

He chuckled. 'You're no lady.'

The smile disappeared and, momentarily, she looked hurt.

'How old are you?' he repeated.

'Twenty-two,' she answered quickly.

'And the truth?'

'I'm twenty-two.' She looked away.

'And I'm Father Christmas.'

He ran his calloused hands down her neck. It was so thin

and narrow he could probably have snapped it with one hand. But where would the fun have been in that?

'You're one ugly bitch, do you know that?'

'What?' she asked, tears pricking her eyes.

'And when did you last have a bath? You're ripe.'

'You don't have to insult me, you know.'

She tried to walk away but he grabbed her and slammed her against the tree. The sound of her head hitting the trunk echoed around the wood.

'Ow, Robert. Look, are we doing this or not? If not, can you drive me back so I can make some money tonight?'

Robert laughed. 'You're unbelievable, you women, do you know that? I've insulted you, I've hurt your feelings, yet you're still offering yourself to me so you can earn a few quid. And you wonder why people have no respect for hookers,' he spat.

'What's got into you tonight?'

He squeezed her neck hard. He could feel the blood rushing to his fingers as they clamped around her throat. Her bony fingers grabbed at them and tried to prise them off her, but she was no match for him. It was an unfair contest. He let go and she dropped to the ground like a stone. She coughed and spluttered and gasped for breath as Robert took a step back and watched as she came back to life.

'Oh my God, are you trying to kill me?' she asked as she gulped in the cold air.

'Trying? No. Succeeding? Yes.'

'Shit. You're him, aren't you? You're the one.'

He smiled at her. 'The penny finally drops.'

He grabbed her by the throat once more, pulled her up, and squeezed. When her eyes rolled back and the eyelids began to flutter, he let go once more and she dropped to the ground. She was losing her fight for life. She was on the brink of death, but somehow, she managed to pull herself back.

She coughed, dragged herself onto her hands and knees and braced herself on the cold, hard ground as she gasped for fresh air.

Robert leaned down, wrapped her lank hair around his huge hand and pulled her to her feet. It must have hurt, but she didn't scream. He lifted her up off the ground then threw her like a piece of rubbish. She landed at the foot of a tree. She groaned as she moved and tried to stand up. She immediately fell back down.

Lisa didn't look back. She didn't waste a moment before he came back and finished what he started. She began to drag herself along the woodland floor, dirt under her bitten fingernails, dead leaves and twigs catching her clothes, tearing at her bare legs. With every movement, she hurt that little bit more as her broken body struggled.

Robert followed her and watched. He kept looking around him to see if there were any late-night dog walkers or fitness fanatics jogging through the woods, but there was nobody there. He had the whole place to himself.

He looked down as Lisa struggled to get away from him. She hadn't got far. He wondered how she was feeling right now: scared, petrified, fearful, panicked, all of the above.

From his back pocket, he took out a ten-pound note, leaned down and rammed it in her mouth. She almost choked as his thick fingers found the back of her throat. Tears ran down her face. She tried to beg and plead with him, but she couldn't speak.

Robert had had enough now. She was boring him. He looked down at his feet. They were size eleven and he was wearing heavy steel-toecapped boots. He pressed his right foot down on Lisa's back, trapping her like a spider. He increased pressure, slowly at first, but as the bones began breaking, he pressed harder, squashing her under foot. She coughed and blood shot out of her mouth. He'd broken her ribs, which had obviously punctured a lung. He continued to stand on her until she no longer moved or made any sound.

He stepped off her and looked down at her stricken body. He decided not to bury this one. And he was sure forensic officers would get a good sample of his footprint, so he'd have to throw the boots away, which was a shame as they'd been good boots.

He headed back for the car, hands in his pockets, a spring in his step, as if he'd just stopped on his journey home for a quick pee among the trees. As he reversed out of the woods he wondered if he'd pass a McDonald's drive-through on the way home. He'd missed his tea and was feeling peckish.

Chapter Thirty-Four

Thursday 24th October 2019

Matilda: Don't take any crap from Danny Hanson in the interview. You don't have to answer his questions. You can stop it at any time.

Sally: Thanks. Pat's been here since first thing. Between us we'll be able to handle him.

An email pinged on Matilda's laptop. She read the message. Paul Chattle had not been found but uniformed officers had discovered more than enough drugs in his flat to charge him with intent to supply once he was found. She stood up and went over to the doorway leading into the main suite.

'Is everyone here?'

'Yes. All four of us. It's a full house,' Christian said with sarcasm.

'I can't get used to us being such a small team,' Matilda said.

'It's a good job we are a small team. I don't think we could fit any more officers in here.'

'I've been thinking about that. Look, I know we left the other suite to try and keep the ghosts at bay, but this room really isn't working. Would any of you find it difficult if we moved back?'

Christian folded his arms and chewed the inside of his mouth.

Nobody said anything but all eyes turned to Scott. He and Rory were best friends and former flatmates. If anyone was going to struggle, it would be him.

His face was impassive. He sat behind his desk in a slim-fitting grey suit, his hair neatly combed, his complexion smooth. He had the fresh-faced expression of an innocent young man who was eager to please, but appearances were deceptive, and his eyes gave him away. Since the shooting, he looked lost and haunted. The sparkle had gone and at times he looked as if he would burst into tears if someone said the wrong thing.

'I think we should move back,' Scott said quietly. 'We need the space. Besides, this office reeks.'

There was a ripple of laughter around the room. Christian sighed and shook his head slightly.

'I'll have a word with the ACC. Right then, let's get the morning briefing started. How are things going at Plantation Woods? Any news from the dog handler?'

'You'll want to ask Sian,' Christian said. 'She's got a crush on Sergeant Inneson.'

'Sian! And you're a married woman,' Matilda joked.

'You should see him. He's like an action hero and a supermodel rolled into one. And the way those trousers tighten around his bum, wow!'

'You do realise what you just said could be construed as sexual harassment in the workplace?' Finn said.

'Could it?' He nodded. 'Oh my God.' She looked genuinely worried. 'Have I offended anyone?'

'He's joking, Sian,' Matilda said.

Sian turned to Finn, who had a grin on his face. 'You sod. I was scared I'd actually said something offensive then.'

'Do you need anyone to go out to Plantation Woods in case the cadaver dogs uncover something?' Zofia asked.

'Are you volunteering?'

'I might be.' She blushed.

'I'm sure you'll make a great impression with that shiner,' Christian said.

'It's fading, and I've put concealer on it. You can hardly tell.'

'I'm sure if this hunk finds anything, he'll let us know,' Matilda said. 'In the meantime, our main concern is finding Paul Chattle. I didn't have him marked down as our killer, but he did try to strangle Bev and as strangulation seems to be a favourite of our killer, he can't be ruled out. Chat to his neighbours, friends, if he has any. I want him found now. Christian, can you sort that out?'

'Sure,' he said, downbeat, not looking up from his notepad.

'Also, Bev told me about a man who seems to like taking care of the working women on the streets. A bloke by the name of Dermot Salter who lives out towards Bradfield. Sarah says he's a harmless old man. Bev disagrees. He brings them flasks of soup when it's cold and allows them to use his bathroom.

Scott, Finn, as two young red-blooded males, find his address and pay him a visit. Don't treat him as a suspect, just find out what his deal is, if he has been with any of the women sexually, and if he's seen anything suspicious around the time of the murders.'

'Will do,' Scott said, making a note on his pad.

'Zofia, where did you get with the traffic cameras around Plantation Woods?'

She rolled her eyes and reached for her pad. 'That was a task and a half. Do you have any idea how many cars drove around those woods that night? I've managed to extract all the registration numbers and as soon as I've got all the contact details, me and a few of the uniforms are going to pay them a visit. The ones in Sheffield, anyway.'

'Thank you, Zofia. I know it's a shit task, but we can't all be ogling dog handlers.' She winked at Sian. 'Finn, when you've finished with this Dermot bloke, I'd like you to pop along to Watery Street and see how the post mortems are going. I want the two victims identified as soon as possible. Scott, I'd like you to—' Matilda's phone rang, cutting her off. She answered, and said a cheery hello when she found out who was calling, but it wasn't long before the smile dropped. 'Shit. Thanks for letting me know.' She ended the call and composed herself. 'Another body has been found,' she said, her voice respectfully low.

'Where?' Christian asked.

'In woods close to Grenoside Crematorium. Sian, let's go and take a look.'

'Do you want me to go out?' Christian asked.

'No. I'll take it.'

Christian leaned back in his chair. 'Fine. I'll stay here and guard the stationery cupboard.'

Matilda had been caught off guard. She hadn't expected another victim to be found, especially so soon after Carly's murder on Monday night. The killer had left a gap of thirteen months and suddenly he's killed twice within two days. As Sian drove towards the crime scene, Matilda thought of the other victims: all young women, all driven to prostitution by circumstances beyond their control. As if they didn't have enough problems to contend with, now they had a killer targeting them. Sian pulled up behind a car that Matilda immediate recognised. It was Adele's. Her heart sank.

'Are you okay?' Sian asked when Matilda made no effort to get out of the car.

'Yes. Fine.' She slowly removed her seatbelt.

As Matilda walked around the front of the car, she couldn't take her eyes from Adele's.

'What happened between you two?' Sian asked.

'Sorry?' she answered, absent-mindedly.

'You and Adele. You were best mates. You were closer to her than you are to Harriet, yet now there seems to be this frosty atmosphere between the two of you. I know for a fact she doesn't call round to the house anymore, and now you've gone pale just looking at her car.'

'Nothing, Sian. Just drop it, will you?'

They headed along the grass towards the woods. A uniformed officer led the way.

'A dog walker found her,' the officer said. 'She was just lying there in the middle of the ground. There was no sign that the killer tried to hide her.'

'ID?'

'Nothing on her, I don't think.'

'Okay. Thanks.'

A white forensic tent had been erected around the body. It was easier to access than the site at Plantation Woods. Matilda and Sian struggled into their paper suits against the stiff breeze. Any extra time was fine by Matilda. She could see shadows inside the tent moving around. She knew Adele would be in there.

'Ready?' Sian asked.

She put her hood up and pulled the mask over her mouth, then nodded.

Inside the tent, forensic officers were taking soil samples from around the body and photographs of the stricken victim. She was lying face down, her arms out in front of her. Adele, on her knees, her back to Matilda, was gently cutting open the woman's shirt.

'Oh my God,' Matilda said out loud when she saw what was revealed.

Adele looked up. Her eyes widened when she saw Matilda, then turned back to the body.

Opening the shirt had revealed a large and detailed footprint on the woman's back.

'Can you take a photo of that, please?' Adele asked. She leaned back out of the way. She then produced a tape measure, placed it along the length of the print and asked for another picture to be taken. 'Size eleven boot.'

'Not a shoe?' Sian asked.

'The tread is very deep. You're looking for a heavy work-type boot, probably with steel toecaps,' she said with solemnity in her voice.

'Why would he stand on her?' she asked.

'To kill her.'

'She wasn't strangled?' Matilda asked.

'She was.' Adele reached for a torch, turned it on and aimed it at the woman's neck. 'You can see finger indentations around the neck. Similar to the others, but I'll get a clearer look back at the lab. However, that's not what killed her. Every single one of her ribs has broken. He stood on her while she was still alive, the ribs punctured her lungs and she choked on her own blood.'

'Jesus!' Lucy muttered, turning away.

'Would she have been in pain?' Sian asked.

'Yes. A great deal of pain.' Adele leaned back. She didn't look up at the detectives. 'She also had a screwed up ten-pound note in her mouth.' Adele held up an evidence bag.

Sian took it from her. 'Why would he do that?'

'To show his contempt for her profession,' Matilda said. 'She's a prostitute. He's disgusted with them, that's why he's killing them. By ramming the money down her throat, he's showing how little respect he has for them as people.'

'Isn't killing them enough?'

'Obviously not.'

'Have you seen enough?' Adele asked, still not looking up. 'I'm ready to move her if you have.'

'Okay,' Matilda said. She backed away out of the tent.

The exchange between Matilda and Adele had been cold and harsh. Sian and Lucy exchanged glances. Lucy shrugged.

Matilda was peeling off her gloves and unzipping the paper suit when Adele came out of the tent.

'DCI Darke?' she called out.

Everyone stopped and looked. They all knew how close Matilda and Adele were. To hear the pathologist use her title rather than her name was alien.

'I have the report on the two women found at Plantation Woods yesterday. I was going to email it over first thing, but this came through. I can give you the ID on the second victim now if you like?'

'Sure.'

Adele headed for her car with Matilda following at a distance.

Adele tore off her gloves and pulled down the hood of her oversuit, revealing hair that badly needed a trim and the roots touching up. She removed her iPad from the back seat and flicked through it.

'I found a match almost straightaway from dental records,' Adele said, glancing up at Matilda and quickly looking away. 'Fiona Bridger. The address she gave the dentist is a flat in the Wicker.'

'Thank you. Do you know cause of death yet?'

'Yes. Manual strangulation. The trachea was practically crushed.'

'My God, he has superhuman strength.'

'He could just be very angry. You're certainly looking for a strong man. The other victim buried alongside her – we've identified her through dental records even though she did have a driving licence with her. It was Lucy Fletcher and her cause of death wasn't strangulation like all the others.'

'Oh?'

'No. She suffocated. There is evidence of manual strangulation, but there was soil in her mouth and throat. When he buried her, she was still alive.'

'Jesus. Would he have known that?'

Adele thought for a moment. 'I'm not sure. The soil down her throat suggests she choked so maybe he did. He could have thought she was already dead when he was burying her, and she came to during the burial.'

'The man's a sadist,' Matilda said, almost to herself.

'I'll do the PM on your latest victim this afternoon. I have a lecture at one,' she said, opening the car door and climbing in.

'Erm ... how are things going with the new job?' Matilda asked.

'Fine,' she replied, icily.

'Adele, could we...'

'PM around half past two then.' She slammed the door closed, started the engine and roared away at speed without looking back.

Matilda remained impassive at the side of the road. Her father was dead. Her best friend hated her, and she didn't trust Harriet enough to open up to her in case she told her mother everything. She needed someone to talk to, to laugh with, to unwind with, and she had nobody. And it was all her own fault.

Chapter Thirty-Five

Scott sometimes felt like a chauffeur ferrying Matilda to and from work every day so when the opportunity arose, he liked to take the passenger seat and let someone else do the driving. Finn didn't mind. He was happy to get out of the office.

They headed for Bradfield to interview Dermot Salter and uncover the cause of his strange obsession with the street prostitutes of Sheffield.

Bradfield is the largest parish in England and occupies one third of the land covered by Sheffield City Council. It's a picturesque rural part of the city on the cusp of the Peak District National Park and features the grand Church of St Nicholas with an imposing mediaeval window which contains fragments of glass dating back to the fifteenth century. It was this building Scott was marvelling at when Finn broke the silence.

'Have you noticed a change in the atmosphere back in the office?'

'You mean that smell?'

'No. I meant between Matilda and Christian.'

Scott turned quickly to look at the DC. 'No. In what way?'

'There seems to be something between them. I was thinking about it in bed last night when I couldn't sleep. It's like Matilda is undoing all the things Christian has done in her absence, like she's putting her mark back on the team.'

'How?'

'Well, she wants us to move back to the old suite, and when the ACC came in yesterday and they were all talking in Matilda's office, Christian was coming up with ideas and Matilda just cut him off. She wouldn't have done that before.'

'You think she's trying to undermine him?'

He took a breath. 'Remember a couple of weeks before she came back to work, and you brought her in for her meeting with the Chief Constable and she came into the office to see us all?'

'Yes.'

'Well, she was asking me what we'd been working on. I was telling her all about the cases in the past nine months and she kept asking how Christian was coping, how he was as a boss, whether I thought he'd been a good DCI.'

'What did you say?'

'I told her the truth. Christian's coped brilliantly while she's been away. The thing is, I'm wondering if she's worried he'll try and go for her job, so she's finding a way to make him seem not as capable.'

'Matilda would never do that. We're a team. She's always said that.'

'I'm not saying she's consciously doing it.'

'Are you going all psychological on me again? I don't think this course is such a good idea if you're going to start analysing the people you work with.'

'Maybe I'm reading too much into it.'

'No shit. Turn left here. Hang on, though, what are you thinking about me?' Scott asked, wide-eyed and worried.

'Nothing,' Finn replied quickly.

'I'm not quite sure I believe you.'

Finn turned off the tarmacked road and went down a single-laned track that had been well worn over the years. Tall trees either side loomed over them, their thick, gnarled branches tapping on the roof of the car. A mile along, the road opened up into a makeshift driveway, at the top of which was an old, neglected-looking double-fronted farmhouse. Dark stonework, a tall dull green front door with stained glass in the windows. At each side of the front door were impressive church-style windows, the white-painted oak chipped and peeling. It would make the perfect front cover for a haunted house ghost story.

Finn parked and they both looked up at the house. 'I'd love to live here,' he said with a smile.

'It looks like it's about to fall down.'

'It's lived in.'

'It's fucked.'

Despite it being mid-morning, the surrounding trees made it dark and gloomy. Lights were on in the downstairs rooms. They entered the open porch, Finn rang the bell, and they stepped back.

They were surrounded by silence. Traffic from the road could no longer be heard down here, just the sound of the bare branches striking each other in the stiff autumnal breeze.

'Do you think it's haunted?' Scott asked, looking up at the building.

'By the ghosts of all the prostitutes he's murdered?' Finn asked with a sly grin.

The front door opened before Scott could answer. A man in his early seventies stood in the doorway, lit by the light from behind. He was tall and very slim with a thick mound of light grey hair. He was clean shaven and wore a charcoal grey cardigan over an off-white shirt, open at the neck, beige trousers and carpet slippers. There was a panicked expression on his face, as if the sound of the doorbell ringing had come as a shock. Living this far out in the middle of nowhere, it probably had.

'Dermot Salter?' He nodded. 'I'm Detective Sergeant Scott Andrews. This is DC Finn Cotton from South Yorkshire Police,' he said. They both showed their ID. 'Could we have a word?'

'With me?' he asked in a soft, quiet voice.

'Yes.'

'What for?'

'Your name has come up in an investigation and we'd like to ask some questions.'

'What kind of investigation?'

'We're investigating the murder and disappearance of a number of street prostitutes working in Sheffield and we've been given your name as someone who is well acquainted with the women.'

'Oh.'

'We won't take up much of your time.'

'Do you need me to come down to the station?'

'No. We can talk inside.'

'Oh,' he said again, looking over his shoulder at his house. 'I haven't vacuumed this morning.'

Scott smiled. 'You don't need to worry about that, sir. I haven't vacuumed all week.' It was a lie as he liked to keep the flat neat and tidy.

Dermot flashed the hint of a smile before he stepped back from the threshold and beckoned them both in.

The hallway was grand and dark. The ornate woodwork of the staircase was an impressive feature, and the tiles were original Victorian. The walls were in need of a lick of paint, and there was an underlying smell of something that suggested fresh air didn't come into the house very often, but it was a stunning entrance to an old property.

Dermot Salter led the detectives into the living room. It was a huge room with a high ceiling and detailed cornicing and ceiling rose. A warm-looking fireplace with a tall mantel immediately drew the eye. The carpet was threadbare, the sofa and furniture dated and the television in the corner was an old box-style dating from the 1990s, maybe even earlier. Despite the ceiling light being on, it was dim inside the room.

Dermot indicated they should both sit down and took his place on the armchair in front of the television.

'Can I offer you a tea or coffee or something? I haven't done a shop this week, but I think the milk should be okay.'

They both declined.

'Mr Salter,' Scott began. 'I don't know if you've seen any news lately, but we've launched an enquiry into the unsolved deaths of five women who work as prostitutes in Sheffield. We've also identified a further five women who are missing. We've been told you see them on a regular basis, you give them soup in the winter and allow them to come to your home to use your bathroom. Is that correct?'

Dermot looked lost in the large armchair as his slight frame sat in the middle. He pulled his cardigan tight around his chest. It was a while before he replied and he glanced towards a framed photograph on the wall before he did. 'It is correct, yes.'

'Can I ask you why you do that?'

'Because they need looking after,' he said incredulously.

'Do you know any of the women? Are you related to them?'

'No.'

'Then why do you do it?'

'Because … it's the right thing to do,' he said firmly.

'Do you have sex with these women?' Finn asked.

'Certainly not,' he replied with severity.

'Then what's in it for you?' Scott asked.

'I'm helping them. Women who work as prostitutes are the forgotten members of society. They're looked upon with scorn and revulsion but they're still people, they still have feelings like you and I do. If I can make them feel better by giving them a hot meal or a nice clean bathroom to use or a fiver to top up their phones with, then it makes them feel better.'

Finn looked around the desolate room and took in the impersonality of it all. 'Are you married, Mr Salter?'

'Widowed,' he replied flatly.

'Any children?'

'I had a daughter. She died.'

'I'm so sorry,' Scott said.

'Was your daughter a prostitute, Mr Salter?' Finn asked with sympathy.

'Certainly not. She had a very good career in banking, a lovely flat in Derbyshire, and she changed her car every two years. She was doing very well for herself until…' He tailed off.

'What happened to her?'

'Nothing that need bother you. Look, I'm on my own and I don't have any friends left. I didn't think helping our fellow man was a crime.'

'It isn't.'

'Then why do I feel I'm being accused of something?'

'Mr Salter, as I'm sure you can understand, some of these women have been through a great deal in their lives, and they have a lot of mistrust. When they see someone being kind to them and expecting nothing in return, it makes them suspicious. Nobody is accusing you of anything, but we wouldn't be doing our job properly if we didn't follow up on their concerns,' Scott said.

This seemed to resonate with Dermot Salter as he began to thaw and relax into his armchair.

'You're going to want to know my alibi for the dates the women were killed, aren't you?'

'That would help.'

'I'm afraid I can't tell you. I get up, I potter around the house, have my meals, watch television, read and go to bed. When I go out, it's to do some shopping, or to talk to the women on the street. I haven't done anything since my Cath was taken.'

Finn looked around the room again. There was a solitary photograph on the wall by the television. It was black and white and in a cheap frame. It showed a young woman smiling to the camera, wearing a flowing ankle-length dress.

'Is that Cath?'

'Yes,' he smiled.

'How long has she—'

'2002,' he interrupted. 'Breast cancer. She was two weeks away from her sixtieth birthday.'

'I'm sorry,' Finn said.

'She was my whole life,' he said, tears welling up in his eyes.

Finn looked to Scott and raised a questioning eyebrow. Scott frowned in reply.

'Mr Salter, when you've been visiting the women, have you noticed anyone strange hanging around, or have the women mentioned someone they're frightened of?'

'Someone like me, you mean?'

'No. An aggressive punter, perhaps.'

'No. They don't talk about their work. They mention that they're cold or have no money. I think some like to have someone to talk to occasionally. Look, if the women want me to stop visiting them, I will. I don't want to scare anyone, and I don't want them to be uncomfortable around me. I just ... well, I suppose I'm lonely.'

'I'm sure they appreciate your kindness,' Scott said.

'Should I stop going to see them?' he asked, looking at the detective with glassy eyes.

'It was your wife, wasn't it?' Finn asked.

'I'm sorry?'

'Your wife. She was a prostitute, wasn't she?'

'Finn!' Scott exclaimed.

A small smile swept across Dermot's face. 'Yes. She was. I'd never been confident with women, so I paid to go with one. I went with Cath twice and then a few months later she turned up and told me she was pregnant. I asked her how she knew I was the father, and she said the condom had burst. I had a feeling it had at the time, but embarrassment got the better of me and I couldn't get away fast enough. It was only after she died that I plucked up the courage for me and Linda to have a DNA test. I told her I was her father, but I wasn't. I didn't mind. Cath saw me as someone who could love her and help raise her child. I was. And I did. She had her demons, but she stopped doing what she did after we were married. We had a happy life together, of sorts.'

For the first time since Scott and Finn had arrived, Dermot looked relaxed, almost serene, as he spoke.

'And you've been visiting the women because you want them to be safe?' Finn asked.

'Yes. I'd never harm them. Never.'

————————

'How did you know it was his wife who was a prostitute?' Scott asked as they made their way back to the car.

'There was only one photograph in the whole room, the one of his wife, but none of his daughter. Despite him saying he loved her, I think if she'd been his real daughter, he would have had her photo up.'

'Look at you, Miss Marple,' Scott teased. 'This psychology course is really going to your head, isn't it?'

'So, are we crossing him off our list then?' Finn asked as they climbed into the car.

'Yes. There's no way he could have strangled them. Did you see his hands, all bony and thin? I doubt he'd be able to overpower any of the women.'

'I felt sorry for him,' Finn said, as he performed a tight three-point turn and headed down the bumpy lane.

'So did I. It's strange, isn't it, how people turn out? I mean, you don't start out in life thinking you'll marry a prostitute and raise her illegitimate daughter as your own, yet there he is.'

'How do you see your life panning out?'

'I've no idea. I certainly didn't think I'd be living above my boss's garage, grieving for my murdered boyfriend and best friend before I reached thirty.'

'I suppose if we know the end it spoils the surprise.'

'There are some surprises I can do without.'

As they drove away, Finn looked in the rear-view mirror at the spooky house they'd just left. He could make out the figure of Dermot Salter in the living-room window, staring out at the retreating car. He pulled the curtains closed in one swift movement.

Chapter Thirty-Six

The HMCU was a hive of activity as phones continued to ring. Zofia and three uniformed officers had dragged two tables together so they could sit around and consult on the arduous task of getting names and addresses of people who drove past Plantation Woods on Monday night. Judging by their facial expressions, none of them could wait until they'd finished.

Scott entered the room and Sian beckoned him over to her desk. He smiled and helped himself to a Mars Bar from the snack drawer.

'What's going on between Matilda and Adele?' she asked in a loud whisper.

'That's funny. I was going to ask you what's going on with Matilda and Christian.'

'Matilda and Christian? What are you talking about?'

'Nothing. Just something Finn was testing his psychological skills on. Go on.'

'Well, we ran into Adele at Grenoside. Adele could hardly

look at Matilda and the atmosphere was frosty. She even called her DCI Darke.'

'Bloody hell,' Scott said, sitting on the edge of Sian's desk. 'There's definitely something going on between them. Adele hasn't been to the house once since Matilda was discharged from that rehab centre.'

'What? That was in March.'

'I know.'

'It's now October.'

'I'm aware of the month.'

'So, what's going on?'

'You tell me. I've tried asking Matilda a couple of times, but she's always changed the subject. Although Harriet did tell me that Adele visited her once in hospital just after she'd come out of the coma. Whatever was said between them was not pleasant as Harriet said Matilda was crying her eyes out when she came back from the toilet. Adele hadn't stayed more than five minutes.'

'They've had a falling out then?' Sian asked.

'It looks like it. Not sure how, though. Unless something happened before the shooting.'

'But if it had then surely it would all be forgotten. The shooting would bring them closer together.'

'I've no idea. Ask Finn. He's the one hoping to take Jeremy Kyle's place.' He sniggered to himself.

Sian thought for a moment. She looked past Scott and saw they weren't being overheard before continuing. 'Scott, while you're here, could I ask you a personal question?'

'Sure.'

'You know when you told your parents you were gay, what did you actually say?'

He frowned, wondering where this was going. 'I just told them I was gay. Why?'

She picked up a framed photo of her family and handed it to him. 'Last night, Belinda told us she was going out on a date with her friend Tina. She just said it all nonchalant as if it wasn't such a big deal.'

'Which one's Belinda?' he asked, looking at the photo.

'There are two women in that photo, Scott, and one of them is me. Which do you think is my only daughter?'

'Oh yes, sorry.'

'You've really earned the promotion to DS, haven't you?' she asked, snatching the picture back from him.

'Well, is it a big deal if she's gay?'

'No. Not really.'

'What did Stuart say?'

'He was fine with it. He drove Belinda over to Tina's. I was going to ask him about it when he got back, but I must have fallen asleep. I was bloody shattered last night. The thing is, I thought Belinda would have sat us down and we'd have had this deep conversation about it.'

'Would you want such a conversation?'

'God no. I worked myself into such a frenzy talking to her about periods I thought I was going to have a stroke.'

Scott laughed. 'The thing is, Sian, people of Belinda's age don't see sexuality and gender as an issue. It's just accepted with them. Belinda discovering she fancies girls is the same as you discovering a new flavour of KitKat.'

Over Scott's shoulder, Sian saw Matilda enter the room. She went straight up to the murder board.

'Thanks, Scott,' she said, placing a hand on top of his. 'And I'll try to do some digging about Matilda.'

'Can I have everyone's attention, please?' Matilda asked. She waited while the room settled down. 'I've been going through the forensic and autopsy reports of the two women found in Plantation Woods and although time of death cannot be accurately estimated, we can put our victims into some kind of order and try and look for a pattern.'

She looked at the faces of her team and the assembled uniformed officers. She had their rapt attention. Picking up a marker pen, she wrote a list of the victims:

Ella Morse. Aug 2016. Strangled.
Lucy Fletcher. Dec 2016. Buried alive.
Rachel Pickering. Feb 2017. Strangled.
Deborah Monroe. July 2017. Beaten and strangled.
Fiona Bridger. Jan 2018. Strangled.
Jackie Barclay. Missing since Apr 2018. ?
Caroline Richardson. Missing since June 2018. ?
Monica Yates. Missing since July 2018. ?
Denise Jones. Sept 2018. Strangled.
Carly Roberts. Oct 2019. Strangled.
? Oct 2019. Crushed?

Matilda stood back and looked at her shaky handwriting. The list was lopsided, but she'd get someone to type it out for her when the briefing was over.

'We have three women unaccounted for. Jackie, Caroline and Monica. All three were reported missing in 2018 and haven't been seen since. Are they dead and buried in Plantation Woods or somewhere else or still alive and well? Any news?'

'Nothing,' Finn said. 'I've contacted the parents for Jackie and Monica. They haven't heard from their daughters since before they were reported missing. I can't find any information for Caroline yet.'

'Scott, how did it go with Dermot Salter?'

Scott told her all about him. 'So he doesn't have hands like monkey's paws then?' She smiled. 'Sorry, I was watching an old *Miss Marple* in the early hours,' she said looking at the blank faces staring back at her.

'I know it's a little far-fetched, but how sure are we these are the work of the same killer?' Scott asked. 'I mean, say they're all dead, eleven victims is a lot for one person, especially for us not to know about it before now.'

Matilda sighed. 'We can't be sure.'

'So we're just putting them together because they all worked as prostitutes?'

She nodded.

'If you take Lucy and our latest out of the list, you're left with six women who have been strangled. They were mostly buried or dumped where they'd be difficult to find but Lucy and Fiona were buried almost in the same place. Why weren't the others buried in Plantation Woods if it was such a good spot for Lucy and Fiona?' Scott asked.

'Please don't expect me to answer that,' Finn said.

'All I'm wondering,' Scott continued, 'is if it's possible we have two killers: one who is strangling his victims and is now leaving them out in the open for us to find, and one who is burying them?'

'Sian, I need a chocolate fix,' Matilda said.

Sian reached into her snack drawer, pulled out a couple of packets of Maltesers and tossed them to her.

'I'll be honest,' Matilda admitted, 'I hadn't thought of that. I was looking at the victims and assuming we had one killer.'

'If we are looking for just one killer,' Finn began, 'it could be possible that Ella Morse isn't victim number one. He's targeted prostitutes as they're an easy group to target, but so are the homeless, for example. Should we be looking at victims from other groups?'

Matilda emptied what was left of the first bag of Maltesers into her mouth and chomped down on them hard.

'Okay,' she said. 'We need to put together a list of all cold cases. We're looking for any murder victims who have been strangled or who fit into any vulnerable group. I also want a list of anyone who is missing who fits the same demographic. I want everyone working on this. Any news on Paul Chattle?'

'No,' Christian said.

'Keep looking,' she almost barked at him.

Matilda turned to the board and looked at the faces of the victims. She wanted them, and those they'd left behind, to be at peace and knew they wouldn't be until she found their killer.

'If Finn's right,' Christian said, coming up beside her. 'We could be looking at, I don't know, another ten victims, maybe more.'

'I know.'

'This could be bigger than anything we've ever dealt with before.'

Matilda folded her arms tightly, hugging herself. 'It already is.'

'The press will roast us for not seeing this until now.'

'Well, fortunately, the press is busy with Carl Meagan, and let's hope it stays that way for a few more days. By the time he falls off the front pages, maybe we can have this solved or at least a person of interest in for questioning.'

'Should you be working so hard this soon?' he asked, concerned.

'It's the only way I know how to work,' she snapped, shooting him a daggered look before retreating to her office and slamming the door behind her.

Chapter Thirty-Seven

The call had come through the second Matilda sat down at her desk. Danny Hanson was in reception and he'd brought Alistair Tripp with him. She rallied Finn and they both went to see what the journalist-in-training had to tell them.

When she opened the door to the interview room, she found Danny and Alistair sitting at the table with a cup of tea each. She rolled her eyes.

'Danny, out,' she instructed.

'Why?'

'Are you Alistair's legal representative?'

'No.'

'Is Alistair under the age of eighteen?'

'Of course not.'

'Then he doesn't require a chaperone. Out.'

'I want to hear what you're going to be accusing him of.'

'Then he can tell you all about it in the pub afterwards. Out.'

Reluctantly, Danny stood up. He made a point of taking a lingering sip of his tea before putting the cup down on the table and breezing out of the room. Once clear, Matilda slammed the door behind him and sat down in front of Alistair. She gave him a weak smile.

Alistair Tripp was in his early twenties. He was tall and slim with bony features and pale skin. His hair was an untidy mound of mousey curls. He wore an oversized sweater and skinny jeans. He had the lived-in look of a student.

'How do you know Danny?' Matilda asked.

'There's a closed Facebook group for Sheffield journalists.'

'Are you qualified?'

'I will be next year.'

'So why are you in this group when you're not qualified?'

'I'm doing my work experience on *The Star*. One of the reporters on it got me invited.'

'How did you and Danny start chatting?' Matilda asked, sitting back and folding her arms.

He stuck out his bottom lip as he thought. 'I'm not sure. I probably commented on something and he commented back, and it went from there. I don't remember.'

'Okay. So, who brought up the subject of the story around the prostitutes first?'

'That was me,' he said, leaning forward on the table. 'I've got a twin sister. She's studying English in Lincoln. She texted me to tell me a girl on her course had turned to prostitution to make some extra money as there were no jobs available and it's not cheap being a student. She said there were a few at her uni who were doing it. I asked around at Sheffield and some had heard of girls here doing it too. I mentioned it to my editor, and he said there's a story there if I was interested in doing some digging. It would be my first investigative piece,' he said with a grin. 'I didn't know where to start so I posted on the closed Facebook group and asked for some advice.'

'That's when Danny Hanson got in touch?' Matilda asked.

'Yes. He said he'd written an article for *The Guardian* about women turning to prostitution due to ten years of austerity thanks to the Conservative government. He said me looking into students turning to prostitution was an after-effect of their cuts.'

'So, he sent you down to the red-light district in Sheffield to interview them?'

'Not at first. He said he'd go as the women were more likely to talk to someone they knew, and they'd know him as he was on television.'

Matilda rolled her eyes.

'Yeah, I thought the same thing. Being on telly has really gone to his head. Anyway, we met up one day in the pub and he said it would be better if I interviewed them as it could look weird if he was caught in the red-light area.'

'Did you believe him?'

Alistair shrugged. 'Sort of. I didn't mind going anyway. Journalism isn't all about interviewing celebrities and royalty, is it?'

'What did you think when you first went down there?' Matilda asked.

Alistair sat back and looked up. 'I'm not sure. It wasn't what I expected.'

'What do you mean?'

'I think I expected the women to be hard, bitchy and nasty, but they weren't. Not at all. They were quiet, reserved, sad. Most of them looked like they wanted to burst into tears. I found it upsetting.'

Matilda nodded to Finn. He opened the folder and took out a photograph of Denise Jones.

'Do you recognise this woman?' Finn asked.

Alistair nodded.

'She's dead,' Matilda said.

'I know.' He shook his head and looked genuinely upset.

'Denise told a fellow worker that she liked you.'

A smiled crept along his face. 'We chatted a few times. She was … sweet. I liked her.'

'She also said it made a change to go with someone who smelled nice for a change.'

Alistair started to blush. 'We did… I mean, she…'

'She sucked you off,' Matilda finished his stuttered sentence.

'You make it sound sordid.'

'Whereas dropping your trousers at night in public and allowing a prostitute to blow you off is romantic?'

'That's not what I meant. She was pretty. She was sweet and kind and … she wasn't like the others. She was naïve, vulnerable. She shouldn't have been out on the streets.'

'And you thought you'd take advantage of her naivety and vulnerability for your own sexual gratification?' Matilda was losing patience with him.

'No. It wasn't like that at all,' he shouted. He jumped up from the seat, which clattered to the floor. 'I liked her. She hated what she was doing, but there was nothing else for her. I was offering ten pounds to the women to talk to me. I gave her a little more. She came on to me.'

'And you let her?'

'I'm only human, for crying out loud.' He turned to Finn. 'Are you telling me that if you were offered sex, no questions asked, you wouldn't take it?'

'No, I wouldn't. For two reasons: one, I'm happily married, and two, you were working while chatting to these women.

You said yourself that Denise hated what she was doing yet you still took advantage of her.'

'You're only saying that because your boss is right next to you. You'd have dropped your trousers within seconds. You're a bloke.'

'And we all know what blokes are,' Matilda said. Daniel immediately popped into her head. He was one of the good ones. She missed him. 'Mr Tripp, where were you on September the fourteenth last year?'

'Why?' he asked, hands on his hips.

'Just sit down and answer the question.'

Reluctantly, he picked up his chair and sat back down. He took a battered iPhone with a cracked screen out of his jeans pocket and began to scroll through the calendar.

'September the fourteenth was a Friday. I don't have lectures on a Friday. I was probably in bed.'

'Alone?'

'I can't remember. What's so special about that date anyway?'

'That was the date Denise Jones was murdered.'

'And you think...? Oh for fuck's sake, you really are clutching at straws if you think I could have killed her, and all those others.'

'Why am I?'

'Okay, I will admit that it doesn't look good, and, I suppose, in a way, I did abuse my position, but just because we slept together doesn't mean I killed her.'

Matilda allowed the silence to grow.

'What?' Alistair asked.

'You slept together?'

'I... No. It's a figure of speech.'

'I don't think it is.' Matilda folded her arms once again. 'Why don't you unburden yourself, and tell us everything?'

Alistair took a deep breath. He ran his bony fingers through his knotted hair a few times. 'We had sex.'

'I gathered that. How many times?'

'Twice.'

'Where?'

Alistair closed his eyes and shook his head. 'There is a field behind where the women work, just over the train track. We did it in there.'

'Classy.'

'It wasn't a date. We weren't making love. It was just sex. That's all.'

'Moving on, for a moment, how long did your research take?'

'Erm, a few weeks I think.'

'And after these few weeks, how did you leave things with Denise?'

'How do you mean?'

'Oh my God,' Finn said. 'You just left, didn't you? You didn't say goodbye or thank you for your help with my research or compliment her on her oral skills, you just stopped going down there, didn't you?'

Reluctantly, Alistair nodded.

'Well, you're certainly doing the reputation of journalists a power of good,' Matilda said.

'Denise liked you,' Finn added. 'She told the other women that she genuinely liked you and she thought you liked her, too. The others commented on how brighter she was while you were around, how much more she smiled, then you just disappeared. Do you have any idea how that made her feel?'

Alistair swallowed hard. His face paled. 'I didn't know.'

'Of course not. Why should you? She was just a prostitute. Her feelings didn't matter, did they? As long as you got what you wanted,' Matilda said.

'I'm sorry.'

'No, you're not.' Matilda took the folder from Finn. She opened it and took out a single sheet of paper and almost threw it across the table at Alistair. 'This is a list of dates all the women went missing. I want you to go away, remember where you were and let us know. We've wasted enough time talking to you.' She stood up and went to the door. With her hand on the handle, she turned back around. 'If you don't want to turn into a twat like Danny Hanson you need to remember that the people you interview are actual people with feelings. And you need to treat them with the respect they deserve. Danny is going to grow up into a lonely old man. By the time he's fifty he'll be an alcoholic and suddenly realise he's missed out on marriage and a family. Now is the time for you to decide what kind of a person you want to be. You only get once chance; don't fuck it up.' Her voice almost broke.

Matilda stormed out of the interview room, slamming the door behind her.

Chapter Thirty-Eight

Bev had a comfortable night in the Royal Hallamshire Hospital. She was given a prescription for strong painkillers and discharged as soon as a doctor had been to see her. She couldn't get out of bed and dressed fast enough. She hated hospitals, and despite the mattress being more comfortable than her own at home, she couldn't wait to get back to the flat. She sent a text to Sarah, telling her she was coming home, and her partner in crime appeared on the ward within ten minutes.

'Where did you spring from?' Bev asked. Her voice was still hoarse.

'I didn't want to go home. I kept moving around the hospital from one waiting room to another.'

'Haven't you slept? You look shocking.'

'I've had an hour here and an hour there.'

'You silly cow. Why didn't you go home?'

'You know I don't like being on my own, especially with how that front door lock is and Paul Chattle still out there.'

'Hasn't he been arrested?'

'Well, Matilda said she'd be in touch and she hasn't been, so I guess not.'

'I'm sure they'll pick him up soon. Come on, let's get off home. I'm gagging for a cuppa that isn't stewed.'

Sarah called for a taxi and one was waiting for them by the time they'd made their way to the reception through the labyrinth of dull corridors. Bev and Sarah lived not far from the red-light district in Kelham Island. There was a row of shops with flats above them. Most of the shops were now boarded up. A newsagents and sandwich shop remained open for the local factory and office workers, but the hairdressers and eyebrow bar hadn't lasted long. The flats had deteriorated over the years despite the rent continuing to increase. The secure intercom buzzer had long since broken and the main entrance was permanently left unlocked as one of the occupants of the flats was a drug dealer and he had customers coming at all hours of the day and night. It was understandable why Sarah hadn't wanted to spend the night alone. It wouldn't have bothered Bev, however. She'd stand up to anyone who tried anything.

The taxi pulled up outside the entrance. Sarah climbed out first and offered her arm to Bev.

'There's nothing wrong with my legs, Sarah, I'm perfectly capable of walking. Cheers, Grigor,' she said to the taxi driver. 'I'll drop you a text when I'm better.'

They made their way up the single flight of stairs, trying not to breathe in the stale smell of sweat and piss. The walls were covered in graffiti and crisp wrappers, and fag ends and little plastic bags that had contained drugs littered the stairs. Bev often wondered why the druggie in the next but one flat didn't just put a neon sign above the front door advertising what he did. He wasn't exactly subtle in his business.

'How are you feeling?' Sarah asked as she unlocked their flat.

'Pissed off. I could have made a hundred quid at least last night. How far behind are we with the rent?'

'A couple of weeks.'

'It's due again soon, isn't it? We need to pay him a full month or he'll want us out. We'll have to go out tonight.'

'You can't. You can hardly talk. And look at your neck, it's still red raw.' Sarah closed the front door behind them. The bolt didn't meet up with the housing on the door frame so the door would only be secured by the chain.

'I've got one of those knock-off silk scarves I can put on to cover it up.'

Sarah went into the kitchen and flicked on the kettle. 'There's a killer out there strangling his victims and you're going to meet him with a scarf on. Talk about handing yourself to him on a plate.'

'You're being paranoid. Besides, I can look after myself. I'm going to have a shower. I reek of hospital.'

'Do you want me to do you something to eat?'

'What have we got?'

'Nothing.'

'Oh. I'll have a plate of that then,' she said with a smile.

'We've got some ice-cream left. That'll be good for your throat.'

'I'll have a nice big bowl, for medicinal purposes only, obviously.'

She pushed open the door to the bathroom and screamed when she saw Paul Chattle sitting on the edge of the bath.

Chapter Thirty-Nine

Pat: Interview went well. S and P were very good. That Danny Hanson is a smooth talking shit. I wanted to slap him a couple of times but S put him in his place. Special programme on BBC1 tonight.

The interview had been on Matilda's mind all day. She kept looking at her watch wondering how it was going, if it was over with yet and how far Danny had pushed them. She felt relieved after reading Pat's text and made a mental note to tune in and watch the interview tonight.

'I've just had a call from downstairs,' Christian said, opening the door without knocking. 'A woman has come into the station to report her sister missing. She matches the description of the woman found in Grenoside this morning, and she works as a prostitute some nights.'

'Jesus,' Matilda said. 'Is she still here?'

'No. She made a statement and left.' He looked down at his

iPad. 'Lisa Temple is twenty-three years old and lives on London Road with her sister. She has a seven-year-old daughter, Belle, and works at a supermarket in town.'

'Why does she go out prostituting if she works?'

'Well, childcare costs a fortune and she can't get benefits as she's working more than sixteen hours a week yet she's on minimum wage. She can't get any more hours at work, so she's having to do this a few nights a week to pay bills and childcare.'

'Welcome to twenty-first-century Britain. Did she leave a photo?'

'Yes. I've asked Adele to email me one of the body across. I'm still waiting.'

'I can't seem to get my head around this,' Matilda said, looking frustrated. 'He leaves a gap of thirteen months yet kills two in forty-eight hours. It makes no sense.'

'Maybe Finn's right and he was in prison for a lesser crime. Is there a way to check to see if anyone in Sheffield has been released from prison recently?'

'I don't know, but that's something for you to look into,' she grinned.

'Thanks. I do love a menial task.'

Matilda's mobile started vibrating on her desk. She looked at the display and saw it was Bev calling. She swiped to answer.

'Bev, what can I do for you?'

'Matilda, I think I've killed Paul Chattle.'

Christian drove Matilda to Kelham Island at speed. It didn't take long to get there from HQ. Matilda hadn't wanted to ask too many questions over the phone and when she ended the call she didn't think to ask if an ambulance was required.

Even though they had the address, it was difficult to find the flat. The area was a labyrinth of narrow roads, abandoned cars and buildings. Windows were either smashed or boarded up, the whole of the surroundings were in decay and it was difficult to tell which buildings were occupied and which had been left to the elements. Matilda noticed Sarah standing on a doorstep, looking out for them. Christian pulled up and they both jumped out of the car.

'What happened?' Matilda asked.

Sarah took one look at Christian and froze.

'This is DI Brady. He's with me. He's okay, Sarah.'

She turned and ran up the stairs to the flat.

'Is she okay?'

'She doesn't trust men,' Matilda said.

'I suppose I do look intimidating with my shaved head.'

Matilda stifled a laugh. 'Christian, you couldn't look intimidating if you were surrounded by dead bodies and holding a liver in each hand.'

She followed Sarah up the stairs and into the flat, where Bev was stood in front of a door holding a small wooden bat aloft.

'We arrived home and I went to take a shower. I opened the bathroom door and there was Paul Chattle, sat on the side of the bath as if he belonged here,' Bev said as soon as she clocked Matilda.

'He broke in?'

'I don't know. The lock isn't that great. I suppose he could have picked it. Who's that?'

'DI Brady, ignore him.'

'Thanks,' Christian said.

'Where is he now? Why do you think you've killed him?'

'He came at me. I kicked him between the legs and tried to close the door, but he grabbed the handle. I pushed the door hard and I think it hit him in the head. I heard a bang like he'd fallen against the toilet or something. I haven't heard anything since. I didn't dare open the door.' She spoke nervously but rapidly, despite the injury to her throat.

'Okay, Bev, step back. We'll deal with it.' Matilda eyed Christian and nodded for him to take over.

Christian tentatively made his way to the bathroom door. He knocked on it.

'Mr Chattle. My name is Christian Brady. I'm a Detective Inspector with South Yorkshire Police. Are you hurt?' He listened intently but couldn't hear anything. 'I'm going to open this door now.' He looked to Matilda and nodded. He placed his hand on the plastic handle and slowly pushed it down. He eased the door open carefully. There was no resistance. When it was open enough for him to peek around, he leaned in.

'Fuck,' he said to himself.

'What is it?' Matilda asked.

He closed the door on the bathroom and seemed to take a while to compose himself.

'Mat, take Bev and Sarah, go downstairs and stay there. All three of you,' he said firmly.

'What? Why?' She frowned.

'Just do it. Then call Sian and have her ring my mobile.'

'Christian, what's going on in there?' she said, defiantly putting her hands on her hips.

He closed his eyes and took a deep breath. 'He's got a gun.'

Matilda's face paled and her eyes widened. She took a step back.

'Mat, go downstairs. Please,' Christian said slowly. There was an urgency to his voice despite it being low and quiet.

Matilda didn't move. She was frozen to the spot.

'You're a survivor, aren't you, Matilda?'

Bev stepped forward. She put her arm around Matilda's shoulder and eased her towards the door. 'I'll get Sian to ring you.'

'Thank you.'

Christian waited until all three had carefully made their way out of the flat before he pushed open the bathroom door again.

Paul Chattle looked shocking. His eyes were barely open and there were thick dark circles beneath them. His face was sallow, and he had at least three days of rough stubble. His hair was a mess, and he was giving off an odour of sweat and desperation. He was sitting on the toilet seat, his legs jiggling, both hands wrapped around a handgun, the barrel pressed firmly under his chin. He was wearing dirty ripped jeans and an old Adidas jacket. There was a sheen of sweat on his forehead. Christian surmised he was suffering withdrawal symptoms from his illegal drug of choice.

'Paul, there's nobody else in the flat. It's just you and me. Now, why don't you put the gun down and we can have a chat. Tell me what's on your mind.'

It was a while before he answered. His eyes were darting left and right as if unable to focus. 'I didn't kill Carly.'

'I know you didn't, Paul.'

'Them two bitches were trying to get her to leave me. They said she could do better than me.' A tear rolled down his cheek. 'I loved her.'

'I know.'

'It's drugs. You start taking them and you think they're

amazing, and they are, but you get addicted and when you don't get any, you look around and you see what they've done to you. Do you have any idea of what we've had to do to get money for drugs?' He asked. His voice was shaking with emotion and the effects of going cold turkey. 'Carly's pulled all kinds of tricks for a fiver here and a tenner there. There are people out there into all kinds of sick shit and they think because they're paying for it, they can do what they want. Carly's had all kinds of shit rammed inside her. She's been spat at, beaten, pissed on, gang-raped, and it's like it's fine because she's just a drugged-up whore.'

'We'd never think that, Paul. You should have come to us and told us.'

'What's the point? What is the fucking point? You don't care about us. Nobody does. We have to look out for each other in this world because nobody else will.'

'There are people who are trained to help you, Paul. We can get you into a drugs programme to help you kick the habit.'

'I don't care about any of that now. If Carly was still here, I'd say it was worth it. Without her, I don't give a toss. I loved her. I'd have died for her.' His eyes were like pinholes, and he could hardly focus. He was swaying side to side.

'Paul, what happened to Carly was terrible. We are moving heaven and earth to find her killer, and we will find him.'

'I miss her,' he said through tears. He didn't wipe them away.

'I know. I lost someone earlier this year. It's painful, isn't it?' Christian asked, edging slowly into the bathroom.

'I can't describe it.' He was looking at the floor. His arms were weakening, and the gun was no longer pressed so hard against this throat. 'It's like the end of the world, like everything's just ended, and there's nothing left.'

'The thing is, Paul, there are still people out there who care for you.'

'There aren't. My dad was never on the scene. Mum couldn't cope and put me into care. My first foster family took me back after a couple of weeks. They changed their mind. Can you believe that? They just changed their minds like I was a fucking jumper or something. My second foster family thought they couldn't have kids. A year after I turned up, she got pregnant, so they dumped me. My third foster family, the husband used to beat me. I ran away and was put into care, but that was even worse. The bloke running the care centre, Richard-fucking-Ashton OBE, had Friday night parties with all his other fucking holier-than-thou friends. They gave me sweets and five-pound notes then took me into the bedroom and fucked the living daylights out of me. I was eight years old, for fuck's sake.'

Christian could see the hurt, torment and horror in his small eyes. He'd had an evil start in life and never received any kind of help. Was it any wonder he'd turned to drugs to dull the pain? When he found Carly, and fell in love with her, he must have thought he could get his life on track, but the lure of the ecstasy of drugs was too much and he was soon pulled back into it. Her murder was the key to unlock the door of his nightmare past.

'Paul, let me help you,' Christian said, softly. 'I'd like to help.'

He reached out for the gun, his eyes firmly fixed on it in Paul's hands.

'What the fuck do you think you're doing?'

Christian looked up; their eyes locked.

Matilda came off the phone to Sian.

'She's sending armed response.'

'Is there anything we can do?' Bev asked.

'I can't believe I froze like that. I didn't even see the gun. As soon as he mentioned it, I was right back to being in the car park and looking down the barrel of the sodding rifle. I thought I was over it.' She ran her hands over her short hair.

She turned and saw Bev and Sarah staring at her. Why was she opening up to two virtual strangers? She would never have done that a year ago.

You really need to get a grip. You're no use to anyone as a complete basket case.

'It's always going to come back to haunt you, Matilda. It was a big thing that happened to you,' Bev said. 'You can't just wake up one morning and think it's all behind you.'

'I know. I'm finding that out the hard way.'

'So, what do we do now?' Bev asked.

Matilda looked up at the flat. Behind that grubby window in urgent need of washing, Christian was alone facing a drugged-up gunman. This was a nightmare scenario. She felt powerless.

A gunshot rang out.

Chapter Forty

Matilda rapped lightly on the door with a knuckle. She pushed it open and called through the gap.

'It's Matilda. Am I okay to come in?'

Scott pulled the door fully open. He had a grave expression on his face. He nodded.

Matilda entered the men's changing room and was hit by a disturbing odour: a mix of cheap deodorant and feet. Christian was sitting on a bench wearing a white forensic suit, his clothes ruined by the spray of blood and brain matter when Paul Chattle put the gun in his mouth and pulled the trigger.

When she heard the gunshot, Matilda leapt into action. The safety of her colleague was at the forefront of her mind. She felt like she was back in the car park in January as Jake Harrison was shooting at them from the roof of the building behind the station, but rather than stand there, staring, this time she ran to help, though looking back she had no idea how her legs had carried her up the stairs.

She burst into Bev and Sarah's flat and saw Christian stood in the doorway to the bathroom. When he turned to face her, covered in blood, she was relieved he was still alive. There was no way she could lose someone else.

Sitting on the bench, Christian had the blank innocent look of a child. His face was pale, and faint worry lines ran across his forehead. He was staring somewhere into the distance.

'Scott, can you leave us for a minute?'

'Sure. Jennifer's on her way with a change of clothing.'

'Okay. Cheers.' She waited until Scott had left before she sat next to her DI and took his hand in hers. It was freezing cold. She rubbed at it hard.

'Richard Ashton,' he said.

'Sorry?'

'Richard Ashton. OBE.'

'Who's he?'

'He ran a children's home. Paul went there for a while when he was young. He abused him.' Christian's voice was a monotone, and he continued to stare at the back wall, not once turning to face Matilda. 'He told me all about his life, abandoned by his parents and foster parents, getting beaten and abused right, left and centre. Drugs were the only thing that dulled the pain. Then he met Carly. He genuinely loved her. They needed each other. With her dead...' he trailed off.

Matilda didn't know what to say. She put her arm around his shoulders, and he fell into her.

'Why didn't they seek help?' Christian asked. 'There are all kinds of drug rehabilitation programmes and therapies they could have used, but they tried to sort it all out between them. It doesn't work. You have to talk to people.'

'We all deal with things in our own way.'

'But they were ignoring it. You can't do that.'

There were many unresolved issues Matilda had from the aftermath of the shooting. She hadn't warmed to her therapist,

Diana Coopersmith, and often held back for fear of being judged, or potentially being placed on a sabbatical. She had snapped at her mother only last night. Where had all that resentment come from? Christian was right. Burying emotions caused more damage. Her long chat with Scott the other night seemed to have helped him. He had a positive air about him recently. Should she give in to her misgivings and open herself up to Diana Coopersmith, or maybe try to repair the bridges with Adele?

'Are you all right?' she asked.

He looked at her. His eyes were red and full of tears. 'I will be,' he said with a hint of a smile. 'Talking to Jennifer helps. And I see a therapist once a month to have a sort of debrief. I'm not given breathing exercises or told to write a journal or anything, it's just talking, but I always feel lighter after each session.'

'You're doing everything right.'

'I like to think so. It's a shame others aren't or can't. But then…'

'What?'

'Well, I think people have to want help. Maybe Paul was embarrassed to talk about being abused with a professional. Maybe he thought drugs would permanently help him to forget one day. I'd like to track down this Richard Ashton OBE and show him what damage he's done.'

'We will.'

Christian swallowed hard. 'The thing is, I…'

Scott poked his head around the door and told them Jennifer had arrived.

'This can all wait, Christian,' Matilda said. 'Go home, spend the evening with your family.'

They stood up. Christian hugged Matilda tight, wrapping

his arms firmly around her and squeezing her. It seemed to last for a long time.

'I don't know what's happened between you and Adele, but if you're not talking to anyone, you really need to change that.'

She nodded. Christian said he'd be in work tomorrow morning, despite being told he could take a couple of days off. Matilda remained in the men's changing room on her own. He was right, she did need to talk.

From her back pocket, she took out her mobile and scrolled through the contacts for Adele's number. Her finger hovered over it. She was about to press when the door opened.

'You really need to come and see who is on *Sky News* right now,' Scott said.

Chapter Forty-One

Matilda followed Scott into the HMCU suite where Sian, Finn and Zofia were standing in front of the television. On screen, a blacked-out silhouette of a female was sitting in front of a window of what looked like a generic hotel room.

'...*and none of us deserve that,*' the young-sounding woman said in a thick Sheffield accent. '*I've been working the streets for just under three years. In that time I've been kicked, beaten, raped, bitten, mugged and threatened. I used to report every incident t'police, but they dint care. You shudda seen the looks they gave me. I've known some of t'women who've gone missing. I knew Ella and Denise and Carly. I was frightened. We all were. They took me statement, when they could be bothered, and that were it. They couldn't get me out of t'station fast enough. I bet they threw it straight in the bin. I don't bother reporting anything now. There's no point.*'

'Who is this?' Matilda asked. Her face was like thunder, her eyes fixed on the screen.

'I've no idea,' Sian said. 'I don't recognise her voice at all.'

'Are Bev and Sarah still here?'

'Yes.'

'Get them in here.'

Finn led Bev and Sarah into the suite, carrying what meagre belongings they could collect from their flat before it was turned into a crime scene and sealed off. They looked around them tentatively as if merely being in a police station made them guilty of something.

'Bev, do you recognise this woman?' Matilda asked.

'Have you seen an increase in police patrolling the area since the killings started?' the interviewer asked.

'No more than usual. Thing is, they come round, and punters bugger off. If I don't earn, then I can't pay me rent, can I? I've been cautioned that many times I know most of the coppers by name. But I'm back on the streets as soon as I'm released. What else can I do?'

'That's Becca,' Bev said. 'Rebecca Sloan. Don't believe a word she says. She's trouble.'

'How do you mean?' Sian asked.

'She'll stab you in the back as soon as she looks at you. She's lied, cheated, stolen. She's turned some of the regular punters off us so they'll only go with her. We've had many a run-in with her, haven't we, Sarah?'

Sarah nodded.

'Whether she's a liar or not, she's on national television saying we're not doing our job properly,' Sian said.

'Rebecca Sloan has got a charge sheet as long as the M1,' Finn said from his desk. 'Assaults, thefts, drunk and disorderly, drug use.'

'Yes. She's as high as a kite. To be honest, I'm surprised she's still alive,' Bev said. 'Sometimes she comes on the streets and it's like she doesn't know where she is. She gets in the car with anyone. I bet she doesn't know what's being done to her half the time.'

The door to the suite opened and ACC Ridley walked in.

'Ah, Matilda, I'm glad you've seen this.'

Becca started talking again on screen. Matilda picked up the remote and turned it off. 'Sian, could you show Bev and Sarah out?' Matilda waited until they were out of the suite. 'Sir, I know this doesn't make us look good, but Bev has identified the woman and she's an unreliable source. I'm guessing the journalist flashed his wallet and she told him what he wanted to hear that would make good news.'

'Be that as it may, whether it's true or not, it's out there and making us look like amateurs.' He must had felt his mobile vibrate because he reached into his inside pocket and pulled out an iPhone. 'Shit. I've got the Chief Constable phoning me now.' He sent the call to voicemail.

'Shouldn't you have taken that?' Matilda asked.

'Not until I have something to tell him. Where are we in the investigation?'

'We're looking through cold cases. I think there may be more victims out there.'

'Jesus Christ, Matilda, how big is this going to get? Are we talking a new Suffolk Strangler here?'

Matilda looked around her. Finn and Scott were watching her with blank expressions. She looked over to the murder board, at the row of faces staring at her, begging her to find the person responsible for killing them.

'To be honest with you, sir, I think it's going to be worse than that.'

He visibly paled. 'I didn't want to hear that.'

'I didn't want to say it. Of the two victims we found in Plantation Woods, one was buried alive.'

He shook his head in disgust. 'Are you sure they're from the same killer?'

'Prostitutes going missing and found killed? How many serial killers do you want on your patch with the same MO, sir?'

He didn't answer. 'How many victims have you got?'

'So far, we have eight confirmed. I'm expecting it to go higher the more we research.'

'I want this man caught, Matilda,' he said firmly.

'I know. So do I. What do you want to do about this TV interview?'

He sighed.

'Rebecca Sloan has a long charge sheet,' Finn spoke up.

Ridley was silent for a moment as he thought. 'Okay, I'm going to call the Chief Constable, tell him that she's lied. We'll issue a press conference saying similar but using much more succinct language. I'll get uniform to increase patrols in the area from tonight. I was hoping the good news of Carl Meagan being found would keep the press from our door for a while. Matilda, you and your team need to work around the clock on this.'

'I don't have the staff for that.'

'I'll get some drafted in from CID to help you. He's been out there killing for at least three years. He needs to be stopped. *You* need to stop him.'

Matilda didn't like the emphasis on 'you', but she knew what the underlying statement meant. This was her first big case since returning from sick leave. She needed to solve it at any cost to prove to herself, and her doubters, that she was still the major force to be reckoned with.

Ridley turned on his heels and left the room, closing the door firmly behind him.

'Wow,' Scott said, running his fingers through his short hair.

'I know,' Matilda replied. 'Finn, how are you getting on with the cold cases?'

He hesitated. 'I'm ... getting there.'

'Okay, I know this is a cheek, but can you do that tonight? Then tomorrow morning at the briefing we'll put them all in some kind of order then go and knock on as many doors in the city as we can. Somebody out there has to know something. I also want Bev, Sarah and every other woman working as a street prostitute interviewed and at least a description of a person of interest.'

'Me and Steph have got a table booked at—'

'Then you'll have to cancel it, won't you?' she barked.

Finn threw his pen down on the table. He kicked his chair back, picked up his phone and headed for the door, making a call as he went.

'I don't mind staying...' Scott began.

Matilda held him by the arm and took him to one side. 'I need you to drive me home. And I need to ask your opinion on something delicate.'

Chapter Forty-Two

Matilda had forgotten about Bev and Sarah until she opened the door to head for the toilets. They were sat in the corridor, nursing their belongings like evacuated children at the height of World War Two wondering where they were being sent for their own safety. It was dark. It was late. There was nowhere to send them tonight. There was only one solution.

Scott was driving Matilda's Range Rover with her in the front passenger seat. In the back, Bev and Sarah sat silently, their bags on their laps, marvelling at the luxury of the plush car. Matilda glanced across at Scott and saw a sly grin on his face.

Matilda had told Bev in the station that they could stay at her place for tonight, making it perfectly clear it was for one night only. Surely the council could offer them emergency accommodation if they were unable to go back to the flat tomorrow for whatever reason.

When they arrived at the old farmhouse, Matilda asked Scott if he wanted to have tea with them. He politely refused, wished them all a good evening and headed for his flat with a bounce in his step.

The house was warm and well lit. Bev and Sarah stood in the hallway, gazing open-mouthed around them as if they'd never been in such a beautiful home before. Matilda had sent a text to Harriet on her way home, informing her of the situation, and she was there to greet them.

'Kettle's on and I've made the beds in the spare rooms,' Harriet said. 'I'm afraid I'm not much of a cook. I can follow a recipe, but we don't have much in the house and I'm no Mary Berry where I can whip up something amazing out of an avocado, a couple of tomatoes and a bag of pasta, so I thought we'd order in.'

'I could do with a bath, if that's okay?' Bev asked.

'Of course,' Matilda said. 'I'll take you up.'

Bev used the en suite in the guest bedroom Harriet had made up while Sarah used the main bathroom. Her room didn't have an en suite.

Downstairs, Matilda and Harriet set about making mugs of tea for them all.

'Are you all right?' Harriet asked.

'I'm fine.'

'Did you see any of the ... you know?'

'Blood? You can say it, Harriet, I'm not going to freak out.'

'I just wondered how you reacted to a siege.'

'It wasn't a siege. He was suicidal, bless him. Besides, it was Christian who witnessed it all. I was outside. Christian told me that he sees a therapist once a month, to get things off his chest. He says it helps.'

'Well, it will do. When I found out Brian had a secret family I went to see someone,' she said, throwing teabags into a pot.

'Did you? You never said.'

'I wanted to speak to someone who didn't know me or Brian. Besides, I knew that whatever advice you gave me wouldn't be impartial.'

'Did it help?'

She thought for a moment. 'Yes, it did. It gave me the confidence to leave him.'

'I don't get that with Diana Coopersmith.'

'Whose fault's that?'

'What's that supposed to mean?'

'Well, is it because you resent her because of what she might represent or because you're not telling her everything?'

She sighed. 'A bit of both, I think.'

'There you go then. On your next session, either end it and find another therapist, or sit down, open up and let it all pour out.'

'Then she'll need a therapist,' Matilda smiled.

Matilda's guest bedrooms were designed for visitors, with spare dressing gowns on the back of the doors and pairs of slippers by the bed. She had no idea why she went to so much trouble when decorating as she didn't have guests. Adele had crashed out a few times when she'd had a few too many bottles of wine to risk driving home, but she didn't count. The added touches of comfort were now being used and Bev and Sarah both came into the kitchen wearing matching white dressing gowns.

'You have a gorgeous home, Matilda,' Bev said. 'Aren't you worried that it's a bit out of the way?'

'That's what I love about it.'

'My sister is the only recluse who's never at home,' Harriet smiled.

'Do you live here as well?' Bev asked.

'No. I'm just staying here while Matilda fully recovers.'

'I'm fine,' she said.

'I'm moving back to Sheffield, though. I'm recently divorced.'

They all sat down at the stripped oak kitchen table. Harriet brought over the teapot, a tray of mugs and a biscuit barrel while Matilda laid out a pile of takeaway menus and asked them to pick their favourite.

'I was married,' Bev said, reaching for her tea and spooning in a couple of sugars. 'No kids, though.'

'I've got two boys,' Harriet said.

Bev smiled, though it didn't reach her eyes. 'We tried, but it didn't happen. I remember in my teens my mum was always telling me to find a nice man, settle down and have a big family. Family was important to my mum. I saw how much my parents struggled. I'm one of eight. I told her there was no way I was going down the same path as her. I fancy Indian,' she said, passing a menu to Sarah. 'The problem was, when I did find a bloke and we got married, try as we might, kids didn't appear.'

Matilda sat back on the chair and watched Bev's hard face soften as she opened up.

'It turns out it was me. There's something wrong with the lining of my womb, or something. It was so long ago, I've forgotten. Anyway, Clark said it didn't matter, we had each other, we didn't need kids. We'd be one of those power couples with a nice house, a car each, three holidays a year and jealous friends.' She gave a hollow laugh. 'Less than a year later he's moving out because he's knocked up someone in his office. They ended up having four kids.'

'I'm so sorry,' Harriet said.

'Two of my sisters fell pregnant at the same time. Two people I worked with had kids close together and it seemed to get to me that I couldn't have any.' Her bottom lip began to wobble. 'All I could hear was my mother telling me how important family was and there I was in a big house and nobody to share it with. Then Clark said he wanted to sell because he needed the money for his new family. The house sold sooner than I expected so had to accept the first shitty flat I could find. He screwed me out of my share of it, I know he did, but I couldn't prove it. Six months later, I get fired and I'm in arrears with my rent and no references.'

'Why did you get fired?' Harriet asked.

'I was an accountant for a steel manufacturer down Attercliffe. Clark leaving me and all that baby talk was crushing me. I turned up for work with a hangover, though, looking back, I think I was probably still pissed from the night before. I made a massive error which I tried to hide and that just made things worse. Next thing, HMRC comes sniffing around and slaps the firm with a huge tax bill. I'm out on my ear and before you know it I'm on the streets offering blow jobs for a tenner.'

She slumped onto the table, head in her hands. 'People look at us and think we're scum, the lowest of the low. It's the same with the homeless, but there aren't many of us who have savings accounts they can dip into during the lean months. There are so many living on the breadline. All it takes is to be out of work for a couple of months before you risk losing everything. And once you've lost it, it's not easy getting it back.' She wiped away a single tear before it fell.

'What about your family? You said you were one of eight, couldn't they have helped?' Harriet asked.

'When you hit rock bottom, you find out exactly who the genuine ones are out there. A couple of my sisters helped. The odd mate let me sleep in their spare room. But when you slip up again, they turn their backs. After about a year, I was getting myself sorted. I was sober, I had a part-time job in the Co-op and I wasn't overdrawn. I took a short cut back to my sister's house one day through the park and who did I see enjoying themselves but Clark and his new wife coochy-cooing into a pram. They looked like an advert for a building society. As soon as I clocked them, my heart fell through the ground. It killed me. I landed on a snake and I went right back down to square one.'

'Couldn't you have sought help? Counselling?' Matilda asked, her voice hardly above a whisper.

'I did actually.'

'It didn't work?'

'It might have done.'

'What do you mean?'

'Who do you think gave me my first tenner for a blow job?'

'Your therapist?' Harriet asked, wide-eyed.

'He saw how desperate I was, and he abused his position. Lesson learned. Trust no one but yourself.'

Bev had been outvoted when it came to choosing something to eat. Matilda fancied a pizza, as did Sarah and Harriet. They ordered from an app on Harriet's phone and while waiting for the food to arrive, Bev questioned Matilda about her recovery from the gunshot wounds. Once they were eating, the conversation soon turned back to Bev and Sarah's life working the streets.

'I really do think one of the punters is a killer,' Matilda said. 'You have regulars, I'm guessing. Who stands out?'

'None of them stand out, love,' Bev said. 'They turn up, you get in the car, they drive you somewhere secluded, you do the business, they give you the money, they go home to their wives. You don't chat, you don't get to know them, you don't ask how their day's been. It's a simple transaction.'

'You don't chat to any of them?'

'A couple. I know a few of their names, but it's obvious they've made them up. Anything they do tell you, you take with a pinch of salt.'

'Speaking of salt, we paid a visit to Dermot Salter,' Matilda said.

'Find any dead bodies in the boot of his car?' she asked, a hint of a smile on her lips.

'No. His wife worked as a prostitute years ago. That's how they met. When she died, he started coming to see you all for company. I think he's just incredibly sad.'

'See, what did I tell you? I told you he was lonely,' Sarah said. 'He reminded me a bit of...' She stopped dead.

'Who?' Matilda asked.

'Nobody. It doesn't matter.' She reddened.

'You're going to say he reminds you of your Jack, aren't you?' Bev asked. 'He looks nothing like him.'

'Not looks, but how kind and caring he is.'

'Listen, if your Jack was kind and caring, do you think he would have left you? No, he'd have stuck by you. Time and again I've told you, all men are selfish bastards,' Bev said harshly.

'Are you all right?' Harriet was sitting opposite Sarah and noticed as a tear escaped her left eye. She didn't reply, but merely nodded.

'She gets maudlin,' Bev said, tearing a chunk off a slice of garlic bread. 'She was married for six years, had two kids, then she was—'

'Bev!' Sarah snapped.

'You don't have to tell us if you don't want to,' Harriet said, placing a hand on top of hers.

Sarah swallowed hard. She took a deep breath and braced herself. 'I went out with some friends to celebrate my birthday. I'd just turned twenty-eight. We all got into a taxi to go home. Anyway, we're dropping one of my mates off and I get out of the taxi and it drives off. I only lived about a five-minute walk away and thought the fresh air might sober me up a bit so I set off on foot.'

She pushed her plate away, picked up her glass of water and emptied it in a single gulp.

'I didn't even see him,' she continued, wiping a tear. 'One minute I'm walking on the pavement, next minute I'm on the ground and this man's... Well, you can guess what happened. By the time I'd got home, Jack had gone to bed. I went straight in the shower and scrubbed myself clean. I didn't tell him. I didn't tell anyone. I thought that if I could act like it hadn't happened then maybe it would be all right.'

'It wasn't, though, was it?' Matilda asked.

'I couldn't get it out of my head. Every time I closed my eyes, I could see him,' she said, looking directly at Matilda. 'He was there, constantly, looming over me, breathing, panting. I could feel his warm breath on me, smell the stale fags. I felt sick. I stopped going out for drinks, I stopped going out on my own, and I started being scared of the dark. Jack kept asking me what was wrong, but I couldn't tell him. I should have done. I should.'

'It wasn't your fault,' Bev said, placing a hand on her shoulder.

'I started drinking. I stopped going to work. Me and Jack were arguing. I was scaring the kids.' Sarah broke down. She pushed her chair back, jumped up and ran out of the room.

'Shouldn't you go after her?' Harriet asked Bev.

'She just needs a few minutes to gather herself. She's permanently sad. She'll have a few good days then it seems to just flick like a switch, and she bursts into tears. She misses her kids so much.'

'They don't want anything to do with her?' Harriet asked.

'Their mother is an alcoholic who sells her body. Would you? I'll go and check on her,' Bev said. She stood up, grabbed a handful of chips and left the room.

'You don't realise what other people are going through, do you?' Harriet asked. 'You see people in the streets, and you have no idea of their personal lives. It's like when you see homeless people in shop doorways, you assume it's their own fault they're there, but it's not always, is it?'

'If only Sarah had told her husband about the rape,' Matilda said.

'"If" is such a small word with a huge meaning.'

Matilda took a deep breath. It quivered as she let it out. 'When I next go to see Diana Coopersmith, will you come with me?' she asked.

Chapter Forty-Three

Matilda was in bed, but she was unable to sleep. The house was dark and silent. It seemed strange for it to be so full. There was, however, a feeling of safety and security in having three other people under the same roof. What was the point in living in such a large house if only one person was going to be rattling around in it, every breath and footstep resounding off the walls, like a security guard walking around an empty museum in the dead of night?

Giving in to her insomnia, Matilda sat up and turned on her bedside light. She might as well utilise the time and do something she enjoyed, read, rather than stare at the ceiling, willing sleep to come.

Despite being declared physically fit for work, Matilda was still taking medication, and each little pill of varying shape, size and colour was neatly arranged in a plastic weekly organiser. She always associated them with the elderly and begrudged having one by her bed, reminding her constantly of what had happened. Not that she needed a physical reminder. She pushed the box out of view and picked up the paperback

Agatha Christie novel she was enjoying. She hadn't even read a page when her phone beeped the signalling of an incoming text.

The time on the alarm clock said 1:18. Who would be texting at this hour? She looked and saw it was from Pat Campbell. It had been sent five hours ago but had not come through thanks to the intermittent signal which came from being surrounded by trees.

Did you see the interview? What did you think? Ring me. I need to tell you something.

Matilda had forgotten all about the interview with Sally and Philip Meagan. She had been caught up in Bev and Sarah telling their life story. By the time they'd finished, and the pizza had been eaten, they were all drained. She put the book down and picked up her iPad. The interview would be on the BBC iPlayer. She grabbed her earbuds from the top drawer and settled down to watch it. As soon as she heard Danny Hanson's annoying voice, she could feel her blood pressure rising. She wondered which coloured pill calmed her down; she could do with a handful right now.

'*In 2015, every parent's worst nightmare was realised for Philip and Sally Meagan when their seven-year-old son, Carl, was kidnapped for ransom from the safety of their home. When the police operation to secure his release went awry, Carl vanished. He was never heard from again. His parents, however, tirelessly kept their son's name and image alive and the search for their only child went global. After more than four years, a vigilant neighbour in Sweden spotted a young boy and made the call Sally and Philip had been waiting for. Earlier this week, Carl returned to England, and home to his parents. Tonight, in an exclusive interview, Philip and Sally*

Meagan will explain how they managed to hold on to the belief their son would return when the odds were stacked against them, and what the first twenty-four hours have been like since his return.'

Matilda rolled her eyes. The introduction was glossy and saccharine. She had heard programme announcers warn audiences of scenes of violence and bad language, and she wondered if the one who introduced this interview warned viewers they may be diagnosed with diabetes following Danny Hanson's sugared tabloid bollocks.

The camera turned to Philip and Sally. They were sat side by side, holding hands in the living room of their home in Dore. Sally looked like a new woman. She was radiant. There was a twinkle dancing in her eyes. There was colour in her cheeks. She sat up straight and proud and looked a decade younger now the worry for her son had dissipated. She wore a cream-coloured shirt, open at the neck, a subtle gold chain with a delicate pendant resting on her breast. She was wearing make-up for what was possibly the first time in four years. Matilda couldn't help but smile at this vision of hope and positivity.

Next to her, Philip was dressed smart but casually. He wore a blue suit jacket over a white shirt, again unbuttoned at the neck. He was clean shaven, his hair neatly combed, and there was a relieved expression on his face.

'There have been many false sightings of Carl around the world over the years. Can you tell us where you were and how you felt when it was confirmed Carl had been found?'

Sally took a deep breath and smiled. *'I was ironing. It was just another normal day and the phone rang. I hadn't given up hope that Carl would be found, but I no longer jumped for the phone every time it rang. I answered and it was Matilda, who had been leading the original investigation. She said she had some news and she'd be* right over. I knew straightaway that it was good news. There was something in her voice. Philip was upstairs getting ready for work and I shouted to him to come down. I just knew this time it was something positive.'

Matilda felt a warmth grow inside her as she saw the joy on her face.

'When Matilda told us,' Philip took over, 'it was like a massive grey cloud hanging over us disappeared. I can't tell you how I felt. I want to say relieved, but it doesn't seem enough. I tried telling myself not to get my hopes up until Carl came through the front door, but I knew from the look on Matilda's face that it was definitely him. We just ... we couldn't stop smiling and crying ... could we?'

Sally wiped away a tear. 'No. The longer time went on with Carl missing, realistically, the more I knew it was less likely we'd get him back. Each day was like a decade without him, but I never gave up. We never gave up. It was the best news we could ever receive.'

Matilda was crying. She had never seen such happiness and relief on anyone's face before. She knew the image of the two of them would be plastered over the front pages of the newspapers in the morning, and they deserved to be. In a world of Brexit, climate change, political uncertainty and terrorist acts, news like this had to be shared with the world.

She leaned back, resting her head against the padded headboard, and let the tears flow. She was so happy for the Meagan family. The past four years had been horrific for all of them, but they could now begin their lives again. The darkness had lifted. That was why Matilda was crying. The end of the darkness.

Chapter Forty-Four

Friday 25th October

Matilda and Scott were the last to enter the suite. Matilda had wanted to have a quiet chat on the journey over, but Scott couldn't stop talking about the interview with the Meagans on television last night and how it seemed that good things do happen following a tragedy.

She turned to look at him. 'When bad things happen, it changes everything,' she said. 'But it doesn't mean they can't change again. Sally and Philip had their lives turned upside down when Carl was kidnapped. They probably thought they'd never get him back, and in the intervening years they were living in limbo. Now look at them. Carl's back. They can't return to how life was four years ago, and they won't want to, but they can be happy once again.'

'I'm not in limbo,' Scott eventually spoke. 'I know I'll never get Chris back. I know there'll never be another friend as special as Rory, but there will be others, won't there?' he asked, looking at her hopefully.

Matilda saw in his eyes he was asking for her permission to be able to continue with his life. 'Of course there will. When you're ready, there'll be others.' She reached over and placed her hand on top of his. 'I am so proud of you,' she smiled.

'What for?'

'For not giving up. For realising you still have a life to live.'

He smiled back. 'What about you?'

'What about me?'

'You still have a life to live, too.'

She took a deep breath and held it for a long while. 'I know I do.'

'So, are you going to live it?'

She turned to him again. 'I'm going to try my bloody hardest.' She smiled weakly.

Matilda was heading for her office when she noticed Finn slumped at his desk. 'Has he been here all night?' she asked Zofia.

'Yes.'

'Finn,' she called out.

He jumped and looked up, wondering who had called his name. He had a hint of stubble. His hair was a mess and his eyes looked heavy.

'Sorry, I was just… What time is it?'

'Have you had any sleep?'

'I think I had an hour around four.'

'Look, Finn,' she began then noticed they weren't a full team yet. 'Sian's not in yet?'

'She's taking one of her sons to the hospital to have his cast removed,' Zofia said. 'DI Brady knows about it.'

She went into her office and squeezed through the small gap between her desk and the wall to get to her seat. There was a knock on the glass.

'Can I interrupt?' Christian entered the office and closed the door behind him.

'I wasn't expecting you in today. How are you feeling?' Matilda asked.

'Fine. I had a long chat with Jennifer last night. Surprisingly, I slept well, too. I've been awake since about five, though. I want to run something past you.'

'You want to look into this bloke with the OBE who abused Paul Chattle when he was a kid?'

'How did you know I was going to say that?'

Matilda sat back in her chair. 'Firstly, I know you. Secondly, I was thinking the same. If this guy has an OBE, he's not going to be some chancer who abused Paul to get his kicks. He'll be in a position of power and who knows who else knew what he was up to.'

'Me and Jennifer said as much last night.'

'There's nothing we can do about it now. I'm sorry. We're short staffed and currently working on one of the biggest cases we've ever seen. It'll just have to go on the back burner.'

'I know how busy we are, but if I got the ball rolling—'

'Christian,' she interrupted. 'I cannot afford to lose one single detective. This is too important.'

'So is a man with a history of sexual abuse. You said yourself he'll be someone in a position of power seeing as he's got an OBE.'

'It can wait,' she said firmly.

'Can it? How do we know he's not still abusing kids? How do we know he isn't part of a bigger network of paedophiles? You know the stick South Yorkshire Police came under for not investigating the abuse network going on in Rotherham. If we have another scandal on our hands, we could be seriously in the shit this time,' he said, raising his voice.

'Christian, I know you're upset at seeing Paul kill himself in front of you and I sympathise, I really do. However—'

'We've always had more than one investigation going at the same time,' he interrupted. 'We've managed that in the past. It's what we do. It's what we were set up for.'

'We are three detectives down, Christian,' she said slamming her hands down hard on her desk. She stood up. 'Not to mention you giving Sian permission to ferry her adult son to hospital to have his fucking cast removed. My answer is no. For now, just leave it.'

Christian stared at her in disbelief. He'd never known her to swear like that, and certainly not at him.

'Fine,' he said calmly.

Matilda turned to come round from the back of her desk but caught her leg on an open drawer. She cried out in pain.

'Fucking office!'

'Are you all right?'

'No. We're moving back into the old suite as soon as possible.'

'I really don't think that's a very good idea. Sian can't look out of the window overlooking the car park. It'll bring back—'

'Christian, I really don't give a fuck,' she said quietly through gritted teeth. 'If you want to run more than one large investigation at the same time, we're going to need space. This is an over-sized rabbit hutch, and it smells like one, too.'

Christian remained silent for a moment. 'Whatever you say,' he grudgingly said. 'You're the boss,' he added as he left the office.

Finn rapped lightly on the glass door. Matilda looked up and waved him in. He looked fresher after a shower but the dark circles beneath the eyes needed more than a wash to fade.

Matilda had been left undisturbed for half an hour. Her face was no longer red with rage, but her lips were pursed. She seemed to be sitting on a knife edge.

'I thought you might be interested in what I discovered last night,' he said, his arms folded tightly across his chest, an annoyed expression on his face.

'Go on,' she instructed.

'Nothing.'

'What?'

'Nothing. Absolutely nothing. I found one strangulation, but she's an estate agent in Beighton and the killer used a rope.'

'Ah.'

'Yes. I said something similar at four o'clock this morning.' There was an edge to Finn's voice. A lack of sleep was making him tetchy. 'Still, I can always take my wife out for a meal tonight, can't I? Oh no, wait, I can't, because wedding anniversaries only come round once a year.' He slapped the very thin report on Matilda's desk, turned on his heel and left the office, slamming the door behind him.

'Nothing,' Matilda overheard Finn saying to Zofia at the drinks station. 'No thanks for staying all night. No apologies for making me cancel my night out with Steph. Just a blank expression. I don't know why I fucking bother.'

Matilda spun around on her chair, her back to the door. She'd never heard Finn swear before. She shouldn't have forced him to pull an all-nighter. It was wrong of her. She should apologise, but she felt as if she couldn't. It would mean admitting she was wrong, that she had made a rash decision because the ACC was on her back and it hadn't paid off. She was losing her judgement, and her grip on the team.

Matilda leaned back in her chair and turned to look out of the window. This high up, she couldn't see much of Sheffield: the tops of roofs, the cranes working on the seemingly never-ending regeneration of the city centre. There seemed to be a third crane in her sightline today. Yesterday, there were only two. It was strange how you never saw cranes being built or dismantled, they just seemed to appear. Would this be to erect a new block of student accommodation or perhaps another unnecessary hotel, which Sheffield seemed to be collecting plenty of lately?

'Scott,' she called out when she saw him pass by her door. He smiled and opened the door. 'Sit down, I need to talk to you. Actually, I don't trust how thin these walls are. Shall we pop outside for a fag?'

'Neither of us smoke,' he said with a frown.

'I know. Don't you feel short-changed about all those breaks we're missing out on?'

Matilda had been back at work for just over two weeks. It felt longer. While in a coma in hospital, she had missed the funerals of her friends and colleagues. She'd even missed her father's burial. When she was at the Dame Charlotte Montgomery Rehabilitation Centre, she had missed the memorial service for her fallen colleagues. She'd heard all about it, seen the footage on the news and the photographs in the newspapers, but she hadn't visited the memorial for herself.

It was only when she pushed open the back doors and stepped out into the cold, dull autumnal morning and her eyes went straight to the shrine that she remembered this was the scene of utter devastation nine months ago. How could she have forgotten so quickly?

The memorial was a stone plinth. On top, there was a glass case in which a blue flame would flicker eternally. There was a brass plaque on the stone in which the date of the shooting and the names of the dead were etched. Matilda approached it slowly and placed her hand on the glass.

ON TUESDAY 8TH JANUARY 2019, SEVEN SERVING POLICE OFFICERS AT THIS STATION DIED IN THE LINE OF DUTY. THIS FLAME WILL BURN ETERNALLY AS A SYMBOL THAT THEY WILL NEVER BE FORGOTTEN AND THE FIGHT FOR JUSTICE WILL FOREVER CONTINUE.

ASSISTANT CHIEF CONSTABLE VALERIE MASTERSON
SERGEANT JULIAN PRICE
DETECTIVE CONSTABLE RANJEET DESHWAL
DETECTIVE CONSTABLE RORY FLEMING
POLICE CONSTABLE ROBIN MORLEY
POLICE CONSTABLE FIONA LAVERY
POLICE CONSTABLE NATASHA TRANTER

'It must have been a very difficult day,' Matilda said.

'I don't think any of us did much work that day,' Scott said.

'Is there a memorial at the school for Chris?'

He nodded. 'There were more people there. The whole school of teachers and pupils, the family of the dead, news crews, the lot. There were hymns and prayers. It seemed to go on for ever.'

Matilda stood in silence looking at the memorial.

'Are you all right?' Scott asked. 'I heard you shouting at Christian. We all did. That's not like you.'

'I'm tired, Scott,' she answered honestly. 'I'm not trusted anymore. People are questioning me, doubting me.'

'They're not.'

'My name should be on that plaque.'

'Don't even think that.'

'I should never have come back.'

'Yes, you should. You belong here.'

Matilda placed her hand on the glass box. It felt warm to the touch. She took a deep breath. 'This really is beautiful.'

'We'll be able to see this every time we look out of the window when we move back to our old offices,' Scott said.

'Will you be okay?' She turned to him.

'Blinds were invented for a reason,' he smiled. 'What did you want to talk to me about?' he asked.

Matilda moved away from the memorial, plunged her hands into her coat pockets and walked around the car park. 'I want to ask your opinion on something and it's not one hundred per cent moral. However, you're the only person I feel I can confide in with this.'

'What about Sian?'

'Sian's very much a by-the-book woman. As is Christian. You, I know, are a bit more like me. Blinds can be closed. As can books.'

'Something tells me I'm not going to want to hear this,' he said, shivering slightly in the cold.

'I want to send Zofia undercover as a prostitute. Do you think she's up to it?'

Scott didn't hesitate. 'With the right coaching, yes. She's eager to learn and she wants to fit in and prove herself. I think, after the whole Paul Chattle business, she realised she needs to be part of the team. She'd never take a huge risk like that again.'

'Good,' she smiled.

'You're going to say something more, aren't you?'

'I don't want Zofia out there on her own. However, I can't risk a car with undercover officers parked nearby watching her. Our killer is very clever. He's been doing this for so long, he'd spot a new car, and he'd certainly spot a car with a couple of plain-clothes detectives sitting inside. I need someone to look after her who can be right there on the street.'

'You want me to be a punter?'

'No. The killer would notice you hanging around. I was thinking of sending someone out there to be a fellow prostitute, someone who could be in the background but doesn't fit into our victim range of young and naïve.'

He frowned. 'Sian?'

Matilda shook her head. 'My sister.'

From a window in the corridor of the station, Christian looked out at Matilda and Scott talking in the car park. They looked as thick as thieves. Why couldn't whatever they needed to discuss take place in her office? Why the secrecy? Matilda talked about the unit being one team, everyone banding together, but she was the one driving a wedge between them all.

Christian was pleased Matilda had recovered from her physical injuries, but right now, he was wishing she hadn't returned to work at all. Everything had been calm and smooth while he'd been in charge. Not anymore. The whole team was falling apart.

Chapter Forty-Five

'Hi, Pat, it's me. Sorry I haven't called you sooner. It's bedlam here at the moment.'

Matilda was sat in her cramped office. Finn had returned from having a shave and a shower and looked better for it. Matilda was jealous. Finn was only in his mid-twenties. He could survive on a few hours' sleep and look fresh and raring to go. Matilda needed a full eight hours, several coffees and a cold shower to look halfway decent. The perils of ageing.

'I've seen the news. Sheffield seems to be dominating at the moment. I'm guessing that anonymous interview with a prostitute hasn't helped much.'

'Not in the slightest.'

'So, did you see the interview last night?' Pat asked, obviously sensing the need to move the conversation on.

'I did. They both handled it very well.'

'I thought so too. I'm pleased they cut out Danny Hanson being an arse with some of his questions. Hopefully the director gave him a bollocking.'

'Was he rude?'

'No. Just far too intrusive for my liking. Still, they didn't make it to the final interview.'

'Good. So, you said you wanted to mention something to me.'

'Yes, I did. It's about Carl. I know it's going to be difficult for him returning home after all this time, but he's incredibly withdrawn. He spends all his time either in his room with the dogs or in the back garden with them. He's hardly talking and when he does, he's snapping. When the film crew had gone yesterday, we were all having a cup of tea and Carl came down for a snack. He left the fridge door open and Sally told him to close it. He slammed it and when Sally told him to be careful, he told her not to be such a bitch about it.'

'Bloody hell!'

'I know.'

'What did Sally and Philip say when he left the room?'

'Philip didn't say anything, but Sally looked really hurt. She looked…'

'Go on,' Matilda prompted.

'It was only for the briefest of moments, but she looked at me and I swear to God if we'd been on our own she'd have said she wished he hadn't come home.'

Matilda walked out into the suite, where everyone was waiting for her. Finn was stood by the murder board, ready to begin. The conversation with Pat sat heavily on Matilda's mind. Counselling was scheduled to begin early next week and there was a whole raft of interviews for Carl to give with the police. Fingers firmly crossed, he would soon see an end to this horrific journey he'd been forced to endure.

'Right then, before we begin, I've had an email from Sian's favourite dog handler.'

All eyes turned to Sian and she blushed slightly.

'He and the dogs have finished their sweep of Plantation Woods and they haven't detected any other bodies buried there. However, I've asked him to go to Chelsea Park, where Denise Jones was murdered, and then to the site where Lisa Temple was killed. Now, Finn,' she said, placing a hand on his shoulder; there was no warmth in the gesture at all, 'bless him, spent the whole of last night in this crappy room searching through our backlog of unsolved murders to try and find any links to our current workload. Unfortunately, or fortunately, however you want to look at it, he didn't find anything new. So, we have to assume his main target is, and always has been, prostitutes. Where are we with our three missing women?'

'Still missing,' Sian said.

'Thanks for that insight, Sian,' Matilda said.

'Look, I know I couldn't add more victims to our list,' Finn began. 'Which, obviously, I'm pleased about, but I had a good look at the victims we do have and we can see a pattern emerge. Firstly, he strangles his victims and hides them so they're not found. He's obviously going to be nervous he'll get caught. When he doesn't, it increases his confidence and he starts to really enjoy himself. He moves from strangulation to beating and strangling. He's verging on torturing his victims: getting a thrill out of watching them in agony before killing them. He's also started leaving them out in the open. He wants us to find them. He wants us to know how clever he is. So, the next step is that he's going to involve himself in the investigation.'

'Wait, before you go all *Silence of the Lambs* on us,' Christian said. 'Lucy Pickering wasn't strangled. She was buried alive.'

Finn nodded. 'Re-reading the post-mortem report I found that she was strangled before she was buried. It is just possible that the killer thought she was dead when he buried her.'

'You can't know that for sure,' Christian said.

'No. But looking at all the other victims, there is no evidence to suggest he buried the others alive. As horrific as it is, I think it's an anomaly.'

'I'm sure her parents will be comforted by the fact the agonising death of their daughter was an anomaly.' Christian rolled his eyes.

'Finn wasn't being flippant, Christian,' Sian said. 'He's made a valid point. We know that serial killers sometimes stand among the crowd when a body is discovered and watch the police at work. We've had gawkers here. Maybe he's been among them.'

'If he hasn't,' Finn said, 'I think we can expect a call from him very soon.'

The room fell silent while they all took this in.

'The press conference, that Rebecca woman giving the interview, the police presence at the woods, he knows we're onto him, doesn't he?' Sian asked Finn, her face grave. He nodded a reply. 'And he'll know we're no closer to him so he'll up his game again to the next level.'

Finn gave another nod.

'He's going to start playing with us, isn't he?'

'I think he may do, yes,' Finn said, subdued.

'Bastard,' Sian spat.

'In that case, we need to catch him before he starts with his mind games,' Matilda said. 'Zofia, did you get anywhere with the registration numbers of the vehicles surrounding the area Carly Roberts was killed?'

'Yes,' she said, scrabbling around on her desk. 'All the

vehicles we identified have been checked out. Not all were local, obviously, but they all have alibis.'

'So, how did the killer get to and from the murder site?' Sian asked. 'He had to have used a car.'

'Maybe he did. Maybe he lied. And maybe he got someone to cover up for him,' Matilda said. 'Zofia, how many cars were identified?'

'Two hundred and eleven.'

'Jesus!'

'One of them has to be our killer,' Matilda said.

'So what do we do? Bring all two hundred and eleven in for questioning?' Christian asked.

'No. Zofia said not all of the vehicles were driven by local people. However, we can assume our killer is a Sheffielder. He knows the area. He knows where to hide the bodies without being detected. I also think this isn't a young killer we're looking for. This is a very confident man who, for whatever reason, feels slightly demeaned in his life and needs the killings to boost his masculinity.'

'Why would he do that?' Scott asked.

'There are all kinds of reasons. He could have been made redundant and ended up losing his car and house. Maybe he was married and his wife left him for a younger man. I don't know, Scott.' Matilda was growing agitated.

'All serial killers want to get caught. Some know they do, others don't,' Finn said. He looked cool and calm, the antithesis of Matilda.

'That makes no sense,' Scott said.

Finn gave a wry smile. 'Some want to get caught so they can enjoy the fame and glory of being a prolific serial killer. Others don't so they can continue killing for as long as possible. However, when they're caught, there's a whole other level of notoriety that goes with being a killer. Once this guy is caught, he'll get an even bigger buzz out of being such an infamous murderer.'

The room fell silent while they all took this in.

'So, where do we go from here, then?' Sian asked.

'If he's going to step up his game to the next level, we have to step up our game too,' Matilda said. 'I will not let this man claim another victim.'

Chapter Forty-Six

'You wanted to see me?' Zofia asked from the doorway to Matilda's office.

'Yes. Come on in. Close the door and sit down.'

'Have I done anything wrong?' she asked. She had a look of fear on her face.

'Not at all,' Matilda smiled. 'You did excellent work on the registration numbers. It can't have been an interesting task.'

'No, but it was an important one.'

Matilda's smile grew. 'Zofia, I've been given the go-ahead by the ACC for an undercover operation and I'd like to know how you'd feel about taking on the role of a prostitute to try and catch the killer.'

Zofia's face lit up. 'I'd love it. Wow. Thanks for trusting me.'

There's no one else for me to trust.

'You're welcome. The thing is,' Matilda said, lowering her voice and leaning closer, 'I'm going to ask something of you that needs to remain private between us.'

'Oh?'

Matilda nodded. 'I'd like you to stay behind this evening when everyone has left. There are parts of this operation that need to be strictly need-to-know.' She looked over Zofia's shoulder and out into the suite. Her eyes met Sian's. Sian's face was grave. It was Matilda who looked away first.

'Do you have anything planned for this weekend?' Scott asked Zofia. They were the last two officers in the suite.

'My bathroom needs cleaning, but that's about it,' she said with a hint of a chuckle.

'Are you seeing anyone at the moment?'

'No. I had a date a few weeks ago. As soon as I told him I was a detective he went white.'

'Oh.'

'Not the first time that's happened either. Some men can't seem to accept a woman in a powerful role. You wouldn't think it was the twenty-first century when you get chatting to them. There are still some men who think women should stay at home, clean the house and have babies.'

'Not very modern of them.'

Matilda came out of her office putting her coat on. 'Are we ready?'

Zofia looked to Scott.

'Don't worry, he's part of our conspiracy,' she smiled.

The drive to Matilda's house was conducted in relative silence. Scott was driving with Matilda in the front passenger seat and Zofia lounging in the back. It was early evening, not quite six o'clock, yet it was dark outside, and a cold wind was blowing. In the early hours of Sunday morning, the clocks would go back by one hour, making the nights longer than the days. Matilda loved this time of year. Although, this year, she wasn't revelling in the isolation of the dark winter months as much as she did in previous years. Getting shot had knocked her confidence. She was more fearful of her surroundings. Thank goodness her sister was staying with her and Scott lived above the garage. She'd be a total basket case if completely alone. Yet there were times when she looked forward to being alone again. Why couldn't her mind settle, for crying out loud?

'Wow, you have a gorgeous house, ma'am,' Zofia said as the Range Rover turned the corner, triggering the sensors and lighting up the building.

'You don't have to call me ma'am outside of the station. In fact, I'd rather you didn't call me it in the station.'

'What do I call you?'

'Call me Matilda.'

'While she's in earshot,' Scott smiled.

Scott pulled up in front of the garages. There was no point in parking inside as he was going to be driving Zofia home.

Matilda turned around in her seat. 'Zofia, are you one hundred per cent happy about working undercover? This is where you can back out if you're not comfortable with it.'

'I am,' she said firmly.

'You will be looked after. I promise you.'

Matilda had spent most of the afternoon on the phone with her sister explaining her plan and asking if she would help. She said yes straightaway, then changed her mind, then changed it back again. 'It's about time I did something daring and exciting,' she'd said.

Once inside, drinks and snacks offered, Matilda and Zofia

stood in front of the fire and Matilda introduced everybody. Bev and Sarah she already knew. She hadn't met Harriet and they shook hands.

'Right then, down to business.' Matilda clapped her hands together.

'Why do I get the feeling we're plotting a heist?' Scott said.

'First of all,' Matilda began, 'I want to say that whatever we discuss in this room stays between us six. Understood?' She looked around at the nodding heads before continuing. 'Now, before this week, we knew of four confirmed dead women and three missing. Now, that combined number could be as high as eleven. We are dealing with a very dangerous man, and he needs stopping before more lives are lost. My boss has approved an undercover operation and Zofia here has agreed to play the part of a prostitute.'

'We'll look after you,' Bev said.

'Now, this is where we go off the book, and nobody outside of this room must know. That includes Christian, Sian and Finn,' she added as an aside to Scott and Zofia. 'As I said, our killer is dangerous. He's also highly intelligent to have got away with it for so long. He will definitely notice a couple of plain-clothes detectives parked nearby. So, Scott and I will be nearby, but not so close as to be seen. However, although Bev and Sarah will keep an eye on you, Zofia, they will occasionally need to work. You need someone with you who doesn't match the demographic of our victims so will go unnoticed by him, but who also has your back.'

'That's where I come in,' Harriet chimed up.

'Harriet will be on hand in case any regular punter tries it on with you, or the killer is spotted. We don't know who he is, or what he looks like, but any punter who seems to want to desperately get you in the car will be a person of interest to us.

Scott and I will then approach him and bring him in for questioning. How does that sound?'

Zofia looked nervous. 'Fine.'

'Are you sure?'

'Yes.'

'I'll make sure you're wired, and you'll have a tracking device fitted, though I hope we won't have cause to use it. We'll start tomorrow night and every night until we catch him. Now, who's for a glass of wine?'

Chapter Forty-Seven

Sian and Stuart had the house to themselves. Anthony, on his first night out of plaster in eight weeks, had called his mates and arranged a night out. Belinda was out with her girlfriend. Danny was at a sleepover and Gregory was staying with his grandparents. It was rare for them to have a night to themselves. When it did happen, they usually curled up on the sofa with a takeaway and a Bruce Willis film. However, tonight, Sian had decided to give the kitchen a scrub down.

'Is everything all right?' Stuart asked, entering the kitchen.

'Fine. Why?' she asked, her head in the oven.

'You've been quiet since you came home.'

'Have I?'

'Yes. And you're cleaning that oven like it's the most important job in the world. What's on your mind?'

'Nothing,' she said, her voice echoing inside the oven.

'Sian, as much as I love staring at your arse, is there any chance you can come out of the oven so I can talk to you properly?'

Sian stood up. She wiped her brow with the back of her hand. She had grease stains on her face.

'What's wrong?' she asked.

'That's my question to you.'

'Nothing's wrong,' she said, going over to the sink to wash her hands.

'I know that's a lie. You hate cleaning the oven. You only go mad with a sponge like that when there's something bugging you.'

She dried her hands on the towel. 'I got the feeling today that I'm being shut out.'

He frowned. 'At work? Who by?'

'Matilda.'

'Why would she do that?'

'I've no idea. She's always told me everything before, kept me in the loop of everything that's going on, but today she had secret meetings with Scott and Zofia. And she had this look on her face like she's planning something.'

'Such as?'

'I don't know,' she said, throwing the towel down in frustration.

'It can't be the case you're working on, can it? I mean, you need to all be on the same page for that.'

'Exactly. It's just… Oh, I don't know. Maybe I'm reading too much into it.'

'Come here.' He held out his hand for her to take.

It was a while before she moved away from the sink. She reached her arm out and he wrapped his hand around hers. He led her into the living room and sat her down on the sofa, then went back into the kitchen and returned with a bottle of white wine and two glasses. He poured a large measure in each and handed one to his wife with a smile on his face. She smiled back, took the glass and had a very large swig.

'Erm, you're not planning on getting drunk, are you? You're supposed to be picking Belinda up at eleven.'

'I'm having one, to be sociable,' he smiled.

'Make sure it is only one.'

'Do you think Matilda's changed? Since the shooting, I mean?' Stuart asked, getting back on topic.

'We've all changed.'

'I mean with her approach to work. Is she still the right person for the job?'

Sian frowned while she thought.

'Did you hear me?' he asked when she didn't reply.

'I did. I'm just not sure how to answer.'

'So, she has changed then.'

'Yes.'

'And you're worried her judgement is being impaired?'

'Yes,' she replied quietly.

'What are you going to do?'

'I don't know. Before the shooting I would have said I'd chat to Adele, but they're not talking anymore either.'

'Why not?'

'I don't know. It's like she's cutting everyone out of her life.'

'Well, from her point of view, you can understand that. She nearly died in that shooting. She's probably frightened of letting people get close in case something like that happens again and they'll be left hurt. Or maybe she thinks something will happen to them and if she isn't close to them, she won't feel the pain. Don't forget, she had a miscarriage, and she didn't know she was pregnant. It's going to have deeply affected her.'

'And she pushed Daniel away too.'

'It sounds like she's got major trust issues.'

'But I've known her for years. I've worked with her for so long. I didn't think she'd push me away.'

'I hate to say this, Sian, but I think you may have to go over her head. Tell that new ACC what she's doing.'

'I can't do that. Mind you…'

'What?'

'Well, when I got back this afternoon, Scott told me that Matilda had given Christian a good shouting at in her office. She's never shouted at Christian.'

'It sounds like she's on the verge of a breakdown. You really need to talk to the ACC. Take Christian with you. It'll look better if you both voice your concerns.'

She took another large drink. 'I'll think about it.'

Chapter Forty-Eight

Dermot Salter pulled up in his ancient Volvo on Hicks Street. He was dressed for the cold night, wearing black corduroy trousers and walking shoes, a thick padded anorak that had seen better days and a bobbled beanie hat that was a size too big. He climbed out of the car, locked it with the key then went to the boot. Inside was a large plastic tub of sandwiches and two Thermos flasks of tea. He loaded the flasks into a backpack and struggled to get it onto his shoulders. He grabbed the tub, slammed the boot closed and looked around to see anyone in need of something to eat and a hot cup of tea.

He noticed a few cars driving slowly but couldn't see any of the women. What those two young detectives had said to him was running around his mind. Was it possible one of the punters was killing the women, his friends? He hoped not. There were a couple who were unpleasant towards him, some who often took advantage of his kind nature, but most were happy to see him and grateful for a hot drink on such a cold night.

He saw Becca first. Despite her face being blurred on the news, he'd recognised her voice as she gave an interview saying how the police didn't care for them. She was one of the women who'd taken advantage of him. Every time she opened her mouth, she was pleading for any spare cash he had. And he was pretty sure she'd stolen from his house when he'd taken her back to his to have a bath and a nap in the spare room.

'Hello, Becca, are you keeping well?' he asked. His voice was shaking in the cold.

'As well as usual. Got some sandwiches for me? What flavour?'

He removed the lid from the tub. He'd spent all afternoon making them. 'There's cheese and pickle, cheese and ham, plain ham, and chicken.'

'I'll have one of each.' She grabbed them and stuffed them into her tiny handbag.

'I've got a cup of tea if you'd like.'

'Anything stronger in it?'

'No.'

'You should put a tot of whiskey in it, Dermot, it's parky out here at this time of year. Here, you couldn't lend us a tenner, could you? I've got no gas at all in the flat.'

'I haven't got any money on me, Becca.'

'I tell you what,' she said, rummaging in her bag. 'Here's me gas card. You can put money on it at most shops. Premier will still be open.' She was interrupted by a car flashing its headlights at her. 'That's for me. Here.' She gave him the card. 'You may as well put twenty on it while you're at it. I'll pay you back next week.'

She trotted off towards the car on impossibly high heels. She didn't even thank him for the sandwiches. He looked down at the gas card and tucked it into his pocket. He'd put money on it, but knew he'd never get the cash from her.

He walked further along the road looking for other street workers he could provide with refreshments. An Audi pulled up at the side of the road and turned its lights off. As Dermot approached, he leaned down to look into the car. He smiled as he recognised the man behind the wheel. He rapped on the window with his glove-covered knuckles. Slowly, the window opened.

'I thought it was you,' Dermot said. 'Another new car? Very nice.'

'What do you want, Dermot?' He asked.

'I had the police come to my house yesterday.'

'Oh?' This piqued his interest.

'I'm sure you know about some of the women being killed, and some have gone missing as well. The police wanted to know if I knew anything about it, what with me coming down here most weeks.'

'What did you tell them?'

'Well, I told them I didn't know anything. I don't. The thing is though, well, I don't mean to be personal, but I've seen you here more than any of the others, and I wondered if you'd seen anything, or if any of the women had mentioned to you about being scared of a particular … you know, punter?'

'No,' he answered quickly.

'Are you sure? These women need protecting. We need to keep our eyes and ears open for anyone who might harm them.'

'Dermot, let me ask you a question. When you're in the supermarket buying your fillings for your sandwiches, do you think about the woman at the till serving you?'

'What? Erm, no.'

'Do you worry about her? Think she needs protecting?'

'No.'

'There you go then. These women are doing a job. They're providing a service and I'm paying for it. They take the risks with the job. Now, take your charity elsewhere, all right?' The window smoothly closed.

He watched as Dermot walked away, sandwich tub in hand, backpack with flasks of tea weighing him down. Sad fucker.

He waited, his mind whirring with possibilities. If the police were finally sniffing around, and they'd already clocked Dermot, how long would it be before Dermot told them about regular punters, about him? He used a different car every time so Dermot couldn't give them a registration number, but he could give them a very good description of him.

There was a tap on the window, making him jump. He looked across and saw Jodie smiling at him. He unlocked the door and she pulled it open.

'Hello Ed, I thought I recognised you. Loving the new car.' She slammed the door behind her. 'Are these heated seats?'

'Yeah.'

'Thank God. It's perishing out there tonight. Are we going somewhere more private or do you want to do it here?' She asked when he didn't make an effort to move.

'Sorry, I was just thinking about something.' He turned on the engine. 'We'll just go over onto Stanley Fields tonight; I've got to get back.'

Fucking Dermot. All day he'd been looking forward to coming out tonight, squeezing the life out of another bitch. If he did it now, the police would go back to see Dermot and he'd tell them about him, and the hunt would be on.

He didn't like Jodie. She made too much noise. She

obviously thought it sounded like she was enjoying herself, but it annoyed him. While he leaned back in his seat and she was sucking him off, making noises like she was enjoying a hot cup of tea, an idea came to him; he'd kill Dermot. And he wouldn't be strangling him either. It would really throw the police off the scent.

Chapter Forty-Nine

Matilda woke up with a start. Her duvet was half hanging off the bed. Her hair was wet with sweat and her breathing was heavy. Another bad dream. She tried to think what this one was about, but it had already faded. *Thank God for that.*

The nightmares scared her. Sometimes they were real. She was standing in the car park, looking up at the gunman as he pointed the Heckler & Koch at her. He squeezed the trigger and she dropped to the ground. That had happened. She'd read the reports and seen the CCTV footage. Other times, the nightmares were a product of her overactive imagination. She'd be in her hospital bed late at night, unable to sleep, and Jake would enter her room. He'd be covered with the blood from his victims, a gun in each hand. He'd tell her who was dead and that it was all her fault. Then he'd begin slowly killing her: a bullet in the foot, one in the ankle, another in the knee, moving slowly up her body. She'd be in agony, screaming for help that wouldn't come before the final bullet in the centre of her forehead put her out of her misery.

She kicked off the duvet and climbed out of bed. It was still pitch black outside so could only be the small hours of the morning. A long time to be awake. She struggled into her dressing gown, pushed her feet into her slippers and padded downstairs. She needed a drink. Alcohol was tempting, but a milky cup of tea was probably best.

There was a light on in the living room, which cast an eerie shadow in the crack at the bottom of the door. It still felt strange having a house full of people. She pushed the door open and saw Bev sitting on the sofa.

'Bev?'

'Sorry? Did I wake you?' she asked, her voice hoarse.

'No. I had a bad dream. A side effect from a bullet to the head,' she smiled. 'What are you doing up?'

'I couldn't sleep. I made myself a cup of tea. You don't mind, do you?'

'No. Of course not. I'm going to make one myself. Fancy another?'

She smiled and held up her empty mug.

When Matilda returned, she had two mugs of tea on a tray and a packet of Bourbon biscuits.

'You can't have a cuppa without a biscuit,' Matilda said, placing the tray on the coffee table.

'I was reading through some of these cards,' Bev said, indicating the pile of letters and cards Matilda had received in the wake of the shooting. 'People have said some lovely things.'

'Yes. I really must reply to them at some point,' she said, sitting down and grabbing a few of them. She leaned back on the sofa, tucking her legs beneath her. She read a card and smiled. 'I have no idea who this is from: *We wish you all the best in your recovery. If you need anything, give us a call. All our love,*

Edward and Jane. I don't know an Edward and Jane,' she laughed. 'I'm sure it will come back to me.'

'Do you have memory loss?'

'I did. I couldn't remember anything of the day of the shooting when I woke up. I had no recollection of why I was in hospital. I get flashbacks, which can be quite frightening, especially if they happen while at work.'

'How do you cope, knowing that there was someone who wanted you dead?'

Matilda thought for a long moment. 'You know you're not going to be loved being a police officer. I suppose if Jake was still alive and in prison, I'd be apprehensive. Knowing he's dead helps with the healing process. I think.' She frowned.

'His brother's in prison. He orchestrated it. Doesn't that scare you?'

She swallowed her emotion. 'It does. Fortunately, Steve Harrison is now in a supermax prison. Fingers crossed he won't slip through the net or there isn't an admin error that puts him on day release.' She gave a hollow laugh.

Bev studied Matilda for a while. 'You're still frightened, aren't you?'

Matilda looked up from her mug of tea. 'I'm petrified,' she said, her voice shaking. 'A door slams and it sounds like a bullet and I think someone is shooting at me again. Every time the phone rings and I don't recognise the number, I think it's someone taunting me like Jake did.' She wiped away a tear as it fell down her cheek. 'What can I do?'

Bev shrugged. 'Have you considered changing career?'

'I'd still be scared of the phone ringing.'

'Are you seeing a therapist?'

'I am. I have a session next Thursday. I need to be more open with her. Tell her absolutely everything.'

'Have you been holding back?'

Matilda smiled and nodded. 'I have major trust issues when it comes to therapists.'

'I have major trust issues full stop,' Bev said with a pained smile. 'Matilda, can I ask you a massive favour?'

'Sure.'

'Will you help me?'

'How?'

'Me and Sarah, we're too old for this game. The flat we're renting isn't exactly above board. We really shouldn't be living there. We can't get a proper job because we don't have an official address. Could you help us get a council flat?'

Matilda smiled. 'I'll have a word with someone. If I don't know anyone, Sian definitely will. She knows everyone.'

'Thanks,' she said, smiling warmly.

'I suppose I'd better see if I can get back to sleep or I'll be no good to anyone tomorrow.' Matilda stood up and headed for the door.

'Matilda,' Bev said.

Matilda turned around. Bev was in front of her.

'I appreciate everything you're doing,' she said. Tentatively, she stepped forward towards Matilda, her arms opening. She gave her a hug which was stilted and awkward, but it meant more to them both than words could ever say.

Chapter Fifty

Saturday 26th October

'Guess who was waiting for me bright and early in the car park?' Finn asked Matilda as she entered the suite.

Matilda looked DC Cotton up and down. He was in a clean, crisp suit, his hair was neat, and he looked fresh and ready for whatever the day had to throw at him. Standing beside him, Matilda felt like Vera Stanhope.

'If you're taking anything to look so bright and breezy so early in the morning, I promise not to suspend you as long as you give me some of it.'

'Ten hours sleep and a fry-up,' he said.

'Bloody hell. It takes me three nights to have ten hours sleep.' She walked past him and headed for her office. 'So, who was waiting for you in the car park?'

'Alistair Tripp.'

'Please tell me he had a dead prostitute over his shoulder.'

'No such luck. He gave me a very detailed account of his whereabouts for the dates we gave him.'

'And?'

'A couple are suspicious as he doesn't have much of an alibi, but what he does have is concrete.'

Matilda sat at her desk. 'Well, I didn't think he was a credible suspect anyway. If it had been Danny Hanson, I would have had him locked up in minutes, alibi or no alibi. Hang on a minute, it's Saturday, what are you doing in on a Saturday?'

'I just wanted to check something.'

'I don't think so, Finn. Look, you're doing sterling work on this case, but you've already spent a full night here, which I'm grateful yet also incredibly sorry for. Take the day off. Take that lovely wife of yours to lunch or something.'

'I don't mind.'

'Well, I do. Go on, go home.'

She watched from her office while Finn turned off his computer, grabbed his coat and left. The door closed, plunging Matilda into silence. She sat back in her chair and looked around her tiny office. She hated this suite and the cramped space she was forced to work in. She knew it was this that was having a negative effect on her and caused her to fly off the handle at Christian yesterday. She really should apologise to him, too.

Her phone vibrated in her pocket. She pulled it out and saw it was Harriet calling.

'You left early this morning,' Harriet said.

'I couldn't sleep.'

'Where are you? Or shouldn't I ask?'

'It's probably best if you don't ask,' Matilda said with a smile.

'I thought as much. Do me a favour, take a look out of your window.'

'Why?'

'I wish you wouldn't question everything. Just look out of your window.'

Matilda stood up, pulled back the blind and looked out to see her sister sitting on the bonnet of her Range Rover.

'What are you doing here?'

'I've come to rescue you. We're going to drive out to Bakewell and have lunch in a gorgeous restaurant and go walking in the hills, get some fresh air into you.'

'That sounds lovely, but I have work to do.'

'You're working tonight. You can take today off. It's Saturday after all.'

'Harriet…'

'I should also warn you that failure to leave that building and get in the car will force me to continue to sit here and my great big arse will leave a lasting and expensive impression on your lovely car.'

'I'll be five minutes.'

Matilda ended the call. She needed a day away from dead prostitutes, and the autumnal countryside air sounded perfect. She felt herself relaxing already. She was about to leave the suite when she saw Christian enter.

'Christian, it's Saturday, what are you doing here?'

'I … erm … I wanted to go through the timeline of victims again. It kept me awake last night. I can't seem to get my head around there being possibly eleven dead people out there and we didn't realise they were the work of one man,' he said, stealing a glance down the corridor.

'I know. It's hard to fathom,' she said. 'Listen, Christian, I want to apologise for snapping at you yesterday like I did. It was unprofessional and uncalled for. You've done an amazing job of leading the team while I've been recovering, and I appreciate your efforts.'

Christian had been softening through her speech until she said efforts, as if he had tried his best, bless him, but hadn't quite succeeded. He knew he'd performed excellently as acting DCI.

'Thanks,' he smiled, reluctantly.

'So, am I forgiven?'

'I've already forgotten it.' His smile grew.

'Well, I'm being kidnapped by my sister. She's taking me to Bakewell for lunch, and then I'm going to have a nap and prepare for the undercover op tonight. Don't stay here all day, you've got a family who'd like to see you from time to time.'

'I won't.'

He watched as Matilda left the room and turned right heading for the stairs. He visibly relaxed.

Less than a minute later, the door opened, and Sian entered.

'I saw her as I came out of the toilets. I thought it best to hang back.'

'I had no idea she was coming in this morning.'

'Me neither. She didn't say anything yesterday.'

'Another item to add to the list,' Christian said.

'Right then.' Sian clapped her hands together. 'Kettle on, strong coffees and a bloody good chat about this before we do anything, agreed?'

'Agreed.'

Chapter Fifty-One

The tension was palpable as the time drew nearer for the undercover operation to begin. The sun hadn't risen at all today and heavy clouds had hung over the steel city, threatening to unleash a heavy rainstorm. It never materialised. As afternoon turned into early evening, the clouds began to disperse, and a cold breeze picked up.

Zofia was sat on one of Matilda's sofas in the living room. She'd arrived an hour early. Her nervousness was etched on her face. She was wearing more make-up than she usually did, and it made her look older, as if she was trying to hide the signs of ageing and the ravages of a painful past. She wore a thin white shirt. It was tight and the first two buttons were undone, revealing an ample cleavage. Her skirt was short, and she kept pulling it down, obviously uncomfortable in showing too much flesh. She was a very attractive young woman. Matilda hoped she was what the killer would go for.

'Here you go,' Matilda said, entering the room and handing her a hip flask. 'I've filled it with whiskey. Keep taking the odd sip and it'll warm you up. Pop it in your bag.'

'I haven't brought a bag,' she said, her eyes wide with fear.

'That's all right. I think I might have one you can borrow.'

'I'm so sorry,' she said nervously.

'Don't worry about it.' Matilda gave her a reassuring smile. 'It's not too late to back out if you're worried.'

'No. I'll be fine. It's good of your sister to volunteer to come out with me.'

'She'll be with you the whole time. You have nothing to be concerned about.' Matilda sat down next to her. 'When we were young, I was going out with this lad. Adrian Shepherd. He was almost ten years older than me, but I was going through my rebellious teenage phase. Anyway, I thought I knew everything and was being very sophisticated. Looking back, I was being a pain in the arse. Harriet could see this bloke was no good. I can't remember what I told her, but something must have resonated with her as she followed me. We were in his car, and he was trying to... Well, I don't need to go into all the details. Next thing, the car door opens, and Harriet drags Adrian out and gives him a good kicking.'

Zofia was smiling. 'She was looking after you.'

'She was. And now she's doing it again,' she said almost wistfully. 'And she'll look after you, too.'

'Thank you for saying that.'

'You're welcome.'

Scott entered the living room. 'Right, Zofia, I've got the wire working if you'll just—' He stopped when he saw what she was wearing. 'Ah.' He blushed.

'Maybe I should fit her wire,' Matilda said.

'That's probably for the best.' He handed it to her and quickly left the room.

'Aren't men pathetic?' Matilda said.

Bev and Sarah had gone on ahead. For them, it was a regular night at work. An hour later, Harriet and Zofia joined them at the junction where Hicks Street joined Mowbray Street. It was pitch dark. The surrounding offices and factories were closed, shutters down, car parks empty. What streetlights were working were all dim and offered very little protection. There were many side roads and back alleys the women could use to take a punter. It was yet another rundown area of Sheffield the council had lost interest in.

'Are you two warm enough?' Bev asked. She was wearing her trademark faux zebra print jacket.

'I'm freezing,' Zofia said. 'I don't know if it's nerves or the cold.' Her arms were folded tight against her chest.

'We just received a dirty look from that woman down there,' Harriet said, nodding towards a tall, slim woman with badly dyed black hair who kept staring in their direction.

'That's Becca. Ignore her. She's the one who gave that interview to Sky. I bet she's pissed because they didn't give her much for it and she'll have already spent it.'

'She was probably hoping being on TV would have got her on the next series of *I'm a Celebrity*,' Sarah added.

'Well, she's halfway there. She went with that footballer, didn't she?'

'I'm surprised she didn't sell her story once his wife got pregnant.'

A parked car flashed its headlights, causing them all to turn. Bev looked at her watch.

'He's early. He said he wouldn't be here until ten. I'll see you lot in a bit. Take care.' She trotted over to the car precariously on such high heels. The front passenger door was unlocked. She opened it, smiled and seductively climbed in, flashing her long, skinny legs.

'Alan Parker,' Sarah said once the car had driven away. 'He's been going to Bev for years. His wife's disabled. She had a car crash, barely recognises him, but he looks after her round the clock. Bless him. Just popping over to see Josie. She owes me a fiver. I know she's got it.' She trotted off over the road.

'I don't know how they can do this,' Zofia said. 'I know they're getting paid so it's earning them a living, but… I mean, it's sex, isn't it? It's supposed to be enjoyable. They can't be having fun.'

'Well, they're not having fun. It's work,' Harriet said.

'But sex is such a personal thing. It should be romantic and special. Not something you do in the back of a car for a tenner.'

'I certainly couldn't do it. They're very brave women.'

A car slowed down next to them. The driver leaned over the passenger seat, looked at Harriet and drove on.

'Bloody hell, this doesn't do much for your self-esteem, does it?'

———————————

Matilda and Scott had taken to the warmth of a nearby pub, the Kelham Kitchen and Wine Bar. They could hear everything Zofia and Harriet were saying and warned them of such as they let them out of the car, in case either of them wanted to say anything nasty.

Matilda found a quiet table by the window and Scott brought over the drinks: half a pint of lager for him (his only alcoholic drink of the night) and an orange juice for Matilda. She shouldn't be drinking alcohol with the amount of medication she was still taking following the shooting, but the odd glass was fine. Not tonight, however. He also threw down on the table several packets of crisps. They were in for a long night.

'How do you think they're getting on?' he asked.

'I think they're bored.'

'Why?'

'They're naming films beginning with every letter of the alphabet. I can't believe they've both got stuck on G.'

'*God's Own Country, Ghost, Guardians of the Galaxy, Green Zone, Galaxy Quest*—'

'Do you want to swap places with one of them?' Matilda interrupted.

'I don't have the legs for what they're wearing,' he smiled.

Matilda smiled and took a sip of her orange juice. She looked out of the window. It was Saturday night, but the streets were relatively empty. Where were the drinkers, the partygoers, the nightclubbers, the punters and the killers?

'Did you have a nice day in Bakewell?' he asked.

'Lovely,' she smiled. 'I haven't had a meal like that in months. It's good to breathe in some country air, too.'

'So, are you going to tell me what's going on between you and Adele?' Scott asked.

'What are you talking about?' she said, looking inside the open packet. 'Look at this,' she showed Scott. 'I'm sure there used to be more crisps in a bag. Fewer crisps and more money.'

'Stop changing the subject. We're stuck here for the night. I'm not going to spend the next few hours talking about crisps. What's happened with Adele? She hasn't been to the house at all this year. She only visited you once in hospital. You two were closer than you are with Harriet.'

Matilda chewed slowly. She swallowed, took a drink of cold orange juice and leaned back in the wooden seat.

'She'd been drinking.'

'Who had?'

'Adele. When she came to see me in hospital. I was sat up in bed and she just stood in the doorway. She had a face like thunder. I smiled, said I was pleased to see her, but she just stood there. I could see a vein throbbing in her neck. I knew she was angry. I tried to speak, but the words wouldn't come. I told her I was sorry about Chris and sorry I couldn't be at the funeral. She didn't say anything. She didn't move.'

'Adele, come and sit down.'

'I'm not staying.'

'Adele, I'm so so sorry for what…'

'Don't. I don't want to hear it. I'm tired of hearing people say how sorry they are. He was after you, Matilda. Jake was trying to kill you. Why did he have to kill my Chris?'

'I don't know.'

'If he'd done it, if he'd killed you, that would have been it. He'd have left. Job done. There was no need for him to go to the school.'

'That's not what would have happened, Adele. He went there to kill his wife. He went there to cause carnage.'

'They'd have caught him sooner. Christian and Sian and your team would have caught him much sooner if they hadn't been worrying about how you were doing. They wasted valuable time concerned for your health. If you'd just died in that car park my Chris would still be alive now.'

'You can't believe that, surely.'

'He was coming for you, Matilda. And he killed my son.' Tears were streaming down her face. She was barely audible.

'If I could take his place, I would, in a heartbeat, but I can't change what happened.'

'Chris is dead. And it's all your fault.'

'She actually said it was your fault?' Scott asked.

Matilda nodded. There were tears in her eyes. She didn't dare risk speaking in case they fell.

'I've spoken to her loads; she's never mentioned any of that to me.'

Matilda shrugged.

'I can't believe that's what she thinks.'

'I tried ringing her, texting her, many times since I was discharged. She's ignored them all.'

'Do you want me to have a word with her?'

'No. She needs to realise the truth herself. I'll be there for her, whenever she wants me. There's nothing I can do until then.'

'But...'

Matilda's phone beeped an incoming text. She looked at it and smiled. 'Harriet's been offered ten quid for a blow job. She wondered if it was good value for money or not.'

They both laughed.

Chapter Fifty-Two

Monday 28th October

The undercover operation on Saturday and Sunday night wasn't a success. In fact, Sunday night had been relatively quiet, and it had been Bev's idea to finish early. Matilda gave Zofia the day off. They'd try again tonight.

The morning briefing didn't reveal anything new to add to the investigation. The dog detection team had been to five different areas of woodland in Sheffield and hadn't uncovered anything. Matilda was keen for the search to continue but Sergeant Inneson was worried all the negative results would have an impact on the dogs. They'd think they were failing in their duties and that would result in lacklustre performances in the future.

Matilda was sat in her office, once more flicking through the files of the victims, when her mobile rang. She looked at the screen and saw it was Pat Campbell calling.

'Good morning, Pat, what can I do for you?'

'Matilda, I need you to come to Philip and Sally's house straightaway,' she said, the concern evident in her voice.

'Why? What's happened?'

'Carl's run away.'

Matilda didn't tell anyone where she was going. She grabbed her coat from the back of her chair and ran out of the room, leaving everyone watching her with their mouths open. Christian looked to Sian, gave her the nod and left the room. Five minutes later, Sian followed.

'I don't like this,' Sian said quietly as she met Christian outside the ACC's office.

'Neither do I, but he needs to be made aware of what's going on. This is a massive investigation and if it goes wrong because of Matilda's actions then we're all screwed. I will not risk my career for her. Not anymore.'

'You're right,' she nodded, though it was clear from the rabbit-caught-in-the-headlights look on her face that she would rather be anywhere else in the world right now.

Christian knocked lightly on the door. He was asked to come in.

'Christian, Sian, lovely to see you both. Have a seat,' ACC Benjamin Ridley said. 'I was going to pop down later to see how the undercover operation went over the weekend.'

'Oh,' Christian said. 'Uneventful, I'm afraid. Still, we can't expect results on the first night.'

'No. Well, as long as it doesn't go on too long. Undercover work is incredibly costly. How's ... what's she called, the one posing as a prostitute?'

'DC Zofia Nowak,' Sian said.

'Yes. How was she?'

'She seemed to manage very well.'

'Good.' He sat back in his tall chair and knotted his fingers together as he studied Christian and Sian. 'Something tells me you're not here for operational purposes.'

They both exchanged glances.

'I didn't think so,' Ridley smiled. 'Come on then, out with it.'

'Sir, with all respect,' Christian began. 'Sian and I have worked with Matilda Darke for a number of years. She's an incredibly capable detective and her record speaks for itself. However, we both think that she's still suffering the effects of the shooting, that maybe she's returned to work too soon.'

'Okay,' he nodded. 'Can you elaborate?'

Christian took a deep breath. He looked uncomfortable and cleared his throat three times before speaking. 'She's become very quick-tempered. She's undermining my capabilities. She's hiding things from the team; we're sure there's more to this undercover operation than she's letting on. When she's alone in her office I look up and she's just staring out of the window as if she's a million miles away. Her mind isn't settled.'

'I see,' he mused. 'DCI Darke's physical and psychological evaluation cleared her to return to active duties.'

'I'm aware of that—'

'The thing is,' Sian interrupted, 'Matilda hated being off work. The day she returned home in March after being discharged from the rehab centre, she was itching to get back to the station. She will have known everything that was going to be asked of her during the assessment and she'd have answered them accordingly.'

'You think she lied?'

'I think she lied to herself that she was well enough to return to work. She's convinced herself she's fine when she's anything but.'

Ridley thought for a moment, frowning, a deep furrow

appearing on his forehead. 'This investigation into the murdered prostitutes is all over the newspapers. I'm fielding calls all the time for an update and the Chief Constable is breathing down my neck for a result. I can't take DCI Darke off the case at such a crucial stage. It would look incredibly bad for the force.'

Christian looked crestfallen. 'Sir, I admire Matilda immensely, I don't want her taken off the case, but I think you need to be aware of the situation and the possible ramifications if this goes on without a result.'

He looked away while he chewed his lip, deep in thought. 'Okay, here's what we'll do. I want you to report to me, Christian, at the end of every day about DCI Darke's behaviour and performance, and we'll evaluate the situation on a day-by-day basis. I shall also get onto the police psychiatrist and ask them to have a succinct chat with her. In the meantime, if anything happens that warrants immediate attention, call me straightaway. Is that all right by you two?'

Christian nodded.

'Yes, sir,' Sian said.

Once out in the corridor with the door closed behind them, Sian leaned back against the wall.

'I feel like crying,' she said. 'I never thought I'd have to report Matilda of all people.'

'We haven't reported her.'

'No? It bloody feels like it.'

'It's for her own good, Sian. You said yourself that you're worried about her.'

'I am, but...'

'She needs help. She's not well enough to be back. You only have to look at her to see she's not getting enough sleep. Who knows what's going around her head late at night?'

'I hate myself for this.'

'I know. I hate myself, too. Still, look on the bright side, it's nearly Christmas,' Christian said with a false smile.

'And we could both be out of a job by then.'

Chapter Fifty-Three

The gates to the Meagan house in Dore were wide open when the taxi carrying Matilda pulled up at the side of the road. She threw a twenty-pound note at the driver, told him to keep the change and jumped out. She didn't even know how much the fare had been. She ran up the gravel driveway. The front door was opened by Pat before she even reached it.

'Pat, what's going on?'

'Come on in.'

In the hallway, the door closed behind them, Matilda expected to be greeting by two excitable Labradors. She wasn't.

'Sally got up this morning, came downstairs to make a coffee and she found this in the kitchen.' She handed Matilda a piece of paper torn from a notebook.

I shouldn't have come back home, I'm sorry. You expected me to be the same and so did I and we're all disappointed. I've seen you looking at each other and I can tell you're not happy. It doesn't feel right either when you hug me. It's like you're scared of something. I don't want to be the one to make you sad. You know I'm alive and that's the main thing. Thanks for looking for me.

Carl.

'He doesn't put any kisses on the bottom,' Pat pointed out.

'He doesn't address it to Mum and Dad either.'

'What do you think that means?'

'He doesn't consider them to be his parents anymore,' she said, looking at her. 'Has he taken the dogs with him?'

'Yes. There's food missing from the cupboards and money from Philip's wallet.'

'Shit.'

'Oh, Matilda, thank God you came,' Sally said as she came out of the living room. She looked pale and frightened. It took Matilda back to the early days of Carl's disappearance in 2015 and the agony of the unknown. 'He's run away. Why? Why would he do that?' she cried.

'I don't know, Sally. Did he say anything that gave you an idea he'd do something like this?'

She shook her head.

'He's barely spoken to us,' Philip said from the doorway to the lounge. He was wearing a creased rugby shirt and jeans. He looked gaunt. 'We've tried everything we can think of to get him to open up, tell us what's happened to him. We've given him space, told him everything that's been happening while he's been away, but he gave nothing back.'

'He's been so distant,' Sally said. 'I can feel him tense up when I hug him. He's not my little boy anymore. What did they do to him, Mat?'

Matilda held Sally by the shoulders. 'They didn't do anything to him, Sally. They looked after him. He's not been physically or mentally abused in any way, but you have to realise how scared he must have been for four years. It's a long time to be separated from you all. Now he's back, it's … well, it's strange and unfamiliar.'

'You need to find him for me, Mat. I can't lose him again, I can't. It'll kill me.'

Philip stepped forward. He grabbed his wife by the shoulders and held her tight. Her cries were muffled against his chest.

'I doubt he's gone far. I think he'll just want some time on his own, try and get his own head straight. I'll call the station and get as many officers as I can looking for him.'

The doorbell rang and they all froze. Pat, who was the closest, went over to it and looked through the spy hole.

'Shit. It's Danny Hanson.'

'What's he doing here?' Matilda asked.

'He was going to do an interview with Carl,' Philip said.

'I'll get rid of him,' Pat said. She opened the door just wide enough to squeeze through and closed it behind her.

'Can you think of anywhere he'd go?' Matilda asked.

Sally shook her head.

Philip looked up at her. 'It feels wrong saying this, but we don't know him anymore,' he said despondently.

Chapter Fifty-Four

As Matilda's office was empty, Christian took the opportunity to use it. He'd just sat down when there was a tiny rap on the glass door. He beckoned for Zofia to enter.

'Am I going undercover again tonight?' she asked.

'I believe so. Why? Don't you want to?'

'No. It's not that. It's just... Well, DCI Darke was going to have a word with me and I haven't seen her since this morning, and, well, time's getting on,' she said looking out of the window at the darkness.

Christian looked at his watch. He hadn't realised how the day had slipped by so quickly. Another day of being no closer to solving the case, not even a person of interest. He hadn't seen Matilda himself since before lunch. Where the hell was she?

'I tell you what, Zofia, go home now and get ready for going undercover this evening. If Matilda isn't back in time, I'll step in and monitor you,' he said, running his hand over his stubbled head.

'You?'

'Yes. Is that a problem?'

'No. It's just … no. Thank you.'

She quickly left the room and went over to Scott's desk. She leaned down and lowered her voice.

'Scott, Matilda's nowhere to be seen and DI Brady said he'll monitor me going undercover tonight if she doesn't come back. He doesn't know about Harriet being on the streets with me. What are we going to do?'

'Shit. I'll give Matilda a ring, see where she is.'

'Okay. I need to go home and…'

'Is there a problem?' Sian asked.

They both turned to look at her, guilty expressions on their faces.

'No,' Scott said.

'Anything I can help you with?'

'Not … that I'm aware of,' he said.

'I'm going to pop home and get changed for tonight,' Zofia said. She grabbed her coat and bag and couldn't leave the suite fast enough.

'Is everything all right, Scott?' Sian asked.

'Yes. Why? Shouldn't it?'

'You seemed very secretive with Zofia.'

'I think she's still a bit bothered by all this Paul Chattle business. She keeps asking how she's doing and if Matilda is happy with her work. I don't think she has as much self-confidence as she likes to make out.' He impressed himself with his quick-thinking lie.

'Should she be working undercover then?'

'Oh, yes, she's absolutely fine. A good result and she'll buck right up. I'm just going to the toilet,' he said, standing up, grabbing his mobile and leaving the suite.

Sian sat back in her chair, a perplexed look on her face. Something was going on. Things were being kept from her. Matilda was at the heart of it and she'd roped Scott and Zofia into it as well.

'Finn,' Sian said as her gaze landed on the young DC. 'Why don't you have an early finish, catch up on some sleep.'

'Are you sure?' he asked, looking at her with heavy eyelids. He didn't wait for her to reply, he was already logging off his computer and grabbing for his jacket.

She waited until he'd gone before she stood up from behind her desk and went into Christian's office.

'What the hell is going on?' she asked in the doorway. 'Why are Scott and Zofia acting so shifty and where the bloody hell is Matilda?'

'I've no idea,' he said as he released a heavy sigh. 'I'm supposed to be the DI and I haven't a sodding clue what's going on in this department anymore. Two weeks ago, I was in charge, I knew what everyone was doing, now I feel like I'm being ostracised for something I've done wrong, but nobody's told me what.'

'What did Zofia say to you? Because when she came out of the office she looked decidedly shifty.'

'Nothing. She asked if she was going undercover still despite Matilda not being around. I said yes and that I'd monitor her if Matilda didn't come back.'

Sian frowned. 'Did you get the impression that she didn't want you monitoring her?'

He thought for a moment. 'Her eyes did widen a little. I didn't give it much thought.'

'You don't think... No.'

'What?'

'You don't think Matilda's pressuring Zofia to go further

undercover than she's comfortable with, than is even legal, in fact?'

Christian couldn't answer that. He had no idea what Matilda was capable of anymore.

Matilda stood in the Meagans' living room, looking out at the darkened front garden. Nobody knew what time Carl had woken up that morning and decided to leave so they didn't know how long he'd been missing. He had money and food with him. He'd been planning something similar in Sweden, so he knew what he needed to survive. He could be out of Sheffield by now.

Matilda had made a call to Sergeant Teresa Childs and told her of Carl's disappearance. She'd texted her a recent photo, one of him in the back garden playing with the two Woodys, and asked her to get uniformed officers to patrol the city and keep an eye out for them. There was one important detail – nobody could know he was missing. If it got out to the press, they'd have a field day and Sheffield was already spending far too much time on the front pages. As far as Matilda was concerned, Carl had merely panicked. He was struggling under the weight of expectation to settle back into his home and needed some breathing space. He'd fled with his dogs, his only friends, and would return home when he was ready, or cold, or hungry. She hoped.

It had been six hours since she made the call to Teresa and despite the constant texts and calls for an update, there had been no sign of him.

'Any news?' Pat asked as she entered the room.

Matilda turned to look at her. 'No. Nothing.'

'I can't believe nobody has seen an eleven-year-old walking two Labradors and not remembered.'

'How are Sally and Philip?'

Pat shook her head. 'In pieces. It's like being back to square one for them.'

'Where the hell is he, Pat?' She moved away from the window and slumped down in an armchair.

'I've no idea. I asked Philip if Carl had any special places he liked to visit but he said not. Even if he had, it's been four years, would they still be special?'

Matilda leaned forward, her head in her hands. She looked back up and had tears in her eyes. 'I never thought something like this would happen. It's like he doesn't want to be back at home. Surely he didn't prefer living in Sweden.'

Pat sat on the sofa next to her and lowered her voice just in case Sally and Philip could hear in the next room. 'Sally said he's been prickly since he came back; hardly talking, snapping when he does, spending most of his time in his room.'

Philip tapped on the living room door. 'Sorry to interrupt. I've taken Sally upstairs, told her to have a lie down. Is there any news?'

Matilda shook her head.

He came in, closed the door behind him and perched himself on the edge of the coffee table. In the space of a day he'd gone from beaming with pride at his son's return to looking deathly pale and on the verge of tears.

'I didn't want to say anything in front of Sally. I was hoping, when the counselling started, it would all be ironed out. The night before last, I couldn't sleep, and I got up to get a glass of water. I saw a light on in Carl's room. I was going to knock, see if he was all right, and I heard him talking, obviously to the dogs. I listened.'

'What did he say?' Pat asked.

'*This isn't my home anymore. Nothing has changed but I don't recognise it. I don't even recognise Mum and Dad either. Their faces are the same but they're not how I remember them. The walls and the gates, they're all new. It's like a prison in here now. And I can't go in the living room without seeing Gran lying there, dead. I hate this house so much.*'

'He started crying then,' Philip said. 'I couldn't hear any more of what he said.'

'I'm so sorry,' Pat said. 'What are you going to do?'

'We need to have a sit down, all three of us, work out what to do for the best, as a family. If that means selling this place and moving, then so be it.'

'Do you think he'll want to leave Sheffield?'

'I've no idea. Look, Matilda,' he said, turning to her, 'I need you to find him. I will do whatever it takes to make Carl happy and safe. If that means selling this house, selling the restaurants and leaving the country, I'll do it. But I need you to bring him back to me. Tonight.'

Matilda looked at him. She felt sick. Her hands were cold. She was screaming inside and could feel her heart pounding loudly in her chest. She'd let the Meagan family down once before. There was no way she was going to let that happen a second time.

'You have my word,' she said.

Chapter Fifty-Five

Matilda: Undercover op cancelled for tonight. Tell Zofia and Harriet for me. I'll explain everything tomorrow.

S cott read Matilda's text twice. He stared at his phone, wondering what it meant. He forwarded the message to Zofia, who didn't seem bothered and said she'd get an early night. Harriet replied asking if he knew what was going on. He didn't even want to think what Matilda was up to. Slumped on his bed, he looked over at the bedside table and saw Chris's smiling face. He missed him so much that it was physically painful. Despite the lateness of the day, the darkness outside and the falling temperatures, he decided to go for a run.

Sarah climbed out of the Ford Focus and slammed the door closed. She pocketed the two ten-pound notes, zipped up her jacket against the cold and trotted across the road to where Bev was waiting. She took the bag from her, rummaged inside for a packet of Polos and threw two in her mouth.

'No Zofia and Harriet tonight?' she asked.

'It doesn't look like it,' Bev said. Her voice was shaking slightly she was so cold. 'Matilda did say it wouldn't be every night. Mondays are usually dead anyway. How much did you make?'

'Twenty.'

'He doesn't usually want more than a hand job.'

'I know. Last few visits he's asked for more. Apparently, his wife's off sex completely now.'

'More money for you.'

'Exactly,' she said with a smile. 'No Becca tonight?'

'She was around earlier. She got a phone call then got in an Uber. Probably her dealer.'

'She should be more careful.'

'I've tried telling her till I'm blue in the face, but she won't listen. I wouldn't be surprised if the killer hadn't recognised her on the news and eyed her up for his next victim.'

'Don't say that, Bev. She might be a bitch, but no one deserves killing.'

Bev looked up and down Harvest Lane. 'Not many out tonight. What do you reckon – because it's Monday, because it's cold or because there's a killer on the loose?'

'Don't make jokes, Bev, it's frightening. Do you think Matilda will help us get a council flat?'

Bev's face soured. 'I don't know. She said she'd help, but she been quiet ever since.'

'It was nice of her to take us in until we got the flat cleaned.'

'She did it because she needed our help. She wants us on her side while that detective goes undercover.'

'I thought you liked her.'

'I do, but, remember Sarah, it's us and them. She's using us to get what she wants. If we can get a council flat out of her then great, but I'm not banking on it. We can't trust anyone, Sarah, I've told you that countless times before. Speaking of people you can't trust,' she said, nodding up the road.

Sarah turned and watched as a Volvo pulled up.

'What have you got against him? He's lovely, kind, and he makes a great cup of tea,' she said as she returned Dermot's wave.

'Nobody does anything out of the goodness of their heart. He's playing the long game. Yes, he's all smiles, hot tea, sandwiches and sympathy, but it won't be long before he's asking for a shag in return for a bacon butty.'

'You're so cynical.'

'Yes. And you should be, too.'

'Good evening ladies,' Dermot said as he approached, a huge smile on his thin lips, a heavy rucksack on his back and a large plastic tub full of sandwiches in both hands. 'You're hardy being out on a night like this.'

'Bills have to be paid, Dermot,' Bev said with a fake smile.

'If you're short, I can lend you some until you get more money. I know you've been out of action for a couple of days after what happened with—'

'I'm fine, Dermot,' she cut him off. 'I don't need a handout, thanks all the same.'

'Well, the offer's there any time. How are you doing, Sarah? Fancy a cuppa?'

'I'd love one. I'm chilled to the bone tonight.'

Dermot placed the tub on the cold, wet ground and shook off the rucksack. Bev watched him out of the corner of her eye. He might look and sound pious, and dress like a countryside vicar without the dog collar, but it was just a façade. There was something dark and sinister lurking underneath, she'd bet her life on it.

Bev's phone vibrated in her pocket. She looked at the text. 'Pete's parked around the corner. I'll be about twenty minutes,' she said, giving Sarah the shoulder bag they shared. 'Look after yourself,' she said with concern in her voice.

'I'll hang around until you're back, Bev. There doesn't seem to be many out tonight. I don't mind waiting,' Dermot smiled.

As Bev was about to turn the corner, she looked back and saw Dermot and Sarah laughing animatedly. Why was Bev the only one who distrusted the do-gooding tosser?

Chapter Fifty-Six

Time was ticking by slowly. Matilda's phone had been silent for more than an hour. Outside, darkness had fallen, the sky had cleared and the temperature had plummeted. The weather presenter had said it was unusually cold for late October and the forecast for Halloween was for a hard frost. Wherever Carl was, he would be freezing cold. He'd survived being kidnapped, being sold and moved abroad, but could he survive below-zero temperatures?

'I've taken Sally a mug of tea up,' Pat said, entering the living room.

'Is she coming down?' Philip asked.

'Not yet.'

'I think I might go up and sit with her for a while. Do you mind?'

'No, of course not.' Pat waited until the door was closed and Philip was out of earshot. 'I sometimes think things like this are harder on the men. People always ask how the mother is, how she's coping with losing a child, and they expect the bloke to take it on the chin, be a man. It's his child too, he's going to be feeling the pain as much as the mother, yet they think because you're a bloke, you can cope. Philip isn't, is he?'

'Sorry?' Matilda asked, looking up.

'You weren't listening, were you?'

'I... Sorry, no, I wasn't.'

'Well, I'm not saying it again.' She sighed and flopped down into the comfortable sofa. 'It seems strange being here and there being no dog sniffing at my pockets,' she half-laughed.

Pat couldn't settle. She crossed her legs and uncrossed them. She picked up a magazine, flicked through it and threw it back down on the table. She stood up and began pacing the room. There was a silver-framed photograph on the mantelpiece. It showed Philip, Sally and Carl on a beach somewhere hot and warm, a brilliant blue sky in the background, not a cloud in sight. They were all grinning to the camera. The definition of a happy, loving family.

'I love this photo. I've often looked at it when I've come into this room. It was taken less than a year before he was kidnapped. Look how happy they all are,' she said wistfully as she gazed at the photo. 'They had everything: a thriving business, a beautiful home, a healthy child, and it all went wrong so suddenly. I wonder if there was a trigger.'

'What?' Matilda asked.

'Well, the kidnappers, they must have seen Sally and Philip at some point and thought about kidnapping Carl for ransom. I wonder when that was. It's a shame we can't go back in time to the point where everything went wrong.'

'Oh my God, Pat,' Matilda said, standing up. 'I think I know where Carl is.'

'What? Where?'

'Where it all went wrong.'

'Where's that?'

'Have you got your car with you?'

'Yes, but…'

Matilda headed for the door.

It was a long shot, but Matilda couldn't think of any other place Carl could be. She'd spent the last few hours going over everything in her mind that she'd learned about the Meagan family from when she first met them in 2015 – the things they'd told her, the photographs she'd seen, the witness statements – and nothing had come to mind, but Pat had hit the nail on the head when she mentioned the place where everything had gone wrong. It was Graves Park. The site of the ransom drop where Matilda should have handed over the money and taken Carl home. When they first met in Manchester airport, Carl had even told her he'd heard her screaming his name. That was where it had gone wrong.

Graves Park wasn't far from Dore and at this time of night, the roads were quiet. Matilda made sure she went to the correct entrance this time. In 2015, she went to the tennis courts and waited, wondering what was taking the kidnappers so long to arrive, only to find out they were in the car park by the animal farm. She would not make that mistake again.

Pat slowed down as they turned into the park and up the narrow incline. There was very little lighting and her headlights illuminated the concrete rectangle of the car park. Matilda breathed a sigh of relief as the white light shone on a figure in the distance, small, wearing a thin jacket, two dogs walking beside him.

'It's him,' she said, a hand on her chest.

'I so wish you'd been on my team when I was still working, Matilda,' Pat grinned.

'I'll go and talk to him. Text Philip, tell him we've found

him, and we'll bring him home. You'd better ring Teresa at the station, too.'

Matilda unclipped her seat belt and climbed out of the car. The cold hit her straight away and she shivered, pulling her jacket around her. Carl had seen her; he noticed the headlights when the car turned into the park. He didn't run so fleeing was not on his mind. Matilda had been right in guessing he just needed some space.

She stepped onto the grass, her shoes crunching the frost that had already formed. The first Woody recognised her and came bounding over to her, tongue lolling, tail wagging. She knelt down to stroke him.

'Hello, Carl,' she said once she was close enough. 'I've been looking for you all day.'

He turned to look at her. Pat had left the headlights on and they were both standing in the middle of the beam. He looked cold, pale, his lips almost blue, his eyes wide and frightened.

'Have you been here since this morning?'

He nodded.

'Why here?'

He shrugged.

'This is where it went wrong, isn't it? I should have met you here with the ransom money and I didn't.'

'I heard you shout my name,' he said in a soft voice, the emotion stuck in his throat.

Matilda stood next to him and watched as he picked up a stick and threw it for both Woodys to chase and fight over. 'Come and sit down,' she said, eyeing up a bench close by.

As they sat on the cold wood, both Labradors trotted over to them and sat at their feet.

'Before you were kidnapped, my husband was diagnosed with brain cancer. There was nothing the doctors could do, and we just had to wait,' she began, tears in her eyes. 'I didn't tell anyone as I didn't want people being all sympathetic around me, so I carried on working. On the day of the ransom drop, my husband, James, died. I was devastated. It felt like the end of the world for me, but I had a job to do. Looking back, I should have said I couldn't do it and let someone else make the drop, but I didn't. My mind wasn't on the case and I went to the wrong car park. I went to the one by the tennis courts. When I knew I made a mistake, I came charging up here carrying the money, and I missed you by seconds.

'I have relived that day over and over and over again. I made so many errors and you were paying the price for it. In all that time, your mum and dad didn't once stop looking for you. They did everything possible to make sure your name, your photo, was in the papers and magazines, on the television and all over the internet. They wanted the whole world looking for you.

'I can't even begin to imagine how you're feeling right now. Everything has changed for you. You're four years older. You've been through so much, but your mum and dad are still your mum and dad and their love has never stopped.' She paused and watched as Carl took in everything she said. His face was impassive. She hoped he was understanding it all. 'I am so sorry I couldn't bring you home that night. I will never forgive myself.'

It was a while before Carl spoke.

'I wanted to come home so much. I thought I'd be happy, but I'm not.'

'Why aren't you?'

'Because it doesn't feel the same.'

'It isn't the same. It looks the same, but it isn't. You've changed. You've had to grow up so quickly, but your mum and dad are still who they were before. My dad died earlier this year. I was heartbroken. My mum is still alive, but we don't have the same kind of relationship. We're not close at all. But she's still my mum, and I know she loves me. And I love her. And I need her in my life. I'm forty-four years old, and I still need my mum.'

'I love my mum,' Carl said, wiping away a tear. 'And my dad.'

'I know you do.'

'I just… I can't get what happened out of my head. And every time Mum hugs me, it feels like she doesn't want to.'

'Oh, Carl, she does. She wants nothing more than to hold you and never let go, but she's scared.'

'Of what?' He sniffed.

'She's your mum and her job is to protect you. From her point of view, she failed when you were kidnapped. She's blaming herself and she's worried you'll blame her too.'

'I wouldn't,' he cried.

'Can I give you some advice?' He nodded. 'You know all about the shooting earlier this year, don't you?' He nodded again. 'Well, I was badly injured, and I lost some good colleagues, close friends, and my dad. I was also pregnant, though I didn't know it at the time. I lost the baby, too. The man I was seeing, Daniel, he wanted us to still be together, but I pushed him away. The people who are left, my friends, family, I've pushed them away, too. I've done that so if anything else bad happens, I won't be hurt. But that's not the way to live our lives. We need people. We need support. We can't do this on our own. You've been through so much that none of us can understand, but you've got so many people around you to help: your mum and dad, me and Pat, your two dogs. Don't push them away.'

Tears were rolling down Carl's cheeks and he didn't wipe them away. He squatted and stroked the panting dogs. He looked up at Matilda. 'Will you take me home?'

She smiled through her tears and nodded.

'What are *you* going to do?' Carl asked, standing up.

She took a deep breath. 'Well, as soon as I've taken you home, I'm going to go and see my mum. I need a hug. And tomorrow, I'm going to start making it up to my friends.'

'Do you think they'll forgive you?'

'I really do hope so.'

Matilda put her arm around Carl and led him to the waiting car. The two Labradors followed behind them.

Chapter Fifty-Seven

'Do you want to come in? Warm up?' Matilda asked Pat as they pulled up outside Matilda's house.

'No. I'd better get back home. Anton will be wondering where I am; not that he's phoned or texted, selfish bugger, but that's men for you. Besides, I'm emotionally spent after today.'

'Me too.'

'Do you think they'll be okay now?'

Matilda thought for a moment. 'Eventually. They've a long way to go.'

'Do you think they will leave Sheffield?'

'It might be for the best if they did. A new start. It's just...'

'What?'

'While we were in their living room and you were looking at that photo of them all happy, you said you wondered what the trigger was for the kidnappers to decide to take Carl. We still don't know, do we? I need to know.'

'Well, hopefully, when Carl begins counselling, and you interview him again, something will be revealed. It'll take time.'

'Hmm. Even though he's back home, it's not over, is it? You think you can lay your demons to rest but you can't. You just keep adding to them.'

'Are you all right?' Pat asked, turning towards her.

She took a deep breath. 'I've no idea. Talking to Carl made me realise what I've lost. I've lost my father, my baby and my best friend. I've never felt more alone than I do right now.' She was struggling to contain her tears.

'Matilda, you are not alone. You have so many people around you who'll be there for you. You just have to let them.'

'I don't want to burden them,' she choked.

'You won't. They say that you find out who your true friends are in the aftermath of a disaster. Your sister has moved in with you. Your mother has moved closer. I'm not far away. You have Scott above the garage and Sian and Christian at work. And, if you work at it, you have Adele. That's a good support network to have. But if you keep them all at arm's length, they'll walk away, and they'll be gone for good. If you were a burden, they wouldn't still be asking how you are.'

'I more or less said exactly that to Carl.'

'Then follow your own advice.'

Matilda digested Pat's words. She nodded. 'I will. Thanks, Pat.'

'You're welcome.'

Matilda climbed out of the car, closed the door behind her and waved goodbye. She watched as Pat reversed and made her way down the driveway, before fishing for her keys in her coat pocket. She unlocked the front door and stepped into the warmth.

She heard voices coming from the living room to her left and assumed it was Harriet staying up late watching television. When she entered, she saw her mother and her sister on opposite sofas chatting. They both jumped up.

'Oh my God, Matilda, what happened? Did you find him?' Harriet asked.

She nodded. 'Yes.'

'Where was he?'

'Long story.'

'You're frozen solid,' Harriet said, holding Matilda and walking her to the sofa. 'I'll go and get you a stiff drink and put the kettle on.'

She left the room, leaving Matilda and her mother alone for the first time since she was in hospital.

'What are you doing here?' Matilda asked softly.

'Harriet called. She was worried about you.'

'I didn't see your car out front. Or did I?' She frowned.

'I'd had a few glasses of wine. I got a taxi.'

'Mum,' Matilda began. 'I'm so sorry,' she said with a broken voice.

'What for?'

'For everything. For being so cruel and a complete bitch to you.'

'You were closer to your dad than me, you always were, even as a child.' She stood up and moved to sit by Matilda. She took her hand in hers. 'You're my daughter. I love you. I'm here for you and I always will be.'

'I've messed everything up, Mum,' she cried, leaning into her mother.

'You haven't.'

'I have. I'm pushing people away. I'm being horrible to those who are my friends. I'm shouting at my colleagues and I don't think I can cope anymore.'

'Of course you can cope. I've never heard so much nonsense. Your surname may be Darke now, but you're a Doyle. You've got your dad's stubborn determination, his strong drive and character. You can cope with anything. Even bullets don't stop you.'

Matilda looked up at her. 'What did I get from you?'

'You've got my magnificent bosom,' she smiled.

Matilda laughed. 'I can't do this anymore, Mum,' she said, lowering her head onto her mother's shoulder.

Penny tightened her hold. 'In this past year, you have been through more heartbreak than most people experience in a lifetime. You've had to learn how to walk and talk again. You've lost so many people you care about. You've lost a baby. The fact you're still functioning and getting out of bed in the morning is testament to your strength. During your recovery there was no doubt in my mind that you wouldn't make it. It's who you are. But there is one thing you need to take from all this: you can't do it by yourself. You need to allow those around you who love and care for you to help. There's nothing to be ashamed about in asking for help. Me, Harriet, Scott, Adele, we're all there for you.'

'Adele pushed me away,' Matilda said, her words muffled in the embrace of her mother.

'Because she's hurting. You've been friends for over twenty years. You don't just throw that away. Don't give up on her. She wouldn't give up on you.'

Matilda sat back up. She wiped her eyes. 'I need help, don't I?'

'No. You've got help. You just need to realise it. Promise me one thing, though.'

'What's that?'

'Don't milk it,' she smiled.

Matilda cried and buried herself in her mother's embrace. It felt warm and familiar. Her eyes grew heavy.

Chapter Fifty-Eight

Dermot Salter headed back to his car. Mondays were always quiet nights, but this one was quieter than usual. Was it the cold weather or the fact a serial killer was stalking the streets of Sheffield picking off prostitutes that kept the women, and the punters, away? His flasks were empty; he and Sarah had drunk most of the tea waiting for Bev to return. He hadn't given away many sandwiches. He hoped they'd still taste fresh tomorrow night.

He unlocked the boot of his Volvo and placed the plastic tub carefully in the back and laid down the flasks. He changed out of his walking shoes into something more comfortable to drive in and slammed the door closed. It was so quiet, the noise resounded around the empty streets. As he looked about him, he realised he was alone.

The roads were narrow in this part of town. The businesses had small car parks attached to their properties, all of which were empty. Shutters were down on all the buildings that were occupied, while those that had been abandoned looked eerie and menacing in the dull lighting. Nobody knew who or what was lurking in them: the homeless, drug addicts, underaged drinkers. They could be watching him, and he wouldn't know about it. He shivered, partly from the cold, partly from fear. He was getting too old to keep coming down here on a nightly basis. He didn't want any of the women to go hungry or cold. Society deliberately ignored them, but he wanted them to know there was at least one person who cared for them. He promised his wife he would take care of her, and he did, but he didn't want other women suffering like she had, until he came along and rescued her.

'Dermot!'

His name was called in a loud whisper. He turned quickly but had no idea where it was coming from. Out of the shadows stepped a familiar face: one of the punters he had spoken to on a regular basis, the only one who would actually talk to him. When he attempted to talk to the others, they either ignored him or told him to piss off and mind his own business.

'Hello. I think they've all gone home now. It's getting late.'

'I know. It's you I wanted to talk to.'

'Oh. Why?'

'I've been thinking about what you said with this killer on the loose. We should be looking out for these women. They're vulnerable and doing a dangerous job.'

A small smile crept on Dermot's face. He began to thaw. 'They really are.'

'Exactly. As you know, I've been coming down here for a few years now. I like to think I know one or two of them quite well.'

He stepped closer. Dermot hadn't realised how tall he was. He'd only ever chatted to him while he'd been sat in his car. He loomed over him.

'Well, I think the best thing we can do for them is simply to keep our eyes and ears open for anything out of the norm and offer support when they need it. We're in a much better position, financially and socially, than they are. I'm sorry, I don't know your name.'

He smiled. 'It's Kevin.'

'Nice to meet you, Kevin.'

'The thing is, I think I might know who the killer is.'

'You do? How?'

'The one who was killed last week, Carly, I was in the sandwich shop on the corner... I work close by here so I'm often around during the daytime, and I overheard a bloke, one of the regulars, talking to the man behind the counter. The thing is, what he was saying...' He shivered. 'Look, we can't talk here properly, I know it's late but are you free to chat now?'

Chapter Fifty-Nine

Tuesday 29th October

'For the first time in as long as I can remember, I didn't want to come into work today. Even in the aftermath of the shooting, I wanted to be here to do whatever I could to help, but now, well, let's just say I was tempted to turn the alarm off this morning and go back to sleep,' Sian said, standing by the window in the HMCU suite and looking out at the grey city before her.

She and Christian were first in, purposely so. Christian had texted Sian late last night telling her he'd heard from Zofia informing him the undercover operation was cancelled for the night. Nobody knew why and Matilda wasn't answering her mobile.

'What are we going to do?' she asked, turning her back on the view and looking to the DI for answers.

Christian sighed. He was sat on his desk, feet on his chair, and the weight of the world on his shoulders. 'If we weren't in the middle of one of the biggest investigations we've ever faced, I'd say we have a quiet word with Matilda and see what happens, but this case is massive, and we need a functioning leader. I think it's obvious that Matilda isn't fully functional right now.'

'We're not saying she's not capable though – she is. Look at what she's achieved over the years. She's just … she's not fully recovered.'

'But she thinks she is, otherwise she wouldn't be back at work.'

'This shouldn't be our fight, though. The ACC should be doing this.'

'He's just looking at this from a PR point of view.'

'Meanwhile we're walking on eggshells. God, I feel sick,' she said, rubbing her stomach. 'I haven't had breakfast this morning, I couldn't face it.'

'Okay.' He ran his hands roughly over his face. 'I'm going to talk to Matilda. She needs to realise how toxic the situation is.'

'Do you want me to be there with you?' she asked.

He looked over to her, saw the look of horror on her face. 'No. She might think we're ganging up on her.

The door to the suite was pulled open and Finn entered. He wrinkled his nose but didn't say anything about the smell.

'Good morning, you two,' he said with a smile on his face. He shook off his coat and hung it up. 'Did you see the news last night? The prostitute killings was the lead item on the ten o'clock news and it dominated *Look North*. I've been checking in with the calls to see if anything interesting's come through and I think I might have got something.' He went over to his desk and picked up his iPad. He switched it on and began flicking through the pages of the screen. 'Lisa Temple's sister said there was one particular punter that she saw on a regular basis. He was called Robert and he was over six feet tall, a shaved head, stubble, and was big but not fat, sort of, naturally muscular. The sister didn't know what kind of car he drove. Anyway, a few of the calls that came through overnight said we should be talking to one of the punters who matches the description of Robert, but they all gave him different names. If it's the same person, he obviously gives a different name to whichever woman he sees on the streets.'

'I bet ninety-nine per cent of the punters don't give their real names,' Sian said.

'No, but we have a basic description now. If we have a word with Bev and Sarah, they might be able to give us more on this bloke. They may have even been with him themselves. And I know for a fact Bev makes a note of the majority of registration numbers.'

'Good work, Finn,' Christian said.

Sian's desk phone rang.

'Maybe they can even put a composite ID together for us and we can give it to the media. If he's a regular among the women, someone is bound to recognise him,' Finn said, the excitement evident in his voice.

'That was uniform,' Sian said, hanging up. 'A body has been found in Stanley Fields.'

'Stanley Fields? Where's that?' Finn asked.

Christian looked crestfallen. 'Just over the railway line from the red-light district.'

'Jesus Christ, not another one.'

Chapter Sixty

Stanley Fields was an open area next to Pitsmoor Road. When Sian and Finn pulled up, they could already see the white forensics tent erected over the body in the corner by the trees and scene of crime officers combing the area for clues.

Despite the strong wind and cold temperature, a crowd of rubberneckers had gathered, as close to the cordon as they were allowed. As Finn climbed out from behind the wheel of the pool car, he stood and watched them.

'What are you looking at?' Sian asked.

'Remember what I said about the killer making himself part of the investigation? It's not unusual for the killer to join the crowd and watch the police at work. In fact, they get a kick out of it.'

Sian joined Finn and looked at the mixed bag of gawkers: the elderly, young parents on the way home from taking their kids to school, students, middle-aged people who had pulled up in their cars as they were passing to nosy at what was going on.

'Do any of them match the description?' Sian asked.

'I've no idea, Sian,' he said, turning away. 'You could go mad if you looked at everyone and thought they were a killer.' He put his hands in his pockets and walked slowly to the crime scene with his head down. 'I'm not sure this criminal psychology course was such a good idea. I don't want to send myself doolally by trying to fit normal members of society into the pigeonhole of a serial killer.'

'You won't. You're only doing it now because we're working on a serial case. Trust me, when this is over, you'll be able to walk around Meadowhall without giving the rest of the shoppers a second glance.'

They approached a freezing-looking PC who wrote down their names and rank from their IDs and handed them the white paper forensic suits. Finn pulled back the flaps of the tent and entered. He stopped in his tracks when he saw what awaited him.

On the ground in the overgrown grass, just before the copse of trees began, a man lay on his back, his head severed from his body which had rolled a few feet away to the base of a huge oak tree.

Finn froze, his right hand clasped to his mouth.

Sian looked down with wide-eyed horror, then over to Adele Kean who was on her knees by the side of the corpse. She didn't say anything. There was nothing to say.

Adele handed Sian a plastic evidence bag that contained an open wallet.

'Dermot Salter. Why do I know that name?' she asked as she read from the driver's licence.

Finn swallowed hard. He was deathly pale. 'Me and Scott went to see him the other day. He visits the street workers most nights; takes them sandwiches and cups of tea, lends them money when they're short. I felt sorry for him. He was ... sad.'

'What happened?' Sian asked.

'It's a single cut to the throat,' Adele began. 'A wide cut, too. I don't think it was made from any knife or other weapon I've seen. You could possibly be looking at a sword, but I don't know...'

'What are you thinking?'

'There is evidence of the skin being pulled, dragged, as if the blade was blunt. If you're going to behead someone with a sword, you make sure it's sharp, don't you?'

'Why would you behead someone?' Sian asked. 'It's barbaric.'

'It's symbolic,' Finn said. 'We associate beheadings with Islamic extremists but it's about annihilation. If you want to kill someone, you shoot them, stab them, this is the destruction of the man. It could be that by removing the head you're removing the thoughts he had. His ideals are wrong and so they needed to be taken away.'

'So, what were his ideals?'

'Well, we know he cared for the prostitutes. He was looking out for them. He was lonely. I don't think he had anything else in his life. He certainly didn't seem to do anything other than bring them food and drink, offer them shelter.'

'You think this is the work of the same killer?' Sian asked.

'It has to be,' Finn said. 'It can't be a coincidence he was killed at a time when we're investigating the prostitute murders.'

'So why not strangle him like the others?'

'Because that's an intimate form of killing. He enjoys the suffering of the prostitutes. Maybe Dermot knew who the killer was, and he killed him in this way to show his contempt for the person who could stop him doing what he's enjoying.

I'm sorry, I can't stay in here.' Finn turned and quickly left the tent.

'He's really getting to grips with this whole psychology thing,' Sian said to Adele.

She gave a hint of a smile then turned back to the body.

'Are you all right?' Sian asked.

'I'm fine. Rushed off my feet, but fine.'

'When will you be able to do the PM?'

'It'll have to be this afternoon. I'm busy at the moment,' she said, standing up.

'Okay. Adele, I know it's only Tuesday, but do you fancy coming round to mine on Friday night for a bite to eat?'

'I can't. Sorry,' she said without making eye contact. She left the tent, leaving Sian in the company of Dermot Salter and a masked crime scene investigator.

'Do you ever get the feeling it's going to be one of those days?' she asked him.

'Every day I'm on duty,' he replied softly.

By the time Sian and Finn arrived back at South Yorkshire Police HQ, the HMCU suite was full. Matilda was in her office, and the door was closed. The morning briefing had been delayed until their return. Finn quietly went over to his desk, head down, while Sian headed straight for the kettle.

'Bev and Sarah are downstairs giving a statement about any regular clients,' Christian said. 'They think they know who this six-foot bloke is, but if it's the same man, they know him under different names. Bev called him Andrew; Sarah called him Jeremy.'

'He can change his name, but he can't change his

description,' Sian said, putting two heaped teaspoons of coffee in her mug. 'Do you want one?'

'Please. How was it?'

'Horrible. He was beheaded, Christian. How can someone do that?'

He shook his head. 'I don't know, but I think we can take this as a positive that he's getting scared. We're so close to him. He's bound to make a mistake sooner or later.'

'Can it be sooner, please? I want this over with.' She turned to look over her shoulder into Matilda's office. The DCI was sat at her desk, glaring out of the window. 'Has she said anything?' Sian asked, lowering her voice.

'No. She headed straight for her office as soon as she came in. According to Scott, Carl Meagan ran away yesterday. She was at their house most of the day and night.'

'Oh my God. Did they find him?'

'Yes. I think he's a bit overwhelmed with everything that's going on and needed some time alone. He's back home now.'

'That's a relief. Poor kid. Where does that leave us with...?' She trailed off but nodded her head in Matilda's direction.

'Let's leave it for today and see how she goes.'

Sian nodded. The kettle boiled and with a shaking hand she began pouring hot water into her mug.

'Are you all right with that, Sian?'

'I'll have to be,' she said, on the verge of tears.

———

The briefing lasted less than an hour. There was a huge amount of calls to go through, generated from the footage on the news last night, and Dermot Salter's murder added another layer to the investigation. Until forensics were finished, they wouldn't know what clues, if any, they were working with, but maybe this was a turning point in the case.

'I think we can assume Dermot Salter was murdered because he knew too much,' Matilda began. 'He knew the women, and he knew, or at least recognised, some of the regular punters. Maybe he knew the killer. If he did, who did he tell?'

'I don't think he will have told anyone,' Scott said. 'He was a loner. When his wife died, he more or less gave up. His house was certainly a shrine to the past. I think he only went out when he needed to shop for essential supplies. Apart from that, all he did was look after the street workers.'

'Okay. I want a team out to his house, just in case. Maybe he kept a diary or something. Scott, can you sort that out?'

'Sure.'

'Once Bev and Sarah have finished giving their statements and talking to the photo ID people, hopefully we'll have a good composite of the killer. I'll talk to the ACC about another press conference and we'll ask for people to contact us if they recognise him. This is a man who has been killing for more than three years.'

'On and off,' Christian interrupted.

'Well, yes. I'm still interested to know why he stopped for thirteen months. However, we all know that killing someone is going to deeply change a person's mental capabilities. Somebody will have noticed a change in his behaviour. We need to blanket Sheffield with this information. Together, with a decent composite, hopefully, we can catch him.' She gave a brief smile. 'Now, the undercover operation will go ahead tonight as planned. As per before, myself and Scott will be monitoring with Zofia on the streets. Any questions?'

'I have one,' Finn said. 'Why couldn't the undercover op go

ahead as planned last night? The killer was obviously out there. Dermot Salter would still be alive if we'd been out.' There was a bitter edge to his tone.

Matilda visibly reddened. She looked around the room at the faces staring at her. 'Carl Meagan ran away from home yesterday morning. I was asked to look for him. Fortunately, he was found safe and well.'

'But that didn't mean the operation couldn't go ahead. Zofia wasn't involved in the hunt to look for Carl; neither of us were. DI Brady could have substituted for you.'

'Logistically, it was too late in the day to make any changes,' she said, uncomfortable at having her decisions questioned. 'Look, we didn't know Dermot Salter wouldn't have been killed. Bev and Sarah were out last night. They didn't see or hear anything. It's obvious it happened when they'd gone home in the small hours.'

'But had we been out there, we could have caught the killer,' Finn said, raising his voice. 'We know for a fact that Monday is a quiet night. The killer might have seen Zofia, a new face, and approached her. We could have caught him. Instead, another person is dead.'

'Finn, calm down,' Sian said quietly.

'Finn, I understand you're upset,' Matilda said. 'Dermot's death is a tragedy, but there was nothing I could do about last night.'

'There was,' he said, almost through gritted teeth. He was gently seething and struggling to contain his emotions. 'That's why you have a DI. That's why we're part of a team. You deputise and rely on each other, share the jobs. This is a unit, or at least it used to be.'

'What's that supposed to mean?' Matilda asked, her hands on her hips.

'The atmosphere in this room has changed dramatically in recent weeks.'

'Since I returned?'

Finn took a deep breath. 'DCI Darke, I admire you immensely, but I think you're taking on far too much work on your own and you're not showing the rest of us the respect we deserve by keeping us out of your decisions.'

'Finn, that's enough,' Scott called out.

'I'm sorry, but I can't help thinking Dermot Salter would still be alive had we been out there last night. He was a kind old man and he's been beheaded, for crying out loud.'

'And you're blaming me?' Matilda asked.

'No. I'm simply saying that you're different. You're not treating us like a team anymore. You're acting like none of us are capable of anything without you holding our hand.'

'In case you hadn't noticed, DC Cotton, I was shot in the head.'

'I know. And here you are, less than a year later, back at work.'

'What's that supposed to mean?' she asked, folding her arms.

'I don't think you're fully recovered.'

Matilda looked out at the team. Nobody said anything. Heads were lowered and eye contact not met.

'I see,' she said after a lengthy pause. 'Maybe you'd feel better, DC Cotton, if you returned to CID. The same goes for anyone else who can't understand what I'm trying to achieve with this unit.'

Instead of returning to her office, Matilda turned and left the suite, slamming the door behind her.

Chapter Sixty-One

Matilda went for a long walk to clear her head. Finn was right. She wasn't showing her team any respect whatsoever and as much as she wanted to open up to them, apologise for how she was behaving and try to go back to the glory days before the shootings, she couldn't find the words to even begin.

She walked into town and decided against a chain coffee shop. If anyone was looking for her, they'd head straight for the nearest Costa. She ducked into Marmadukes on Norfolk Row, ordered the strongest black coffee they could make and retreated to a quiet corner, well away from the window.

It was warm and she shook off her coat. The coffee was brought to her, placed on the rustic table, and she wrapped her hands firmly around the mug. She wished she could spend all her days like this, sat drinking coffee, reading books, and not having to worry about the stress of being in the police. She didn't need to work – James left her very well off and the sale of their bespoke home added to her bank balance – but she needed to be a detective, she enjoyed the job. She used to.

She leaned back, her head hitting the wall, and released a sigh. She thought about Carl, took out her phone and sent a text to Sally, asking how everything was this morning. A reply came almost straight away.

We stayed up until about 2am talking. Carl told us everything. We all cried. Philip has taken Carl and the two dogs out into Derbyshire for a good long run while I make us a big lunch. Me and Philip were talking in bed last night. We're going to leave Sheffield. We think it's for the best. Fresh start.

Matilda smiled as she read the text. She didn't reply, but thought a fresh start was probably for the best for all of them. She hoped it was a long time before they sold up and chose a new place to move to, though. She'd like to understand Carl's recovery more so she could try to make sense of her own.

Two women had come into the coffee shop while Matilda had been lost in her thoughts. They sat by the window, a coffee in front of them, and seemed to be enjoying each other's company. They could have been sisters, lovers or just best friends, but they were relaxed, smiling, and laughing. That's what she and Adele used to be like. They both had a strange sense of humour and enjoyed making fun of each other. They'd look out of the window and rate passing men out of ten. The relationship Matilda had with Adele had been beautifully honed over more than two decades of friendship and it was now lost. Matilda decided what they had was too precious to leave to the pages of history. She wanted Adele back in her life. They needed each other. She picked up her phone and began to compose a text.

Adele, please don't delete this without reading it first. I am so very sorry for what happened to Chris. I watched him grow up. I often thought of him as a son and I would have died for him. I miss him. I miss you. I need you back in my life. I know you're in pain, it's understandable. I'm in pain too. But we can help each other. We can support each other. Please, say you'll meet me. We can chat, scream, cry, whatever you want, but we need to talk to each other. Call me any time.

There was nothing more Matilda could do. The ball was in Adele's court. She placed the phone next to her on the table and picked up her mug. She felt better for sending the text. Hopefully, she'd get a response.

Adele wasn't far from Marmadukes when Matilda sent the text. She was a few feet away in Marks and Spencer's Food Hall buying the ingredients to make herself something substantial to eat when she went home tonight. She was scanning her items in the self-service check-out when she heard the text come through. As usual, Adele had bought more than she'd expected and struggled under the weight of two full carrier bags. She left the store via the back entrance and struggled to rummage through her bag for her mobile, the handles of the plastic bags cutting into her wrists.

When Adele saw it was a text from Matilda, her heart sank. Would it be work-related or was it personal? She didn't have the strength for another plea to repair their destroyed friendship. As far as she was concerned, Chris was dead because of her. She didn't want anything more to do with Matilda.

She headed down Chapel Walk towards the car park, reading the text, struggling under the weight of her shopping, when she was knocked to the ground. Her bag was ripped from her shoulder, the phone torn from her hand. She looked up to see a man, no, a boy, hurtle down the street at speed.

People ran towards her to help her up. Others picked up her shopping that had spilt out of the bags and rolled away. Adele leaned against the wall of a shop, her face blank, tears streaming down her face. She wasn't hurt and she didn't care that her purse had been stolen with cash and cards inside, but her phone was gone. The final voicemail message from her son before he was killed was on it. She would no longer be able to hear his voice again.

Chapter Sixty-Two

How do you do this night after night in all weathers?' Harriet asked Bev. They were standing on the pavement on Harvest Lane beneath a dim streetlight. It was dark, a fine drizzle was falling, and occasional gusts of wind tore straight through them.

'You get used to it,' she said with a smirk. 'You become hardened.'

'I suppose it's like anyone who works outside,' Zofia said, hopping from foot to foot to keep warm. 'Look at people on building sites. They're building all year round. They can't go inside in the winter months.'

Bev looked at her with a blank expression. 'Yes, it's exactly like being a builder, except they don't have to violate themselves several times a night in order to pay for their next meal.'

'Shit. Bev, I'm sorry,' she said.

'I'm joking,' she said with a grin. 'Don't worry about it.' She put her arm around the young DC and pulled her close. 'Another thing you have to have working the streets, and that is a sense of humour. If you can't laugh, you may as well throw yourself into the Don.'

A few feet up the road, a car squealed to a halt. Sarah climbed out, slammed the door closed and stuck two fingers up at it as it drove off at speed.

'You all right?' Bev asked as Sarah joined them.

'Dirty bastard. I've told him many times I don't pull tricks like that, but he keeps trying it on.'

'Creepy Clive?'

She nodded.

'What did he want you to do?' Zofia asked.

'You don't want to know,' Bev replied quickly.

'Is he violent?'

'No. Nothing like that,' Sarah said reassuringly. 'He's just got a few kinks that not everyone's into.'

'And certainly not for twenty quid.'

Bev handed the shoulder bag back to Sarah. She rifled through it and took out a bottle of mouthwash. She gargled and spat it down a nearby drain.

Zofia and Harriet looked at each other with frightened eyes. They were getting a glimpse into a world they'd only ever seen dramatised on television. The reality was not what they had expected. Neither of them understood how people like Bev and Sarah could put themselves through such degradation on a nightly basis.

———

At the Kelham Kitchen and Wine Bar, Matilda and Scott had claimed their regular table in the corner of the pub. The table was littered with empty glasses, the dregs of orange juice and cola sticking to the sides, and with screwed-up empty crisp packets. Scott was debating whether to risk the perils of a packet of pork scratchings.

'The name alone is enough to put you off,' he said. 'Should something edible be called scratchings? I used to love them as a child, but then I had one with a hair on it and it put me right off. I just don't think I can face another packet of crisps. Matilda, are you listening?'

Matilda was staring out of the window, not at anything specific, but at something far off into the distance. She hadn't had a word from Adele. The text had been read, but no reply. What else could she do?

'Sorry?' she asked, turning to Scott. 'Sorry, I was miles away.'

'I can see that. You've been off all day. What's on your mind?'

'Nothing,' she croaked.

'It's what Finn said at the briefing, isn't it?'

She nodded, biting down hard on her lip. 'I've been beating myself up all afternoon wondering if Dermot Salter could have been saved had we been out last night. Then I started thinking about what Finn said afterwards, about not sharing with the team. He's right. I haven't been. I've hardly spoken to Christian and Sian since I came back. I mean, that's not like me at all, is it?'

'Not really.'

'And I don't think I thanked Finn for pulling an all-nighter. I shouldn't have even asked him to do that. I've changed, haven't I?'

'Of course you have. You were shot in the head. You can't expect something as big as that not to change you.'

'Scott,' she said, leaning forward and lowering her voice. 'Do you think I'm up to still being a DCI?'

'Yes, I do,' he replied honestly. 'But you need to keep telling yourself you're not the same Matilda Darke as a year ago. Things have changed. You're behaving like nothing has, but it has, everything has changed. You have nothing to prove, yet you're piling on work like you're a one-woman police force. You've built up a strong team around you. You can trust every single one of us, you know you can, but you need to remind yourself of that. We're your colleagues, but we're also your friends.' He placed his hand on top of hers.

A tear rolled down Matilda's cheek. 'What can I do?'

'You can start by being honest. Tomorrow morning, stand up in front of the whole team and apologise for freezing them out.'

'I tried to do that today, but my bottle went.'

'Do it tomorrow.'

'You make it sound so easy.'

'It is.'

'Not from where I'm sitting.'

'It is. You're making it bigger than what it is. Do you think everyone is going to point and laugh at you?'

Scott's mobile started to ring. He struggled to take it out of his jeans pocket. He saw that it was Lucy Dauman calling and swiped to answer.

'Hello, Lucy, how are things?'

'Not good, Scott. Where are you?' There was a panicked tone to her voice.

'I'm at a pub with Matilda. We're on an op. What's wrong?'

'Oh God, Scott, it's horrible. Adele disappeared around lunchtime and didn't come back to work. I phoned and phoned, and it went unanswered. I went round and the back door was open. Scott, she's tried to kill herself,' Lucy said, her voice giving way to a barrage of tears.

Scott was struck dumb. He stared at Matilda, his eyes wide in horror.

'What's going on?' Matilda asked.

'Scott, are you still there?' Lucy asked.

'I'm still here. What happened? Where is she?'

'She took an overdose. I don't know how many. I'm at the Northern now. Can you come?'

'Yes. Yes. I'll be there as soon as I can.' He ended the call and remained seated. The shock was evident on his face.

'Has something happened?'

'That was Lucy. Adele's tried to kill herself.'

Matilda's mouth fell open and she visibly paled.

'Lucy's asked me to go to the hospital.'

'Go,' Matilda said firmly. 'I'll stay here. Just go. Take the car.'

'I can't. You let me have a couple of pints. I'll call for an Uber,' he said, taking his phone out again. His fingers were shaking while he struggled to locate the app. 'How will you get home?' he asked.

'Harriet can drive me.'

'There's one about a minute away,' he said, heading for the door.

'Scott,' Matilda called after him. 'Keep me updated, won't you?'

'Sure.'

He ran out of the pub to the waiting taxi with Matilda stood in the doorway looking on in horror. She should have seen this coming. Adele had blamed Matilda for her son's death. Scott had told her more than once that she was quiet, rarely texted, and he'd had to initiate all conversations. She was withdrawn and no longer took care of her appearance. If she hadn't been so consumed with her own issues, Matilda thought, she would have seen the signs of Adele's breakdown.

The door to the pub closed on her and she slowly returned to the table. She hoped Adele was going to be all right. She needed her. They needed each other.

Chapter Sixty-Three

Matilda sat at the table in the pub, lost in her thoughts. She could hear the conversations Harriet and Zofia were having but tuned them out. She couldn't stop thinking of Adele, of how desperate and lonely she must have been feeling at the loss of her son. In the early days of James's death, Matilda had felt exactly the same. There were many occasions she wanted to end it all as the pain was so raw, but there was one person who saved her – Adele. And how had Matilda repaid her? By turning her back on her when she needed her the most.

You're a selfish bitch, Matilda.

Matilda had been waiting for Adele to come to terms with Chris's death and realise that even if Matilda hadn't been shot on that day in January, there would have been nothing she could have done to save him. Adele was a sensible, intelligent woman; she would have understood eventually. All she needed was a little time.

It's been nine months; how much time were you going to give her?

'You all right, love?'

Matilda looked up and saw someone had come to the table to collect glasses.

'Sorry?'

'You've got tears streaming down your face. Is everything all right?'

Matilda wiped her cheeks. She had no idea she'd been crying.

'No,' she said, standing up and grabbing her coat. 'Everything is not all right.' She stormed out of the pub, slamming the door behind her.

'I keep expecting to see Dermot's car pull up,' Sarah said.

Harriet and Zofia had been to a nearby petrol station and bought them all a takeaway coffee from a Costa machine to warm them all up.

'I was wrong about him,' Bev said. 'I thought he had some kind of ulterior motive. He was just being nice.'

'We went round to his house this afternoon,' Zofia said. 'His bedroom was like a shrine to his wife. He obviously couldn't get over her death.'

'Poor man.'

'I can't believe he had his head cut off,' Bev said, her face souring at the thought. 'Who does that? What kind of a sick bastard does something like that?'

Zofia shook her head. 'I don't know. I don't want to know either. I just hope we catch him.'

'If I get my hands on him,' Bev seethed. 'I swear to God, I'll rip his balls off with my bare hands.'

Sarah shuddered. 'And to think we could have actually had

sex with him.'

'Did our descriptions help?' Bev asked Zofia.

'Yes. Definitely. They're tidying up the image and doing a couple of versions with longer hair and shorter and they've arranged a press conference for tomorrow morning. Fingers crossed someone recognises him.'

'Harriet!'

They all turned at the sound of Harriet's name being screamed. They saw Matilda running towards them. As she reached them, they could see the redness of her eyes, the dried tear tracks running down her face.

'What is it? What's happened?' Harriet asked.

'I've been so selfish. I should have seen it coming.'

Harriet grabbed Matilda by the elbow and led her away from Zofia, Bev and Sarah.

A car pulled up and flashed its headlight. They all turned. Bev squinted to read the registration number.

'That's for me.' She handed the shoulder bag to Sarah. 'I'll see you in about half an hour.'

As she approached the car, she saw Becca had got there before her and was already leaning into the driver's window.

'Oi, Becca, move on. He's not for you.'

Becca stood upright and unzipped her jacket, revealing huge breasts under a tight off-white T-shirt. 'I think we should let him decide who he wants, don't you?' she grinned.

'Oh God, this is going to get ugly,' Sarah said to Zofia. 'Hold my coffee, will you?' She handed Zofia the drink and headed for the car.

Zofia moved away. She didn't want to get involved in a squabble over whose punter he was. This undercover operation was being a real eye-opener for her. She was seeing a whole different side to how people lived, and it was making her flesh crawl.

'How much, love?'

It was a while before Zofia realised she was being spoken to.

'I said, how much do you charge, love?'

'Oh,' Zofia gave a friendly smile. 'I'm not actually… I'm just … I'm with my mates. Sorry.'

The driver of the black Land Rover looked her up and down. 'Come on, love, there's no need to be shy, hop in.'

'No. Honestly, I'm not one of them.'

'First time out? I thought as much. I haven't seen you here before. You've no need to worry about me, love. They all know me. I'm as gentle at they come.'

Zofia looked around her. Matilda was crying in Harriet's arms and Bev and Becca were physically grappling with each other while Sarah was trying to pull her best friend off. It was a futile fight as their punter had already driven off.

When Zofia looked back to the car, the driver had got out and was standing in front of her, a smile on his face. He was tall, broad-shouldered and well-built. He loomed over her. The smile didn't reach his eyes and made him look sinister. She hadn't been able to tell in the darkness of the car, but under the whiteness of the streetlight, he looked very much like the photo composite of the killer they had in the station.

'Come with me. I'll show you all the tricks.' He grabbed her arm and pulled her towards the car.

'No. I don't want to.' She dropped the coffee cups she'd been holding, which splattered and spilled on the pavement. She tried to pull away from the man, but she was no match for him.

He opened the front passenger door and threw her inside.

He slammed it closed and locked it. As he went around to the driver's side, he unlocked the car and climbed in.

Zofia screamed as loud as she could and banged on the window as the car was driven away at speed. She saw Matilda and Harriet look towards her, helpless as the Land Rover took the kerb and disappeared around a corner.

Chapter Sixty-Four

Matilda and Harriet stood at the side of the road in disbelief at what they had witnessed. They had been turned away for less than a couple of minutes while Matilda told her all about Adele trying to take her own life. A split second, that's all it had taken for the killer to grab Zofia off the street and drive away with her at speed. He must have been watching out for his opportunity to strike.

'Car!' Harriet screamed. 'Car. Matilda, where's the car?'

'Shit. It's still at the pub.'

'Fuck!'

'Was that Zofia?' Bev asked as she and Sarah ran towards them.

They ran towards the pub, all four of them. Matilda was in comfortable shoes so managed to get a good lead on the other three, who were struggling in heels.

As she ran along Burton Street and up Ball Street to where her Range Rover was waiting, she tried to think of what the car looked like, the colour and make. Had she noticed the registration number? Nothing came to mind. All she could picture was the look of sheer torture on Zofia's face as she'd been kidnapped.

She saw her car up ahead and scrambled in one pocket for her keys while trying to grab her phone out of the other. She needed to call the station and get uniformed officers and armed response looking for Zofia.

There was a tracking device in Zofia's left shoe. It shouldn't take long to locate her, but it was the time it took to get there that was the problem and what the killer could be doing to her in the meantime.

She unlocked the door and remained at the side while the other three caught up with her.

'Terry, it's DCI Darke,' she said into her phone. She was struggling to hide the panic in her voice. 'I need a location on a tracking device placed in DC Zofia Nowak's shoes. I've lost her, Terry,' she croaked.

'It's okay, we'll find her. What do you want?'

'Uniform and armed response. It's the killer, it's got to be.'

'Where are you?'

'Look, don't worry about where I am, just find Zofia. Let me know the moment you get her location. I'm in my own car, I'll probably be the closest.'

She ended the call. Harriet, Bev and Sarah had already climbed into the Range Rover.

'Did you see who it was?' Harriet asked, panting.

'No.' She turned around to look into the back seat. 'Look, you've both seen this bloke. You've both been with him. Where does he take you?'

They looked at each other.

'He likes Plantation Woods,' Bev said.

Matilda had no idea how to get to Plantation Woods from where they were. As she started the car and backed out of her parking space, Harriet went online and found the fastest route. At this time of night, with very little traffic, it would take twenty minutes, less if Matilda broke every speeding rule in the book, which she had every intention of doing.

'Jesus Christ! He could have killed her in twenty minutes,' Matilda said.

'If it takes us twenty minutes, then it'll take him twenty minutes, too,' Sarah said from the back seat. 'There's probably only a couple of minutes between us.'

Matilda couldn't argue with that logic. She slammed her foot down on the accelerator and drove through a red traffic light.

You're a survivor, aren't you, Matilda?

The last thing she needed was Jake Harrison haunting her. She shook her head to try and get rid of the dark thoughts.

'Oh my God!' Matilda exclaimed. She was driving at speed along Penistone Road and had just overtaken a refrigeration truck far too closely.

'What is it?' Harriet asked.

'I'm not supposed to be driving. I'm not cleared to drive.'

'Shit! Okay, don't panic. Calm down and do those breathing exercises that Coopersmith woman told you about. It's not much further. Are you all right?'

Matilda swallowed hard. 'I don't know.'

'You can't stop, Mat.'

'I know I can't.'

'Then just calm down and breathe.'

'I need some air.'

Harriet pressed the controls and Matilda's window opened a crack. A blast of freezing cold air filled the car.

At the junction with Hazelshaw Spring Wood, Matilda

slowed down, but not enough, and she struggled to maintain control of the car as she turned right into Westwood New Road. Harriet didn't take her eyes from her sister. She was looking for signs of her breaking down, but all she could see was a steely determination. This had been missing from Matilda since she was shot. She needed to think about someone else. Usually it was Carl Meagan, but now he was back home, she didn't have that to occupy her mind and there was only herself to worry about; that was the cause of her dark thoughts. Now, however, Zofia was in trouble, and Matilda would move heaven and earth to save her.

At Westwood roundabout, Matilda didn't even slow down. A car swerved and a truck beeped as Matilda went over the roundabout and straight ahead. In the back, Bev and Sarah were holding hands and both had their eyes closed.

The road stretched out ahead. Once again, Matilda slammed her foot down on the accelerator and reached a speed of almost one hundred miles per hour. When she saw the turning into the woods, she slammed on the brake, threw the wheel to the left and the car left the road and went onto the bumpy track. Beneath the cover of trees, the inside of the car was even darker.

Ahead, a dark-coloured Land Rover was found next to a tree. Its lights were off. There was nobody inside.

Matilda pulled up and jumped out. She ran over to the car. The bonnet was still warm. She cupped her hands around her eyes and peered inside. There was nobody there. She looked around her. She couldn't see anyone.

'Shit, where is she?'

She dug out her phone and dialled again.

'Terry, it's Matilda. I'm at Plantation Woods. I've found the car but there's no sight of Zofia.'

'I've got a team on the way to you. I suppose there's no point in me telling you to stand by until backup arrives.'

'Afraid not. I need you to run a registration number for me. Yankee Romeo six five Kilo Kilo Echo. I'm looking at a dark grey Land Rover.'

'I'll get back to you.'

She ended the call.

'Where is she?' Harriet asked.

'I don't know.'

'Should we shout for her?' Bev asked.

'Not yet,' Matilda replied as she rotated and looked around the dark woods. 'We should be able to see movement or hear them at least. The car's here for fuck's sake.'

Ahead, Matilda saw something move. She alerted the others to keep quiet. She went back to her car, got a torch and telescopic baton from the glove box and made her way along the uneven ground. She extended the baton, held it aloft and raised the torch. She could make out two figures but nothing else.

Matilda's mouth had dried. She could feel her heart pounding and the blood gushing in waves through her body. She turned on the torch.

'This is the police…' She stopped when she saw it wasn't the killer and Zofia but two men having sex against a tree. They quickly pulled up their trousers and ran as fast as they could. Matilda didn't bother giving chase.

She scanned the woods with her torch.

'Matilda!' She heard her name being screamed. It sounded like Bev.

She ran back through the woods and saw Harriet with her arms around a petrified-looking Zofia, and further along, Bev and Sarah sitting on top of a man, his face in the ground.

'We got the bastard,' Bev called out over her shoulder.

'Are you all right?' Matilda asked Zofia.

The DC had tears streaming down her face. She nodded.

Sarah stood up and Matilda approached when the man found strength from somewhere. He kicked out at Bev, jumped to his feet and grabbed Bev by the hair. He wound it around his fingers, kicked her hard between the legs, kneed her in the stomach and kneed her once again in the face. He tossed her to the floor like she was a piece of litter and was about to move to his car when he saw Matilda and stopped dead in his tracks.

Matilda looked at him with disbelief.

Oh my God.

He broke eye contact first and ran to his car.

'Matilda, what's wrong?' Harriet said, running to her sister.

Matilda didn't reply. She couldn't. She was struck dumb with fear.

It's not. It's not. It can't be.

Sarah ran to Bev, who was lying on the cold, wet ground in agony, blood pouring from her broken nose.

The engine to the Land Rover was started. Zofia stood in front of it, blocking his way. He revved the engine urging her to get out of the way, but she held her ground.

'Matilda, what's wrong?' Harriet asked her stricken sister.

No. No. No. No.

He threw the car into reverse and backed up at speed and started to turn the car around. Zofia ran to her left to get in front of the car when the Land Rover turned to the right, moved forward, but couldn't go any further as there were trees in the way. He put the car into reverse, slammed his foot down on the accelerator and crashed into a tree.

Above the sound of the engine, a scream rang out. Harriet turned and saw Zofia pinned between the car and the tree.

'Zofia!'

The DC was leaning over the back of the car. Her face was pale, and she was shaking in shock.

'Zofia, can you hear me?'

She nodded slowly.

'Matilda. Quick,' Harriet called out.

Matilda came back from her reverie and ran towards Zofia.

'Okay. I need you to stay calm,' she said as she shook herself out of her coat to put around the injured DC. 'I'm going to call for an ambulance. You need to stay awake. Harriet, talk to her.'

Matilda went to the front of the Land Rover and opened the door to the driver's side. The man hadn't moved. He remained sitting in the car, his hands stretched forward gripping the steering wheel.

'You have got some serious explaining to do.'

'I'm so sorry, Matilda.'

Once again, he slammed his foot on the accelerator. The closing car door hit Matilda and she was thrown to the ground.

Zofia fell, her shattered legs buckling under her weight. Harriet caught her and eased her gently to the woodland floor.

Sarah looked up and saw the Land Rover hurtling towards them. She screamed, grabbed Bev and tried to drag her out of the way. It was too late. Sarah was thrown to one side as Bev was pulled under the car and dragged with it as it exited the woods.

'Bev!' Sarah screamed as she stood up and ran after the car.

Matilda followed, limping slightly from where the car door had hit her.

'Terry, we need an ambulance at Plantation Woods,' she screamed into her mobile. 'We have an officer down.'

As she reached the clearing of the woods, she looked up the

road. About fifty feet away, Sarah was crouched down, her cries echoing in the darkness. Matilda walked slowly towards her. It was obvious even from this distance that Bev had suffered fatal injuries.

'Matilda. Matilda. DCI Darke,' Terry was calling down the phone.

'Shit, sorry,' she said, coming back to the present. She turned and ran back towards the woods and her car. 'Terry, DC Zofia Nowak is seriously injured.'

'Ambulance is on its way.'

'Bev's been killed. The car ran her over and dragged her at speed. I need you to put an alert out on the registration to the Land Rover I gave you.'

'I'm on it. It's registered to a Richard McLean from Brightside.'

'It's not him driving,' she said as she fished her keys out of her pocket and unlocked her car.

'How do you know?'

'Because I've seen the driver. I know exactly who the killer is.'

'Who is it?'

She put on her seat belt and turned the key in the ignition. Before she set off, she put her phone on hands free and pressed it into the holder on the dashboard. 'Jesus Christ. I can't fucking believe this. It's Stuart Mills,' she said solemnly. 'It's DS Sian Mills's husband.'

Chapter Sixty-Five

Matilda Darke had no idea where Stuart had gone, but she had a pretty good idea where he was likely to end up – home. She needed to get there before he did. If he arrived home knowing there was an entire police unit after him, he could turn on Sian and the children. He'd worked hard at keeping his other life secret for so long, he wouldn't want them to suffer the indignity of knowing what he had been doing. Could he kill Sian and their four children just so they wouldn't know the truth? Matilda shivered at the thought.

She grabbed her phone from the holder and tried to make a call. She was driving well over the speeding limit and the road was wet. She entered a roundabout without looking at what was coming from her right. She heard the squeal of brakes, the sound of metal crashing into metal, and dared not look through the rear-view mirror in case she felt compelled to stop. Matilda was determined to beat Stuart to his house.

'Terry, it's Matilda. I need an armed response … fuck!' She dropped the phone as she used both hands to quickly swerve around a Nissan Micra that reversed out of a driveway without checking to see if any traffic was on the roads. 'Wanker!'

The phone was on the floor. She could see the screen and could hear the faint sound of Sergeant Terry Atkin calling her name. She couldn't reach it and she didn't want to waste valuable time pulling over to pick it up.

Matilda activated the video screen on the dashboard. Terry had disconnected the call. She had no idea of his number so used the voice activation to call him. Unfortunately, Terry's number was not stored.

'Fuck!' she screamed to herself.

You're a survivor, aren't you, Matilda?

'Too fucking right I'm a survivor,' she said to herself.

———

Stuart pulled up outside his house. He remained seated behind the wheel of the Land Rover he'd borrowed from work. He never used the same car twice when visiting a prostitute. That was the benefit of working for a garage; different cars came in all the time, and many were left for a day or two. The owners never checked their mileage, and if they questioned it, he gave an excuse that he needed to test it to make sure it was working as it should be.

He looked up at his house. It was plunged into darkness. It was after midnight; everyone would be in bed, fast asleep, unaware of what horror they would be waking up to.

He and Sian had lived in this house since they married twenty-six years ago. They'd decorated many times, had an extension put on the back for a bigger kitchen and an extra bedroom upstairs. They'd celebrated birthdays, Christmases and exam success and failure in that house. They'd laughed and cried and watched world-changing events play out on the television, but one thing had remained a constant – Sian had always been by his side. She had supported him through everything: his cancer scare in the late 90s, being made redundant in 2004, his sister dying in a motorway pile-up in 2007. It didn't seem to matter what life threw at him, Sian was there to hold his hand and live through every moment with him. That's what a marriage was. He'd had everything. And it wasn't enough.

He closed his eyes and all he saw was the look of horror and disappointment on Matilda's face when she saw him in the woods. His secret was blown. The truth was out. He was a serial killer. His family could never know the truth.

He unbuckled his seatbelt, climbed out of the car and slammed the door behind him. It resounded around the quiet neighbourhood. As he walked up the path to the front door, he looked around him; this unassuming street in Sheffield was about to become infamous for being home to a serial murderer.

Stuart unlocked the door and stepped into the warmth. He closed it behind him and remained in the hallway, his back to the door. He listened intently for any sound of life: Sian snoring, the tinny sound of Belinda listening to music until the small hours. There was nothing.

He pushed open the door to the living room. It was an untidy vision of family life. Cushions scattered on the sofa, a furniture catalogue open on the coffee table, wireless controllers for the PlayStation charging, a half-eaten packet of biscuits abandoned on the shelf of the wall unit. This was a homely place and he'd destroyed it with his murderous actions.

The door from the kitchen opened and Sian entered the living room carrying a mug of tea. Her hair was a wild mess, and her over-sized dressing gown was tied in the middle.

'Jesus, you scared the life out of me,' she said. 'I didn't hear you come in.'

'I didn't want to wake anyone,' he said, remaining in the doorway.

'How was it?'

'What?'

'Games night with Dean, Shaun and his brothers.'

'Oh. It was … fine. What are you doing up?' He tried to look at her, but he couldn't. She was perfect. She was his loving wife. She looked so warm, cuddly and innocent in her dressing gown and novelty bunny slippers. How could he tell her he'd committed mass murder? It would destroy her.

'I couldn't sleep. I thought a hot drink might help,' she smiled. 'There's plenty of water in the kettle if you'd like me to make you one.'

'No. I'm fine. Thanks.'

'Okay.' She headed for the door, but he didn't move. 'Are you coming up?'

'Yes.'

'Is everything all right?' She frowned. 'You look … I don't know, distant.'

'I'm … I'm just tired, that's all. You go on up. I won't be long.'

'By the way, we won nine pounds eighty on the lottery. I was thinking the Maldives this summer,' she grinned. 'Are you sure you're all right?'

'I'm fine. Honest.'

'Okay. Well, I'll be upstairs.'

He stepped out of her way and she left the room.

She hardly made a sound going up the stairs. Stuart waited until he heard the bedroom door opening before moving. He went into the kitchen, and, without turning on the light, went over to the cutlery drawer and took out the largest knife he could find.

Chapter Sixty-Six

Matilda turned into the road at speed and slammed on the brakes as soon as she saw the Land Rover ahead. She pulled up close behind, grabbed her mobile from the floor and climbed out, closing the door behind her. She ran up the garden path and looked around her. All was quiet. The neighbours hadn't been woken by any arguments or screams for help. Surely that was a good sign.

She rang the doorbell and banged on the door with her fists.

Inside, Stuart was on the landing. He was standing in front of the main bedroom, carving knife in hand, when the sound from downstairs caused him to stop dead in his tracks. The door opened and Stuart quickly put the knife behind his back.

'What the hell's that?' Sian asked. There was an angry look on her face.

Stuart didn't reply. He was frozen in confusion. He had no idea what to do for the best. On the one hand, he didn't want Sian and the children to know what he'd been doing, but he didn't have the heart and the capacity to kill them all.

Sian ran down the stairs and quickly opened the door. She shivered as a cold blast of air hit her.

'Matilda, what the hell are you doing here? It's gone half twelve.'

Matilda pushed past Sian and entered the house, heading straight for the living room.

'Where's Stuart?'

'What? He's upstairs. Why? Matilda, are you all right? You look—'

'Are you hurt?' Matilda asked.

'No. Why, should I be?' she asked, looking confused. 'Matilda, you're not making any sense. What's going on?'

'Sian, I need you to—' She stopped when she saw Stuart enter the room.

'Matilda, what are you doing here at this time of night? What's so urgent? You could have woken the whole house up.'

Matilda stared at him. 'Stuart Mills, I'm arresting you on suspicion of murder. You do not have to say anything—'

'What?' he exclaimed.

'Murder?' Sian stepped back from Matilda and looked at her with her mouth open. 'What are you talking about?'

'—but it may harm your defence if you do not mention, when questioned, something you later rely on in court. Anything you do say may be given in evidence,' she said quickly.

'Matilda, what's got into you?' Sian asked.

'Sian, I'm so sorry. Stuart's the one who's been killing the prostitutes.'

She gave a burst of laughter. 'What? Oh, come on, you're not serious, surely.' She saw the look of intensity on Matilda's face and turned to her husband. 'Stuart?'

'I have no idea what she's talking about.'

'Tell her where you were tonight,' Matilda said.

'She knows where I've been. It's games night. I was with Dean and Shaun and his brothers.'

'Liar,' Matilda said. Her voice was quiet, but there was a venom behind her words.

'Matilda!' Sian said. 'He's not lying.'

'Call them. Phone this Dean and Shaun and ask them if he was there tonight.'

'It's gone half twelve, they'll all be in bed,' she said. 'Look, Matilda,' she said, stepping forward and placing a hand on Matilda's shoulder, 'you've been through a lot lately. I know it's not been easy for you, but this is … well, it's beyond incredible. How can you honestly think my Stuart has killed — how many is it, eleven people? Come on, don't you think I'd know?'

Matilda wiped a hand over her face. She could feel the sweat prickling at her armpits. 'Sian, he's been lying to you all these years. Ask him. Ask him right now where he was tonight.'

'I don't need to.'

'Do you think we should call someone? Maybe she's having some kind of breakdown,' Stuart said. 'You said yourself she's been weird, snappy and secretive lately.'

'What?' Matilda looked at Sian. 'Is that what you think?'

'What's going on?'

They all turned to see Belinda standing in the doorway. Her dressing down was hanging off her shoulders, her eyes barely open.

'Belinda, go back to bed,' Sian said.

'Oh, hi, Mat,' Belinda said, looking past her mother.

'Belinda, go on back upstairs,' Stuart said, ushering his daughter out of the living room.

'Belinda, no, don't go upstairs,' Matilda called out. 'Wake your brothers. You need to leave this house.'

Stuart closed the door. 'Matilda, I think you should leave,' he said firmly. 'I don't mind what you say to me, I can take it, but I won't have you upsetting Sian or my kids.'

'I'm not going anywhere. Tell Sian what you've been up to tonight. Tell her!' she screamed.

'I'm phoning Harriet,' Sian said. 'This can't go on, Matilda. You've come back to work too soon; we've all said it. You should have taken longer off to recover. Maybe come back after Christmas.' She went to the television unit where she picked up her phone she'd left plugged in to charge overnight.

'Sian, no, listen to me,' Matilda said, snatching the phone from her. She grabbed her hard by the shoulders. 'He's hurt Zofia. He ran the Land Rover into her. He's crushed her legs. He ran over Bev, dragged her along the road. She's dead, Sian.'

Sian frowned in confusion. 'We don't have a Land Rover. Matilda, are you still taking your medication? You're not drinking as well, are you?'

'You're not listening to me!' she shouted.

'Ok, I've had enough of this,' Stuart said. He grabbed Matilda. 'I know you've been through shit this year, Mat, but I will not have you disturbing my family like this. I want you out. Now.'

'Stuart, let me phone her sister,' Sian pleaded.

'No. You come home from work, night after night, worried about her, covering for her, no. It's over. It ends tonight. I don't want you in this house again.'

He forcibly dragged Matilda into the hallway, pulled open the front door and pushed her out into the cold air. He slammed the door behind her, locked it with the Yale and put on the security chain. He returned to the living room and found his wife sitting in the middle of the sofa. Her eyes were filled with tears.

'I can't believe I just witnessed that,' she said. 'I know she's still recovering, but I had no idea she was so close to snapping. Accusing you of murder and saying you'd injured Zofia and killed Bev? Where did she get all that from?'

'I've no idea,' he said, sitting next to her, putting his arm around her shoulders.

'What should I do?'

'I think you need to speak to the new ACC and have her suspended. It's for her own good. Come on, let's go upstairs to bed.'

'I won't go back to sleep now,' she said softly.

'You will once I've got you in my arms,' he smiled.

Matilda stood on the doorstep. Her mind was spinning at a million miles per hour. She couldn't believe she'd been thrown out like that. Stuart was a killer. She'd seen him beating Bev with her own eyes. She watched, helplessly, as he reversed into Zofia, pinning her against the tree, then speeding off, knocking Bev down and dragging her along the ground. It happened. She knew it.

She ran her hand over her short hair as she walked slowly down the path. What Sian had said had been like a slap in the face. Had she really been thinking Matilda wasn't up to her job? If so, who else had she been talking to, Christian, Scott, Finn? Had she been to the ACC?

She turned back to look at the house that was now in darkness. She had known Sian for so long, watched the family grow from the sidelines, shared in the highs and lows. They'd been through so much together, professionally and personally, and she'd turned her back on her, just like Adele.

Oh my God, Adele.

Matilda turned back to the house.

You're a survivor, aren't you, Matilda?

'I am,' she said out loud. 'I really am.'

Chapter Sixty-Seven

When Sian had gone running down the stairs to answer the door, Stuart had stood frozen on the landing. When he'd heard Matilda's voice, he'd known he had to get rid of the knife. He'd hidden it in the gap between the bookcase and the wall. Now, as Sian went into the bedroom, he bent down to pick it up and followed her in.

Sian was sat up in bed, her eyes wide.

'You're shaking,' Stuart said from the doorway.

'I can't get over what I just saw,' she said.

Stuart climbed onto the bed next to her. He pulled the duvet up to warm her and put his arms around her.

'We can't really blame Matilda. She's ill,' he said quietly. 'She needs help.'

'I thought I knew her,' she sniffled.

'What are you going to do?' he asked as he pulled his wife into his arms and began stroking her hair.

'I honestly have no idea. I should phone Christian.'

'He'll be asleep. Call him first thing.'

'No. I need to talk to him now. I'll never sleep with this on my mind.' She pushed the duvet back and tried to get out of bed, but Stuart pulled her back.

'Sian, leave it until morning. There's nothing any of you can do tonight.'

'I need to talk to someone,' she said, looking at him with tear-filled eyes.

'Talk to me,' he smiled.

She thought for a moment, chewing her bottom lip. She shrugged off her husband and climbed out of bed.

'Where are you going?' he asked.

'To get my phone. It's downstairs.'

'No. Wait.' Stuart jumped up and headed for the door. As he did so, the knife he'd been hiding beside him fell off the bed and onto the floor.

'What's that?' Sian asked.

'Erm, nothing.'

'What's a knife doing up here?' she asked, not able to take her eyes off it.

'I … don't know. Oh, yes I do. I was cutting some bread earlier and Anthony shouted for me. I came up and must have left it up here,' he said, his voice having increased an octave in panic.

'No. I used that knife this evening to prepare the tea. I washed it and put it away.'

'You must be mistaken.' He looked at her.

'I'm not. That's not even a bread knife. Stuart, why is there a carving knife in our bedroom?'

He couldn't say anything. He looked down at his wife, his eyes wide, his mouth slightly open, a sheen of sweat on his red face.

'Stuart, what's going on?'

He looked as if he wanted to say something, but the words were stuck in his throat.

'Stuart, where were you tonight?'

He eventually replied, but his voice was quiet. 'I was with Dean and Shaun and his brothers,' he said unconvincingly.

A tear rolled down Sian's face. She didn't wipe it away. 'I don't believe you,' she said. 'Oh my God.' She started to back away. 'Matilda was right, wasn't she? It is you. You've been killing all those women.'

'No…'

'I don't understand. How, Stuart? How could you possibly have done that without me knowing?'

'I haven't done anything,' he pleaded. 'Matilda's sick, she's all screwed up and she's got it so so wrong.'

'Then why is a knife in our bedroom, Stuart?' she said in a loud whisper. 'What were you going to do with it?' The realisation dawned. 'Oh my God, you were going to kill me, weren't you?'

'What? No. Of course I wasn't. I wouldn't do anything like that.'

'You were.' She nodded, tears streaming down her face now. 'You were going to kill me so I wouldn't find out the truth. What then? Were you going to kill the kids, too? All four of them?'

'Sian, no. What do you take me for? I'm not a killer.'

'Then tell me where you were tonight.'

'I was with Dean and…'

'Look at me and say it,' she said firmly.

He looked at her. His jaw was set firm, a vein throbbing in his neck. He opened his mouth to speak, but no words came out.

'Oh God, no.' She buckled, and held out her hand to steady

herself on the bed. 'I can't believe this. I can't... I don't... I feel sick.'

Stuart came round to the side of the bed and held her by the shoulders.

'Don't touch me,' she screamed. 'I don't want you to touch me or be anywhere near me.'

'Sian, please, let me explain,' he said impassively.

'Explain? This should be good. Go on then. Explain to me why you've felt the need to murder eleven people.'

'Eleven? No. I haven't... It's not... Sian, you need to understand.'

'You can't. There is nothing you can say that can justify what you've done. My God, Stuart, you buried one of them alive, for fuck's sake.'

'What?' His face paled. 'No. I didn't.'

'You did. You buried one of them alive in Plantation Woods. I saw her body with my own eyes. She choked on the soil. She suffocated because you buried her alive. What kind of a monster are you?'

'Sian, no, I didn't. I didn't bury anyone alive.'

'And Dermot Salter. Was that you, too?' she asked, wiping her eyes. 'Did you kill him?'

She looked up at him. The heavy silence built between them.

Stuart gently nodded.

'You decapitated him, Stuart. How? Why? What had he done?'

'He knew. He guessed. He knew it was me. I had to...' he trailed off.

'You cut his head off,' she said, looking down at his hands. 'How could you?'

'I wasn't... I wasn't thinking... I... When you're doing

these things, when your mind is somewhere else, it's like someone has taken over your body. I'm not that person, Sian, honest.'

'Wrong. You're a killer, Stuart. You're a cold-blooded murderer. Oh my God, how can I be married to a killer? I'm a detective, for crying out loud. How am I going to go into work now? What am I going to tell the kids? What the fuck have you done to this family?' she screamed. She barged past Stuart and headed for the door.

'Where are you going?'

'To get the kids.'

'No.' He ran after her. He bent down to pick up the knife from the floor. He grabbed Sian by her hair and pulled her back into the room, throwing her down on the bed. 'You can't tell the kids, Sian, I won't allow it. They can't know. I don't want them to,' he said, looming over her.

'Who the hell are you?' she said, looking up into his eyes. 'I don't recognise you anymore.'

'I'm your husband, Sian,' he said with a hint of a smile.

'No. You're not.'

They remained silent. Their eyes were locked on each other.

'I really didn't want to have to do this, Sian,' Stuart said, raising the knife. 'I love you.'

Chapter Sixty-Eight

'Terry, it's me,' Matilda said into her phone as she looked around the garden in the door for something to use as a weapon to break into the house. 'I need an armed response unit to DS Sian Mills's house right now.'

'I thought you wanted them at Plantation Woods.'

'I did, but the killer is… I told you who the killer was,' she seethed. 'Surely you deployed someone to go to his home, the home of a fellow officer, for fuck's sake.'

'Erm … no.'

'Jesus Christ, Terry, Sian and her four kids are in that house with a man who has killed up to eleven people. Am I expected to barge in there on my own?'

'Look, stay put. I'll get onto—'

Matilda ended the call.

Two doors along, one of the neighbours had a small rockery in the front garden. Matilda ran up to it, grabbed the biggest rock she could manage and went back to Sian's front door. She threw it into the glass window. The sound of shattered glass resounded around the quiet neighbourhood. She reached inside, unlocked the Yale, yanked off the chain and kicked the front door open.

She ran for the stairs and stopped as she saw Belinda stood at the top. She was holding her arms tightly around herself. She looked so young, so cold in her thin pyjamas. There was a look of pure horror on her face.

'They're arguing,' she said, quietly. 'I've never heard them like that before. Is it true? Is it true what he's...?' She couldn't say it.

Matilda, one hand on the bannister, one foot on the stairs, nodded.

'Oh my God.' She clamped a hand to her mouth.

'Belinda.' Matilda began walking up the stairs slowly. 'I need you to get your brothers and, as quickly and quietly as you can, you need to get out of the house.'

'What's going on? Did I hear smashing?' Anthony asked as he limped out of his bedroom. 'Oh, hello, Mat, what time is it?' He looked to his sister. 'Bel, you all right?'

'Anthony, go and wake your brothers up. You need to leave the house right now,' Matilda said.

'Why? What's happened?'

'I'll explain everything. Just, please, do as I say.'

Matilda walked up the stairs. She grabbed Belinda by the hand and pulled her gently. When they were halfway down the stairs, Matilda handed her her mobile. 'Look in the contacts for Christian, ring him. Tell him everything that's going on and to get here right now.'

She looked back and saw Anthony coming down the stairs with his two younger brothers following. They were all in dressing gowns and slippers, their hair a wild mess, their faces unreadable as they tried to make sense of what was going on.

'Is the house on fire?' Danny asked.

'Anthony, look after them,' Matilda said as she pushed past them to go back upstairs.

'What's going on?' he asked.

'Please – just do it. I'll explain as soon as I can. Close the door behind you.'

Matilda waited at the top of the stairs until the front door was closed and she was plunged into silence. She went over to Sian and Stuart's room and listened intently. There was no sound coming from inside. She knew she should wait for armed response to arrive, but Sian was in danger. Who knew what was happening to her on the other side of that door? Matilda had lost so many people she cared about this year; she wasn't going to lose another.

'Stuart, it's Matilda. Are you both all right in there?' she called out. She was hoping her voice would be calm and controlled, it wasn't. It gave away her fears.

'Go away, Matilda.'

'Sian, are you all right?'

'She's fine,' Stuart answered. There was venom in his voice.

'Sian?'

The door was unlocked.

Matilda waited a few long seconds before stepping forward and pushing the door open. The room was dimly lit by the streetlight outside coming in through the thin curtains. Stuart was standing by the wardrobe. Sian was in front of him. He had one hand wrapped around her and the other was pointing a knife to her throat.

'Stuart,' Matilda said, slowly entering the room. 'You don't want to do this. You don't want to hurt Sian. Put the knife down.'

'I didn't want to kill any of them,' he cried. 'It just happened.'

'Stuart, put the knife down and we can talk. You can explain everything to me.'

Matilda looked at Sian, but she didn't look back at her. She appeared to be in shock. Less than an hour ago her life was perfectly normal. She had a husband she loved and four children. Now, she had discovered her entire married life had been a lie. She was married to a serial killer. She'd given birth to a monster's children. She'd slept with a murderer.

'It was all her fault,' he said.

'Whose?'

'Ella Morse,' he spat. 'She started it.'

'She was your first victim?'

He nodded.

'What did she do?'

'She saw me. I was in Meadowhall with Sian. She saw us. She kept looking at us and smiling. She was with some friends and showing off. I'm a good man, Matilda, you know I am. She got complacent, asking for money, wanting favours. When I said no, she said that she knew where I lived. She was going to tell Sian. I couldn't...' His words were lost to his tears. 'I didn't know what I'd done until I saw her lying there. I hid her.'

Matilda needed to keep Stuart calm. While he had a knife to his wife's throat, he was volatile. She also needed answers.

'I can get my head around that, Stuart, I really can. But we have eleven dead—'

'I did not kill eleven women,' he shouted.

'Why, Stuart?' Sian asked. 'Why did you go and see a prostitute in the first place? I thought we loved each other. I thought we had a good sex life.'

'Sian, I'm lucky if we do it once a month. You either come in late or you're too tired or you're not in the mood. And lately, it's like you just can't be bothered. I need ... I need to feel something.'

Sian squeezed her eyes closed. 'So you paid someone. You paid a complete stranger. How could you go behind my back like that?'

'It's just sex, Sian. It doesn't mean anything.'

'I means everything,' she seethed. 'How could I have got you so wrong? I see the crap people do to each other every day. I see husbands kill wives. I see wives kill husbands. I see fathers kill children and I think, well, at least I can go home to my loving family, to my loving husband. You've been lying to me all this time. You've brought your filth and your lies and your sickness into my house, you bastard,' she screamed through the tears.

'I love you,' he said, his mouth millimetres away from her ear.

'You disgust me.' She squirmed to free herself from his grasp.

'Stuart, put the knife down. Let Sian go and let's sort this out between the three of us.'

'There's nothing to sort out,' Sian said. 'How can I face my children and tell them what their father's done? How can I go into work with everyone knowing I'm married to a man who killed eleven women?'

'It wasn't eleven,' he pleaded.

'You've got the knife to my throat, Stuart, do it. Kill me. Put me out of my misery. I can't live knowing what you've done.'

'Sian, no,' Matilda begged.

'Do it, Stuart. You say you love me. If you do, then kill me. Don't let me live in agony.'

'No. Stuart, don't listen to her,' Matilda said. 'Sian, think of your kids. They'll need you now more than ever.'

'Do it, Stuart. DO IT!' she screamed.

With one swift movement, Stuart sliced the knife across Sian's throat.

Chapter Sixty-Nine

Wednesday 30th October

Stuart declined to have a solicitor present. He intended to plead guilty to what he had done. However, when he was read all the charges and found out he was to be charged with twelve murders, he immediately called for a lawyer. He couldn't remember how many people he'd killed, but he knew for a fact it was nowhere near twelve people.

Members of the Homicide and Major Crime Unit were reeling from the shock of Sian's husband being revealed as the killer. How was it possible the killer was in their sights all this time from the moment Ella Morse had been found three years ago and none of them had known about it? That was one of many questions Matilda wanted the answer to.

It was a little after eleven o'clock when Matilda and Christian entered interview room one. Stuart was sat at the table next to the wall. He was wearing trousers and an old jumper given to him, his clothes having been removed for evidence. He hadn't slept or eaten. He was unshaven and looked ill. Next to him was Juliet Simpson, his solicitor. She was dressed in a navy suit and cream shirt. Her dark red hair was tied back into a neat bun. She sat, pen poised, over a legal notepad. She'd already made extensive notes.

As soon as Matilda entered the room, Stuart shot up out of his seat.

'I did not kill twelve people,' he stated.

'Sit down, Mr Mills,' Juliet said.

'I didn't. I didn't kill twelve people.'

'You'll have time to defend yourself,' Matilda said. 'Please, sit down.'

Christian went through the preliminaries and stated that the interview would be recorded and videoed. Everyone said their names for the benefit of the recording and Matilda began the interview.

She felt sick. Matilda had interviewed many people over the years, and in some cases she would have staked her house on them not being a killer. Stuart would have been one of those people. She'd been in his house for dinner on many occasions. She'd called after the birth of all four of his children to offer congratulations. She went to his twenty-fifth anniversary party last year. He'd been living a double life and she hadn't picked up on it. How? Why?

'Mr Mills, you've been arrested and charged for the murder of twelve people. We need to go through each victim one by one for you to talk us through the events surrounding their deaths. As you know, some of the victims are still listed as missing. Any help you can give us in finding and identifying them will reflect on your character when it comes to sentencing. Do you understand?'

'I didn't kill twelve people,' he said with very little energy behind his words.

Matilda opened the thick folder in front of her. She looked up at Stuart. Their eyes met. She felt sick and reached out to pick up a plastic cup of water and take a large drink.

'Why did you start using prostitutes, Stuart?'

'Is that relevant?' Juliet asked.

'In order for me to understand why someone killed a woman working as a prostitute, I need to understand the mindset of a man who uses them in the first place. Stuart Mills, as we know, has been married for twenty-six years and has four children. From that we can gather he and his wife enjoyed a full sex life. I'd like to know why he decided to turn to paying for sex.'

Stuart swallowed hard. 'Me and Sian … we don't have sex very often.'

'You'll need to speak up for the benefit of the recording,' Matilda said.

'I said that me and Sian don't have sex very often.'

'How often?'

'I don't know. Once a month maybe. If that.'

'And how often would you like it?'

'Really, DCI Darke?' Juliet asked.

'Really, Ms Simpson.'

'A lot more than that,' Stuart replied.

'Once a week? Once a day? Once an hour? Every fifteen minutes? Help me out here, Stuart.'

'I don't know. I just… I really need sex. A lot.'

'But surely, as a man who has been married for twenty-six years, you have the kind of relationship with your wife where you can talk to her about these things. You can ask for sex whenever you want it.'

'When we had our youngest child, Danny, Sian was in a

great deal of pain. Afterwards, sex was always uncomfortable for her.'

'How long after Danny was born was it before you started looking elsewhere for sex?'

He shook his head, as if disgusted with himself. 'A couple of months.'

'A tad louder for the recording, please.'

'A couple of months.'

'And Danny is how old?'

'Twelve next birthday.'

'So you've been using prostitutes for twelve years?' Matilda asked.

'No. I went to pubs first, picked up women. I met women through apps.'

'Why change to prostitutes?'

'Because the women in bars wanted to meet up again; go for a meal, on a date. I didn't want that. I have a wife for that. I wasn't looking to have an affair. I just wanted sex. That's all.'

'Oh, is that all?'

'There's no need to be flippant, DCI Darke,' Juliet said.

'Right, let's turn to our first victim, shall we? Ella Morse. She went missing in August 2016 and was discovered in woodland in Endcliffe Park in October 2016.' Christian had opened a folder and placed a photograph of Ella Morse in the middle of the table. 'Can you tell us what happened?'

'I told you last night.'

'We need it on record.'

Stuart swallowed hard and began to tell his story once again. He had to stop several times as his emotion occasionally made his words inaudible. Matilda was losing patience with him.

'Next, we come to Lucy Fletcher...'

'Do you think we could take a break here?' Juliet asked.

'Not yet. Lucy Fletcher went missing in December 2016 and was found last week in Plantation Woods. She was buried alive.'

Stuart shook his head. 'No. I did not bury her alive,' he said slowly.

'What happened?'

'I strangled her,' he began quietly. 'I was scared, nervous. I thought she was dead. She looked dead, but ... I don't think I checked.'

'You don't think you checked?' Christian asked, revulsion in his tone.

'I did afterwards.'

'What do you mean by "afterwards"?'

'With the others. I always checked afterwards. With ... Lucy, I, well, I was digging the grave to put her in. I rolled her into it and as I was shovelling the mud back, I saw her move. Or, I thought I saw her move. Look, I know what happens to a person when they kill someone. Their mind goes all over the place. I thought I'd imagined it. I thought I was seeing things. I covered her up as quickly as I could, and I ran. I just... I ran.'

'You buried her alive, Stuart,' Matilda said. 'There was soil in her mouth, up her nose, in her throat, in her stomach. She swallowed it. She was gasping to breathe, and you left her there to suffocate and die a slow and horrible death.'

Stuart wiped away a tear.

'Don't you dare,' she said. 'You have no right to cry for any of your victims.'

'I really think we should take a break here,' Juliet said. 'I think we're all allowing our emotions to get the better of us.'

'Agreed,' Christian said.

Matilda left the interview room and opened the door to the

observation room next door. Sian Mills was sat by herself, her eyes fixed on the large window looking into interview room one. She held her arms rigid around her body. Tears were running down her face and there were several crumpled, soggy tissues by her feet. She had a large, thick bandage around her neck.

When Stuart sliced the knife across her throat, it was a shallow cut. She didn't even require stitches. He'd thrown his wife to the ground and that's when Matilda pounced. She ran for him, slammed him against the wardrobe and knocked the knife out of his hand. In order to subdue him, she kicked him between the legs, and while he was bent double, she jumped on his back, so he collapsed to the floor. Moments later, Christian Brady ran into the room and saw Sian with blood dripping down her throat and Matilda sitting astride her husband.

Matilda knelt down beside Sian and wrapped her arms around her, pulling her close.

'He's admitting it,' Sian said.

'I know.'

'I'm sorry I didn't believe you.'

'Sian, if I hadn't seen him with my own eyes, I wouldn't have believed it either.'

'How could I not have known?'

'Because you weren't looking for it.'

'I'm a detective. I should have noticed.'

'Don't blame yourself. He's mastered the art of manipulation.'

Sian pushed herself out of Matilda's embrace. She wiped her eyes and blew her nose. 'What do I do now?'

'You go home and comfort your children.'

'My home's a crime scene.'

'Harriet's in my office upstairs. She's waiting for you. She'll take you to your house for you all to grab what you need, then you're going on to mine. You can spend as long as you want there.'

'But I've been so horrible to you these last couple of weeks.'

'You haven't. You've been concerned. There's a difference.'

Sian tried to smile, but the tears would allow her. 'Any news on Zofia?'

'Not yet,' Matilda lied. There was no reason to tell her just yet that Zofia had permanently lost use of her legs.

They both looked through the thick glass at Stuart Mills, his head on the table, a look of incredulity in his eyes. Neither of them recognised him.

'I didn't think after the shooting that life could get any worse,' Sian said. 'This is a whole new level of hell, isn't it?'

'It is,' Matilda said. 'But we'll find a way to get you out.'

Matilda wanted to take Sian away from this nightmare. She needed to visit Adele in hospital, but first, she wanted to make sure Sian was with her sister and out of the station.

'Do you mind if I just stay here on my own for a minute? I don't think my legs will hold me right now.'

'There's no rush. Can I get you anything?'

Sian shook her head.

Matilda left the small room, closing the door behind her.

Sian felt numb. She felt sick. She didn't know how she felt. She had met Stuart thirty years ago in a pub around the corner from Bramall Lane. Sheffield United had won, that was all Sian knew, and the atmosphere was raucous. She was out with a few friends and she hardly gave the louts at the bar a second glance. It was only when she had to force her way through them to the toilets and one of them started making lewd suggestions that a man stepped forward to save her. She looked up at this stocky, hunky gentle giant and straightaway felt a prickle of excitement. Four years later, they were husband and wife.

A door to the interview room was opened and Stuart was led out by uniformed officers to be placed in a cell. Sian stood up. She opened the door of the observation room a crack and looked down the corridor. Stuart was walking, head down, shoulders hunched, as if he was on his way to the gallows. She waited until he was out of sight before following.

As Sian walked silently down the corridor, she could feel the eyes of everyone she passed burning into her. She was the centre of attention, her name was on everyone's lips, and she hated that. She knew exactly what they'd be saying, too; in their position, she would be saying exactly the same. How could she have not known?

The truth was Sian was berating herself. She should have known. She'd been living with a killer for four years. How was that possible? She had shared a bed with him, been on holiday with him, made love to him, wrapped herself in those big strong arms and felt comforted as his calloused hands caressed her – and all the time those same huge hands had been used as weapons to squeeze the life out of so many poor defenceless women.

Sian held out a hand against the wall to steady herself. She felt ill. She wanted the ground to open up and swallow her whole. She didn't look up, but she could hear the hushed whispers as people passed her. How would she be able to return to work as a detective sergeant after all this?

'Terry,' she said as she entered the custody suite.

Terry Atkin was a huge barrel of a man. He was wedged in behind his desk, his white shirt straining against his girth, buttons threatening to shoot off like missiles at any moment.

He had an uncontrollable mound of wiry dark grey hair. His face was craggy and the broken capillaries beneath his eyes and along his bulbous nose were evidence he enjoyed more than the odd drink in the evenings.

'Sian, oh my goodness, Sian, I don't know what to say,' he said with genuine sympathy. He reached over the desk and took her hands in his. 'You must be going through hell right now.'

She nodded. 'Can I ask a favour?' she asked quietly.

'Of course, anything.'

'Can you let me see Stuart?'

'Ah…'

'Just for a few minutes. I need to see him. I need to ask him something. I know it's not allowed, and I'll take full responsibility if his solicitor finds out, but, please, Terry, I'm begging you.'

He quickly looked around him. 'I can give you five minutes. No more.'

She nodded.

Terry struggled to climb out of his chair and headed for the cell corridor. Sian followed. It felt strange knowing the man she had promised to love and cherish for the rest of her life was behind one of these strong steel doors. None of this seemed real.

Terry unlocked the door and stepped back. 'I'll be waiting at the entrance. If you need me, just shout,' he said, placing a huge hand on her shoulder before walking away.

Sian stood in the doorway to the cell and looked down at her husband on the blue mattress. When he looked up, he had tears in his eyes.

'Sian…'

'Don't say anything, Stuart. It's my turn to talk now.' She

had her arms folded firmly across her chest. She leaned slightly against the door frame. Her legs were shaking, and she worried they'd give way and she'd collapse to the floor. She was cold, scared and wished she was anywhere else in the world right now other than here.

'Why?' she asked. 'Why did you do it?'

He shook his head. 'I honestly don't know.' His voice was weak, cracked.

'You must do. Jesus Christ, Stuart, you're married. You have four kids, isn't that enough for you?'

'I love you and the kids with all my heart...'

'You can't do, otherwise you wouldn't have killed all those people. Serial killers often have something missing from their lives which they need to fulfil by murdering. What the hell was missing from your life?'

'I don't know,' he shrugged.

'You do,' she said, quickly wiping away a tear. 'You can't love me. You can't love any of us if you were prepared to throw it all away like that.'

'I do love you all. I promise you. My love for you hasn't faltered since the moment I met you.'

'Don't. I don't want to hear it, Stuart.'

'I'm sorry.'

'No. Don't apologise. Back there, in the interview room, when you said you saw Ella Morse in Meadowhall and she was pointing and laughing with her friends, I almost felt sympathy for you.'

'You were watching?'

'I was in the observation room next door. I think I could have forgiven you seeing a prostitute. I could probably have understood why you killed her, but to go on and kill all those others... Why, Stuart? Did you enjoy it?'

'No.'

'You must have done. Twelve people are dead.'

'I didn't kill twelve people.'

'You buried one of them alive.'

'I didn't know she was still alive.'

'You rammed a ten-pound note down Lisa Temple's throat. You stood on her back and crushed her like you were killing a spider. You decapitated Dermot Salter, for crying out loud. You're sadistic.'

'That wasn't me, Sian. None of that was me. I can't explain it, but it's like something takes over you and you become someone else.'

'No. Stop. I don't want to hear this. I will not have you trying to justify what you've done. You need to take responsibility. Own up to your crimes. You killed them. You strangled, beat, crushed, buried and destroyed each and every one of them. Don't even think of looking for a way out.'

'Sian, I...'

'Why the gap?'

'Sorry?'

'You didn't kill for thirteen months. Why did you stop?'

Stuart wiped a tear away with one hand and used the sleeves of his second-hand sweater to wipe both eyes. 'You were stabbed. I thought I was going to lose you. I needed to look after you. And then the shooting happened earlier this year, and I wanted to be there for you.'

'Then life settles down and you start killing again.'

'I couldn't stop.'

'But you did. You stopped for thirteen months.'

'Because I had you to look after. You mean the world to me, Sian. And when I thought I could have lost you...'

'No. No, don't do this,' she said. 'How can you sit there and show such humanity about losing me when you were mercilessly killing people? You're a psychopath.'

'I'm not.'

'You are.'

'Sian,' Terry called out from down the corridor.

Sian breathed in and wiped her eyes. 'This is the last time I'll be seeing you, Stuart.'

'No.'

'I'll be seeing a solicitor and starting divorce proceedings as soon as possible.'

'No, Sian, please. I'm begging you,' he cried.

'I won't be coming to see you in prison, and I don't want you phoning or writing to me. I can't stop the kids from contacting you, but whatever they decide will be a decision of their own making. However, I don't want anything more to do with you.'

She turned on her heel and walked away.

'Sian. No. Please. Don't do this to me,' Stuart called out as Terry closed the cell door with a loud bang.

As Sian headed down the corridor, she could hear her husband slamming his fists on the door, screaming and shouting for her to return. It was over, as far as she was concerned.

Terry caught up with her and handed her a crumpled handkerchief from his pocket. She thanked him and wiped her eyes.

'Is there anything I can do?'

She shook her head.

'Are you going to be all right?'

She took a breath. 'No, Terry. I don't think I am. But I will be. In time.'

Chapter Seventy

The lift doors pinged open and Matilda stepped out into the stifling corridor. She walked past a few nurses she recognised from her many visits to the Northern General Hospital but continued, head down, towards a private room. She stood outside and looked through the window. Her best friend, Adele, was sat up in bed. She looked frail, tired, pale, defeated. She knocked and pushed the door open. Scott was sitting by the bed and stood up, an awkward smile on his face.

'Hello, Adele,' Matilda said.

Adele smiled, but it soon quivered and the tears flowed.

Matilda leapt forward and perched on the edge of the bed. She wrapped her arms around her and pulled her into a tight embrace.

'What am I going to do with you, eh?'

'I'm sorry,' Adele said, her voice muffled in Matilda's chest.

'You have nothing to apologise for.'

'I blamed you.'

'I blamed me, too.'

'I just... I couldn't...'

'You don't have to explain. I understand.'

'It was getting mugged and having my phone stolen. Chris's voicemail was on it. It was the only recording I had of his voice.'

Matilda looked at Scott. He shook his head. He knew what she was about to ask him – any news on the phone being found?

Adele pushed herself out of Matilda's hold and looked up.

'Can you ever forgive me?'

'I've nothing to forgive.' She snuggled up to her on the bed and they held hands. She looked up at Scott. 'This has been a nightmare year for all three of us, hasn't it?'

'You can say that again,' Scott said. 'Finn called me earlier. Is it true the killer is Sian's husband?'

'I'm afraid so.'

'I can't believe it.'

'Poor woman,' Adele said.

Matilda looked at them both. 'Look, we can either wallow in our own self-pity or we can take life by the balls and do something positive.'

'Such as?' Adele asked.

'I've no idea. All I do know is that life is a fucker at times and the only way we can survive it is by being honest and open with others. My goodness, James has been dead nearly five years and it's taken me all this time to work that out,' she said with a smile.

'I've been in a daze this past year,' Adele said, wiping her nose with a wet tissue. 'Everything has been so numb, so raw, I don't know how I've got through each day.'

'I know that feeling,' Scott said.

'Neither of you are on your own. You have to remember that,' Matilda said.

'I think I'm going to move,' Adele sniffed. 'That house is too big for me on my own. And I keep seeing Chris everywhere.'

'I've got plenty of room,' Matilda said. 'Harriet's going to be moving out soon when she finds a house. I'll be on my own again. You're more than welcome to move in with me.'

'Permanently?' Adele asked.

'Why not? We know each other. We get along. It's a big enough house so that if we ever get on each other's tits we can move to another part of the house.'

'You could try it for a few months and if it doesn't work, you can always start house hunting,' Scott added.

'I tell you what,' Matilda said, getting up from the bed. 'Think about it and let me know. I won't be offended if you don't want to.'

'Thank you.'

Matilda looked deep into Adele's eyes. 'Are we okay?'

'We are,' she said with a weak smile.

The door opened and a nurse entered. She asked Matilda and Scott to step outside while Adele was checked over.

'I need to get back to the station. I'll come and see you tonight,' Matilda said.

'Will you bring me some Ferrero Rocher?'

Matilda smiled and rolled her eyes. 'You're going to be fine.'

Chapter Seventy-One

Christian was exhausted. They all were. He sat back in his chair and loosened his tie. He looked across the table. Juliet Simpson, a vision of professionalism when she first arrived, looked worn out. Her hair was no longer tied back in a severe bun. Her jacket was slung over the back of her chair and her sleeves rolled up. She looked drained of all emotion. They had both spent the last two hours listening to Stuart Mills tell his story, talk through his nine victims and explain everything in minute, painful detail.

Stuart was to be charged with nine murders and appear before Sheffield Magistrates' Court tomorrow morning. The possibility of bail was never mentioned. There was no chance of him being allowed to go free pending a sentencing hearing. Until then, he would be held on remand at a maximum security prison.

Christian pushed his chair back and hoisted himself to his feet. He felt drained.

'Christian, can I ask you a favour?' Stuart asked, looking up with a hopeful expression on his face. 'Could you give this to

Sian for me, please?' He looked to his solicitor who gave him a folded-up piece of paper. 'She's made it perfectly clear she doesn't want to see me again. I can understand that, but I need to explain everything. Will you let her read this, when she's ready?'

Christian looked down at the single sheet of paper that had been torn from Juliet's legal pad. 'How will I know when she's ready?'

'You're her friend. You'll know.'

Reluctantly, he took the paper, and left the interview room, instructing the uniform officer on guard to take Stuart to his cell.

Finn was alone in the HMCU suite. He wasn't working, simply staring out of the window at the darkening Sheffield skyline. He looked up when he heard the door open and saw Christian enter, dragging his feet.

'Coffee?' Finn asked.

'Intravenously, please,' Christian said. 'I'm drained.' He flopped down into his seat. 'I've just listened to the husband of a colleague talk me through nine murders, and I still can't believe he's done them. Stuart, of all people. I can't... It just doesn't seem real.'

'I've been sat here thinking about Sian and her kids. I've always thought of them as being such a close family.'

'They are.'

'For him to have such a dark secret, and for so long, how is that possible? How can they have not known?'

Christian shrugged.

Finn made a strong coffee and handed it to his boss.

'He's asked me to give this to Sian.' Christian held up the letter.

'What is it?'

'An explanation. I don't think she's ready to read it yet, though.'

Finn looked at it and licked his lips. 'Have you read it?'

'No.'

'It's not in an envelope, is it?'

'You want to read it, don't you?'

'Well, it might help us to understand. You know, the mind of a serial killer written in his own words.'

'My God, you're almost salivating.'

'Aren't you interested? From a detective's point of view?'

'Here,' he said, handing over the letter.

Finn practically snatched it from him. He unfolded it and looked at the letter before he began reading. The writing was legible but had a childish scrawl to it. Stuart had pressed hard as he'd written, evidence of a determined man, eager to impart his words. This wasn't a thought-out confession, planned and written after several drafts; it was a one-off.

Finn sat down at his desk and read:

Sian,

This is the hardest thing I'm having to write, but I need you to know everything. I need you to understand why I did what I did. You heard about why I killed Ella Morse. I thought she was going to tell you I'd been sleeping with her. I didn't want you knowing, not like that, not from her. I killed her to silence her. Straight afterwards, I couldn't believe what I'd done. I couldn't even remember doing it. I remember you coming home from work saying you were investigating a missing prostitute and it took me ages to realise it was me you were talking about. I was petrified I was going to get caught. As time went on and you said you'd hit a brick wall I thought I'd got away with it. The relief was immense.

The problem was, in the back of my mind, I wondered if I could do it again. Not purposely, of course, but if I was ever in that position, could I possibly kill again? That question kept me awake at nights. It was constantly running around my mind. Am I a killer? Did killing Ella awaken something inside me that had been lying dormant all these years?

The answer was obviously yes. The second time I killed I was much more lucid. I remember everything about it – putting my hands around her neck, squeezing hard, looking into her eyes, watching the horror and the fear and the life start to fade away. There really is no other feeling like it in the world. It's orgasmic.

I was worried you'd notice a change in me. You've told me many times that killers change, and their families notice something is wrong. But you didn't. Why didn't you? We've always been close. You've always known when something has been bothering me, but not this time. Why? Looking back, I don't think it has anything to do with you not seeing the change, but me being able to hide it so well. People will tell you it was manipulation, but I don't think it was. I've never manipulated you before in my life. I was just so good at killing and hiding what I'd done. I'm not trying to justify what I've done but explain that I was obviously born this way and it was always going to be released at some point. I'm just glad that it wasn't you and the kids who were on the receiving end.

I never wanted to ruin what we had. I love you. I love all four of our children. I was happy and content, but there was obviously something missing. I do regret what I've done because I know that I've lost you now, and I'll lose the kids, too. For that, I am sorry and always will be.

Love, Stuart

'Oh my God,' Finn said, sitting back in his chair and letting out a heavy sigh.

'Do I want to know?' Christian asked, looking at him over the top of his coffee mug.

'He's apologised to Sian for what he's done, but he's not shown any remorse for his victims. He says that's he knows he's lost her and the kids and for that he's sorry, but he's not apologised for killing anyone.'

'Sian certainly doesn't need to read that,' he said.

'What are you going to do with it?'

'I have absolutely no idea, Finn.'

Chapter Seventy-Two

It was pitch dark outside and the lights were on in the HMCU. Finn and Scott were the only members left and they were busy making teas for them all. Matilda and Christian were in her office with the door closed.

'What's going to happen to Sian?' Christian asked.

'Nothing. She knew nothing about what Stuart was up to, that much is obvious. There's no reason why she can't come back to the unit.'

'Do you think she'll want to?'

'I hope so.'

'So do I.'

'She's on compassionate leave for as long as she wants. Let's take it a day at a time. Listen, Christian, I need to say something to you,' she said, shuffling her feet, slightly uncomfortable. 'Actually, I need to say it in front of everyone. Come on.'

She opened the door and went out into the main suite. Finn handed her a tea. Surprisingly, nobody took anything from Sian's snack drawer.

'Firstly,' Matilda began, 'I popped in to see Zofia when I left Adele. She's unconscious and I spoke to her mother. Despite the efforts of the surgical team, they were unable to save Zofia's legs and she will be paralysed from the waist down. I've told Zofia's mum that when she wakes up, she just needs to concentrate on recovering. There will always be a job for her in this unit.' She paused and allowed everyone to take in the horrific news. 'Secondly, I want to apologise to you all, especially to Christian.'

Matilda was finding this difficult, but it needed to be said. 'I can't believe I've only been back at work for just over two weeks, so much has happened, but I've been a complete bitch to you all. Christian, I think I must have felt threatened by you. You did such an amazing job as Acting DCI while I was away that I thought you were after my job. I've undermined you at every opportunity to try and show you were incompetent, and I was the better choice for the role. It was wrong of me, and I'm sorry. I hope you'll forgive me.'

'Of course,' he said, looking embarrassed.

'I'm saying the same to you two, as well,' she said turning to Finn and Scott. 'You're both excellent detectives and I'm proud to have you on my team – our team,' she said, looking to Christian. 'I'm sorry I've been difficult these past couple of weeks. We've got a lot to contend with in the coming months – Zofia coming back, hopefully Sian returning and the subsequent fallout from Stuart's sentencing. I hope we can return to the team we once were, only stronger.'

'And with less members,' Scott said.

Matilda looked around the room. 'Yes, I think we need to try and poach a few people from CID.'

'What's the latest with Stuart?' Finn asked.

Matilda turned to the murder board. 'Well, he's admitted

killing eight women, and Dermot Salter. But we still have three women who worked as prostitutes listed as missing persons – Jackie Barclay, Caroline Richardson and Monica Yates.'

'Do we think he killed them?' Scott asked.

'I don't know. Maybe when Sian is feeling a bit more lucid, we can chat to her, find out his whereabouts for the dates when they went missing. So long as they are missing, Stuart has no reason to admit to their murders.'

'I still can't understand why,' Scott said, shaking his head.

'I hate to say this,' Finn began, 'what with him being Sian's husband, but I think he simply enjoyed killing and getting away with it. He was never on the radar as a suspect. And even if he popped up on CCTV or something we wouldn't have given him a second glance because he was married to Sian and she's spent years saying what a good husband and father he was.'

'True. Also, Sian's gone home every evening and told him how her day's been,' Christian said. 'In all that time he's stored away information on what killers she's investigated and how they tried to cover their tracks. He's known to use a different vehicle for each murder, and he's had perfect access working in a garage. He's done everything right to evade capture.'

'Poor Sian,' Scott said, looking over at her empty desk.

'He's a cold, calculating, psychopathic murderer,' Finn said.

They all reflected, silently, on Finn's statement.

Matilda clapped her hands together. 'Right then, I think we should all have an early finish. Lots to do tomorrow. We have three missing women who need to be found. Life goes on. The world keeps turning, and all that bollocks.'

Everyone turned off their computers and grabbed their coats. They all left the suite and Matilda told Scott she'd meet him in the car park. Before she turned off the lights, she stood in the doorway and looked at the empty room. There was still a rancid smell – she couldn't quite figure out what it was – and she'd be glad to move back into the old offices. But as she flicked off the lights and plunged the room into darkness, she smiled. Matilda Darke was back.

Epilogue

Wednesday 13th November 2019. Two weeks later. City Road Cemetery, Sheffield. 10:30

There were only three mourners standing around the open grave. The vicar read from his book as the coffin was slowly lowered into the ground, and the three women stepped forward to throw a handful of dirt on top of the oak box.

Matilda stepped back from the grave first and shook hands with the vicar, thanking him for the service.

'Would you like us to leave you alone for a few minutes?' Matilda asked Sarah.

'No. I'm fine,' she said, wiping her eyes. 'I just wish she'd have had more people come to say a final goodbye. I thought her ex-husband would have turned up.'

Matilda didn't tell her that she'd contacted him and he'd hung up on her.

They walked away, Sarah in the middle, and headed for a

bench. Matilda looked up and saw a taxi pull up at the entrance. A man and a woman stepped out. She nodded to them.

'How are you getting on in the new flat?' Harriet asked.

Matilda had stuck to her word and had arranged for Sarah to be given a flat by the council. She had signed up for a job programme with the job centre and had enrolled in a computer course at the city college to brush up her skills. She was also working three evenings a week cleaning a betting shop, cash in hand.

'Fine. It seems strange living on my own again after all these years with Bev, but I'm getting there. There's an old dear living next door who I chat to. I'm not on my own.' She gave a hint of a smile.

The man and woman who entered the graveyard had sat on the bench nearby.

'Sarah, I've been doing some research,' Matilda said, taking Sarah's gloved hands in her own. 'I found out where your children were living, and I gave them a call. When your husband left you, all those years ago, he told your children you'd died.'

'What?' Her eyes widened in horror.

'They didn't try to look for you because, from their point of view, you were dead. When I told them you were alive, they were over the moon.'

'They thought I was dead?' She cried and fished in a pocket for a tissue. 'Why would he do that? They must have been heartbroken.' She wiped her eyes and blew her nose. 'Well, what did they say when you told them I was alive? How are they?'

Matilda nodded to the bench behind her. She turned to look

and immediately recognised the man and woman as her grown-up children.

'Oh my God,' she cried. 'It's them. It's really them.'

Sarah stood up, holding onto the bench for stability. Her children hurried over to her, arms open, and they both scooped her up.

Harriet was in tears and Matilda choked up. They stepped back and allowed the family to catch up.

'That was a lovely thing to do,' Harriet said.

'I've been surrounded by death and destruction for so long I almost forgot what goodness felt like,' Matilda said, a hand on her heart.

Harriet looked at her watch. 'I've got those houses to look at with Mum in an hour. Are you coming with us?'

Matilda thought for a moment. 'Erm, no. I think I'll just go home and have an hour or two to myself.'

'You're not going to see Carl, are you?' Harriet asked, her lips squeezing tight so they were almost white.

'No. It's Wednesday. Carl has therapy on Wednesdays.'

'Good.'

'What does that mean?'

'It means I think you're going around there too often. You should give them some space.'

'I just want to make sure he's happy and settled.'

'And Sally and Philip will let you know if he isn't.'

Matilda turned and walked away.

'Where are you going?'

'I just said, I'm going home. Here.' She tossed Harriet the car keys. 'Take the car. I'll get a taxi.'

'Matilda, I didn't mean …'

Matilda was already out of earshot.

12:15

Carl was always quiet after his therapy sessions. They had talked a great deal and he had so much to process that he could only do that in silence. The journey home in the car was spent with Carl gazing out of the front passenger window, not looking at the view of Sheffield whizzing by in a blur, but looking through it, somewhere into the ether.

Sally had been told his recovery was going to be long and complex, and she had to give him space. She shouldn't force him to reveal what he talked about in his sessions, but to let him know that she was there for him whenever he wanted to talk. Her role was to provide a stable and relaxed environment. She was doing her best, but it was eating her up inside that she didn't know what was going on inside his head. He looked hurt, as if he was screaming but couldn't make any noise. She wished the three of them could move away right now and start afresh but Sally had been told that was the last thing Carl needed at the moment.

Once in the house, Carl went to his room, shadowed by the two Woodys. He needed to write in his thought journal about his feelings following his latest therapy session, so that they could be discussed next time.

'Would you like me to make you a snack?' Sally called after him.

'Okay.'

'Anything in particular?'

'I'm not bothered,' he said, an edge to his voice.

He slammed the bedroom door and sat on the edge of the bed, stroking the two dogs.

Carl had no intention of writing in his journal. He'd make something up before the next session. It wouldn't take him long. He wasn't sure what to make of his therapist. He seemed like a nice bloke, but he had a permanent smile on his face, as if everything was all sweetness and light.

Carl took his iPad out of his bedside cabinet and turned it on. He logged onto the Facebook page his parents didn't know he had. He used a different name and lied about his age but it was fun to talk to someone who didn't know who he really was.

A message was waiting for him.

Hello again.

Hi.

How are things?

Not good.

Parents still giving you grief?

Something like that.

Annoying, isn't it?

Big time.

Are you able to go out much on your own?

Sometimes. I like to walk my dogs.

That reminds me, I got a new dog last week. A golden Labrador.

I've got two of those.

Cool. Something else we've got in common.

What have you called yours?

I've let my nephew name him. He's a big fan of the *Toy Story* films at the moment. He's called him Woody.

OMG. That's what mine are called.

Both of them?

Yes. Long story.

You should tell it me sometime.

Maybe.

Listen, does anyone else use your computer?

No. Just me.

That's good. You should probably delete our chats, just in case. You know how nosey parents can be.

True. I will do.

So, Carl, where do you take your dogs for a walk?

14:30

It was the first time Matilda had entered her home to find no one else there since the day she was shot, back in January. Harriet was with their mum looking at houses, Sian and her kids had gone to stay with her mother for a few days and Adele was at her house, packing, getting ready to move out and in with Matilda. It wouldn't be long before the house was bursting with people. Matilda decided to enjoy the solitude while it lasted.

The wind had picked up outside and it whistled around the house. She lit a fire in the living room and went into the kitchen to flick on the kettle. Although it was growing dark outside, it was too early to think about having a big meal; a mug of tea and a handful of Bourbons would be enough for now. She went into the lounge and sat on the Chesterfield sofa. She sat back and sighed.

Her eyes fell on the pile of cards and letters on the coffee table in front of her that needed answering. Most were from family, friends and ex-colleagues scattered around the country. A few evaded her memory and took some probing to remember who they were. People she hadn't seen for more than a decade had got in touch to wish her a happy recovery. She smiled and felt a warmth grow inside her at how many people she obviously had in her life who were keen to see her return to full health and be back at work. It was touching.

She picked up a white envelope and ran her finger under the seal. She pulled out the card, which showed a scruffy grey teddy bear holding out a bunch of flowers. Matilda smiled. She opened it and read the message:

'You're a survivor, aren't you, Matilda? But what's the point of surviving, when everyone around you is dead?'

Matilda grabbed the envelope and looked at the front. There was no stamp on it. It had been hand delivered.

Acknowledgments

The creation of a book isn't easy. When I think of all the people who are involved in putting one together, my task of arranging all the words in the correct order seems simple. The Coronavirus pandemic has made publishing harder with many working from home and not having the large offices and face-to-face interaction. I want to say a huge thank you to everyone at HarperCollins and One More Chapter for their Herculean efforts over the past year. A special mention to Charlotte Ledger and Bethan Morgan. Also, Tony Russell and Lok Yee Liu for their work on *Survivor's Guilt*.

My esteemed agent, Jamie Cowen at Ampersand, for his advice and behind-the-scenes role in keeping my writing career moving forward. We have so much more planned over the next few years.

Pathologist, Philip Lumb, thank you for replying to my weird questions with even weirder answers. Andy Barrett for forensic information, Simon Browes for all things medical and Neil Lancaster and Mr Tidd for police procedure. Any factual errors in this book are all mine and not the fault of these wonderful people.

Additionally, thank you to Craig Denial, for allowing me to use his photographs of Sheffield during the promotion of my work. I'll buy you a pint someday.

A shout out to those who I interact with on a daily basis who support me in my career and life in general, particularly, my mum and also Christoffer Human, Kevin the Beagle, JD (a vase of sprouts), and Maxwell Dog.

Lastly, but most importantly, to my fellow writers who support me, the bloggers and reviewers who champion my books, and finally, to you, the reader, thank you. Without you purchasing this book, I wouldn't be able to continue writing.

ONE MORE CHAPTER

YOUR NUMBER ONE STOP

FOR PAGETURNING BOOKS

One More Chapter is an
award-winning global
division of HarperCollins.

Sign up to our newsletter to get our
latest eBook deals and stay up to date
with our weekly Book Club!
<u>Subscribe here.</u>

Meet the team at
<u>www.onemorechapter.com</u>

Follow us!

 @OneMoreChapter_

 @OneMoreChapter

 @onemorechapterhc

Do you write unputdownable fiction?
We love to hear from new voices.
Find out how to submit your novel at
<u>www.onemorechapter.com/submissions</u>